THE FALLS:
Cupid's Arrow

GEORGE JACKSON

Copyright © 2014 George Jackson

All rights reserved.

ISBN:1505617936
ISBN-13:9781505617931

DEDICATION

This book is dedicated with love to my wonderful wife
Carolyn's immediate family:
Her parents: Frank and Felicia Brzezicke
(Grandma and Grandpa B.)
Her sister: Joann and her husband Donald Trolinger
Their children: Debbie and Scott Leker and their
children Kristie and Nicole
Kim and Richard Tisdal

ACKNOWLEDGMENTS

The cover was created by CreateSpace and the coverpicture was created with a large Thank You to RobertProska (fangol) and the use of his illustration, Destructive Business. The book was Beta read by the author and his wonderful, patient and indulgent wife Carolyn.

Other books by George Jackson:
The Falls small town Mystery Series:
The Falls: In the Dead of Winter
The Falls: Summer Nightmare
The Falls: Fall of the Rotten Apples
The Falls: Mud Season
The Falls: Making a List, Checking it Twice
The Falls: Fourth of July
The Falls: Cupid's Arrow

The Dragon World Series:
Dragon World: Dragon Magic
Dragon World: The Gathering
Dragon World: Dragon Mist
Dragon World: Dragon Legends
Dragon World: Dragon Moon
Dragon World: Treasures of the Ancients

Tales from The Principal's Bench

The Twilight Tea Party

Chapter 1

Jordan Smith-Stone gazed thoughtfully into the front window of Burman's Five and Ten Cent Emporium and smiled, her interest piqued. Her stunning eyes attentively scanned over the assorted heart shaped boxes filled with mouthwatering chocolates and succulent truffles, the sparkling, stylish heart-shaped jewelry and the rows and rows of Valentine's Day cards. The beautiful greeting cards with their sometimes silly, sometimes romantic and sometimes poignant verses filled the display case with their vibrant color and diversity. Her gaze then took in the rest of the wide array of appealing gifts made especially for a sweetheart, each of them artistically and romantically displayed. With a slight flush on her cheeks, she glanced down at the beautiful two carat Princess cut engagement ring and shining wedding band on her finger and her smile widened.

As a chilly gust of winter wind blew a few crystallized snowflakes whirling past her she shivered slightly and pulled her fashionable, while at the same time warm and comfy, winter coat closer around her. Turning and walking past the display window, Jordan glanced at her own reflection in the mirror. There, looking back at her was a beautiful, charming, but also very strong, independent and capable woman.

Suddenly, a joyful thought flitted through her head. Never again would she have to wonder whom her Valentine's sweetheart might be or if she would be receiving a symbol of someone's love and devotion on Valentine's Day. Doctor Malcolm Stone was her love and her devoted husband, and although he was a bit forgetful and far too kind-hearted for his own good at times, he was all hers.

Stepping around a chunk of ice and snow left on the sidewalk since the last snowstorm, Jordan stepped contentedly into the well-snowplowed street that circled the town park. With her spirits soaring, she crossed over to the snow-cleared sidewalk just outside her own pharmacy. Next door to her shop, she spied Doc Stone through a window of his medical office, standing next to a patient. Jordan chuckled to herself. Doc was so kind and caring to the townspeople he served, and they, in turn, loved him dearly. He was a very special man, she mused, her eyes twinkling, in many different ways.

The front three downstairs rooms of the sprawling building were where Doc had his family medical practice. There was a waiting room, an examination room and an office. The rest of the large downstairs and the entire spacious upstairs was their comfortable home: the stylish and amazing home of Dr. and Mrs. Stone! Jordan nodded contentedly to herself. Even though she was a highly focused, self-reliant and smart businesswoman, her heart and soul still treasured being Mrs. Stone.

Jordan hustled up the neatly snow-cleared steps to her pharmacy, decisively unlocking the door and stepping inside. The warmth that greeted her as she shut the door and slipped off her boots and coat was more than welcome. This winter, much like the last, had arrived early and was doing its very best to keep the temperature well below freezing, the stoves and fireplaces blazing brightly, and the citizens of West Sugar Shack Falls safely sequestered indoors most of the time.

Jordan turned on all of the overhead and under the counter lights as she walked through the shop. She carefully hung up her coat and hat after she had walked briskly to the back of the store. Turning the thermostat up a few degrees to its daytime temperature, Jordan slipped on her starched white pharmacy coat and prepared to execute her favorite chore of the day. Slipping a small container of Vermont Select Blend Breakfast coffee into her single cup coffee machine and placing one of her new brightly colored ceramic coffee mugs under the spigot, she enthusiastically pressed the start button. As the fresh, heavenly aroma of brewing coffee filled the air, Jordan breathed deeply and smiled with pure satisfaction and pleasure.

As the cup filled, Jordan stepped behind the pharmacy's front counter and turned on her digital cash register, wiping off the shelf with a sanitary wet wipe as she did every morning before opening. Then, as she efficiently went about her daily routine, Jordan's thoughts slipped back to the Valentine's Day display at the Five and Ten.

At that particular moment, Jordan happened to glance out the frosted windowpane. There, jogging by in a thin thermal, lime green running outfit, frosty breath rising in the cold morning air, was the only other medical doctor in town, Dr. Meg Monroe. Meg's cheeks were bright red and she was jogging a bit faster than normal due to the freezing temperatures. Meg had taken over for Doc Stone as the physician in charge at The West Sugar Shack Falls Regional Medical Facility about a year and a half ago.

To be quite candid, Jordan had been instrumental in firmly pushing Doc to turn his attention to his own family practice, give up his eighty-hour a week job as both a private practitioner and the hospital's physician, and let someone else deal with the day to day medical needs and demands of the small local hospital. Hiring Meg to do just that had been a Godsend, both for Doc's medical career and for Jordan's love life.

Jordan peered curiously out the window once more. Meg smiled and waved when she noticed Jordan staring out the window and Jordan smiled and cheerfully waved back. Meg continued jogging around the corner and toward the hospital.

It was then the idea hit the beautiful pharmacist. Valentine's Day was in two weeks. Meg had been complaining about how she never had any time to have a social life. Cash and Yamato, the sheriff and deputy of The Falls, along with her darling Doc, had also remarked at one time or another that they thought Meg was a bit home-sick and more than a little lonely at times. She smiled and her eyes lit up. It was time to do something about Meg's lack of a social life and she was just the person to do it! Her creative and logical mind began percolating and her plan began to come together.

Jordan strode purposefully back to the coffee machine with a mischievous twinkle in her beautiful eyes. She picked up her steaming mug and took several long sips, closing her eyes and fully savoring the rich, full-bodied flavor. Then, the mischievous twinkle turned to a determined gaze as she resolutely headed toward the front of her shop. Pulling her Rolodex from under the counter, the pharmacist set it on the top of the granite countertop. As Jordan flipped slowly and decisively through the entries, she had an eager focus, a definite purpose in mind.

She was bound and determined to find a special someone who could become Meg Monroe's Valentine.

***

Darlene Pitts sat bolt upright at her desk, at attention as usual. She held the phone an inch or so from her ear, stoically listening while continuing to type up a work order with the other hand. Her face was as inscrutable as ever, but it was easy enough to tell by the rolling of her eyes and the tapping of her foot that she had long since tired of this particular call.

"Yes, Tabitha, dear, I do understand. I'll pass the information on to Sheriff Green. Yes, Tabitha, I'll make sure he gets it as soon as possible. No, dear, there's no need to check back with me in awhile. The sheriff will add it to his list of to do's. Thank you dear. No, no trouble at all, I perfectly understand why you would be offended. You have a good day now. Make sure to say 'hello' to Cora for me. 'Bye."

Darlene placed the phone back on its base and went back to typing with two hands. Cash Green and Ericka Yamato glanced at each other with raised eyebrows and slight grins. Cash leaned back in his office chair and set the police bulletin from Brown Bear Junction on his desk, tipping his head slightly to the side and waiting. Shaking her head in amusement, Yamato focused her attention back on typing up notes on her computer. With a silent chuckle, she placed a bet in her head that Cash would be the one to ask Darlene about the recent call, long before Darlene, the office's senior citizen secretary-dispatcher, would volunteer the information.

Cash stretched his back and took a sip from his steaming coffee mug, his eyes watching Darlene the whole while. If she noticed her boss watching her, Darlene never showed it. She continued typing away, efficiently removing one completed work order from her old IBM Selectric typewriter and replacing it with a blank one.

In the back room, they could hear several large plastic bins being shifted around as Horace Scofield, the other town deputy hollered out, "Does anybody remember where we put the extra heavy duty mittens after the last cold spell? I've got to go walk my rounds, and the mercury in the thermometer has gone and hid. My hands are gonna' be cold without those mittens!"

Yamato pushed her chair away from her desk and walked back into the storeroom, finding Horace sitting in the middle of the back room surrounded by at least ten large, filled plastic storage containers and looking more than a little frustrated. Yamato couldn't help but chuckle as she stared down at the deputy.

Horace was well meaning, hard working, sometimes emotional and slightly inept and self-conscious. He and his wife Millie had two children, Hank and Hillary. Horace was also thoughtful and kind-hearted to a fault. Order and consistency were not, however, a part of Horace's vocabulary or lifestyle.

"Hmmm, my guess would be to try the one labeled winter gear," Yamato grinned and glanced at Horace.

"Labeled? You mean these containers have..." Horace's exclamation trailed off as his eyes widened and he started examining the small raised tapes on the front of each bin.

Glancing up at Yamato, his embarrassment reddening his slightly chunky cheeks, Horace pulled open one of the bins, to find an assortment of bad weather gear such as hats, gloves and scarves.

"Oh, yeah, I see," Horace commented lamely, reaching in to grab a pair of heavy mittens. As he stood up and started putting the containers back where they had been stored, he glanced over at Yamato for a moment, his eyes resembling an imploring puppy for a moment.

Horace whispered, with a quick glance out into the main office, "Can we keep this between us, Yamato? Please?"

Ericka grinned, her eyes twinkling, "No, Horace I won't tell Darlene. I promise. But only if you bring me back one of Federman's hot glazed donuts!"

Horace grinned and his eyes lit up with relief, "Done! You're the best Yamato!"

As Yamato walked back into the main office, Cash was still staring at Darlene. The secretary was still focused on her work orders. With a smile to herself, Yamato sat down at her desk and went back to editing her notes on the computer.

At that moment, Bert Westin, the town's First Selectman stepped through the front door, stomping the snow off his boots and his cheeks rosy from the cold.

"Good morning, everyone! My, what a glorious bounty old man winter has sent us once again! The snow will keep the rich skiers happy, and the chilly temperatures will keep the ski companies happy as well! It's going to be a bumper year for the maple sugar industry and all this snow will fill the streams, rivers and lakes in the spring!" Bert brushed off the snow on his heavy jacket as he stood on the front door mat. Glancing all around the room, he oozed civic pride and good will, as if he had been in charge of the weather himself.

"Morning, Bert," replied Darlene without looking up from her typing.

"Morning, Bert," both Cash and Yamato declared. Cash smiled, rose from his desk and walked over to shake the first selectman's outstretched hand, "and how are things over at the town hall this morning?"

"Just fine and dandy," responded Bert as he gazed around cheerfully at Darlene, Yamato and then back to Cash, "or at least they were when I left! I just wanted to remind you that we're going to need the town square cordoned off for the big Valentine's Day carnival!"

Cash glanced over at Yamato and came close to grinning indulgently, "Oh, yes. I remember you telling me about that a while back, Bert. Can you be a little more specific what will be going on so we can develop a more detailed plan to deal with it?"

Bert sniffed the air, his excellent sense of smell ferreting out the strong, savory scent in the air, "Is that fresh coffee I smell?" His eyes lit up as he smiled broadly and inquired, "Don't suppose I could convince you to pour me a cup, could I, Miss Ericka?"

Yamato grinned and nodded, heading off to the back of the office while Bert continued almost without pause, his eyes widening with enthusiasm and delight, "It's going to be fantastic, Cash! We've decided, the council that is, that we need a little something to liven up the winter months, so we're going to begin an annual Valentine's Day Celebration! It will bring in some money, get people out, and hopefully alleviate a touch of cabin fever at this time of year."

Cash had to nod in agreement. February in Vermont was a bit like being on house arrest. The snow, ice and freezing temperatures tended to keep all but the hardiest citizens indoors and hunkering down with a roaring fire and a good book in the evening. Any respite from the weeks on end of winter weather with its bluster, numbing cold and foot after foot of white stuff was considered a good thing.

"Well, let's see! We're going to have an ice sculpture contest around the town square, a skating rink in the middle of the park, craft fairs in the Congregational, Methodist and Catholic Churches, a local Valentine's Day art show at Mona Castillo's Gallery, and a dance in the town hall on Valentine's Day evening!" Bert was animated and excited as he went over all the trappings and events for their new holiday festival.

Bert fairly jiggled with enthusiasm as he continued, "We're even going to have a wine, cheese tasting and maple syrup on snow buffet in the Garland-Mulroney Funeral Home during the day! Jeb and Zeke told me that they were already planning to have some kind of grand video game contest setup as well! I tell you, it's going to be absolutely spectacular!"

Bert's smile vanished for a moment and he stared at Cash and Yamato quite sincerely, "So we need to make sure that the town square is completely blocked off from traffic of any kind from nine in the morning until midnight on Valentine's Day. Can you do that, sheriff?"

Yamato walked over to the first selectman and handed him a large sturdy paper cup with steam drifting up from it, winked at Bert and interjected, "Three sugars and plenty of creamer, right, Bert?"

Glancing down at the cup in front of him, the first selectman's smile returned, and he glanced over gratefully at the deputy as he accepted the coffee, "Oh my, yes! Thank you, Deputy Yamato! This will most certainly hit the spot as I walk back to the town hall this morning!"

Cash placed his hand firmly, reassuringly, on the selectman's arm, "Bert, we'll be glad to take care of it. We'll put together a plan, then come and run it by you a day or two before the event. Fair enough?"

"Great, can't wait! It's going to be amazing, just wait and see! See you all soon," uttered the obviously enthusiastic and invigorated First Selectman as he turned, waved goodbye and hurried out the front door into the early morning chill.

After all three of them had called out their goodbyes, Cash turned back toward Darlene, studied her for a moment and with a resigned sigh asked, "Okay, Darlene, what did Tabitha Makepeace want on the phone?"

Darlene waited for a few seconds, most probably to emphasize the moment, and then stated in her simple, dry, matter-of-fact way, "She just wanted you to know that some kids are making snowmen in her back yard."

Cash stared at Darlene and then glanced at Yamato in disbelief, scratching his head slowly before he responded, "That's all?"

"Well," added Darlene with a straight face and not missing a beat, "she did say that the kids were making these particular snowmen anatomically correct."

***

Norma McClain was completely absorbed in whipping up a new batch of chocolate on the stainless steel worktable in the front window of The Scoop, the best homemade ice cream and chocolate shop anywhere around for at least three counties. When the front door bell of the shop tinkled, it startled Norma for a moment. Then, as she glanced up, a joyous smile lit up her beautiful face.

Newt Anderson, her British beau and fiancé, was standing there, stomping the snow off his boots and holding up two coffees that he had just bought at Tina's Diner. His cheeks were red and rosy and his eyes were twinkling.

"Top of the mornin' to ya', Sweet Lady!" declared Newt, his British accent mixing in with his attempted Irish brogue, "I thought you'd be ready for your second cup by now, Darlin'!"

Setting one cup on the counter and shoving it toward Norma, Newt winked playfully, "One sugar and a dab of half-and-half, right?"

Norma wiped her hands off on the towel that was slung over her shoulder, chuckled and accepted the caffeine gratefully, "Well, truth be told, it's actually my third cup, but all that matters is that I surely do appreciate it!"

Glancing around behind Newt, a look of curiosity flashing across her face, Norma asked, "Where's Remy? To see one of you without the other, now that doesn't happen very often."

Newt and Remy Renquist had been friends most of their lives and had flown balloons together all over the world for the past thirty years. The two adventurers had accidentally 'dropped in' on The Falls two years ago when they had to emergency land their cherished balloon, Limey. They had come to like the people and the town so well that they had promptly decided to make their home there. Newt's falling head over heels in love with Norma and Remy's infatuation for Trish, Norma's sister and co-owner of The Scoop, did have a good deal to do with that decision as well, of course.

Now, Newt and Remy owned their own business in

town, a business shared with another relative newcomer, Drake McKiernan. 'Dream Rides', half Harley dealership and half balloonist's heaven had definitely given The Falls a financial shot in the arm.

"Well, I can explain that, My Darlin'," smiled Newt as he leaned over the counter to give Norma a sweet kiss on her lips, then winked once again, "Remy is headin' off to make a life-changing decision this mornin'. He's headed up to Burlington at this moment, in fact."

Norma stared at Newt, her eyebrows lifting, as her smile turned into an animated grin. Leaning close to her love, she whispered excitedly, "He's headed up to Jamison's Jewelry, isn't he!? He's finally going to get Trish an engagement ring, isn't he!? Well, isn't he?"

Newt glanced guardedly around making sure that Trish wasn't anywhere within earshot, then grinned and nodded happily, "He's been talkin' about it for a year now, My Love! He finally decided to 'pop the question' as you Americans say, on Valentine's Day, he did! But you didn't hear it from me, you understand? Mum's the word!"

Norma reached over the counter and pulled Newt close, kissing him firmly and ecstatically as she laughed quietly, "Trish has no idea! She's wanted him to ask her for so long now! They'll have a magical Valentine's Day celebration!"

Just as quickly as Norma had been laughing she started crying, large hot tears of elation rolling down her cheeks. Newt's smile vanished in shock as he looked on, uncertain what to do. He awkwardly reached out to hold her, patting her back softly, trying to find some clue as to what had gone so horribly wrong.

Noticing her fiancé's predicament, Norma laughed again through her tears, shaking her head and staring at her well-meaning Newt, "Oh, you silly man! These are tears of joy! I'm not hurt or sad or angry! I'm happy for Trish and Remy! Overjoyed!"

Newt held up his hands in confusion, shaking his head and realizing that no matter how old he lived to be, he would never begin to understand women. Love them, undeniably, with all his heart. Want to be with them, always and forever. But understand them, never.

Chapter 2

Matthew Andrew Morrison sat behind his elegant cherry wood desk gazing thoughtfully at the young woman who was sitting in one of the matching cherry wood armchairs on the other side. Andy, as his close circle of friends called him, was dressed in an Armani suit, wore a Rolex, had his hair cut in a trendy short style and sported solid gold cufflinks. But, as the old adage advised, one shouldn't judge the book by the cover.

Andy was a kind, caring, and 'thoroughly comfortable in his own skin' young man. He wasn't pretentious, but he felt strongly that he should dress the way his firm expected him to while doing his job. On his free time, he was definitely a jeans and t-shirt kind of guy. Andy worked for Brown Bear Junction's most prominent law firm: Lesner, Malkowitz, Freedman and Lister. Andy was only thirty, but through hard work and perseverance, he was already a junior partner.

The obviously heartbroken young woman across from him was Elizabeth Fallon. Elizabeth was twenty-three and had just lost her father. Benjamin Fallon had died of congestive heart failure a mere five days before. Elizabeth's mother had died giving birth to her, and her father had done his best to raise her. Lesner, Malkowitz, Freedman and Lister had represented her father in several business dealings, and it was now Andy's unenviable job to go through Benjamin's will with his only heir.

"Elizabeth, do you understand everything we've discussed?" Andy asked compassionately, as he tried to assess young Elizabeth's emotional state, "Is there anything else I can do to help? I know how hard all this must be right now."

Elizabeth glanced up, her eyes red, her voice quiet and trembling slightly, "No, Mr. Morrison, I understand. I didn't realize how much debt Dad had acquired over the years. It's rather overwhelming. It doesn't look like Dad had much saved either."

Elizabeth glanced out the window for a moment, trying to control her emotions, "It's going to be hard to keep our house. I have a job as a sales person at The Dollar Store in Brown Bear Junction, but the mortgage payments are going to be a little out of my price range. I'm not really sure what I will do." Her voice became softer and quieter as she spoke.

Andy frowned slightly, then glanced back up at Elizabeth, his eyes lighting up with the beginnings of an idea, "Elizabeth, you said you went to business school, correct?"

Elizabeth stared at her lawyer inquisitively, "Yes. I went to Vermont Community College and got my MBA. It was the only college in the area that I could afford. I lived at home to save money. Why?"

"Well, we have a job opening in our paralegal department. You'd have to start at base level, but there's a chance for advancement and I imagine the salary is a good deal more than the salary of the job you have right now. Now, understand that I would have to run it by the managing partners, but I'm pretty sure they would approve. Would you be interested?" Andy was smiling, his eyes twinkling happily as he eagerly awaited Elizabeth's answer.

"Oh, yes! I would be very interested! Oh, thank you, so much!" Elizabeth declared animatedly. For the first time since she had been sitting with Andy a smile broke through the veil of tears and gloom. Elizabeth sat up in her chair, obviously overjoyed at the almost too good to be hoped for opportunity.

Andy grinned and pushed a button on his telephone. A moment later, a rather stylishly dressed young woman stepped quietly into his office. Andy turned to the secretary and smiled warmly, "Jennifer! This is Elizabeth," Andy gestured toward Elizabeth who had stood up by her chair.

"Elizabeth, Jennifer will take you down to human resources, so we can get you started on an application for that paralegal position. While you're doing that, I'll check with the partners and get an okay to get you started. What do you think?" Andy stood and glanced cheerfully back and forth from one young lady to the other.

Jennifer nodded cheerfully to Andy and smiling, she held the door open for Elizabeth. As Elizabeth began walking toward the door, she suddenly stopped and then impulsively strode over to where Andy was still standing. She looked up into the kind and caring eyes of the young man and reached out purposefully. She shook his hand firmly, whispering, "Thank you so much. You don't know how much this means to me. I owe you a debt I'll never be able to repay."

Her eyes filled with tears once more as she quietly added, "I know that my father would thank you if he were still here too, Mr. Morrison."

Andy shook her hand, smiling happily, "You are very welcome, Elizabeth! Welcome to LMFL as we like to call the firm! I know you'll be a great addition to the company!"

With that, an overjoyed and appreciative Elizabeth nodded self-consciously to her lawyer and joyfully followed a smiling Jennifer out of Andy's office and down to personnel.

Sitting back down at his desk, a satisfied grin still plastered across his handsome face, Andy picked up the phone, ready to dial into Glen Lister's office. Just before he pushed the intercom button, his cell phone rang. Glancing at the caller ID, Andy smiled and answered.

"Hey, it's my favorite coffee connoisseur! How are you Jordan?" Andy's face lit up as he leaned back in his office chair.

On the other end of the line, Jordan Smith-Stone chuckled, "Well, I'm not the only one who enjoys the savory secrets of the cocoa bean, young man!" she replied.

"True, true," Andy returned, "I have to admit that where coffee is concerned, I will go to all lengths possible to enjoy the best the globe has to offer! Now, to what do I owe this call from such a charming, beautiful young woman?"

Jordan chuckled once again, "Ever the charmer, aren't you? Well, if you must know, I'm playing Cupid."

Andy stared out the window, his smile fading a bit, "Oh, Jordan, you know I'm not much into dating and all that stuff. I keep trying to tell you that although I have a somewhat engaging, amiable public persona, that's really not who I am underneath. Under it all, I'm just a plain old country boy, and a kind of shy one at that. Sorry, I don't mean to spoil your fun."

Jordan listened, nodding to herself, expecting nothing less from her friend, "I know that, Andy. But the person I'd like you to meet is a lot like you. She's a doctor here in West Sugar Shack Falls. She has no family in the area and works all the time. I think she's a bit home sick and she's wearing herself out. She's also cute and witty and is as sweet as an ear of spring corn."

Andy listened, quietly. He never had liked blind dates. But fortunately he knew who Jordan was talking about. It was Dr. Monroe. He had seen Meg Monroe around the area a few times, and had always thought she seemed sweet and honestly nice with no 'put on' airs. In his heart he hesitated. He really was as shy as he described, maybe more. But the truth was, he was a bit lonely himself. He rattled around in his new house. That's what it was, a house. It wasn't a home like the place where he had lived with his parents. With all his money and success, he still didn't have a home.

With lots of mixed emotions, Andy leaned forward in his chair and spoke quietly into his phone, "Okay, I know the young lady you mean. What are you suggesting?"

On the other end of the line, he could hear Jordan exclaim, "You're saying yes! I just knew you'd say yes!" and he had to shrug and simply grin.

***

Donald Morganstein huffed and puffed as he worked diligently to clean the freshly fallen snow off the front porch of his hardware store. The freezing temperatures had made him bundle up, but now, as he began to sweat heavily, he regretted the choice.

Glancing up, Donald spotted both Lyle Federman, the owner of Federman's Bakery, and Philo Jones who ran Jones' Deli and Market both struggling to clear the front porches of their own businesses as well. Standing up and wheezing heavily, Donald waved and grinned cheerfully at his two friends. They stopped shoveling as well, leaning on their snow shovels, wiping the sweat off their brows and waving back.

"Two winters in a row with enough snow to fill up Owl Creek Gorge twice over! Unbelievable!" hollered out Lyle, arching his back to get out the kinks.

"What do you expect, ya' old geezer!? It's Vermont for criminy's sake!" replied Philo, taking off his wool hunting hat and letting the heat rise off his sweaty head in a steamy vapor.

At that all three friends chuckled in-between gasps of air, nodding silently in agreement and amusement.

"Hey, what are you guys gonna' do for the Valentine's Day celebration?" called out Donald, glancing from Philo to Lyle and back again.

Philo shrugged, glanced over at Lyle and then back again at Donald, "I figured I'd put up some decorations around the deli, and then have a sale on candy hearts, cherries, boxes of chocolates, that sort of thing. What about you?"

Donald kicked a piece of snow and ice that was frozen to his porch railing and glanced around, "I wasn't really sure what to do. A hardware store doesn't really have any gifts especially for Valentine's Day."

Lyle grinned and called out to his two old friends, "I had an idea. How about the three of us put together a flyer to go out to everyone in town? In it we'll put coupons with little cupids on 'em that can be used at each of our stores for ten, fifteen and twenty percent off an item, depending on how much it costs. Whadya' think?"

"That's a great idea!" shouted out an impressed and

relieved Donald and Philo in perfect unison.

Donald's thoughtful frown flashed across his sweaty brow as he added, "Maybe we could get some of the other town businesses to go in with us! We could even extend it for three days, not just Valentine's Day! That way everybody would have a chance to use a coupon or two. It sure could help business!"

The three businessmen grinned at each other and nodded. Refreshed and energized, they dug back into finishing their shoveling. The grins remained on their faces, as they each thought of more and more ways to make Valentine's Day a profitable business venture.

Kitty corner from the three businesses on the snow-covered town square lay the three churches that had long been part of The Falls. The spires of the Catholic church, the Methodist church, and the Congregational church rose proudly up into the clear, chilly February sky. In front of each church, the minister of that particular denomination was busily engaged in the same activity as Philo, Donald and Lyle.

"Mornin' Father," called out Reverend Theo Dunham as he glanced over at Father Flynn O'Flaherty who was grunting and groaning with the weight of too large a shovelful of ice and snow.

Father O'Flaherty plopped the load of snow down onto a nearby snow bank with great difficulty and turned slowly to acknowledge the greeting, "And the same to you Reverend Dunham! The same to you!"

Reverend Marcus Templeton, the pastor of the Methodist church which stood between the Catholic church and the Congregational church stood up and leaned heavily on the handle of his snow shovel, "You know, my blessed father used to say that the snow was a blessing from up above and that we should enjoy every moment of it."

Marcus grimaced and glanced all around the blanketed town square that had been inundated with the snow three nights in a row. "But there is a point when an overabundance of anything gets to be too much of a good thing, don't you agree gentlemen?"

Both Father O'Flaherty and Reverend Dunham grinned and nodded their heads in agreement, "Well, with perhaps the exception of Tina's fabulous turkey dinner," chuckled Reverend Dunham. "There could never be too much of that." Just thinking of Tina's annual holiday dinner made the good reverend's stomach grumble.

"Or a good, well aged, single malt whiskey!" exclaimed Father O'Flaherty, a mischievous twinkle in his eye and a slight lift of a craggy eyebrow.

"And there could never be too many of Lyle Federman's amazingly light and scrumptious raised doughnuts! I can smell their aroma on the breeze right now!" added Reverend Templeton, involuntarily licking his lips hungrily at the thought.

Glancing around at each other, all of their eyes now sparkling merrily, the good reverends made a silent but unanimous pact. They each purposefully stuck their snow shovels in a nearby snow bank and then trudged determinedly through the hip deep snow, until they were striding together toward Federman's bakery with large smiles on each of their faces. There they each would drown their snow shoveling woes with a warm raised doughnut and a good strong cup of coffee.

Sometimes, a snowstorm can have a residual effect that is at once both savory and unexpected.

***

Jeremy Burman hurriedly stomped his boots off and

left them to the side of the welcome mat in front of the entrance to the Elmer Oberman Library and Welcome Center. He was late. He had promised Miss Eunice that he would be here at seven o'clock and it was at least five minutes after. Jeremy now regretted the second stack of pancakes that Grandma Burman had offered and he had hungrily and happily accepted.

"Jeremy? Is that you?" came Miss Eunice's voice from down in the basement of the library as Jeremy hustled through the main room of the library, looking all around, trying to spot the town's librarian.

"Yes, Miss Eunice! I'll be right down!" called out Jeremy, as he laid his coat and hat over the back of a large wooden chair next to the first library table he passed.

Eunice McAllister had been the town's librarian for a number of years. She was excellent at her job. Her one glaring idiosyncrasy had been that she disliked letting her precious books leave the library. Before Jeremy had become her assistant librarian, she had been almost obsessive about keeping her treasured volumes in excellent repair and safe on the library shelves. Since her brother Millard had been killed two winters past, and Jeremy had come to work with her in the library, she had learned to relax a good deal, and now she was actually able to enjoy seeing her prized tomes lent out to the good citizens of The Falls.

"I'm in here," came Eunice's voice, as Jeremy strode along the well-lit corridor that led to the artifacts' room. As he turned the corner and entered the exhibit, he noticed Miss Eunice, over in the corner, on her hands and knees, a rag in one hand and a can of polish in the other. Eunice was attempting to clean and buff an ancient farmer's plow from the eighteenth century. She glanced up and smiled at her assistant, motioning to him.

"Get the other cloth and polish and start on the old tiller over there," Eunice pointed to the tiller and then turned back to the job at hand, "I figure it's going to take us several days of polishing before and after library hours to get this old equipment back into good shape. I'm afraid we've been neglecting them lately."

Jeremy had already started working on the old tiller, rubbing the liquid in and then wiping it off after a few minutes, "Well, we've been busy, Miss Eunice. We catalogued the whole fiction and nonfiction sections and entered them into the computer and all we have left to catalogue is the children's picture books. Then you'll be able to use the wand to check out and turn in every book in the library. That's a big job and it's going to save you loads of time."

"You catalogued the books, Jeremy, I still don't have much of a head for computers. All I did was carry books back and forth and enter the bar codes for them," Eunice's voice was slightly muffled as her head was on the other side of the tiller at this point.

Jeremy grinned, enjoying the praise, a warm feeling trickling through his body, but staunchly defended his boss, "But you understand more and more all the time, Miss Eunice! I'll bet you could enter and catalogue all the children's books without me even around!"

Eunice poked her head out from behind the plow and smiled, "Well I might just be able to, but that's not about to happen, young man! You are this library's biggest asset, and I know enough to value someone extraordinary!"

Jeremy blushed, glad that he was half hidden by the old tiller. Buffing a section of the tiller he had already cleaned and waxed to stay out of sight, Jeremy self-consciously changed the subject, "What are we going to do for Valentine's Day, Miss Eunice? It seems like the whole town's doing all sorts of special things. Shouldn't we do something here in the library?"

Eunice stopped a moment and sat on the floor, resting and adjusting her glasses, "Well, I agree. I've been thinking about what we might do. There are several possibilities…"

As the librarian and her protégé worked and thoroughly discussed the possibilities of Valentine's Day at the library, Jordan Smith was waiting on old Daniel Caruthers at the pharmacy.

"I ain't never taken this medicine before, Miss Jordan," Daniel was saying, rubbing his chin and staring at the prescription bottle he held in his gnarled old hand, "and I ain't sure what this means."

Jordan smiled and gently took the bottle from Daniel, reading off the instructions, "Sure, let's take a look. It says, take one pill before bedtime, Mr. Caruthers. Is there a problem?"

Daniel scrunched up his face, obviously getting more and more frustrated, and shrugged, "Well, I'm in the middle of working on sap collection and boilin' in my little maple grove down the road a bit. It's a twenty-four hour a day kinda' thing, understand? Sometimes I don't sleep for thirty-six hours, sometimes I take catnaps every hour or so. So when do I take the darned meds?"

Biting her tongue to avoid smiling and embarrassing the obviously sincere and earnest old gentleman, Jordan nodded and firmly but kindheartedly stated the obvious, "I understand, Mr. Caruthers. That is a problem, isn't it? If it were me, I would choose one time when you would normally go to bed during your off season and take the pill every night at that time. Does that make sense?"

The old man instantly brightened up, as his frown vanished and he smiled back at Jordan, his blue eyes twinkling merrily, "That makes perfect sense, Miss Jordan! Leave it to you to figure it out. Thanks ever so much. I'm obliged!"

With a wave and a relieved wink, Daniel strode across the pharmacy floor and out the front door. For a moment, Jordan smiled indulgently as she watched the old man walk down the steps and into the snowy street, then she turned and began working on filling other prescriptions from her back counter.

Almost immediately, the front door bell tinkled again and Jordan turned, assuming that Mr. Caruthers had another question or had forgotten something. Jordan's smile flashed across her face and as she turned she called out, "What else can I do for you today, Daniel?"

There stood Matthew Andrew Morrison, a broad smile on his face and his eyebrows raised in mock alarm, "Well either you have just become The Falls' latest case of instant amnesia, or I'm not who I think I am!"

Jordan chuckled and waved off Andy's witty if sarcastic comments, "I was expecting someone else, you foolish man!"

"You mean the old guy who was walking out to the old truck parked out front and kind of mumbling to himself?" Andy grinned as he took a glance around the pharmacy and then settled his gaze back on Jordan.

"Well, yes. But he's a really nice old guy, just gets a bit confused," Jordan raised one eyebrow and nodded at Andy, "as we all do from time to time." Jordan emphasized the 'all do' as she stared at the young lawyer.

Andy raised his hands, feigning submission, grinning from ear to ear, "Okay, okay! I give! He's a nice old man! You win!"

Jordan and Andy shared a light laugh for a moment and then Andy's smile faded slowly, "Okay, I'm here. You wanted me to stop by to discuss 'project cupid' so here I am. But I have to tell you, I'm feeling a little uncomfortable with this."

Jordan's eyes widened as it was her turn to feign surprise, "You?! The rising young hot shot lawyer is feeling uncomfortable asking a beautiful, sweet young woman out?"

Andy blushed slightly and smiled once again, "Yeah. Well. I'm a little out of practice. I've been working so hard at the lawyer thing that I haven't had much time for a personal life."

Jordan stepped out from behind the counter and walked over to the young man, a smile on her face, her eyes kind and compassionate. She placed a hand on his arm gently, "Look, I know you've had kind of a rough time the last few years in your personal life, and that you may not feel exactly 'gung ho' about putting your toe in the dating pool. But trust me. Meg Monroe is a breath of fresh air. She's kind and caring and sweet, smart as all get out, not to mention she's a really beautiful woman."

Andy stared into Jordan's eyes and smiled much like a little boy just waiting permission to stick his hand in the cookie jar, "Okay, okay. You've convinced me. Now, does the young lady know about me?"

Jordan winked, "Well, not exactly, but I intend to take care of that this very morning. So, here's the plan..."

Chapter 3

Wendy Morrison gently slipped the antique porcelain doll out of the heavily padded shipping package and stood it up on the glass counter of her antique shop, Treasured Memories. Her face lit up as she admired the beauty of the doll and the skilled workmanship of the doll maker from almost a century ago.

Mandy Wagner, her part-time clerk, stopped cleaning and polishing one of the assorted used bureaus on the display floor and walked over to get a good view of the new acquisition.

"Oh my! She's a real charmer, isn't she, Miss Wendy?" Mandy smiled and her eyes widened with wonder as she took in the beauty of the well-preserved figure. "Even the clothes are immaculate, and so well made! She'll be a great addition to our dolls collection!"

Mandy's gaze was eagerly drawn over to the exhibit case on the other side of the store that proudly displayed at least twenty-five other porcelain dolls.

Wendy smiled and nodded at Mandy, "You're right, she will. She's easily one of our best 'little treasures'. We'll clean her off and display her today."

As Mandy walked back to the bureau to finish her cleaning, she grinned and replied, "If I'm any judge of a doll's worth, which I like to think I am after all these years, she won't last long before one of our regulars scoops her up and carries her home with them."

Mandy had once been the owner of Treasured Memories, and she had worked there for at least forty of her sixty years. Wendy and her brother Andy had bought the antique store from Mandy a few years ago, and had kept Mandy on partly because of her expertise and mostly because everyone in Brown Bear Junction knew and loved her. Now Mandy had the best of both worlds: she could work part time in the store she loved, enjoy her semi-retirement and take the time to 'smell the roses' when she wanted to as well as having a neat little nest egg in the bank if and when she needed it.

Wendy and her lawyer brother lived in a rather large house that Andy had purchased three years ago, right in the heart of the Brown Bear Junction town square. With their parents dead, and neither Andy nor Wendy having anyone special in their lives, they depended a great deal on each other. Wendy, at thirty-six, was six years older than her brother. She had started raising him when their parents had died. At the time, she had been eighteen and he had been only twelve. For all intents and purposes, their relationship had changed forever at that moment from brother and sister to one more like mother and son.

Wendy fluffed out the wide, flouncy dress and adjusted the jaunty hat on the doll as she carried her over to the display case. Carefully reorganizing the collection to adequately display her new purchase, Wendy smiled as she proudly surveyed the china and porcelain figures.

Adding porcelain dolls had been one of the subtle changes she had made in revamping and updating Treasured Memories. She had also brought in new glass display cases, track lighting to better display the antiques and she had added a coffee counter where shoppers could get a free cup of coffee or tea and munch contentedly on some fresh bakery cookies as they leisurely perused the shop's wares.

Having completed her doll setup, Wendy took a step back and gazed proudly at the beautiful vintage dolls on display. Just then, Wilomena Hargrove, whose family had been one of the founding families of Brown Bear Junction hundreds of years before, stepped into the little shop.

"Good morning, Wendy, Mandy! It's a beautiful day!" trilled the seventy-year-old Wilomena, "A great day to be alive!"

Wendy smiled and nodded to Wilomena, who was one of her biggest customers, "Good morning to you, as well, Miss Hargrove. There's a beautiful sky, but the temperature is still a bit brisk for my liking!"

Mandy glanced over at Wilomena, whom she had known for several decades and grinned, "Any day is a great day to be alive! Right, Wilomena?"

Wilomena chuckled and added, with a wink, "Well it's certainly better than the alternative!"

As Wendy stepped toward her frequent customer, Wilomena carefully took off her coat and gloves and handed them to the shopkeeper. Then, Wilomena began to systematically search the shop with her eyes, looking for anything new, anything interesting. Wilomena Hargrove had a great deal of money, but she didn't spend it foolishly. She took her time and made smart bargains and could never be charmed or cajoled into any purchase, much like her banker father before her.

Wendy and Mandy were used to this method from

Wilomena so they simply gave their patron some time to probe and investigate the shop's second-hand treasures. Mandy poured Wilomena a cup of her favorite tea and placed two shortbread cookies on her plate. She then set it on one of the tall tables that Wendy had placed strategically in the center of the display floor. Wendy stood near Wilomena, quietly ready to respond to any questions or describe any item that Wilomena might have questions on during her storewide search.

Wilomena's gaze finally settled on the new porcelain doll and her eyes lit up. "That doll's new, is it not?" Wilomena turned and glanced curiously at Wendy before immediately returning to stare appreciatively at the beautiful doll.

"Yes, she arrived just this morning, Miss Hargrove. She's traveled around the world, actually." Wendy walked over to the display and picked up the porcelain doll, bringing it over to Wilomena and setting her on top of the tall circular table for Wilomena to get a closer look.

"Around the world?" Wilomena took a moment from studying the figure to glance quizzically at the shop's owner, "Really?"

Happily seeing Wilomena Hargrove's interest in the doll growing, Wendy continued. "Yes. The doll originally was a gift to a teenage girl who lived here in America. But the girl and her family soon moved to London, where her father was a man of quite some importance. When the girl grew older and became married, she handed the doll down lovingly to her own daughter, and the family moved to Venice, Italy. From there, the doll found its way to Russia where it was owned by a thrice removed Russian princess, then on to Switzerland and to a small village in Austria. Ten years ago she found a home in Edinburgh in a small curio shop, and that is where I found her online and brought her back to America."

"Well, well. My, my," murmured Wilomena as she gently stroked the doll's hair and with great admiration touched the silky material of the flawless and skillfully stitched dress.

By this time, Mandy and Wendy knew Wilomena was hooked by both the beauty and the background history of the doll. They glanced at each other with knowing looks and exchanged smiles.

Wilomena, dragging her gaze away from the doll, arched her eyebrow at Wendy and stared at her directly. Then she leaned over the tabletop intently and almost whispering, she murmured softly, "It is a charming little piece, I suppose. If I were to consider this trinket, what, pray tell, would it cost me?"

Wendy took a moment, considering her options. If she asked for too much, Wilomena would most certainly pay it, but their relationship would become more a one of doubt and mistrust rather than the honest and aboveboard one they had always enjoyed. If she charged too little, Wilomena would think less of her, for not getting the true value of the piece.

Wendy gazed at her costumer, her demeanor calm and relaxed, and quietly asked, "Miss Hargrove, you are the most astute customer we have. I have no doubt that what you give me in exchange for the doll will show both your thrifty nature and your generosity at finding a true treasured memory."

At that, Wilomena Hargrove stared hard and long at the shop's proprietor and then broke out in amused and pleasant laughter. After a moment, both Wendy and

Mandy heartily joined in.

***

Leonard Obregon raised sheep. He had a fifty-acre sheep farm about a mile and a half down Owl Creek Road from the town square of The Falls. At the moment, however, he was sitting in the examination room at the regional hospital, holding his hand, which had been hastily wrapped in an old but clean towel, holding it up at an awkward angle in the air. Standing next to him was his daughter, Gypsy Lee Obregon, dutifully holding her father's old hat and wiping away the trickle of blood that oozed from time to time down his tanned and weathered arm.

Meg Monroe stepped briskly into the examination room, clipboard in hand. She smiled and glanced expectantly at both Lennie, as Leonard was better known by the townsfolk, and his daughter.

"Hey Mr. Obregon, Gypsy Lee! What brings you here this beautiful frosty morning?" Meg asked as she closed the examination room door behind her and walked over to where Lennie was sitting.

Leonard glanced up at Meg. He was obviously embarrassed and he let his eyes drop down to the floor. Gypsy Lee, noting her father's discomfort took over the conversation, "Pa hurt his arm, Dr. Monroe."

Meg carefully had Leonard set his arm down on the examination table, all the while waiting for Gypsy Lee to continue her explanation. Unwrapping the towel, Meg found that the sheep farmer's arm had several long, deep tears in the skin. They appeared somewhat uniform in distance and as though something had been dragged roughly along his arm.

Lifting her eyebrows and glancing inquisitively back and forth from father to daughter, Meg replied, "Okay, you need to help me out here so I know how best to treat this. What exactly happened?"

"Well," Leonard began with a shrug, mumbling almost under his breath, "when I went to grab her, she spooked."

Meg again stared at Leonard and then back at his daughter, still waiting for clarification. "Who is she? What did this to your arm?"

Gypsy Lee glanced over at her dad, saw that he still wasn't about to fill in the details, sighed and began to tell the story. "Okay, we were out tending to the sheep. We let 'em out in the daytime if it's not stormin', then bring 'em in at night so they don't freeze, see?"

Meg nodded as she started cleaning out the deep wounds, glancing up at Gypsy from time to time, waiting for any information that might affect her treatment of the rather nasty gashes.

"Well, one of the rams was a little randy, you know how they get, right?" Gypsy Lee continued, her eyes wide and matter-of-fact. Even though Meg didn't really 'know how they got', she nodded and waited for Gypsy Lee to continue as she worked on Leonard's arm.

"Well, this old ram, Jethro is his name, was in full rut. Daddy named him after a man in the Bible, you know. Anyway, Jethro was getting' randy with some of the ewes. One of 'em got pushed into the barbed wire fence while he was mountin' her, and she got caught up in the fence." Gypsy kept talking as quickly as she could, her eyes staring down at Meg as she worked on her father's arm.

"Anyway, daddy shooed Jethro away from the ewe, who was bleatin' to beat the band. Then he reached out carefully to get her untangled. Just as daddy got the ewe set free, old Jethro, who apparently didn't much like bein' pulled off the object of his affection like that, ran up and butted daddy right in the seat of his pants!" Gypsy Lee glanced over at her father who obviously was not enjoying the story in the slightest. Gypsy blushed a bit but finished off the story.

"Long story made short, old Jethro knocked my daddy into the barbed wire, and then stalked away with his head held high, like he was once more the alpha male of his flock. Then he set about finding another ewe to mount!" Gypsy Lee then stepped back a step or two, her lips shut firmly, her eyes anywhere but on her mortified father.

Meg continued cleaning out the wounds that Jethro the ram and the barbed wire fence had inflicted, trying desperately not to giggle and hurt Leonard's feelings any further. She worked quickly, just trying to fix up the poor sheep farmer and not make matters worse with further conversation.

Half an hour later, as a disgruntled but grateful Leonard Obregon and his now silent daughter, Gypsy Lee, were walking back out toward their truck, Meg stepped out of the examination room and glanced down at her watch. Ten-thirty, just in time to do rounds of all the hospital patients, she thought with relief.

Turning to grab her stethoscope and charts, Meg started walking briskly toward the main hospital ward. Just then, the front doors to the hospital swung open and Jordan Smith-Stone walked in. To say that Jordan walked in anywhere however, simply did not do her usual entrances justice. Jordan was a beautiful, voluptuous and charming woman. Her charisma and aura made her positively glow as she entered a room. As Meg watched Jordan climb up the stairs toward her, she wished, for at least the umpteenth time that she could look like and command the attention that Jordan did.

"Hey Jordan! How's your day going? Keeping warm?" called out Meg, her eyes cheerful, her smile wide and sincere.

"Well my day has been busy, but that's not bad. As to keeping warm, well, it's February in Vermont. Since I'm not curled up with a blanket reading a book by the fire with my handsome husband to keep me warm, I'd say 'warm' is an allusion at best! How are you, Meg?" Jordan's eyes twinkled as she reached out and gave the young doctor a firm hug.

"I'm fine, thanks," offered Meg, clasping the clipboard in front of her, staring at Jordan's perfectly curled hair and wondering how long it took each day for the beautiful woman to maintain her exquisite good looks. "Can I offer you some coffee or tea?"

Jordan unwound her scarf and then glanced at the young doctor, her smile perfect, "No thanks, dear. I have a fresh cup of Brazilian Dark Roast waiting for me back at the pharmacy. I have just enough time to hand deliver a dinner invitation for tonight, our place eight o'clock. What about it, 'Miss I never get to go anywhere cause I'm always working'?" Jordan winked and giggled affectionately.

Meg stared at Jordan, her mind racing. She would be over her nightly rounds by seven o'clock, but she still had all that paperwork to catch up on before she went home late to a cardboard-like TV dinner and feeding her cat before tumbling into bed completely exhausted. At least that was her usual, if uninspiring, routine.

Jordan quickly saw where Meg's thoughts were headed. She stepped closer to the young doctor, firmly grasped her shoulders and looked her straight in the eye, whispering, "I'm not accepting a no, young lady. It's time you made a little time for yourself. Is that clear?"

Meg, staring into Jordan's beautiful but commanding eyes, heard herself reply, "Sure, I'd love to. See you at eight then."

A few seconds later, Jordan was stepping briskly and victoriously out the front door, while Meg was left standing motionless at the top of the stairs, wondering just exactly what had happened and if anyone had gotten the license plate of that exquisitely beautiful truck.

***

Sean Frasier stood looking out over the playground full of students. He had on his warm winter parka, his ski hat and his insulated mittens. On his slightly numb feet he had on the same pair of old winter boots he'd been wearing on this playground for the past dozen years.

This was his second twenty-minute recess in a row. Two of his staff members had called in sick, and he was taking their duty, rather than asking other teachers to take up the slack and cover their colleagues' duties. Sean firmly believed that, nowadays, teachers have more than enough to deal with without being asked to do even more.

Sean glanced over by the swings where seven-year-old Potter Jenkins was sitting, having a pity party for himself, in a mound of snow. His eyes were red, his lip trembling and he was staring with great remorse at the swing where little kindergartner Amy Nesbit was pumping back and forth with great relish and delight. Amy and Potter had both run to get the swing. Amy had been quicker than Potter thought. Once she had jumped on the fly onto the rubber seat, Potter had stopped in his tracks, tears welling up in his eyes and had plopped himself dejectedly down in the snow. Sean decided that this was one of those moments to turn a blind eye, and simply walk away. Potter was a bit of a baby and perhaps the lesson of having no one pay attention to his tantrum and pamper him with what he wanted would be a good life lesson.

As Sean walked away, he couldn't help but notice the twinkle in little Amy's eye as she enjoyed the swing, acting for all the world as though she was paying no attention whatsoever to the whimpering second grader. Sean smiled slightly and turned his attention to a group of sixth grade girls who were huddled excitedly, speaking in hushed whispers, over by one of the cleaned off picnic tables.

Meandering closer, acting as though the girls were of absolutely no current interest to him, the principal gazed across the playground as he got within listening distance.

"Yours is just divine!" Mable Mitchell exclaimed breathlessly, "It has awesome glitter and ribbons all over it!"

"No, yours is the one that stands out," giggled Eliza Obregon delightedly, "look at the delicate lace and sequins! It's simply amazing!"

"But look at Suzette's!" declared Mable as the animated girls turned their rapt and envious attention to yet another item, "there are decorations folded in the shape of a swan and a dragon! And it's covered with light purple and pink silk! Wow!"

Suzette Yung spoke up, a bit shy and embarrassed, but with definite pride and joy, "My grandmother taught me how to fold them. It's called origami!"

After a moment's hesitation with the other girls

'oohing' and 'ahhing' she added, "I can teach you how to make them if you want!"

At this all the girls began talking at the same time, excited and overjoyed. Sean took a quick glance at what the girls were talking about, and then looked quickly away, a lopsided grin spread across his face. They were comparing the homemade containers that they had created to hold the Valentine's cards they would each get from their classmates during Valentine's Day parties.

Every Valentine's Day, each classroom at the elementary school had a Valentine's Day party at the end of the academic day. It was a time to open the Valentine's cards that students had been making, shopping for and agonizing over giving and receiving during the week before Valentine's day.

The kindergarteners, first graders and even second graders all enjoyed giving and receiving the cards without any embarrassment or misgivings. They merely gave one to everybody in their class and to their teacher. The teacher made punch and gave out Valentine's candy hearts and the kids opened their humorous and heartwarming cards as they laughed and giggled.

Fifth and sixth graders, however, viewed the whole event in a somewhat different light. All of the fifth and sixth grade girls spent hours and hours and hours designing their card containers, making them look as amazing and as spectacular as possible. They went to great lengths to create Valentine's cards for the boys they pretended not to like, but secretly did. The boys, on the other hand, usually took about a minute or two designing their card containers, which sat on the corner of their desks for the week before Valentine's Day. They were embarrassed by the mere idea of sending Valentine cards to 'a girl' and therefore lived in dread of a frilly, satiny, fabulous card being placed in their container.

Now, there were certain exceptions. For those boys who had actually begun to notice girls, they were in a no win situation. If the girl they liked gave them a special 'Be Mine' card, they were thrilled. But they would also draw down the hoots, guffaws and instant shame and humiliation from all the other boys. They would be 'marked men' for days and weeks to come.

Sean promptly reminded himself of his feelings about Valentine's Day back thirty odd years ago, and simply shook his head, glad he didn't have to go through that agony again. He wondered if that was the first initiation that most kids had into the wild and uncontrollable world of dating, puppy love and crushes.

Setting those thoughts aside, the principal moved toward a group of third graders who thought they were out of sight of all the duty teachers. The foursome had decided to secretly try and exchange a few well-chosen snowballs while the duty teachers were busy across the playground.

Grinning to himself, Sean carefully snuck up in back of Jerome Murkowski and Potter Phelps, as the two boys were hiding behind a large snow bank. Their sweaty yet half frozen little mittens were tightly grasping two snowballs each, just about ready to launch them across the school yard at two other third graders, hidden for the moment behind their own snow bank. Sean moved closer, hunched over and silent until he was just a few feet in back of the two boys. As they rose up to eagerly hurl their missiles, the principal whispered loudly into their ears, "I'd think again, gentlemen."

Both boys gasped with shock, dropped their ammunition and turned slowly around, coming face to face with their principal. Their eyes were wide and stunned, much like the deer in the headlights syndrome.

Just then, two well-thrown snowballs hit Jerome and Potter right in the back of their heads and the boys crashed headfirst in the snowdrift. Standing with empty hands, great dismay and panic written across their faces as they spotted the principal standing right behind their chosen victims, were Ramona Osaka and Philbin Johnson.

As Jerome and Potter climbed out of the snowdrift, shook their heads and wiped the snow out of their faces, Sean stood up and without a single word, he motioned the four third graders to follow him. The stern look on the principal's face made the hearts of each of the culprits sink to their shoelaces.

A few moments later, Sean had the four scalawags seated at the small picnic table by the back door of the school. They each knew what that meant. They had 'time out' for the rest of that day's recesses. They would have to sit and watch the other kids play, one of the worst punishments third graders can possibly imagine.

As Sean walked away he cracked a lopsided grin, remembering how many times he and his younger brother William had served 'time outs' at the same table when they had been students in the very same school. The principal was pretty sure that was not a story to be shared with the kids at this point. He grinned and shook his head. Maybe he would share that story when the kids were in middle school, or high school, but certainly not now. He had to maintain.

The other two duty teachers, Lorraine Phelps and

Nancy Sturgis, were watching him, hardly containing their own amusement at the cowering little group at the time out table. As the three of them winked at each other knowingly, they turned back and stared at the miserable quartet at the time out table, and shared what only educators or parents could truly enjoy as truly a 'Kodak moment'.

Chapter 4

Dr. Serena Messina-Frazier sat in her white wicker rocker glancing back and forth between Beverly Tonga and her stepson Elmer. The mother and stepson were seated on the couch directly across the room from her. Elmer's face was screwed up into a storm cloud scowl, his arms crisscrossed tightly across his chest, his leg nervously moving up and down on the ball of his foot. Beverly was slumped in her seat, eyes red, thin lipped but still determined and hopeful.

"How long have you and Elmer's father been married, Mrs. Tonga?" Serena asked with a cheerful smile on her face, glancing from Beverly to Elmer and back again.

Beverly smiled wanly and sighed before she responded, "About three years. It's the second marriage for both of us. We were living up in Silver Pines until about two months ago, then we moved down here to be closer to," Beverly glanced over at Elmer unenthusiastically, "Herbert's children. They lived with their mother, but now she's remarried as well."

Beverly paused for a moment, deciding how to best word her next remark. "Elmer didn't seem to get along with his new stepfather, so his mother threw up her hands and said she was done. Elmer now lives with us."

Elmer turned and glared at his stepmother and

simply glowered, turning his gaze back to a spot on the wall he had been concentrating on since the discussion had begun. His demeanor was one of selfishness, disdain and superiority.

Beverly shrugged, "Elmer and I aren't doing much better than his stepfather and him. I've just about run out of things to try. You are our last hope, Dr. Messina." A tear ran down Beverly's flushed cheek and she wiped it away quickly. Her eyes reached out to the psychiatrist, hopeful that she might have some psychological magic to alleviate the obviously strained and painful relationship.

Serafina glanced over at Beverly and smiled reassuringly, "Mrs. Tonga, I'd like to talk to Elmer privately, if you don't mind, for a little while. Would that be alright?"

Beverly glanced over at Elmer, and seeing no immediate reaction, she nodded, and immediately let herself out into the adjoining waiting room.

Serafina leaned forward in her chair, laid her clipboard on the coffee table and stared at Elmer, "Well, young man, what do you have to say for yourself?"

Elmer, caught off guard at her insistent and firm tone, stared at the psychiatrist with a shocked look. He had been treated with kid gloves for so long by his parents and step parents and was so used to always getting his way that he didn't know what to make of the sudden change.

"What do you mean?" the boy responded, obviously confused by not being pampered and catered to, "I don't understand." The boy sat trying to size up this new adult, looking for her weaknesses so that he could control the situation with her, just like he did with the other adults in his life.

Serafina quickly got up from her chair, walked over to the couch and sat down uncomfortably close to the wily young Machiavellian. Elmer leaned away from her and scooted back to the end of the couch, But Serafina followed him, purposely moving right next to him, her knees touching his. Her eyes stared deeply into Elmer's.

"Now, young man, we are going to come to an understanding," Serafina's eyes narrowed, a slight frown on her beautiful brow, "unless you can tell me something that your parents or step parents are doing to you that is wrong, things are going to change dramatically."

Elmer's eyes widened, as he trotted out all his best lines, "My parents got divorced! They didn't even ask me! I don't like my stepparents! I want my parents to get back together! I don't like the way things are! I want things back the way they were! I cry myself to sleep every night!"

At this last statement, Serafina's left eyebrow went up in obvious disbelief. "Right. And I can fly and leap over tall buildings at a single bound. What else you got, Elmer, 'cause what I just heard isn't making it," Serafina declared in a firm, clear voice.

Elmer swiftly searched his mind, looking for anything to help him in his cause, but after a few seconds Serafina continued. "I thought so. You've got nothing. You've been a spoiled little brat just to get your parents and step parents to let you have your way, buy you things, and do anything to try and make you happy."

Elmer wiggled uncomfortably on the couch, his cheeks and rather prominent ears reddening. Elmer was not a stupid boy. It was painfully obvious to young Elmer Tonga that his reign of mischief, willfulness and selfishness was coming to an abrupt end.

"Here's what's going to happen, Elmer. I'm going to see you and your stepmother once a week for the next three months. You are going to start repairing your relationship with your mother and father and you will work very hard at building a meaningful relationship with your stepparents. There are three excellent reasons why you will do this. First, your parents obviously love you very much and are feeling terrible because they think you hate them for getting a divorce. They deserve your love and support. It's a hard time for them too."

Dr. Messina continued, never taking her intent gaze away from Elmer's shell-shocked eyes, "Second, you need to start becoming a caring, loving young man, a young man that helps his parents and becomes a kind and considerate part of both your new families."

"Finally," Dr. Messina leaned forward staring deep into Elmer's soul, "You need to prove to me that you are doing those things. If you don't show me that you are trying hard to become the very best son you can be, I will start seeing you for an hour every day. During that hour, you and I will dramatically change your life around. Do we understand each other, young man?"

Dr. Messina stood up and walked back over to her chair, her smile returning, and her manner as charming as usual. But as Elmer studied the psychiatrist, he wasn't foolish enough to overlook the quiet determination and resolve still sparkling from her beautiful eyes. Sighing with the imminent loss of his emotional hold over his parents and stepparents, Elmer Tonga surrendered and nodded in agreement. He realized the harsh reality was that now was the time to make the best of things.

After speaking with a stunned and overjoyed Beverly Tonga, during which Serafina praised Elmer for making great progress during therapy and affirmed over and over again his wanting to make things right with his parents and stepparents, Serafina waved goodbye to the mother and son. As a joyful Beverly took a still shell-shocked Elmer down the stairs to get each of them a large ice cream cone at The Scoop, Serafina saw Elmer turn back and stare inquisitively at the psychiatrist. Serafina smiled, waggled her finger at the conniving young man and winked meaningfully. Elmer's face immediately reddened once more as he slowly and wistfully turned away.

Serafina walked back into her office, smiling delightedly to herself, deciding that it would be a lovely time to treat herself with a strong cup of Irish Tea.

***

The bell at Treasured Memories tinkled as the front door opened. Both Wendy and Mandy looked up from where they were working. Wendy was carefully unpacking a set of antique oil lamps that she had just purchased from a curio shop in Wales. Mandy was in the middle of replacing several old fashioned music boxes, which they had just sold to delighted Brown Bear Junction Mayor Putnam Pierpont, with several more they had stored away in the back room.

"Hey, Sis! Hey, Mandy! How are the two hardest working businesswomen in The Junction today?" Andy Morrison grinned and winked at the two women, walking swiftly over to give his older sister an affectionate peck on the cheek.

"Well, I don't know if we are the hardest working, but we definitely seem to be working harder than my little brother this morning!" exclaimed Wendy, glancing at her brother with a warm smile.

"Thank you kindly, young man. I do believe you're right. We are the hardest working businesswomen in The Junction." Mandy smiled, nodding energetically, and went back to arranging the beautiful, delicate music boxes.

Wendy gazed up at her younger brother inquisitively. Her voice dropped a little lower, "Okay, I can never get you to leave that stifling old law firm. You work a hundred hours a week! So why are you out in the daylight? Give, Matthew Andrew Morrison, tell me what's going on?"

Andy smiled a bit self-consciously and shrugged, his eyes roaming around the shop, never settling on anything for more than a second or two, "Well, truth is, Sis, I've been invited over to Doc Stone's house for dinner tonight."

Wendy stared at her obviously uncomfortable brother and nodded thoughtfully, "You've been friends with Doc and Jordan for several years. So what's the problem?"

Andy finally looked his sister in the eye and took a deep breath, "Well, Jordan has someone else coming for dinner."

"Someone else?" Wendy raised her eyebrows, "Why is that a problem? Is it Cash or Yamato? Maybe Sean Frasier, that nice, sweet principal?"

Andy shook his head, "No it's none of them. It's..."

As her brother hesitated, Wendy finally got where he was going. She smiled and her eyes twinkled, "Ah! Jordan set you up! She invited a woman! A date for you, right?'

"Yeah," Andy sighed, slightly embarrassed, and shook his head as he picked up a china knickknack and glanced at it with sudden feigned interest. "She invited Meg Monroe, the doctor over at The West Sugar Shack Falls Medical Facility. You know Meg."

"Yes," responded Wendy, "I know who Dr. Monroe is. I saw her once for my high blood pressure. Dr. Johnson at the emergency room here in The Junction was sick with the flu, remember? Dr. Monroe seemed very enthusiastic, sweet and quite intelligent." Wendy studied her brother for a moment. Andy was fairly shy, had been ever since high school. He was also a notorious workaholic, which meant he very rarely had dates. She assumed the same was true for Meg Monroe, since she had never seen or heard of Meg going out on the town with any of the local single men.

Wendy chuckled to herself. This arranged dinner, two weeks before Valentine's Day was obviously Jordan Stone-Smith's way of bringing two attractive, nice, and unattached people together. It was Jordan's way of giving Cupid a little shove in the right direction.

Andy glanced up at his big sister, a bit more relieved now that his news was out, and asked a bit uneasily, "So should I take something to Jordan, Sis? You know, like a bottle of wine or something, to show my thanks for her invitation?"

Wendy smiled back and nodded, "That would be a nice gesture. You can never go wrong with a little courtesy and thoughtfulness, Andy. Mom and dad taught us that."

Mandy stepped away from the counter where she had finished arranging the music boxes, glanced earnestly at both brother and sister, then interrupted their conversation. "I know it's probably not my place to say, but I'd bring her one of these!" Mandy pointed at the antique music boxes and winked.

"I know Miss Jordan pretty well. She does like beautiful things. You bring a bottle of wine, you drink it and it's gone and then forgotten. You bring her one of these and it's beauty and sweet sound will be around forever." Mandy put her finger up to her temple and winked again, as if saying 'this is the smart way to go'.

Andy glanced back questioningly at his sister who smiled and nodded her approval. Then the young lawyer walked over to the counter and stared down thoughtfully at the exquisitely crafted antiques.

He glanced up at Mandy, grinned and returned the wink she had given him, "I think you've made yourself a sale, young lady!"

Wendy watched Mandy gift-wrapping the little music box for her brother. As he chatted with Mandy happily, Wendy's mind wandered off. It took her back to the accident that had taken the lives of both her parents one icy winter night. She remembered how hard it had been for a scared and grieving eighteen-year-old version of herself to take over looking out for her little brother.

She was reminded how she went to work as soon as she graduated from high school that year. She waitressed full-time, and then took a second job stocking shelves, just to pay the bills and keep food in the house for her brother and herself. She sang him to sleep each night that first year, as he cried brokenheartedly over their missing mother and father. She became the one he came to in order to discuss, agonize over, and think through every decision or problem. They had taken on the attitude of 'us against the world' those first few years. It was the easiest way to survive, even though the townspeople were caring and offered their help over and over again.

She was further reminded of the years she struggled to help her brother get his college degree, often spending more than she could afford on books and tuition. She remembered the bank rejecting her request, her plea, for several loans. Her credit cards had maxed out several times during those difficult years. Then, finally, her brother had finished law school, passed the bar exam with flying colors and their lives had instantly changed.

He was a much sought after young barrister, who had his choice of well paying jobs with impressive firms. Within two years, he had paid off all the loans she had taken out over the years and had cleaned up her overloaded credit cards. He had been overjoyed that he could finally do something for the sister who had done so much for him. Together, joyfully, they had purchased a beautiful new house, and he had eagerly underwritten her loan to buy the antique store so she would finally have her own business.

They had been each other's whole lives for the past eighteen years. They were so close they very rarely had to talk to get their feelings and thoughts across to one another. They had come to depend and rely heavily on each other in every way.

Just for a moment, as she looked over at her handsome, young brother, Wendy felt a sharp sense of imminent loss. In her head, it only made sense that Andy would eventually find someone to share his life with other than her. But somewhere deep down inside her, she just wasn't sure that she was ready for that moment to be now.

***

Cash Green stared into the open refrigerator, noting that there were only three bottles of wine on the top shelf. On the second and third shelves were assorted salads and casseroles ready for Saturday night Bible supper, along with Father O'Flaherty's two-day-old egg salad sandwich in the crisper.

"You're sure you just didn't use up more of the sacramental wine during services than usual?" Cash asked, shutting the door and turning back to Father O'Flaherty. "I know I often think I have things in the fridge and when I go to get them, they're gone."

Father O'Flaherty's craggy eyebrows rose dramatically as his cheeks reddened. "See here, Sheriff Green! I would most certainly know if I had used an extra eight or nine bottles of wine! What do you think I do? It's only used for communion! Look!" It was obvious the good father did not like his word being questioned, especially about sacramental wine.

He turned and motioned to a nearby shelf. On the shelf there was a chart, detailing the wine that was purchased and then each bottle being crossed off as it was used. Father O'Flaherty pointed to a pair of beautifully carved, ornamental glass carafes sitting next to the sink.

"Each time I use a new bottle of wine, I do three things to it. First, before I take into the sanctuary, I cut it with a little water. Second, I bless it. Third, I empty it into one of these large crystal carafes, which the deacons use to fill the gold chalice in the church during communion." Father O'Flaherty described the process, his eyes glancing back and forth from Cash to Yamato, "The other crystal jug is filled with water and carried into the church along with the jug of wine."

It was Yamato's turn to raise her eyebrows as she stared at the good father and asked, "You cut the wine with water before you mix wine and water during the communion ceremony in the sanctuary, Father? I didn't know that."

Father O'Flaherty nodded firmly, replying, "Our Savior mixed the wine with water to make it go farther with his disciples and the multitudes who came to hear his sermons. I just do it twice. If it was good enough for Him, it's good enough for our little country church!"

Then he added, in a quieter, slightly reflective tone, "Besides, it defrays expenses, and the church can surely use all the help we can get making ends meet these days." Then Father O'Flaherty smiled and whispered, "And we don't want to get in trouble because any of our parishioners get a bit tipsy, doncha' know?!" His sly Irish eyes twinkled with his little attempt at humor.

Cash smiled and then glanced up from the inventory list on the shelf, "According to this, you should have an even dozen bottles left, Father. I see only three in the fridge."

"Precisely why I called you, Sheriff!" Father O'Flaherty straightened up to his full five-foot-six inches, shoulders pulled back, and his slight chin jutting out. "Someone is stealing wine from the church!"

Yamato glanced around at the small kitchenette, and pulled out her notepad, "Is this place ever locked, Father? And if so, who has the keys?"

Father O'Flaherty raised his hand as if to brush away the question as inconsequential, "The church is never locked, deputy. The Sanctuary, the rectory, there is no place in our church that is locked. It is a place of worship. People come to pray, or simply seek refuge, at all hours of the day or night."

Cash and Yamato exchanged glances.

Father O'Flaherty spoke quietly, earnestly with his hands clasped together. "None of the three churches in

The Falls are ever locked. We depend on the innate goodness and honesty of our community members. Leaving our churches open is our commitment to, our leap of faith and our belief in, our parishioners. It is the way things are, the way things have always been, and the way things always will be."

Cash glanced around the room, then asked, "Father, with all due respect, is there anyone that you can think of that might do this?"

Father O'Flaherty leaned against the shelf, obviously reticent to name any names of parishioners or townspeople. Finally, with a sigh, he responded quietly, "Well there's old Milburn Ransom. He pretty much lives by himself in an old deserted ramshackle hut up in the woods. He comes into the sanctuary sometimes when there's bad weather and sleeps next to the broom closet. He definitely smells of stale wine and beer at times. But he's a fairly decent and harmless soul, nonetheless."

Yamato jotted down the name and then glanced up expectantly at Father O'Flaherty, patiently waiting.

"Then there's Isabel Lugavitch. Her neighbors' gossip about the large number of empty bottles she has out in her trash every week on pickup day. Wine, Vodka, Whiskey mostly, they say. But I've never seen her when she was under the influence, thank The Lord."

Father O'Flaherty glanced up into Cash's eyes, shaking his head, "Truth be told, sheriff, I have no idea who's been partaking of the sacramental wine."

The little old white-haired priest looked hopefully at the two officers, took a deep breath, turned on his heel and started nimbly towards the outside door. "That, my dear sheriff and deputy, is where you both come in. Have a good day now. Let me know when you've found something out."

As Cash and Yamato watched Father O'Flaherty walk out into the mid afternoon chill, they turned and stared at each other for a moment. Then, in unison, they both burst out in broad grins and shook their heads incredulously.

Cash whispered conspiratorially, "I've heard about someone stealing the proverbial sacramental wine in jokes and in books, but wouldn't you know that we would be the ones to actually have to try and find the person who did it!"

Yamato chuckled quietly and responded, "And with the church never locked, and townspeople coming and going freely, technically, everyone in town is a suspect!"

Cash nodded and he and Yamato both shrugged as they started checking around for any possible clues. Such was the life of keeping the peace in a small town.

Chapter 5

Doc Stone cheerfully poured a new rich-bodied Hawaiian blend Kona coffee into Blue Willow China cups as a beaming Jordan served slices of hot apple pie topped with a scoop of homemade French Vanilla ice cream from The Scoop.

Jordan had loved both the antique music box from Andy and the bouquet of flowers from The Green Thumb from Meg. As she settled into her chair at the dining room table to enjoy dessert, she excitedly gazed over at their two guests, trying to carefully appraise how each of them felt about the other.

Meg was chatting animatedly with Andy and Doc, laughing at their jokes, attentive and seemed to be thoroughly engaged. Andy was obviously having a great time, and she noticed him taking moments here and there to simply blatantly stare at the beautiful and vivacious young doctor.

Jordan smiled happily as she took a long sip of the savory coffee. Andy, who was usually charming but somewhat aloof in his dealings with new people, was clearly captivated by Meg's innocent openness, wit and charm. Meg was a bit harder to read, but then, she more gregarious, and was always sweet and endearing to everyone she met.

Jordan leaned back in her chair and simply watched

for a few moments, content to observe what her blatant matchmaking had created.

"Well, that was a wonderful meal, Sweetheart!" declared Doc, glancing over at his new bride, winking and reaching out to hold her hand. "And the good conversation and pleasant company has made it even more so!"

Andy glanced over at Jordan, his eyes twinkling, "Yes! I second that motion, Doc! Great food, great conversation," he turned and glanced meaningfully at Meg, "and great company! Here! Here!"

Meg joined in, chuckling, "Well, that's makes it unanimous then! It's been a great evening!"

Andy glanced around the table with a shy smile, "I have to admit, when Jordan first approached me about a dinner party, my first instinct was to say 'no thanks, I have too much work at the office'."

He continued, glancing over at Meg once more. "But I'm really glad I came. I haven't had this much fun since my sister Wendy had the hiccups and the sneezes at the same time and couldn't stop for about twenty minutes! I couldn't stop laughing at her predicament the whole time! That's brotherly love for you!"

Doc chuckled and teased, "Bet your sister just loves hearing you tell that story! And how long ago was that, pray tell?"

Andy frowned thoughtfully, "I think I was fifteen!"

Doc laughed, and teased Andy once more, "Then it's been awhile! Well, I'm glad our little dinner party rates right up there on your list!"

Meg interceded while chuckling, reaching out to touch Andy's hand comfortingly, "Now Doc, be kind! He's not used to your rapier wit and cheerful quips!"

"But we are glad you had a good time tonight, aren't

we Miss Jordan?" Meg smiled warmly at Andy and then glanced over at Jordan with a cheery wink.

"That we are!" replied Jordan as she took a bite of the still warm pie, "We're glad you're both here with us tonight, aren't we Doc?" Jordan glanced at her husband, her eyes glistening with happiness and, in her estimation, a job well done. Cupid had set the pair together, now whatever was to be, would be.

Doc stood up and held out the carafe of steaming coffee, "Indeed we are! All joking aside, it's been great having the two of you here tonight!" Doc glanced first at Andy then over at his partner in the medical needs of the community. Doc had come to care a great deal about Meg Monroe, even though he would never let on. He had sort of become her de facto big brother, and he tended to watch out for her, especially since she had no other family in the area.

Doc looked at the happy smile on Meg's face and felt a bit contented. Meg deserved to be happy, and if it proved out that this young man could do that, more power to her. Doc was not a true fan of his wife's avid matchmaking interests and abilities even though he rarely said so. However, in this case, he just might make an exception.

Later that evening, as Jordan peeked out through the curtains of the front window, she watched breathlessly as Andy walked Meg to her car in the frosty winter air. She watched them smile, exchange 'good nights' and then Andy hesitated. With a shy smile, he leaned over to kiss Meg's lips, and she seemed to immediately blush. Then Meg deftly turned her cheek and allowed him to kiss her there. Moments later they were both gone, their cars billowing white vapor out into the below freezing air.

Jordan stepped away from the cold windowpane, her features thoughtful. Andy had obviously overcome his shyness enough to try and kiss the beautiful young doctor. Meg, on her part, had chosen the more modest kiss on the cheek. Jordan's mind raced. Just what did that mean? Wasn't Meg interested in the handsome young man, or was she simply playing hard to get? No, that was unlike Meg Monroe. With her, what you saw was what you got. Perhaps Meg was simply going slow.

At that moment, as Jordan stood musing in the front room, Doc silently came up behind her, slipped his strong arms around her and hugged her tight, "Okay, I can see your mind going into overdrive, Miss Matchmaker!" he teased softly.

"Just remember, you can lead a horse, or in this case a man and a woman, to water, but you can't make them drink!" Doc chuckled at his own joke and hugged Jordan tighter, kissing her softly on her ear.

Jordan, broken out of her reverie, chuckled back, turned around and kissed her sweet love firmly and passionately on his eager, warm lips. Her eyes twinkling, she pulled off her heels and started to sprint up their stairs, calling out, "I've got some especially sweet water in the bedroom, Doc! Care for a drink?"

As Doc chased her up the stairs, Cupid's arrow suddenly shifted his target from Meg and Andy to Doc and Jordan. In all honesty, however, they were very willing and eager targets.

***

The massive old clock in the tower of the town hall chimed one bell on every half hour, rain, snow or shine. As Jeremy Burman and his first cousin Parnell were walking briskly around the frozen landscape of the town square headed home from The Scoop with large ice cream cones, they immediately glanced up toward the tower in the darkness and stared at each other. It was now 9:30 PM. Their curfew, set by their moms and Grandma Burman, was now officially up! Curfew and meal times were two things that were not to be messed around with in the extended family Burman home.

The two boys had been having such a good time talking with Trish and Norma, and Newt and Remy, who had been loitering about the ice cream shop, that the two boys had forgotten about the time. Sixteen-year-old Jeremy and thirteen-year-old Parnell were well aware that there would be a long and stern lecture waiting for them when they did arrive home. On one hand, the two boys weren't anxious to get there and undergo their punishment. On the other, if they were going to get a lecture anyway, why hurry?

At that moment, out of the corner of his eye, Jeremy saw someone walking out the door of the Catholic rectory. He stopped and turned toward the figure, raising the hand without the ice cream cone to wave at whom he now could clearly see was Father O'Flaherty.

"Good evening, Father, how are you..." Jeremy's voice trailed off and his hand stopped half way up, as he looked closer at the good father. Father O'Flaherty had his eyes open, but only had on a light robe over his pajamas. The priest's fine white hair was all rumpled up and wisps blowing in the cold evening breeze. The good father didn't look left or right, just shuffled almost mechanically toward the back door of the church.

Jeremy and Parnell glanced at each other, both boys frowning slightly as they watched the old clergyman shuffle up the snow shoveled sidewalk to the church's back door.

"Father O'Flaherty must be feeling sick or

somethin'," Parnell whispered, his eyes wide and curious, "'cause he looks awful! Maybe he's got the flu!"

Jeremy shook his head thoughtfully, "No, I don't think he's sick. Even if he was sick, he'd say something to us. Something's wrong. Let's follow him."

"But our curfew! We're..." began Parnell in protest.

"We're already in trouble. Best to make sure the good father is okay, even if we won't be," declared Jeremy as he set off across the street toward the church.

Parnell just shrugged, glanced over toward their house as if half expecting there to be a search party already forming to come find the boys. Then, with a dejected sigh, he followed his older cousin.

About the time that Jeremy had reached the back door of the church and reached for the doorknob, the door swung open and Father O'Flaherty stepped out. Jeremy almost spoke to the good father, but the blank stare in Father O'Flaherty's eyes stopped him. Jeremy smiled and his eyes lit up as he turned to Parnell.

"He's asleep! Father O'Flaherty's asleep! Sleep walking!" whispered Jeremy excitedly to his younger cousin, stepping out of the catholic priest's path.

The two boys watched wordlessly as the priest shuffled slowly back along the cleared path to the rectory. Jeremy glanced over at Parnell and whispered, "I heard that it's not good to wake up somebody who's sleepwalking. Something about shocking their brain or scaring them or something. We'd better follow him and just make sure he gets back inside okay. Then tomorrow, we'll come over and tell Father O'Flaherty what we saw. C'mon!"

Parnell nodded affirmatively and the two boys

trailed along behind the old man. Once he had opened the door to the rectory and stepped inside, Jeremy and Parnell peeked carefully in through the window, using the light from a nightlight to watch the good father as he headed toward his bedroom. Before getting into bed, Father O'Flaherty took something out from under his robe and placed it in the back of his closet. Then he closed the closet door and climbed slowly back into bed.

After waiting for several minutes, Jeremy glanced over at his cousin and sighed, "Seems like he's okay to leave. Looks like his sleep walking is over for the night."

As the two boys jogged toward home, gulping great mouthfuls of their ice cream cones, Parnell panted, "Well, the Father's problem may be over for the night, but I have a feeling ours is just beginning!"

He pointed toward their house, where Grandma Burman stood all bundled up in her parka and winter hat, watching the boys as they now sprinted towards home. Grandma had a smile on her face as she saw the boys racing toward her, but the glint of strength and determination in her eye made the ice cream in the two boys' stomachs begin to churn and gurgle.

***

Wendy sat curled up in a plush antique chair with a small knitted blanket over her legs, reading the latest William Frasier novel, *Christmas is the Time for Taking*, in the small study by the front door of the Morrison's home. In essence, she was waiting as much as she was reading. She was waiting for Andy to get home from dinner at Doc and Jordan's house over in The Falls. More specifically, she was waiting to hear how his 'date' with Meg Monroe had turned out.

Part of Wendy truly wanted her little brother to have

had a wonderful time. Part of her wistfully, and a bit regretfully, wanted him to have had a so-so time. That would eliminate the need for Andy to pursue the relationship with the young doctor any farther, and things would go back to the status quo.

Wendy stared out at the driveway once more and then scolded herself for her rather selfish and egocentric viewpoint on the whole matter. She told herself that whatever made Andy happy she would encourage and work to help make it happen. That's what she had been doing ever since she became his virtual parent at the age of eighteen. That's what she would continue to do.

As she took her eyes away from the driveway, she stared all around at their beautiful home. It was their home now, hers and Andy's. If he ever got married, it would no longer be her home. It would belong to Andy and his wife. Andy's money had bought the home in the first place. Wendy would have to find somewhere else to live, alone. Wendy's mind wandered farther. She might have to give up Treasured Memories, her antique store, if Andy got married and needed to use his money in other ways. Then what would she have?

Wendy's face flushed as she thought of all the years she had taken care of her kid brother, of all the things she had given up so he could be successful. She had mortgaged her life to help him create his. For a moment, a fierce, angry look flashed across her face, then she shook her head. She hated thinking thoughts like that. She loved her brother dearly and wanted him happy.

Just then headlights flashed across the window as Andy's car drove into the three-car garage. Wendy took a deep breath and tried to calm herself, she wasn't going to let her little brother see her like this. She had always put on a brave front for him. It was habit and old habits die-hard.

As Andy strode briskly into the hallway just outside the study, he peered in and winked at his sister. His face was flushed, perhaps with more than just the cold. He wore a broad, excited smile and his eyes sparkled. He was happier and more enthused than she had seen him in some time.

Wendy's heart sank.

Chapter 6

At the same time, on Owl Creek Road, just off the town square in The Falls, Jeremy and Parnell Burman were standing in the kitchen of the Burman home. Grandma Burman and two of her daughters, Maureen and Phyllis, were at the kitchen counter, washing dishes and cleaning up the well used kitchen for the night.

Maureen, Parnell's mom, handed another plate to her sister and then stared back at her oldest child. Her eyes showed annoyance, as if she were frustrated at having to deal with one more thing after a very busy day. "Well, we're waiting, young man. We're all ears to hear why you broke your curfew. Please, proceed."

Phyllis, Grandma and Grandpa Burman's oldest child, took the wet plate, wiped it down and placed it on a pile of newly washed plates that were ready to be put away, "I'm kind of wondering just what it was that kept you from being here on time."

Phyllis glanced over at Grandma Burman, raising her eyebrows, "It surely must be something quite important to make them break their curfew, don't you think, mom?"

Jeremy and Parnell glanced at each other uneasily. At this point sixteen-year-old Jeremy, good kid that he was, had pretty much decided to simply say he was sorry and lay himself open to whatever punishment might be headed his way. Parnell, being three years younger, however, still saw a tiny light in the darkness.

"Well, there was a good reason that we were late, wasn't there Jeremy?" Parnell's voice wavered a bit as he glanced at his older cousin, obviously asking for Jeremy's support.

"Oh? And what might that be?" Maureen stared at Parnell, studying him closely, ready to pounce on any slapdash excuse.

"We saw Father O'Flaherty!" exclaimed Parnell, his eyes wide with determination, hoping for a reprieve. "He was sleepwalking!"

Grandma Burman turned from covering up the leftovers from dinner with plastic wrap to face the two boys, "Is this true, Jeremy?" From years of experience, Grandma Burman knew in her heart that Jeremy would never lie to her. She was not so sure of his cousin, Parnell.

With all three women staring at both boys, Jeremy glanced hesitantly at his cousin, not entirely sure he wanted to go this route, and replied, "Yes Ma'am. He was sleepwalking. He walked out of the rectory and into the church."

Parnell jumped in with more details, "We were about to go into the church to check up on him when he came back out again!"

Jeremy nodded and added, "We watched him walk back to the rectory, and by peeking through the window we made sure he got back into bed. Then we ran home."

At this point, Parnell was beaming, sure that they had escaped any punishment, and perhaps they would even be hailed as heroes for watching over and protecting the good father!

"Is this the truth, all of the truth?" Phyllis gazed down at her son, staring directly into his eyes. Her eyes were filled with kindness, but they also showed the trust and love she had for her son. It was obvious she was ready to take Jeremy's answer as the indisputable truth.

Jeremy couldn't lie to his mother, let alone his grandmother. He hung his head and told the truth, much to Parnell's dismay, "It's the truth. But the town hall bell had already rung when he were starting to walk home from The Scoop. So even if we hadn't seen Father O'Flaherty sleepwalking, we would have missed our curfew. That's the truth."

The three women glanced at each other, trying to hide their smiles and amused looks. Grandma Burman glanced back at the two boys, "You broke your curfew. For that tomorrow night's dishwashing duties will be all yours."

Parnell groaned slightly, shaking his head. He hated washing dishes.

"But," continued Grandma Burman, "you both did the right thing helping Father O'Flaherty, regardless of your own dilemma. That takes a good deal of caring, strength of character and compassion for our community and its citizens."

"Because of your actions, I think I might just be able to persuade Grandpa B to take you boys out ice fishing at the shanty on Lake Pumpkinseed this Saturday. What do you think?" Grandma Burman smiled, her eyes filled with pride and love for her two grandsons.

As Maureen and Phyllis chuckled at the relief on the boy's faces, Grandma Burman offered to get the two boys a large bowl of ice cream. Jeremy and Parnell glanced at each other hesitantly. They had just gulped down three scoops of The Scoop's best on their way home. More ice cream on top of that might cause them to have the collywobbles later that night.

With courageous and eager smiles, the two boys sat down to their second enormous helping of ice cream within the last twenty minutes. Glancing at each other, they shrugged and grinned. If they did have stomachaches during the night, it would be worth it!

***

Early the next morning, Grandma Burman picked her way carefully across the town square, avoiding the stray chunks of snow and ice that either the snowplow or townspeople's shovels had missed. She carried a large basket with a brightly colored kitchen towel over the top. She walked up the small, stone path to the Catholic rectory and knocked three times on the old wooden door.

She heard some mumbling for a few seconds and the padding of sock feet, then the door swung wide open. Standing in front of her was no other than Father Flynn O'Flaherty himself.

"Ophelia Burman! What a pleasant surprise!" declared the good Father, his eyes twinkling good naturedly, "Come in! Come in! You must be freezing out there!"

Grandma Burman smiled and stepped inside as the priest closed the door behind her, "Thank you Flynn! And a very good morning to you!"

Grandma Burman stepped over to the kitchen counter and placed the basket down, tapping the top, "I've brought you some of those scones you love so much Father. I was planning to bake them this morning, and you popped into my mind. You and the hollow leg you have when it comes to pastries, that is!" Grandma

Burman was smiling indulgently, as her eyes took a good look around the small but cozy dwelling.

"Ah, Ophelia! Ya' shouldn't have, but I'm surely glad you did now!" Father O'Flaherty crooned, peeking eagerly under the kitchen towel at the pile of scones within. The delicious aroma from the freshly baked scones was filling the little home.

"Father, you know, you really could use a housekeeper a couple of times a week," remarked Grandma Burman, glancing at the priest over the top of her half glasses. "I hear Anita Stroud is excellent and she has an opening right now, what with Madge Tameridge down in Florida for the winter. You might want to give her a jingle."

"Now, now, Ophelia," replied Flynn O'Flaherty, "I haven't had anybody in to clean since old Nell Winters passed on, and I'm particular about who I let muck about my possessions." His eyes twinkled with both thankfulness for his old friend's concern and the stubbornness that was his basic nature.

Grandma Burman sighed, well aware she wasn't going to convince Flynn Flaherty if he didn't want to be convinced, and moved on to another subject, "By the way. Do you know what my grandsons Jeremy and Parnell saw last night?"

Father O'Flaherty chuckled as he went to the cupboard and got out two coffee mugs and replied, "Well, I guess I'd have to be psychic to know the answer to that, and thankfully, I am but a poor shepherd of my flock."

Raising his eyebrows and holding out his coffee pot, the priest glanced at Grandma Burman and she gratefully nodded affirmatively. The he continued on with a wink, "Why? What did the two young scalawags see?"

Grandma Burman stared straight at her old friend, a concerned look on her sweet face, "An old fool stumbling around in the darkness, fast asleep."

Father O'Flaherty perked up at the news and stared at Grandma Burman. He tipped his head to one side thoughtfully, "Was it Jeb or Zeke? Old Ed Morganstein?"

"Think closer to home," was Grandma Burman's reply.

"Surely not Theo Dunham or Marcus Templeton!?" declared Flynn O'Flaherty with vigor, his eyes widening.

"No, it was neither of the good reverends, Flynn," stated Ophelia Burman flatly. "It was you."

Father O'Flaherty's eyes widened, he turned a shade whiter than he already was and he stepped back from the counter, coffee pot still in his hand. "Me, Ophelia?! Faith and begorrah, that can't be right!"

"Jeremy and Parnell watched you sleepwalk out of the rectory and go into the church," Grandma Burman continued, in a very calm efficient manner. "Then they watched you come back out of the house and go back into the rectory. They watched through the window as you went back to bed."

"Truly!" said Father O'Flaherty as he sat down heavily on a kitchen stool, looking like all the wind had been knocked out of his sails.

"And that's not all," Grandma Burman declared. "They said that before you got into bed you walked over to the bedroom closet and placed something in there that you had hidden under your coat. They couldn't see what it was, though."

Father O'Flaherty looked as though he had just been told that pigs could fly. All the air had certainly been knocked out of him. He sat motionless on the stool for a moment until Grandma Burman reached out and gently touched his arm. "Flynn. It's okay. It's not the end of the world. Get on over to Doc or Meg and see what can be done to help you with this. I'm sure they have things that can help."

Then Father O'Flaherty blinked his eyes and came to. He stood up and finished pouring the two mugs full of steaming hot coffee, "I'm sure you're right Ophelia. Just a bit of a shock, doncha' know."

Grandma Burman nodded her head as she took a sip from her ceramic mug, "I'm sure it was. That's why I came right over this morning to let you know"

She glanced down at the warm scone Flynn had already pulled from the basket, smiled and added, "The scones were to be a bit of a buffer to help you get over the news. Did they work?"

Father O'Flaherty winked and chuckled, "That they did, Ophelia!" His grin faded as he looked thoughtfully back toward the bedroom, "Now I wonder what it was I carried in there?"

Within moments, the good father was at his bedroom closet door. Opening it up, he peered back into the gloom, and started pushing aside a pile of clothes, shoes and assorted items until he stopped and stood up, his eyes white, his mouth in a perfect 'O'.

"Well I'll be jiggered! That's where the sacramental wine has gotten to! Oh, my goodness! What shall I ever tell Cash?" He turned to Grandma Burman, his voice shrill and upset, "I had the sheriff and Deputy Yamato in to report that a number of bottles from the fridge in the church had been stolen! But..." He counted quickly.

"Here they all are! Every last one!" Father O'Flaherty turned and his face looked so stunned and bewildered that Grandma Burman had no choice but to chuckle at her old friend's predicament.

Within moments, as the absurdity of the situation hit the good father, he too began to chuckle. Before long, the two old friends were laughing until the tears were running down their cheeks.

When Grandma Burman finally headed out the door to go to work at the Emporium and Father O'Flaherty picked up the phone to call the sheriff's office to tell them the lost had been found, the cold winter sun was shining brightly across the frozen landscape.

***

Andy Morrison reached his law office even earlier than usual that morning. By the time the first paralegals had made it in, he already had drunk two cups of coffee and gone over three briefs. He was sitting in his office, enthusiastically attacking his pile of work, a passionate gleam in his eye and a huge smile on his handsome face. As the morning wore on, everyone in the office, paralegals, secretaries and even a few lawyers noticed the 'new and improved Andy Morrison'. His attitude was even more positive and eager and he was working like there was no tomorrow.

Jennifer Allen and Teresa Jablonski stood at the copier, exchanging gossip as they worked on the huge stacks of copying their bosses needed done that morning. As usual, everything in a law office was due yesterday, and every hour was accounted for and billed to their clients.

"Pansy Walker said she saw Mr. Freedman out last weekend with a tall, statuesque blonde," giggled Teresa quietly, glancing carefully around for prying eyes and the possibility of being overheard.

"And we both know that Mrs. Freedman is a brunette and only a little over five feet," Jennifer winked and added conspiratorially.

Around the corner from the two secretaries, Elizabeth Fallon, the newest paralegal at Lesner, Malkowitz, Freedman and Lister, was poring over a thick volume on legal precedence. She overheard the two women, but the sound was merely a background buzz as she concentrated on doing a good job. Elizabeth was still terribly grateful that Andy Morrison had gotten her the job, and she was doing everything she could to fulfill his trust in and kindness to her. She had begun to picture Andy as her own personal knight in shining armor, and had come to think of the handsome young lawyer as a very special, thoughtful and wonderful man.

"Mavis down in accounting has decided to start dating Mr. Listor's son again," Jennifer told Teresa matter-of-factly above the click, click, click of the high-speed copier.

"Really?" gasped Teresa, her voice going up an octave, "after the way she caught him cheating on her last year? Why on earth would she do that?" Disgust and a fair amount of annoyance could be heard in her voice.

"Well," Jennifer replied, "he's rich, and then he's rich!"

The two secretaries chuckled in unison for a few seconds, then Jennifer's voice could be heard once again, her tone taking on a dreamy note, "Did you notice how animated and happy Mr. Morrison is this morning?"

Elizabeth Fallon's head popped up as she heard the name of her benefactor. She totally lost her train of thought and listened carefully.

Teresa responded, quiet but heartfelt, "Yes, I noticed. I try and walk by his office whenever I can to see if he'll notice me. And, of course, to stare at him! He's so handsome and sexy. I don't know why he's acting like that, but I sure wish I was the reason!"

As Elizabeth listened to the two women go on and on about what a hunk Andy Morrison was, her mind drifted back to the day she had been in his office dealing with her father's will. She had been completely lost and miserable and Mr. Morrison had been so caring and kind to her. He had even gotten her a job here at the firm so she could begin to dig her way out of the overwhelming debt she had inherited.

Shaking her head, Elizabeth got back to work, trying to push all thoughts about the handsome young lawyer out of her head. After all, she thought, humbly, what good would it do for a poor girl like her to even think about a special man like Mr. Morrison? She would never stand a chance with a man like him.

Meanwhile the two secretaries had turned their catty conversations on to other subjects, and Elizabeth shut them out as well as she doggedly delved back into her time consuming drudgery.

Over in The Falls, Meg Monroe had just finished her early morning rounds of the hospital wards and was heading down to the hospital cafeteria to see if she could scrounge a bagel or a muffin to pacify her grumbling stomach from completely skipping breakfast that morning.

At that moment, Doc Stone caught up with her. He cheerfully called out, "Hey Meg! Good morning! I had to come in and check on old Mr. Woolsey. I sent him here after his ulcers started bleeding again. I'm going to try one of those new pharmaceutical wonder drugs that Jordan told me about on him. How's your day so far?"

Meg grinned, "I'm jealous! As a pharmacist Jordan

gets to hear about all those drugs long before we do! Wish I had my own personal drug encyclopedia!"

Doc laughed as he grabbed a cup of coffee and a Danish from the cafeteria counter. He handed the cashier money for both his and Meg's trays. Meg winked and quipped at her friend and colleague, "Why thank you, Doctor! You wouldn't be trying to buy my affections would you now?"

Doc chuckled, "Nope. One woman in my love life is more than enough! Speaking of which…"

Meg turned and stared at Doc curiously, as he continued, "…how was your kiss with a certain young lawyer last night? C'mon, give me the details, kiddo!"

Meg sat down at one of the tables in the cafeteria and immediately began arranging her tray and started fixing her coffee. With a slight shrug she glanced at Doc and replied, "Nothing much to tell, nosy posy. He kissed me on the cheek and then I went home."

It was Doc's turn to stare curiously at his colleague, "Really? That's odd. Jordan said that Andy called her early this morning, thanking her profusely for the dinner and for the introduction. He said you were fantastic and beautiful, along with a several other things. He said he couldn't remember a better evening."

Meg stared in astonishment at Doc, "Are you pulling my chain, Doc? 'Cause if you are…"

Doc held up both hands, shaking his head, interjecting quickly, "No! Honest! He was all excited. We just naturally assumed that, well, you know."

Meg glared at Doc, raising her eyebrow, "No, I don't know! Nothing happened. He tried to kiss me on the lips, I turned my head and he kissed my cheek. That was it. Truth, I swear."

Doc, now a bit uncomfortable with the whole

conversation, glanced at his friend a bit sheepishly, "Sorry, Meg. Must be Andy got his signals crossed."

"Don't worry about it, Doc," Meg grinned, munching happily on her muffin, "He's a nice guy, really. Kind, sweet and handsome. There's just no sparks. Know what I mean?"

"Yup, now I know," Doc nodded his head thoughtfully as he eagerly bit down on his Danish. "Question is my friend, does he?"

Chapter 7

Jeremy Burman was torn. On one hand, he was in Seventh Heaven, riding on the back of Drake McKiernan's dragon, Scarlett. On the other hand, his nauseous stomach from way too much ice cream eaten just before going to bed was sending fresh waves of cramps and queasiness his way.

As Jeremy climbed off the back of Drake's Harley by the front door of the union high school, he managed a quick smile and an earnest 'thank you' to the tall distinguished biker.

Drake had come to The Falls two years before, as he was riding aimlessly across New England on his beautiful 1997 Harley Davidson Heritage Springer. True Scotsman Drake called his bike his 'dragon', because it rumbled deeply and breathed fire as he rode it.

Interestingly enough, Drake had spent that first night at Maeve McTavish's bed and breakfast. Maeve's old, wise grandfather Taog McTavish had instilled in her all the honor, honesty, stubbornness and tradition from his own Scottish roots. Taog had given Maeve her first dragon sculpture when she lived with him in the family's ancestral home deep in the highlands of Scotland above Loch Ness. Ever since then, Maeve had religiously collected dragons, now owning more than forty of the fire-breathing creatures.

Maeve and Drake had immediately been attracted to each other's kindred spirits. Now Drake was one of the leading businessmen in The Falls, owning half of the new Dreams Rides store that sold Harleys and hot air balloons. The two Brits, Newt Anderson and Remy Renquist owned the other half of the store. The adventurous balloonists had found The Falls, and the McNeil sisters who owned The Scoop, to be the perfect home for them after years of roaming the world.

Drake glanced at Jeremy's pale complexion and noticed that the sixteen-year-old was sweating, even though the temperature was still well below freezing, "You sure about staying, Jeremy? I can bring you home, you know. It's no problem."

Jeremy glanced over at the school, really wishing he could just go back to bed, but knowing there was a big math test today and his anal math teacher, Mr. Forester, would not look kindly on his absence. Feeling his stomach growl once more, he swallowed hard and glanced back at Drake. The tall Scotsman had been mounting his bike just as Jeremy had come dragging himself out of the house, half-heartedly ready to ride his new bicycle down to the bus stop to catch the bus for school.

Grandpa Burman had been on the porch, watching his sick grandson closely. Jeremy had already told his grandpa about the math test when Grandpa Burman had told Jeremy that he probably should go back to bed. When Grandpa Burman had spied Drake, he had asked the tall biker if he would mind giving the boy a ride, figuring that was the only way Jeremy would make the trip in his present condition.

"No, I got this, honest," Jeremy managed to get out, trying to smile at Drake. The tall silver haired biker hid his knowing grin and nodded once in affirmation to the sixteen-year-old. "Mr. Forester will have my hide if I miss his big test and the makeup will be even harder. I just have to suck it up and make it through. Bet you've had a few of those days yourself, Mr. McKiernan, right?"

Drake glanced at the teenager, his eyes twinkling, "You're right about that. I've had a few, Jeremy. See you tonight, then, young fella'. Do well on your test, and may the dragons watch over you." The biker winked and gave Jeremy a quick two-finger salute, then engaged the powerful engine and rumbled out of the parking lot.

Jeremy turned to stiffly walk up the front sidewalk and steps of The West Mount Union High School located in North Beaver Falls Hollow. North Beaver Falls Hollow was approximately four and a half miles as the crow flies from The Falls. Unfortunately, Vermont roads were famous for their curves, double-backs and meanderings, so the actual driving distance was seventeen miles. That was somewhat ironic, considering that there were exactly seventeen different towns that were incorporated into the new union high school. One board member from each town, creating a nightmare of a school board that each succeeding district superintendent and high school principal lost plenty of sleep over.

As Jeremy trudged up the steps along with other students that had been driven by their parents or brought by rural bus routes, he glanced at the front doors. His heart sank. There, standing outside the main doorway was Matilda the Hun.

Matilda Rodriguez was West Mount's Dean of Students. She made it her personal mission to seek out, scrutinize and 'reinvent' any student who she felt wasn't properly utilizing their ability, intelligence and talents. This particular year, that would be Jeremy, along with several dozen other underperforming (at least in her mind) students.

Matilda the Hun's reputation was a matter of legend among the students of West Mount Union. She was not to be denied. Once she had grabbed onto you, the choices were slim to none. You either did what she told you to do, modified your academic or social identity to meet her uncompromising standards, or you were as good as on high school death row. Even the principal of West Mount took a wide berth around Matilda the Hun. Once she sank her determined hooks into you, it was simply best to do what she wanted and try and keep a low profile.

Jeremy glanced up once more and saw with a growing sense of impending doom that Matilda the Hun was staring at and waiting for him. Great, thought the sixteen-year-old as his stomach flipped nauseously one more time. I've got an ice cream hangover and now I've got Matilda on top of a killer math test. Can this day possibly get any better?

***

"So Father O'Flaherty took the wine while he was sleepwalking?" Cash stared at Darlene Pitts, stopped in the motion of pouring his second cup of coffee that morning, "Seriously?"

"The good father's very words," answered Darlene brusquely, her voice a monotone and never taking her eyes off her typing. "He mumbled something about being sorry that he wasted your time and that he was going to drop over and see Doc Stone today to see what could be done to cure his sleep walking."

"Interesting," interjected Yamato as she stood up from her desk and walked over to the window. The glass was frosted over with a late night cold snap, and the light February wind was swirling snow back and forth across the street.

"I had an aunt who had a sleepwalking issue. She would go downstairs, pour herself a glass of milk, get several cookies out of the cookie jar and sit there until all the cookies and milk were gone. Then she'd climb the stairs and go back to bed. She wondered for several weeks who could be doing it. Accused her husband and her son of sneaking out of bed at night and wouldn't listen to them when they said they were innocent."

Cash turned and glanced at Yamato expectantly. When she didn't continue he asked, "So, how did she find out it was her?"

Yamato shrugged, turned back from the window and walked back to her desk, "She stepped on the cat's tail one night on her way back to bed. She scared the cat and herself both half to death. But she finally realized what was going on."

Darlene glanced up from the work order she was typing and declared, "Poor soul. My Grandma Beecham would sleepwalk from time to time. My grandpa would tie a bell to the bedroom door. When it went off, he knew she was on the prowl."

Cash turned and stared at his secretary/dispatcher, "What would your grandpa do? To help her, I mean."

Darlene went back to typing, her face expressionless, "Why he'd follow her down to the kitchen, of course. He said she made much better pancakes when she was asleep."

Cash and Yamato exchanged a grin and then they slipped on their parkas and cold weather hats, "Going out for our morning rounds, Darlene. I've got my two-way. Be back soon."

"Good, I can finally have it quiet enough to get my paperwork done," Darlene announced firmly as the two law officers closed the door behind them.

"Where's Horace this morning, boss?" asked Yamato as she and Cash began striding briskly up toward the white, frosty town square.

"He had to stop out at Kasmir and Ivan Rostov's dairy on his way into work. Seems there has been some vandalism. Somebody spray-painted the back of their main barn," Cash replied turning up the thick collar on his coat and zipping it all the way up. The night had left a cheery little reminder that February in Vermont, even though it might be getting close to Valentine's Day, was still at times a cold-hearted mistress.

Yamato grinned as she kicked at a piece of ice and snow still in the sidewalk, "Did Rostov say what the graffiti was? A picture? Words?"

Cash grinned and glanced over at his deputy, "Seems it was a bright red heart with an arrow through it. Kasmir Rostov claims the lovesick boyfriend of one of his seven daughters put it there. He has no idea who and the daughters aren't telling. Guess Kasmir was mad as a wet hen, and his single brother wasn't helping any."

Yamato glanced over at her boss, her eyes twinkling but inquisitive, "How so?"

Cash chuckled and shrugged, "Apparently Ivan was teasing his older brother, telling him that the heart was a work of art and they ought to keep it on the barn. That was about the time that Kasmir went off the deep end and was shouting and blustering at all his daughters and his brother. That's when Kasmir's wife, Katrina, called into Darlene."

Yamato shook her head, "Poor Horace! Glad he's dealing with that one and not me! I hate dealing with family issues! Just when you think you've got it figured out, they go off again in another direction."

As Cash and Yamato passed by Ed's Pharmacy, they spotted the owner, Jordan Smith-Stone through the front window. They both waved and she smiled happily and waved back.

Jordan was filling prescriptions and working on paperwork that morning. Tasks she usually simply tolerated. But this morning, she was almost enjoying them. That good mood was mostly due to the fact that her dinner party last night had been a rousing success. Or at least that was what Andy Morrison had called to tell her at the crack of dawn that morning.

As Jordan worked along, savoring a new blend of a light Brazilian coffee called Cocoa Sweet from her steaming mug, she hummed. She hummed a late 80's tune she had always loved. Somehow, humming seemed appropriate that morning.

Just then, the phone rang. Jordan reached out, picked up the receiver and still with a smile on her face answered, "Good morning, this is Ed's Pharmacy, how can I help you this morning?"

"Hey, Sweetheart," came her husband's warm and loving voice, "how's your morning so far?"

"Why just wonderful, thank you for asking, Sweetheart!" replied Jordan, glancing out the side window at the large building that housed both their home and Doc's family practice offices. "Are you in the office?"

"Nope, I'm here at the hospital. I'm looking in on a couple of my patients." Doc's voice seemed to have quieted as if there was something on his mind.

"Okay, so what's going on?" Jordan stopped working for a moment, ready to help if her husband needed her.

Doc hesitated and then spit out what he had called for, "Well, I figured I should give you a call. I was talking to Meg this morning."

Jordan beamed happily, "I'll bet she was just full of good things to say about Mr. Andrew Morrison, right?"

"Well," Doc spoke quietly, a little uneasily, "not quite. She thought he was sweet and kind. But Meg pretty much said he wasn't her type. I figured you'd want to know, Sweetheart. Sorry."

Jordan listened carefully and deliberated for a moment. Her smile vanished and her mood changed rapidly. She took a deep breath and spoke quietly back into the receiver, "I see. Well, I do appreciate the call, Doc. That kind of puts a different light on things."

Doc spoke quietly, reassuringly, "Look, Sweetheart, you tried to do a nice thing. It just didn't work out right for these two. At least you tried. I love you, you know." Doc sounded so loving and worried about her that Jordan had to chuckle and smile.

"Hey, its okay, Sweetie. I'm fine. Don't worry. I'm a little disappointed, but all you can do in life is try, right?" Jordan's voice had regained her usual energy and joyfulness. She was also once more truly grateful that Doc Stone had slipped into her life. He was the perfect man for her. She realized that several times a day, as he did of her.

Jordan could envision a relieved Doc, smiling over his cell phone, "Okay Sweetheart, I'll be home in about an hour. Shall we take a few minutes and have a cup of coffee together? I'd like to try that new Brazilian blend you've been raving over."

Jordan smiled happily and responded

enthusiastically, "You bet! Drop by the shop and we'll steal a few minutes! Bye, Sweetheart!"

As she hung up the phone, Jordan's smile vanished. Andy Morrison. The young lawyer was under the impression that he and Meg were 'an item'. Jordan wondered for a moment what she was going to do about that. As she deliberated, she came to a decision. She was going to do nothing, at least for a little while. Who knew? Things sometimes change in life. Stranger things had happened. Why not give the relationship a chance.

Jordan took a deep breath and went back to counting out pills to fill prescriptions. She would see what the day brought.

***

Jordan Smith-Stone wasn't the only one humming that morning. Over in Brown Bear Junction, in the distinguished law offices of Lesner, Malkowitz, Freedman and Lister, Andy Morrison was humming a merry tune as he moved with impressive speed through his load of briefs, impressive speed even for him. The young lawyer had already done a day's work and the sun was only a third of the way up in the bitterly cold February sky.

His actions and attention may have been on his work, but his innermost thoughts were undoubtedly on a certain young female doctor in The Falls. Andy had already called over to The Green Thumb and asked Joe Capone to deliver a dozen red roses to the young lady in question. Then he had almost instantaneously changed his mind and asked Joe to put together a spectacular arrangement rather than just plain roses. Now, Andy's most important decision was when to call and thank Meg for such a wonderful evening. His heart kept urging him to call now, but his head advised him to take it a little slower. Don't overwhelm the young lady, wait until tonight after work to call and express his gratitude.

As law partners, paralegals and secretaries walked by his office door, they stared in at the happily preoccupied young man. Andy was, in essence, a kind, sweet and naturally positive young man. But it was quite obvious that he was somehow much more excited, more enthusiastic and more joyful this cold February morning. Office gossip, much like the gossip in a small town, spreads like wildfire. By nine-thirty that morning, everyone at the law offices of Lesner, Malkowitz, Freedman and Lister knew something was up with Andy Morrison.

By mid-morning, Andy desperately needed to talk with someone. He felt like he was about to burst. Other than a few dates in high school and college, Andy was a neophyte to the world of dating, feelings and puppy love. Unfortunately, the most natural person he chose to talk to was the person least likely to want to hear about his instant infatuation: his sister.

Escaping the office on the pretext of picking up files that he needed at the courthouse, Andy drove the few blocks to Treasured Memories and hurried into the shop, just as Wendy and Mandy were carrying in a small, antique desk they had purchased at an estate auction.

"Hey, Andy!" called out Mandy, grinning and gesturing toward the new addition to their collection, "What do you think? It's about one hundred years old and worth at least $600. We picked it up for just over $150! It came from the old Pritchard house. Not bad, huh?!"

Andy grinned back and nodded, "Just another in a

long line of smart investments, ladies!"

Wendy leaned over and gave Andy's cheek a kiss, a small smile on her face. Although she had been feeling a bit drained and somewhat out of sorts, she always tried to look her best for her little brother.

"Can we talk for a minute?" Andy glanced anxiously at his sister as Mandy moved out of earshot to get the wax and soft polishing cloth to clean up the desk.

Wendy glanced carefully at her brother, trying to assess what he might need. Even though she was pretty sure what he wanted to discuss, she forced a smile and slipped her arm through his.

"Of course," she responded walking with her brother to her small office in the back and then shutting the door quietly. "Okay, what's up?"

Andy smiled broadly, his eyes twinkling uncontrollably, "I know I probably sound dumb, but I just can't stop thinking about Meg!"

Wendy reached out and touched her brother's cheek, a slight smile passing across her face, "I can see that. You must have really enjoyed her company, Andy. I've never seen you look quite like this."

Andy grinned again, beginning to pace briskly back and forth across the antique Egyptian rug on the floor, his voice quiet but intense, "You're right, sis. I've never felt this way before!"

Andy stopped for a moment and stared anxiously at his big sister, "I think I've fallen in love with her, sis! In just one night! I know that sounds crazy! I just needed to talk to you. We've always talked about the important stuff in our lives, made decisions together."

Andy stared at Wendy, his eyes wide and trusting, "I don't know what to do, sis. Can you help me out here?"

Wendy's heart gave a slight tug, as she stared back

at her brother. The brother she had raised and taken care of for the past seventeen years. She had to do and say what was best for him, as always. Her feelings about this situation didn't matter, she kept reminding herself.

"Well," she whispered, reaching out and taking one of his big hands between her two little ones, "you have to do what your heart tells you to do. You have to get to know her. Make sure what you feel is real." A tear rolled down her cheek. It was a tear filled with both joy for her brother, and loss and sadness for herself.

Andy reached out and hugged her tight, "You always know just what to do and what to say, Wendy. I can always depend on you. I love you so!"

With that, and a parting grin and wink, Andy nearly sprinted out of the antique shop. Mandy, polishing the old desk turned and watched him go, then glanced back at Wendy, "What's gotten into him this brisk winter mornin'?"

Wendy smiled and wiped away the tear, watching her brother drive away as she walked over toward the counter to begin the bookwork for the day. Her face was careworn, but filled with happiness for him, as she sighed and glanced back at Mandy, "What is it that gets into most young men at this time of year?"

Mandy grinned back at her boss and friend, nodding her understanding as she continued to polish the old desk, "Ah, that would be Cupid's arrow, my friend. Cupid's arrow knows no rhyme or reason. That pretty much explains it, doesn't it?"

Chapter 8

Jeremy sat leaning over his math test, his face intense. It was second period and although the stomach cramps were still coming and going, they were less severe and the only real discomfort was the gurgling of his stomach and passing of gas from time to time. As Jeremy's stomach produced yet another rumbling gurgle, he glanced quickly around to see who had heard him. Cynthia Schakowsky who was seated next to him was staring at him in thinly veiled disgust. His friend James, on the other side of him, was grinning and teasing him by holding his nose and making a face. Jeremy's cheeks flushed and he shook his head slowly, wishing that his stomach distress, and the embarrassment it was presently causing him, would simply vanish.

Up in the front of the classroom, Mr. Forester was pacing back and forth, his bowtie and large round glasses prominent on his smallish features. Mr. Forester was gazing out across the class, watching every student closely, making sure that no one was pulling a fast one and cheating on his test. His penetrating gaze stopped for a moment on Jeremy, and his eyebrows lowered slightly. Jeremy's cheeks reddened again as he leaned closer to the test, willing himself to focus in on the math problems, trying to take his mind off the embarrassing sounds.

But minds have a way of slipping off to where they want to go, and in time, his mind played out the whole scene with Ms. Rodriguez as he climbed the steps of the high school that morning.

"Jeremy! Oh Jeremy!" Matilda the Hun had called out with great authority as he had attempted to head toward one of the other front doors to the main entrance.

"Yes, Ms. Rodriguez?" Jeremy had answered. He was pale and shaking slightly from his intestinal distress as his stomach continued rumbling.

"If I didn't know better, young man," Matilda the Hun had continued, her brown eyes drilling holes into his head, "I would say you were trying to avoid me." Ms. Rodriguez folded her arms across her ample bosom.

"No Ma'am," replied Jeremy, sighing and realizing that he was trapped with no escape possible. His eyes did not meet hers. Her gaze was so piercing that few students at West Mount could look their Dean of Students in the eye.

As the Dean of Students stepped through the front door of the high school with Jeremy right beside her, she continued to lecture him, in low, firm tones, "I hear from several of your teachers that you don't participate in class as much as you should. You receive excellent test scores, but have very little interaction with your teachers and the other students. Is this true, Jeremy?"

The end of Ms. Rodriguez's sentence made it sound like an indictment of something terrible and unnatural. Inside, Jeremy knew that it certainly was true he didn't participate much. But he was uncomfortable speaking up. He simply didn't like to. And besides, he rationalized, I know the stuff and I get all A's. What more do I have to do to please this woman?

Matilda the Hun stopped in mid-step and turned toward Jeremy, her eyes stern, "Well? Is this true or not?"

Jeremy turned toward the Dean of Students and simply mumbled, "Yes, Ma'am. It's true. I get nervous speaking, answering questions. It's not 'cause I don't know the answers, I do. I just don't like doing it. That's not wrong is it, Ma'am?"

A flash of recognition passed across Matilda the Hun's face and then it was gone. Back was the demanding Dean of Students who always held students accountable, "Well, while I do understand not wanting to participate in classroom discussions, you need to try harder. I want you to work on being more involved in class discussions. I will check back in a few days to see if you have done so."

Just before Matilda the Hun strode away, she frowned and declared in a slightly lower volume, "You can be better than this, Jeremy. You aren't living up to your potential. But you soon will be. I'll see to that! Good day, Jeremy."

As Jeremy's thoughts returned to the math test, he frowned. He had no doubt that Matilda the Hun would be checking up on him, and soon. He would have to make more of an effort to participate in class discussions so that his teachers would give him a good report. If they didn't, he just might end up on Matilda the Hun's Bad List. Her Bad List was both a school legend and a reality. Kids who got on her Bad List found high school to be, in simple terms, 'a living hell', from all reports.

Jeremy's frown deepened. He was not going to be on that list, no way. As he stood up and carried his paper up to the front of the room to Mr. Forester, Jeremy smiled engagingly and whispered, "Excellent test, Sir. I hope I did well. Have a great day!"

That little speech was almost as many words as he had spoken to Mr. Forester all semester. As a grinning Jeremy walked quietly down the aisle and out into the high school corridor, Mr. Forester stood, eyes wide in shock, mouth open, at the front of the classroom, staring after the suddenly relatively loquacious sixteen-year-old.

***

The three old friends huddled together over coffee and hot Danish at a booth in Tina's Diner. They were deep in a serious conversation, each one conscientiously attentive and talking almost at the same time. The three old friends were often, kind-heartedly but amusingly, nicknamed 'the three musketeers' by their congregations and townsfolk in general. The clergymen oftentimes went places together and nearly always believed in and supported the same things.

"My sister Agatha had it occasionally. Father installed a two way padlock on her bedroom door, put a gate across the stairs and had a little bell installed over her door." Theo Dunham nodded his head emphatically as he poured a small amount of half and half in his newly refilled coffee cup, glancing up at both of his colleagues in all earnestness.

"That sounds like it certainly might help," Marcus Templeton, pastor of the Methodist church, replied, contemplating the description of what Theo's parents had done, "although my great aunt Grace seemed more than able to get around any obstacles placed in her way when she slept-walked."

Father O'Flaherty frowned slightly and tilted his

head slightly to one side as he listened, "What do you mean, Marcus? What was done to try and stop her?"

Marcus Templeton shrugged and took another bite of warm, tender pastry, "Well, the usual, I would presume such as locked doors, obstacles in the way. My great uncle even tried tying a rope around her ankle from what I remember."

Both Theo Dunham and Father O'Flaherty waited curiously for Marcus to continue as he took a long sip of steaming coffee, "But whatever they tried, none of it worked. Turns out she was a pretty clever old girl, at least when she was asleep!"

The priest sighed and glanced out the window, "Well, I have no idea how long this has been going on. Doc Stone told me that it isn't uncommon for it to happen only occasionally over your life. It could be set off by any number of things."

Theo leaned forward, gazed directly at Flynn O'Flaherty, after glancing around cautiously at the other patrons eating a mid-morning snack. His eyes had widened as he whispered earnestly, "We do have an idea, my old friend, if you're willing to try it."

Theo glanced over at Marcus, who nodded enthusiastically and added in a near whisper, "Yes, we're willing to help, if you want us to, Flynn."

The good father stared at Theo and then leaned forwards himself. Glancing back and forth between his two best friends, jaw jutting forward, eyes narrowing, he uttered firmly, "At this point, I'm willing to try anything! Can you imagine how mortified I was to call the sheriff over to report sacramental wine being stolen only to find I had been hiding it away on myself?! Let's hear your idea."

Marcus began, motioning to Theo and himself,

"Well, we propose to come to your rectory at bedtime, and stand guard as it were, for a few nights. We'll take two-hour shifts. Then we'll be able to watch over you, and tell you what's going on. Our observations will let you know if this is just a random occurrence or something more regular. Then, you'll have a better idea as to what you need to do in order to deal with it."

Theo quickly added, humbly and with real care and compassion in his voice, "We won't get in your way, and we'll be gone by the time you wake up, Flynn. It will only be for a few nights. We thought that it might provide you with a certain sense of clarity and some factual knowledge in this matter. We only want to be of assistance, to help you solve this puzzle, old friend. Now, you won't hurt our feelings if you say no. What do you say?"

Upon hearing his friends' plan, Father O'Flaherty was struck with two opposing reactions. The first was the 'I can do this by myself' syndrome held by many older New Englanders. Most townspeople over the age of fifty had learned to be self-sufficient and keep their problems and business to themselves. It was the old-fashioned philosophy of life and relationships in the rugged environment of Vermont.

The second reaction was the honest desire to have his old friends help him solve this new conundrum. Over the years, the three friends had worked together, quietly and skillfully, to solve a number of their personal and church related issues in their village. Flynn O'Flaherty had grown to trust Theo and Marcus implicitly. He not only cared deeply about his friends, but they were the closest thing that he had to family.

Father O'Flaherty stared back at his two best friends and hesitated a moment. Then a wry smile passed across his weathered old face and he held out his hands, one to Theo and one to Marcus, "Thank you for your offer. I truly appreciate it, and both of you as well."

The priest grinned and winked, "Let's do this!"

Marcus and Theo reached out and grasped their old friend's hands tightly. Then they all smiled and nodded with confirmation of their latest joint project, and as the original three musketeers themselves would have proclaimed, it was indeed 'all for one and one for all'.

***

Meg Monroe was just finishing up with Nathaniel Johnson. Nathaniel, or Nate as most of his family and friends called him, had been climbing trees in the grove of woods just back of his home. He had been with his best friend, Jimmy Capone, son of Joe and Tammy Capone, owners of The Green Thumb. The two twelve-year-olds had been playing a version of winter tree tag that actually involved chasing after each other up in the boughs of the stark, cold and sleeping trees in their little woods.

Nate was trying to keep from being tagged. In the process of leaping from one icy limb to another, he had slipped and wedged his foot in the fork of a tree. He had been left hanging helplessly there in the frozen limbs of an oak tree until a frightened and stunned Jimmy could run home, get his dad to bring the tall ladder, and get his red-faced friend Nate down.

Not only had Nate badly sprained his ankle and knee, but the skin around his ankle had unfortunately been rubbed raw by the time the relieved boy was rescued by the somewhat amused town landscaper and gardener.

Meg had listened to Nate's mother Agatha as she alternated between fuming, scolding, lecturing and hovering protectively over her recalcitrant son. As she worked on the boy, Meg grinned to herself and gave Nate a slightly less than twenty-five percent chance of getting out of the house to do anything fun for the next month or so.

As Nate was wheeled down to the front door of the hospital by an orderly, Meg watched him go, a small smile appearing on her lips. Her thoughts drifted back to her own childhood. She remembered how caring and wonderful her own mother had been to her when she was a kid. She hadn't really known her dad, but her mother had remarried and Meg's stepdad had been wonderful to her, in every way imaginable.

Of course, whenever she talked to her mom on the phone nowadays, sometime during the conversation the awkward subject of Meg's sparse social life and any prospective suitors would come up. Meg always ended up getting a bit defensive, telling her mom that she had no time to date, and she hadn't meant a Mr. Right anyway. To which her mother would tactfully but firmly counter by saying that if Meg didn't make an effort to meet men, how was she ever going to know if there was a Mr. Right out there for her. It was a conversation that went around and around ad infinitum, much to Meg's frustration at times.

Meg stared after Nate and his mom, and a nagging sense of loneliness settled over her. With a determined shake of her head, Meg promptly banished the gloom and moved on to her next task, making rounds in the hospital ward.

As she passed by the admittance desk, Flora Hendrickson leaned out from behind the counter. Peering over her reading glasses, she called out, "Dr. Monroe, these are for you."

There on the counter was a beautiful bouquet of

flowers. Not your 'run of the mill' bouquets, understand. It was definitely a 'You paid top dollar for this, Sweetheart!' bouquet.

Meg frowned slightly. It wasn't her birthday. Her parents weren't the type to send flowers to their daughter anyway. She wasn't dating anyone. Then it hit her. Last night, the kiss she had expertly slipped onto her cheek. Andy Morrison.

With an unenthusiastic sigh that Flora most definitely heard, even though Meg had wished she hadn't, the young doctor peeked reluctantly at the inscription on the card.

Dear Meg, I had a great time last night. Call you tonight, Andy

Meg shook her head a bit, drew in a deep breath and turned toward Flora, who now was staring curiously at the young doctor, one eyebrow up, her creative brain trying to fill in the blanks.

"It's not what it looks like," Meg declared hesitantly with a small self-conscious smile.

"Oh?" countered Flora, her eyebrow rising higher, her tone low and monotone, "And just what does it look like?"

Meg attempted a confident smile which really didn't work out, "Well it might seem as though they are from a boyfriend," she blurted out.

Flora leaned back in her chair and re-positioned her half glasses, staring straight down her long nose at the young flustered doctor, and announced, "It might."

Meg hesitated a moment and realized with a queasy feeling that she needed to clarify further, "But it's not. I went over to Doc's house for dinner last night and he was there too."

The eyebrow went higher.

"It wasn't a date." Meg glanced at the flowers once again. "But he seems to think it was a date," she muttered.

"I see," replied Flora, her eyes still staring at the young doctor, while Meg could image all sorts of thoughts running through the duty nurse's head.

"Well, maybe he thinks it was a date, but I don't really have any interest in him, you see?" Meg stared back at Flora, hoping that this announcement would clear up the situation.

Apparently, it did not.

After a few protracted seconds, Flora cleared her throat, turned and stared at the bouquet. "A fella' sends a bouquet like that to a woman, he's got more than just a thank you on his mind. That man's got plans." Both of her eyebrows lifted and Flora stared back pointedly at Meg once again.

Meg took a deep breath and let it out slowly, gazing uncomfortably over at the bouquet once again. Flora was right. If a man sent a woman a bouquet like that, for no other apparent reason, he had plans.

Meg leaned over the counter and spoke to Flora in a desperate whisper, her eyes wide with the unvarnished truth, "Oh, Flora! You're right! I can see that now. What do I do?"

Flora glanced both ways down the hallway and toward the entrance of the hospital. Seeing no one for the moment, she gestured for Meg to come around in back of the front desk. There in a few short, whispered terse sentences, Meg learned more about the actual practical workings and mechanisms of the 'birds and the bees' than her mother had ever thought of teaching her.

***

Nancy Sturgis looked up from helping Pansy Herbert with her project and glanced over at her two adult helpers. Her brother, Daniel, was cutting a large red heart out of construction paper for Sherri Schuman. Daniel was concentrating mightily, his eyes narrowed and his tongue was sticking out as he slowly and carefully cut along the pattern lines. Across the classroom Emily Goldstein was grinning, as she was deep in conversation with Jonathon Shimonoseki. The two of them were laughing and attempting to fit all the pieces of the project together with school glue and scotch tape.

All around the classroom, her first grade class was intently cutting, pasting, coloring and aligning the pieces together carefully. Nancy had two classroom moms, her brother, Emily and an EA who had volunteered to help. There were six adults to help seventeen first graders get their Valentine's Day cards for their moms and dads ready for the 'big day'. She chuckled to herself, her eyes twinkling as she quickly reflected.

You would think six adults for seventeen first graders would be enough, she mused. And yet, here they were, 20 minutes into the activity, which was supposed to take 30 minutes tops, and from the looks around the room, most kids were less than halfway finished.

All of a sudden, Nancy started laughing. She couldn't help it. The sheer ludicrousness of the situation had walked up and smacked her in the face. As she giggled harder and harder, all around the room, the kids and adults turned and stared with shocked fascination at her. As Nancy continued to laugh, giggle and chuckle, the kids and the adults glanced around the room at each other at first, all of them desperately trying to figure out what had brought her giggles on. Finally, giving in to her infectious good-humor, several of the kids started laughing along with their teacher.

Within a few moments, everyone in the room was roaring hilariously. They laughed even harder because they had absolutely no idea why they were laughing. Emily and one of the class moms laughed so hard they started crying. Billy Swanson and his best friend Phillip Yung literally rolled over and over on the floor, their giggling turning to guffawing and then to hiccups and back to giggles. Three of the girls in first grade laughed so hard that their noses started running. Then they giggled even harder because their noses were running.

Finally, the classroom door opened and there was the principal, Sean Frasier, staring curiously all around the room, a wide, crooked, but mystified smile on his face.

"Miss Sturgis, is everything all right?" Sean queried, still glancing back and forth at the hilarity that was slowly subsiding all around the first grade classroom. "I heard a lot of noise coming from your room and thought I should..."

Just then, Myron Obermyer, who had been sneaking numerous tastes of the white school paste during the activity, clapped his chubby hands over his mouth and ran to the classroom bathroom. Seconds after the door was slammed shut, everyone could hear the first grader throwing up.

That, plus the appearance of the principal successfully put an end to the laughter and giggles. As Nancy stood up from the low table she had been sitting at, she smiled, her cheeks red with embarrassment and declared, "Sorry, Mr. Frasier! I got to laughing over the Valentine's Day activity we were doing and it just went downhill from there!"

The rest of the somewhat embarrassed, but still cheerful adults in the classroom nodded quickly in agreement.

"I thought my sister was finally going over the silliness edge with all these themes, activities, games and learning projects she comes up with!" added Daniel, glancing over at Sean and winking conspiratorially.

At that moment, a mortified Myron stepped out of the bathroom, a bit pale, his eyes down, and quickly made his way back to his little chair at the third table.

"We'll finish these projects tomorrow, kids," Nancy announced to the class motioning to her adult helpers, "when we are not quite so silly! But," she turned and smiled pleasantly at the principal, "its okay to be silly now and then isn't it, Mr. Frasier?"

As the two room moms, Daniel and Emily stood up and got busy picking up each child's project and placing the pieces in their individual cubbies, Sean glanced all around at the first graders who were staring up at him, eyes wide and innocent, obviously waiting for him to respond.

Sean grinned at Nancy and sat down in the middle of the first grade class. He leaned forward, a twinkle in his eyes, his voice calm and quiet but animated, "Yes indeed, it is quite okay to be silly sometimes, Miss Sturgis. In fact when I was a little boy, my little brother and I used to create these imaginary games. We would pretend that we would be in outer space, or knights at King Arthur's Court..."

Jerry Porter's hand shot up, his eyes wide and filled with eager fascination, "Who's King Arfur, Principal Frasier?"

Sean grinned and explained to the class, "King Arthur

was a king that lived a very long time ago, Jerry. He gathered around him a group of knights with swords and shields and armor. They were called the Knights of the Round Table, and they protected and fought for everything that was good and right in the world."

As Sean got into the story, the children quietly came and sat around him in a large circle, sitting cross-legged on the floor, many of them with their elbows on their knees and their chubby little fists on their chins. For that spellbound moment, the principal was their storyteller and he had their rapt attention.

The other adults in the room clustered together out of the way, over by Miss Sturgis's desk. They all watched, fascinated themselves, at how Sean's story had captured the attention and imagination of every last first grader.

"Neat!" whispered Emily, sitting on the edge of Nancy's desk, cleaning the glue off her fingers with a wet-wipe.

"How does he do that?" breathed Daniel with great admiration, turning toward Nancy while keeping his eyes on the storyteller as he wove his web of dreams and sheer imagination.

Nancy smiled softly, "It's a gift. When he comes in and reads to them it's the same way. It's like he's the Pied Piper. When I read to the kids, at least one or two will fidget or their attention will wander off. But when he comes in, they're like putty in his hands."

"Speaking of putty," whispered one of the room moms, her eyebrow lifting and a wry smile flashing across her face while she lifted up her glue covered hands, "remind me not to show up the next time you want to play with glue!"

The adults chuckled quietly this time as they

continued to watch the Pied Piper weave his magic story-web. Sometimes, thought Nancy Sturgis as she watched her class, in education, you have to take the path where dreams are made and nourished, rather than always dealing with facts, the 'right answers' and the here and now. That's what bureaucrats, governments and legislators always fail to realize. They make it all about 'testing'. They fail to consider that teaching is about inspiring and sometimes inspiring takes the form of imagination. Imagine that.

Chapter 9

The phone call in the early afternoon was not unexpected. In fact Meg had been rather dreading it. As Meg stopped halfway down the hospital corridor and looked at the caller ID on her cell, she sighed heavily and frowned. It was Andy Morrison. She had been fervently hoping that he would let the beautiful flowers speak for themselves. But apparently he had more to say, in person.

In all honesty, she was hoping that she could send a formal and slightly impersonal thank you note telling the young lawyer how beautiful the flowers were and that she appreciated his kindness and thoughtfulness. She also had hoped that the thank you note would excuse her from speaking with the sweet young man and perhaps having to deal with what looked like a potential, but unwanted, romantic entanglement on his part.

Meg took a deep breath and answered the phone, "Good afternoon, Andy! I want you to know that the flowers you sent over were simply beautiful. The duty nurses and the patients have really been enjoying them! I really do appreciate your kindness and thoughtfulness."

At his desk in his office, Andy grinned broadly, his eyes gazing delightedly out his office window, "Oh!

You're very welcome, Meg! I was hoping that they would please you, and not be too..." he scrambled for the word, blushing slightly even though he was alone, "ostentatious!"

Meg smiled to herself. The huge assortment of rare and gorgeous flowers in the bouquet had seemed a bit over the top, but she understood that it was his way of showing her how much the evening had obviously meant to him.

"Well, to be truthful, we haven't seen such a stunningly gorgeous arrangement around here for quite some time. They have been the highlight of our day! So, thank you, and don't worry. The flowers were perfect." Meg's voice was calm, comforting and compassionate. The last thing in the world she wanted to do was to hurt this sweet, kind, obviously sensitive man.

"I was, ah, wondering," Andy hesitated slightly, trying to summon up his courage, "if you would like to have dinner at Luigi's, the Italian restaurant here in The Junction, and then take in a movie this weekend?" Meg could almost hear the anxiety and tenseness in his tone. She felt a world of empathy for the young man. So much so that for a few moments she almost said yes, although to do so would only prolong an uncomfortable and unavoidable situation.

"You know, that sounds wonderful, but I have a heavy shift this weekend, Andy," Meg replied softly into the phone. "I appreciate and I'm flattered that you asked, however. Thank you for being so sweet."

Andy, disappointed, but buoyed up by her sweet rejection, continued, "Well, if you can't make it this weekend, perhaps..."

Meg gritted her teeth, and decided to tell the young lawyer a white lie. She despised lying, but sometimes, as her partner Doc often advocated, 'a white lie used in the right way at the right time is often the greatest kindness'.

"Andy, I should tell you right up front, that I'm at a stage in my career where I just don't seem to have time for much of a personal life. I promised Doc Stone when I took over this job that I would give the citizens of The Falls my very best. That's what I intend to do for the near future. Eventually, there will be time for me. Right now, there isn't. I'm sorry. You're sweet, kind and very handsome. Any girl would enjoy being with you and spending time with you. But right now, I'm just not any girl. I'm Dr. Meg Monroe. I hope you understand." Meg's voice carried with it a sweet wistfulness as she tried her best to let the young man down easily.

There was silence on the other end of the phone for several moments, then Andy's voice, a little too happy and enthusiastic, replied, "Oh! Sure! I understand, Meg. Really, I do. I have been doing the same here at the law firm. I work eighty or ninety hours a week. Get here at five-thirty and leave after dark every day. My sister is always joking with me that the only time she sees me is when I'm coming or going."

Andy swallowed hard and continued, "I get it. And I applaud your hard work and pride. Look, thanks for a great time at dinner. I'd better go, lots to do, just like you! Take care of yourself, Meg Monroe, you are a very special young woman. See you around, I hope. 'Bye."

Before Meg had a chance to say goodbye, Andy was gone. She stared at the cell phone and suddenly felt terrible. She slipped her cell phone back into her lab coat pocket and began striding briskly down the hallway. The faster she got back to work, the easier it would be to deal with the feelings and residual fallout from her phone call. In her head she knew that it was kinder to end it now, in the beginning. In her heart, however, she couldn't help but feel like the mean stepsister in a Grimm's fairy tale.

Back in the law offices of Lesner, Malkowitz, Freedman and Lister, Andy Morrison was staring vacantly out the window. His hand was still holding the office phone, and his eyes were dull and listless. His heart had turned cold and he hurt deep down inside. He didn't blame Meg. He was disgusted with himself. He had jumped into an uncertain situation with both feet, taking a chance. Now, he felt the fool. He suddenly also felt very lonely, very lonely indeed.

At that moment, there came a knock on his office door. Drawing a deep breath and trying to pull himself together, Andy called out, "Come on in!"

Elizabeth Fallon, the newest paralegal at the law firm entered the office hesitantly, almost timidly, with a shy smile on her face. She was struggling to carry in a huge stack of briefs, law books and copies. Andy, who was always the gentleman, rushed over to help her. As he reached out to take her oversized load, he accidently bumped into her, sending the books, folders and stapled papers cascading to the floor.

Eyes wide, staring around at the once neat assortment of articles lying randomly on the office floor, tears slipped down Elizabeth's reddening cheeks. She stammered, "Oh! I'm so sorry! I'll pick it all up, Mr. Morrison! I can't believe how clumsy I am!"

As Elizabeth knelt and desperately began to gather the documents, Andy knelt beside her. He reached out a hand to help and inadvertently touched Elizabeth's arm. She turned to see an amused half-smile playing around his handsome face.

"Elizabeth, it's no big thing, okay? I caused this and I'm sorry. We'll pick it up together, okay?" His eyes were kind and caring, and Elizabeth suddenly felt much better.

"Thanks!" she murmured as she smiled back. Together, they picked up the massive pile of material. By the time they were done, they were chatting amiably, and both Elizabeth and Andy felt a good deal better than they had a few minutes before.

Life is funny. An old proverb is that in life when one door closes, another door opens. But, sometimes, when least expected, a fortunate accident brings our lives some relief, as well as a needed change of direction.

***

Cash and Horace were in the process of shoveling out old widow Haney's front walk and driveway, even though there hadn't been a car in the garage for the past fifteen years. But then, Myrna Haney's sister-in-law Edith came to visit twice a week and needed a place to park. Cash and Horace had worked up a really good sweat by the time the call came for them on the two-way radio.

Yamato was a couple of blocks over, investigating what Turnbull Mystik had classified as a "disturbance" when he had called it into Darlene. The deputy had poked around in the back lot of Turnbull's small meat packing plant, struggling through hip deep snow at times, attempting to find out what the source of the disturbance might be. She had met with Turnbull for a moment inside the packing company, but he had been busy and had hollered out that he didn't know what it was, only that two of his crates with meat products inside had been broken into and pieces of meat stolen. He also yelled loudly over the rumble of the machinery that it had happened twice before in the last week.

As Yamato had begun searching around in several small abandoned buildings, she heard a tremendous growl. The growl sounded like it was made by something the size of a massive mountain lion or perhaps even a tiger. Self-preservation promptly reared its head and she stepped back a few feet, pulling her Glock 9mm and holding it down at her side. Then she immediately had called Cash for reinforcements over the two-way.

Five minutes later a heavily breathing Cash and Horace arrived on scene and Yamato filled them in with a terse, calm whisper, never taking her eyes off the small building where the growling had emanated from. "Deep growls. They were loud and resonating. The sound may be caused by the emptiness of the abandoned building, but it sounded big, mean and not very happy to see me snooping around out here."

Cash nodded, glancing over at a red-faced and panting Horace, "You move to that side," he motioned to his left, "and Yamato you head right. Let's keep whatever is in there from escaping. No shots unless you're defending yourself. Got it?"

Both deputies nodded and moved slowly but deliberately off to each side, Glocks drawn, pointing them at the entrance to the building. Cash waited until they were in position and then took, one, two, three steps forward, handgun held high.

The thunderous growling erupted once again, Cash glanced over at Yamato and shrugged, mouthing silently, "You're right. It sounds big and mean alright."

Horace's eyes grew wide and his mouth opened in pure astonishment. It truly did sound like there was either a ferocious lion or a raging Tyrannosaurus Rex inside the little building. Several nosy townspeople had begun to cluster at the edge of several buildings a few yards away, their eyes wide with shock after also hearing the massive roars.

Cash rolled his eyes and thought, 'Great! Now we have an audience! Could it get any better?' Not more than an instant after that thought popped into his brain, a small, cute little ragged puppy dashed out of another one of the small buildings. The pup ran straight into the building they had surrounded. As the puppy disappeared into the dark shadows of the building, the loud roar sounded yet again.

Shrieks of pity for the possible eminent demise of the cute little puppy immediately erupted from several kind-hearted bystanders, and even from Horace, who immediately clapped a hand over his mouth and peeked guiltily to see if Cash had heard him.

"Great! Just what we need!" whispered Cash to himself. Then, he glanced quickly at his deputies and motioned for both of them to move forward. Together, the three brave officers of the law charged into the dark shadows of the abandoned building.

The townspeople waited one, two, three seconds breathlessly, their wide-open eyes intently trained on the entrance of the small building. Then a shot rang out and they all flinched involuntarily, their anxiety level rising quickly. The suspense lasted another fifteen seconds until Horace Scofield strode out of the shed carrying two wiggling puppies in his arms. His face was pale, but he walked purposefully across the lot toward the sheriff's office without a word to anyone.

Ten seconds later, Yamato emerged with a big smile on her face, carrying three more squirming, licking and whining puppies. She walked out of the shed and then turned and waited for her boss. Cash came out last carrying a large, shaggy, somewhat gaunt and scrawny dog wrapped in a dirty old blanket. He struggled with the weight of his burden in the snow and Miles Federman, Lyle's youngest son, stepped over and offered to help Cash carry the dog.

Cash gratefully accepted. Looking around and seeing all the curious faces staring out at them, Cash declared loudly, "This stray had a litter of pups in that old building, probably been stealing scraps to feed herself and make milk for the pups."

The townsfolk immediately came forward, checking out the little pups and even petting the obviously weary mother gently and with great care.

"But sheriff, what made those horrible growls?" ventured Shawna Morganstein, Donald's sister-in-law, curiously as she patted the mangy dog soothingly.

Cash grinned and looked around at the group of townspeople, shaking his head slightly, "The mother had her babies nestled inside half of an old, discarded, cast iron boiler. It was probably left over from fifty or sixty years ago when the old Duffee Precision Parts Factory was housed here. When she barked, the acoustics were just right so it amplified her weak bark to sound like a huge, savage beast! But, that certainly explains the rash of calls we've been getting lately about wild animals and noise disturbances."

Several of the older citizens, including Lathrop Poole, who had been employed at the factory in his younger days, nodded in agreement. Lathrop leaned forward, and lightly touched the anemic dog, his eyes misting over slightly, "I had me an old dog like this once. Best dog I ever had."

Cash smiled at Lathrop compassionately and then,

seizing the opportunity while he glanced around at the small group, decided to offer up an idea of how to take care of the newly found pups.

"I'm betting that there will be four or five free puppies up for adoption within the next couple of weeks," Cash called out, "so if you want one, you'd better get your names into Darlene pretty quick. The show's over, folks. Go on about your business. Have a good day."

By the time Cash, Miles and Yamato got to the sheriff's office, Horace had already fixed up a makeshift dog bed. It was an old cardboard box with several spare blankets tucked into it in the back room. Darlene warily eyed the three more puppies and their mother as they were carried through the door.

"And just who is going to be taking care of these dogs, sheriff?" she queried pointedly, glaring down over her half-rimmed reading glasses. "Because I'm telling you who will not be doing that, right now. Do we have an understanding?"

"I'll take care of 'em, Darlene," announced Horace, striding out of the back room with the two puppies he had brought in bounding about his heels happily. His eyes were determined and his jaw was set.

Darlene, her eyes widening a bit at the new 'take charge' Horace, stared intently at the deputy for a moment. Then she merely nodded and went back to her reports.

After Miles had left, Cash, Yamato and Horace were gathered around the temporary bed for the five dogs. They had already put down a large bowl of milk, a dish of dry dog food and a bowl of water. Horace glanced over uncomfortably at his boss and colleague, obviously needing to say something important.

His voice was quiet, but filled with humiliation and remorse, "I'm awful sorry about falling on my face on that ice and my gun going off. If you want my gun for a while, or if you want to dock my pay, I'll understand. I know I endangered both of you, and that just can't happen. Whatever you do to me, the way I'm beating my own self up over it will still be worse. I'm sorry."

Horace glanced at Yamato and then at Cash, nodding his head slightly with the sincerest apology he knew. Then he lowered his eyes and simply waited.

Yamato glanced over at Cash and she lifted her eyebrows meaningfully, then she stood up and walked to the front, leaving the two men alone.

Cash stroked the mangy fur of the obviously mistreated and malnourished dog gently. The sad, but somehow hopeful eyes of the dog peered straight up into Cash's face and she whined slightly.

Cash sighed and looked over at his deputy, "Horace, what happened was an accident. We all had our guns out. We were all ready to shoot if need be. You slipped and fell so quickly that you didn't have time to do anything. I saw you deliberately move your shooting hand out away from us. In fact," Cash pointed out the big goose egg swelling on Horace's forehead, "that's why you got that. You moved your gun out of the way and fell directly on your head rather than protect yourself. Isn't that true?"

Horace nodded once, but made no move to respond otherwise.

"Then the incident's over. We won't talk about it again." Horace glanced up, some of the color returning to his face.

"However," Cash continued, and Horace immediately glanced down again, "you need to have your Glock checked out to make sure it wasn't damaged or see if you need to sight it in again."

Once again, Horace's eyes met Cash's and he smiled warmly. "Thanks, Boss," the grateful deputy whispered gratefully, "I sure do appreciate it. You won't regret it, Sheriff, I promise!"

At that moment came a sharp, incensed announcement from the other room, "Horace Scofield! Get yourself out here this very instant! One of your mangy fleabags has made a mess right in the middle of the floor! Get the bucket and the mop! It had better be gone in five minutes or there will be hell to pay!"

Horace jumped to his feet and raced for the storage room, his face whiter than usual. Cash simply chuckled and stared down at the female lying back wearily in the blanketed box. He reached out and patted her head gently once again and she gave her best rendition of a doggy smile, her tail wagging feebly and her eyes filled with friendship.

Cash stared at the dog and mused kind-heartedly, "I'll bet you could tell us quite a tale if you could speak, right old girl?"

The dog simply gave a short, quiet yelp and licked his hand.

***

As Elizabeth Fallon trudged through the snow to her old beat-up car, she was tired. Actually though, for the first time in days, she was feeling a little bit more optimistic. It had been a hard day at work, ten hours of fetching documents, pouring over law books and running hundreds of pages through the copier throughout the day. But her chance encounter with Mr. Morrison, sharing a laugh with him, and his kindness and sweet attitude had warmed her soul just a bit.

As she pulled open the creaky driver's side door, she didn't notice the figure standing in the shadows. Suddenly, that figure stepped forward and a large, mean-eyed man grabbed her wrist roughly.

"I come to collect," he growled quietly, glancing around nervously to make sure they were alone and out of earshot of several other people walking along the artificially illuminated streets near the law offices.

Elizabeth shrunk herself against the side of the car, staring up into the eyes of the large man. Although stunned by his sudden appearance, she remembered who he was. He had worked with her father at one time. The man had quit over an argument about back wages he claimed her father owed him. Tinmouth Pritchard. That was his name.

"You hear me, Missy?" the man growled again, staring at Elizabeth in a very threatening, menacing kind of way, grasping her wrist even tighter, "I come to collect."

Elizabeth forced herself to calm down and deal with the unpleasant situation. "Mr. Pritchard, I believe? Is that correct?" Her voice was wavering, but she hoped he didn't notice.

Pritchard grinned and leered at her, "Well, well. You remember me. You remember old Tinmouth, do ya'? How touching."

Using her wits to try and find a way out of this predicament, Elizabeth pulled her wrist free with surprising strength and stood up straighter, moving away from the car slightly, "Yes, I remember you, Mr. Pritchard. You worked with my father. I'm sorry, but I really don't know what you want. My father has just passed away..."

"Good enough for him!" exploded Tinmouth, spitting

out the words vehemently, "He cheated me out of my money! The old swindler!"

Elizabeth felt a sharp, painful twinge in her heart to hear her father talked about in that manner, but did her best to let none of her feelings show. She continued, gaining a little strength, "I'm sorry Mr. Pritchard, perhaps if you could tell me what this is all about…"

Before she could finish her sentence, Tinmouth interrupted her, "It's about money that your father owed me. It was nearly fifteen thousand dollars, Missy. Money that I earned and that he cheated me out of. I want that money and I intend to have it. That old lying, dishonest coot must have been worth something when he died. I want my money now."

Elizabeth took a deep breath and tried to contain her frustration and rising rage, "My father not only had no money when he died Mr. Pritchard, but he left me with a huge pile of bills to pay! There is no money for you, Mr. Pritchard. I'm probably not even going to be able to keep our house. So, you're out of luck! I don't know what the issue was between my father and you, but it's over. He's dead."

Tinmouth Prichard glared at Elizabeth with narrowed, angry eyes, "This ain't over, Missy. Not by a long shot. Now it's you who owe me, and I fully intend to collect."

He turned and stalked off into the cold, frosty night, turning once to growl over his shoulder, "I'm gonna' collect in full! Count on it!" Then he was gone, lost in the shadows and in the light snow that had begun to fall.

Elizabeth leaned back weakly against the car. Her rage had suddenly vanished and in its place came the sensation of anguish and heartache. A racking sob burst out of her, as hot tears began to stream down her flushed cheeks.

Suddenly, she felt someone next to her and she stiffened up, expecting the worst: the return of the mean spirited Tinmouth Pritchard.

"Hey! What's wrong?" came a soft, tender voice.

Elizabeth turned to find Andy Morrison, who had stopped on his way toward his car, several parking spaces past hers. He walked over to the young paralegal, staring at her with great concern, "What's wrong, Elizabeth? What can I do to help?" His sweet, kind voice and his innocent, caring eyes were too much for Elizabeth. It had been so long since she had been treated compassionately and with thoughtfulness, that she simply couldn't help it. Elizabeth broke down completely, overcome by her sobs and tears, as her boss gently reached over and pulled her to him.

The snow continued to fall as Andy held the obviously upset and heartsick young woman. He glanced around and saw several other employees of the firm staring their way, generously wondering if he needed their help. He smiled and motioned to them that it was all right and that he would handle the situation, and they simply nodded silently and went along their way.

For a moment, Andy thought of Meg Monroe, the dinner party, the flowers and that awkward phone call that afternoon. Then, all that slowly vanished as he stared down at the young woman he held tenderly in his arms.

"Hey there, let's get you tidied up and head over to Mitchell's Café for a cup of coffee. How about that? Then you can tell me what brought all this on. Deal?" He smiled kindheartedly down at the red-eyed young woman who had finally stopped crying.

"I'll buy!" he grinned and winked at Elizabeth.

With a great deal of effort, Elizabeth smiled back through the mist in her eyes. Then, she allowed herself to reach out to this kind, gentle man, "Okay. I must look a sight. But a cup of coffee would taste really good right about now."

"Maybe even a slice of pie if you're lucky!" chuckled Andy.

Elizabeth stared curiously, but gratefully at the handsome young lawyer and whispered, "That's a deal."

Chapter 10

Horace finally had all the puppies quieted down, their full little bellies stretched greedily and safely tucked away into the doggy bed he had made next to their mother. He had mopped up three accidents, chased puppies around the office for a good forty-five minutes and worked tirelessly to make sure the puppies and their mom were fed and felt at home in their new surroundings. All the while Darlene had kept a close eye on Horace and his new charges while finishing up her paperwork for the night.

Finally, when she couldn't hear the puppies toenails clicking on the hardwood floor anymore and all the sounds of activity and eating had subsided, Darlene got up from her desk and quietly walked over and peered into the back room.

There were all five puppies, nuzzling up close to their mom, fast asleep, their swollen little bellies rising up and down softly in rhythm. The mother dog was lying quietly, and turned her head inquisitively toward Darlene when she poked her head around the corner. The large, trusting brown eyes on the shaggy dog were by far her most beautiful feature, at least at this point. She had obviously sacrificed herself to feed, nourish and protect her litter. Darlene thought she could see a hint of hope and a whole lot of determination in those liquid pools of brown.

Next to the temporary doggy bed was Horace Scofield. He had lain down with the puppies to keep them company and probably to try and keep them in the bed. Now he had fallen fast asleep as well. As Darlene stared down at the dogs and the deputy, the mother dog leaned over and gently licked Horace's peaceful face. Horace wrinkled his nose, but smiled slightly and kept on sleeping.

Darlene walked briskly over to one of the holding cells, picked up an old blanket from the cot and came back and laid it over the top of the sleeping deputy. She glanced at her watch. Horace had another hour to go on his shift. She might just let him spend it there with the pups. At least they were quiet and out of her hair.

Darlene turned and walked back toward the front office, turning only once to look back at the heart-warming little scene playing out on the back room floor. For just a moment, a twinkle appeared in Darlene's eye. Now that twinkle might have been filled with pleasure, or pride in a job well done, or simply contentment. Then again, it could have been a glint from the overhead light. Only one person would ever know for sure.

As Darlene walked back to her desk and prepared to clean up for the night, Wendy Morrison was sitting by the front window of her house, reading and waiting for her brother Andy to come home. He hadn't called to let her know he would be late. So she had placed a plate with his supper on it in a warm oven when he didn't show up on time for dinner.

Wendy stared out the window. The book on her lap held little interest to her. Her thoughts were racing. Andy had called her to tell her that things had not gone well with Meg Monroe. Wendy had tried to console her younger brother, but secretly, she had been very relieved that the relationship had not worked out. It had been so long since she and Andy had only had each other that she was uneasy and anxious about what a love interest in his life would mean for her. This was, after all, his house, even though he always said it was theirs. He had also placed a good deal of seed money into her business, Treasured Memories. Would he expect her to pay him back should he start a new life? And if he did, would she be able?

But now, she wouldn't have to worry about those things, at least for a while. Relief had flooded through her even as she tried to comfort her brother over his emotional loss. Even though it embarrassed her, she couldn't change how she felt. She was glad that she had Andy just to herself again. She knew she would have to eventually face the issue again, but she was just happy that it was gone for now. As she stared out into the night, her expression seemed to change from one of weariness and relief to an almost cunning and clever smirk. Just as fast as it had come, however, it was gone.

Lights flashed in the driveway, as a car pulled in. Getting up from her chair, Wendy hurried to the kitchen, eager to get her brother's dinner out of the oven for him. She smiled elatedly. She had made his favorite, sausage lasagna with extra cheese, a garden salad with lots of little tomatoes and cheese sprinkled on top along with fresh baked Italian bread from Travolati's Bakery.

"Hey, Sis, I'm home!" Andy's voice echoed through the large building as he called out to her from the mudroom at the back of the house.

Wendy opened the refrigerator and pulled out an opened bottle of red wine to go with the meal and poured a half a glass into a stemmed goblet by his plate. "In here, just setting out your dinner. How come you didn't call? Your phone die or something?"

Andy strode quickly through the living room and popped his head into the kitchen, "Sorry! I got busy and forgot. I apologize!"

He glanced down at the supper set for him and whistled in surprise, "Wow! Is that sausage lasagna? What's the occasion?" He took a long whiff, smiling broadly, "That sure smells good!"

"Come sit down! It's still warm and just right!" Wendy smiled happily and bustled around the kitchen making everything just so.

"Well, to tell you the truth, I'm stuffed, Sis!" Andy sheepishly declared, "I stopped at the café and had coffee and two pieces of Heloise's Pecan pie."

Wendy's smile vanished as she stopped fussing around with his dinner and stared at Andy, "Why on earth would you stop there when you know I was making dinner for you?"

Andy grimaced awkwardly, "Well, there was this girl, Elizabeth. She's our new paralegal. Remember I told you about her coming in to hear her father's last will and testament read? How he left her with all those bad debts?"

Wendy nodded slightly, vaguely remembered him telling her about the case. He told her everything. Then she glumly readjusted her thinking. He used to tell me everything anyway.

"Anyway, it turns out that she has this former employee of her fathers who is threatening her! Can you imagine that?" Andy reached over and grabbed the wine glass, drinking half the glass in one swallow.

"Anyway, long story short, I found her crying by her

car after he threatened her and I took her to the café to try and see if I could help." Andy eagerly grabbed a slice of Italian bread and slathered butter on it.

"Tomorrow I'll call this guy to work it all out, get a restraining order on him if need be. We talked for over an hour and a half then I drove behind her until she got home." Andy appeared utterly delighted with his heroic intervention and he was obviously in excellent spirits. Perhaps if he had not been thinking so much about his new friend, Elizabeth, he might have noticed the look of hurt and disappointment on his sister's face.

"Just put the dinner in the fridge and I'll take it with me for lunch tomorrow, okay, Sis?" Andy called out over his shoulder as he strode toward the staircase. He turned on the stairway, winked at Wendy and called out, "You're the best, Sis! I promise, I'll call if I get waylaid ever again. I do apologize! But I really need a shower and some sleep! Big day tomorrow and it's going to start early! Night! I love you!"

Andy animatedly blew a kiss to his sister and still grinning, he bounded up the stairs.

Wendy stood for a moment, simply staring after him. Then, slowly, with a heavy heart, she packaged up the dinner into neat little plastic tubs, ready for her brother to take with him early the next morning. She sat herself back down in her favorite chair by the window, bringing the half drunk wine glass with her. As she finished her brother's wine, she stared out the window, and despondently wondered what in Heaven's name life was about to bring her.

***

Marcus Templeton nudged Theo Dunham hard in the ribs. Theo's eyes flew open as he exhaled with a slight gasp. He picked his head up off the throw pillow on the divan and rubbed his eyes, complaining, "What did you do that for…"

Marcus' hand covered Theo's mouth quickly and firmly as Theo opened his eyes up enough to see through the shadows of the Catholic rectory. Marcus pointed toward a figure that seemed to be shuffling quietly out from Father O'Flaherty's bedroom.

Now fully awake, Theo sat up and along with Marcus, watched the good father walk straight toward the front door of the rectory. Theo and Marcus were 'on duty'. This was the first night that they would take turns watching over their old, suddenly sleepwalking prone friend. It had been Marcus' shift to be awake, and Theo's turn to catch some sleep in the rectory's sitting room.

Marcus and Theo glanced at each other and smiled. The first test for their sleepwalking friend was just ahead of him. After the priest had gone to bed, Marcus and Theo had double locked the front door to the rectory. They had set the deadbolt, as Father O'Flaherty did every night, but they had also locked the other lock on the door that required a key. Theo immediately felt his bathrobe pocket. There was the key, right where he had placed it.

Theo and Marcus were seriously hoping that this would keep their old friend locked in and hopefully he would then return to bed. If this worked, it would at least keep the sleepwalking pastor confined to his small cottage.

When the sleepwalking priest reached the door, he reached out and quickly unlocked the deadbolt and reached for the handle. Theo and Marcus stood up and watched with great interest to see what would happen next.

Predictable, the good father reached for the old door handle and turned it. Nothing happened. Theo and Marcus grinned at each other and then glanced back at the sleepwalking priest.

Almost without hesitation, the priest turned and walked to the rector's old desk on the other side of the room. Opening the second drawer, Father O'Flaherty reached in and quickly pulled out a key. Marcus and Theo's grins faded. Walking back to the door, Father O'Flaherty expertly fit the key in its keyhole and turned it firmly. Then the sleepwalking pastor opened the door and stepped out into the frigid February night.

Quickly slipping their feet into their old winter galoshes, the two stymied clergymen followed their sleepwalking friend. They watched as the priest made his way to the back door of the Catholic Church and slipped quietly inside. Once they had followed Flynn O'Flaherty into the darkened church, they quickly moved closer to be able to see where he was headed in the shadows.

As they had assumed, the priest was moving unhurriedly back to the kitchen area of the church. Once there he headed toward the refrigerator. Again, Theo and Marcus glanced at each other, their grins not quite so large as before, but they still appeared somewhat confident. The two pastors had previously taken all of the sacramental wine out of the refrigerator and replaced it with several stuffed animals.

There was a somewhat battered bunny that Theo Dunham kept in his rectory for children who needed comforting. The bunny had been held and cuddled by literally hundreds of little ones in need. There was also a soft, fluffy hippopotamus that Marcus Templeton had used for the same purpose in the Methodist rectory.

The third stuffed animal was a cute little mouse that some child had left on a pew in the Congregationalist Church and had eventually found its way back to the rectory after lying in the 'Lost and Found' box for several weeks.

Father O'Flaherty opened the fridge and reached inside. Theo and Marcus watched eagerly. Would Father O'Flaherty realize there were no wine bottles and instinctively go back to the rectory empty handed? Would that end the sleepwalking journeys of their old friend? Both Marcus and Theo were beginning to feel almost like Sherlock Holmes and Watson, out to solve a great mystery.

Father O'Flaherty's hand came out of the fridge. In his grasp was the lop-eared bunny. Securing his prize under his arm and shutting the door to the fridge, Father O'Flaherty turned and confidently began his trip back home.

Marcus and Theo followed their old friend back to his house and watched as he shuffled back into his bedroom. The priest stopped at the storage closet door momentarily, but then turned and slipped back under the covers, bringing the soft, cuddly bunny with him.

Marcus and Theo stared down at their old friend, asleep and snoring slightly, smiling and squeezing the old bunny tightly. Then they turned and stared at each other, realizing and admitting to themselves that the sleepwalking priest had outwitted them at every turn.

With a sigh, the two clergymen found places on the old divan and the overstuffed chair and wearily tried to get at least a little sleep. The dawn would come early enough, and with it, they would have to get even more serious about helping their old colleague come up with a solution to his sleepwalking.

From the priest's bedroom came the somewhat irritating sound of content, happy and robust snores.

***

The next morning, Cash slipped silently in through the back door of the sheriff's office just as the cold February sun peeked over the snow covered Green Mountains. He was surprised to see Darlene standing in the corner of the back room, hovering over the doggy bed. She was in the act of placing a fresh bowl of milk on the floor beside it. In her arms, she was cradling one of the little pups, and talking softly and gently to it.

"There, that's better, isn't it? I don't know where that good for nothin' Horace is, but you're hungry now, aren't you Sweetie?" Darlene placed the puppy by the side of the bowl of milk and he started lapping the milk greedily. Noticing that their brother was getting a head start on the first meal of the day, the other pups quickly stretched and energetically tumbled down out of the bed to join him.

Cash stood still for a moment, just watching, with a smile and a twinkle in his eye. He watched Darlene reach out and tenderly scratch the mother dog behind the ear. That started the dog's tail thumping a regular rhythm on the blanket in the temporary dog bed.

"Don't you be worryin' about your babies, little Missy," Darlene crooned softly, gazing kindheartedly at the scruffy canine. "They're just fine. We can help you with them now. You gotta' eat, rest and get better, you hear me? My Lord! You're as skinny as my great Aunt Pamela!"

At that moment, the front door of the sheriff's office swung open with a bang and Horace Scofield hustled in, a large bag in each hand. Darlene glanced up, and then unhurriedly walked toward Horace, her eyes raised and a small frown on her face.

"It's about time you got here, Horace Scofield! Those babies were cryin' for some milk! And I had to clean up their business already this morning!" Darlene almost growled with aloofness, "You promised me that you'd take care of those mangy critters! You'd better get to it!"

With that Darlene stomped over to her desk, sat down ramrod straight and quickly began to get out her reports and orders for the day. As she glanced up, she spied Cash standing by the back door. Her eyes narrowed and in a low voice, she inquired, "How long you been standing there, Sheriff?"

"Oh, I just got here, Darlene." Cash promptly lied with a smile. "Why?" He met the accusatory glance of the secretary/dispatcher with an innocent stare as she raised an eyebrow and stared at him inquisitively.

Darlene held his gaze for a moment, then glanced down at her report, responding noncommittally, "No reason. Just wondering. Isn't that allowed?"

Yamato stepped inside out of the brisk February sunrise and glanced around the office. Cash was stomping off his boots by the back door, Horace was hastily pulling food, doggie toys and more blankets out of bags while he fussed over the dogs and Darlene was typing away with particular gusto. None of them even looked up at her as she entered.

"Well good morning to all of you, too!" chuckled Yamato as she hung up her coat and hat.

"Good morning, Yamato," called out Cash as he headed for the coffeemaker, a wry grin plastered across his face.

"Mornin', Ericka," came Horace's anxious voice as he was reaching for the mop to clean up a little more 'doggy business' before Darlene had a chance to smell it or see it.

"Good morning, deputy," responded Darlene, as prim and proper as ever, glancing at Yamato and then turning her gaze back to the report she was typing. "It looks like we might have a thaw. Farmer's Almanac forecasted it. They're hardly ever wrong you know."

As Yamato joined Cash at the back counter, she glanced over at her boss. Her expression was one of thoughtful scrutiny and a vague sense that more was going on than met the eye. Grabbing two mugs off the shelf she whispered inquisitively, "Okay, give. What did I miss?"

Cash chuckled under his breath and then glanced over to where Darlene was typing a mile a minute. He glanced back at Yamato and winked, whispering back, "Nothing of consequence, partner."

As Cash took his first sip of steaming hot coffee and glanced back toward Darlene, he thought he saw, although he had no way of being sure, a slight smile cross her thin lips.

Chapter 11

Over in Brown Bear Junction, Andy Morrison was already in his law office hard at work trying to find a way to help Elizabeth Fallon. He had already spoken to his ace private investigator, C.R. Shanks, and asked the P.I. to find out everything he could about Tinmouth Pritchard. At the moment, Andy was looking into Benjamin Fallon's business records, debts and hidden assets, if there were any.

The more Andy delved into Benjamin Fallon's life and business, the more he realized that Elizabeth was in a very tight financial situation. Her father had left her a wide variety of bad debts and literally no money. The only asset he had left her was his rather dilapidated woodworking shop and tools. The one good thing that Andy had uncovered was that Benjamin Fallon was a wonderful woodworker and had a long list of friends and business associates who agreed that he would give the shirt off his back to help anyone, whether he knew them or not. Unfortunately, it appeared Ben Fallon had been far too kind and generous to everyone but his own daughter.

Andy stared out his office window at the rising sun and his thoughts took over for a few moments. As he and Elizabeth had sat and talked last night, they had seemed to connect. They had talked easily with each other and he had felt very comfortable being around her. They were quickly becoming friends at the very least. Good friends in fact in a very short span of time. He found that he really liked the unassuming, humble young woman. He also realized that he truly wanted to help her solve her financial and personal problems.

That brought him back to Tinmouth Pritchard. Someone would have to have a word with the old reprobate. Andy smiled. He decided that he and C.R. Shanks would do that together. There was something to be said for safety in numbers. And that would get done today, to make sure that Elizabeth would be receiving no more intimidating visits from Putnam.

Andy picked up the phone and made a quick call. On the third ring it was picked up, "Good morning! Did I wake you?"

Elizabeth Fallon laughed nervously, "Good morning! No, of course you didn't wake me. I'm walking out the door to go to work. I'm a poor working girl, remember?" Her voice sounded absolutely thrilled that Andy had called, yet still had a shy and self-conscious component to it.

"I brought in bear claws and bagels for the office staff! So get here before they get picked over! A warning, though! We have a hoard of ravenous and starving interns, secretaries and law partners! See you soon!" Andy hung up the phone. He felt good. He felt more than good. He felt wonderful!

As he munched on a warm bear claw and began searching out more and more information about Tinmouth Pritchard, he found himself actually humming! Humming! Amazing! He would have to call and tell Wendy all about it!

***

THE FALLS: Cupid's Arrow

Tinmouth Pritchard stirred the blackened old stew pot that hung over the crackling wood fire in the ramshackle fireplace. He leaned down and tasted the contents of the pot using the old wooden spoon he had stirring it with. Not bad for three-day-old venison stew, he thought. Not bad at all.

Tinmouth Pritchard was temporarily residing in a deserted hunting cabin on the outskirts of The Falls. The owner, an accountant from New York City, had long since abandoned the rundown hunting lodge. The accountant had brought some of his wealthier clients up on hunting trips two or three times a year, but he had retired a decade ago. Since then, the accountant and the rest of his family had apparently forgotten about the place. Because the cabin was standing vacant and Tinmouth needed a place to live, Tinmouth had been occupying the cabin for several years and would continue to do so until either the local sheriff evicted him or the owner showed up and kicked him out.

Tinmouth stared out the broken pane of glass and decided to throw another piece of wood on the fire. The old rundown cabin had lots of cracks, chinks and holes where the freezing winter winds managed to whistle through and create icy drafts. Luckily, the cabin was in the heart of the deep woods. There was plenty of available firewood nearby. Tinmouth didn't even have to cut down any trees. All he had to do was just gather up what was already on the ground and cut it up to fit the old stone fireplace.

Tinmouth shuffled back to the wobbly table and picked up his dented coffee mug. The coffee wasn't great, since he had to reuse the grounds at least twice given his meager financial situation, but at least it was hot. As he swallowed several long draughts of bitter black coffee, he thought about last night.

He smiled to himself. He had somewhat enjoyed terrorizing the girl, Benjamin Fallon's kid. It was obvious to see that the girl was scared of him. But that was good. She needed to be scared of him in order for his plan to work. Tinmouth was owed money by the Fallons and he was going to collect, one way or another. In Tinmouth's mind, Benjamin Fallon had been the start of all Tinmouth's problems back many years ago. Tinmouth's thoughts flew back twenty years and he scowled with anger.

Two decades ago, he had started working with Ben Fallon. Fallon had owned a small woodworking shop located in the large shed in back of his home. Ben was an excellent woodworker and townspeople flocked to him to have him build them new furniture as well as refinish their old chairs, tables, beds and bureaus. Tinmouth was real handy with tools as well. He had worked as a successful carpenter and a handy man for a number of years before coming to see Benjamin Fallon about a job.

Ben had so much work he couldn't do it all, so he had advertised for a helper, and Tinmouth had been the best man for the job. Tinmouth and Ben got along famously and Tinmouth loved building and refurbishing furniture. It was a natural fit. There was one small problem, however. Benjamin Fallon was a soft touch. His more astute customers could easily persuade Benjamin to give them a healthy discount.

If there was one thing New England Yankees liked to do, it was haggle over prices. Unfortunately, Ben Fallon was the world's worst haggler. His customers found a world of reasons why Ben should cut them a break on his price. Maybe it was because their daughter needed braces, or their wife was sick and they had no insurance. It might be because their crops hadn't done well for three straight years. Whatever the sob story, Benjamin, kind and good-hearted person that he was, would be a good Samaritan and end up charging the customer less. Sometimes a good deal less than the job was worth.

Christian charity was one thing, thought Tinmouth petulantly, but giving away your labor was quite another. Due to his soft heart, Benjamin had less and less money coming in. Of course that meant that Tinmouth was getting less and less in his paycheck as well. Tinmouth got a little less every week for the same amount of work. This became an issue for both men and it dragged on for years.

As Tinmouth figured it, after five years of hanging on, hoping things would get better, Benjamin owed him approximately fifteen thousand dollars. When Tinmouth finally went to his boss and demanded to be paid what he felt his work was worth during that five-year period, Benjamin apologized, but he admitted to Tinmouth that he had no money to pay him. Benjamin honestly tried to get Tinmouth to stay on, promising a bigger paycheck and part ownership in the business, but Tinmouth had already had enough. He stalked away, spouting a number of foul and angry words as he went.

After that, things had just gone downhill for Tinmouth. Without a steady job he couldn't make his mortgage payments and he lost his small but neat little cottage in Brown Bear Junction. After losing his house, he became surly and disagreeable to be around. Because he was so cantankerous, his daughters saw him less and less, eventually disowning him completely. Tinmouth moved from one cheap apartment to another, while his rage and resentment slowly built a white-hot fire within him. He blamed everything on Benjamin Fallon.

The one thing that Tinmouth still had left in his life was hunting. He was an expert marksman with either a bow or rifle. His daddy had taught him to hunt starting when he was five and he had hunted all his life. As might be expected, a man who inhabited other people's cabins illegally, and had very little property of his own, paid little or no attention to state hunting regulations. He hunted what he wanted when he wanted. At that very moment, there were two skinned and gutted deer carcasses and several wild turkeys hanging up in the little shed back of the cabin. Winter made a wonderful freezer.

Tinmouth hunted with a rifle during regulation hunting seasons and with a bow the rest of the year. He found a silent but deadly arrow to be just the ticket to keep from getting picked up by the local fish and game wardens. There were several rifles and three compound bows hanging on the wall of the hunting cabin. He had few possessions, but his weapons were his pride and joy.

Tinmouth grunted and shuffled over to the fire. He scooped out a bowlful of stew, returning to the rickety table to gobble down his breakfast. As he wolfed the venison stew down, he glanced at the scrap of paper on the table. It was the Fallon's old address. Not that he had forgotten where the place was. No, he just kinda' liked staring at it, knowing that soon, he was going to take back what was his. Take back what had been owed him all these years.

He smacked his lips together and hungrily devoured the potatoes, beans and meat in a thick venison sauce.

No siree, he thought eagerly. It wouldn't be long before his life started to change.

***

Tinker LaGrange stared at the mound of paperwork heaped on his desk and sighed. Two months ago when Mayor Putnam Pierpont had appointed Tinker the Chief of Police for Brown Bear Junction, he had assumed that the job would be all swashbuckling action, thrilling stakeouts and following mysterious clues to close exciting cases. By now, the new police chief had a much more realistic view of what the job entailed. He spent most of his time listening to the complaining citizens of The Junction, following up on those complaints and immersing himself in hour after hour of tedious paperwork. Tinker's idealistic vision of the office had long since vanished into the winter landscape, along with his enthusiasm and eagerness for the job.

"Chief LaGrange," called out the loud and often sharp-edged voice of his part-time secretary and fulltime police officer, Myna Lynn Jones, "it's Rebecca Meyers again! Claims that the raccoons are makin' a mess out back of Becca's Bar and Grill again. Wants to know when you're gonna' take care of the problem."

Myrna Lynn hesitated a moment, then with a bit more exasperation, she continued, "What do you want me to tell her? This is her third call this week. Rebecca's stubborn. She's not gonna' let go of it, Tinker."

Tinker got up from his desk, actually relieved to be doing something, even if it was dealing with hungry raccoons. He threw the pen down next to the report he had been editing and pulled his heavy jacket off the back of his chair. "Tell her I'm on my way, Myrna Lynn. Thanks."

As Tinker clomped down the icy steps of the

combined town hall, county courthouse and police station, he glanced around the town square of Brown Bear Junction. There were already several dozen people walking back and forth, on their way to work, shopping or just enjoying the early moments of the day. Tinker made sure to smile and wave to all of them.

Matthew Ferdinand LaGrange had been known as Tinker ever since he had been a kid. His dad had told the rest of the family that his son was always 'tinkering' with something, and the name had stuck. He was now twenty-nine years old and before becoming the police chief, he had been a snow plow driver, worked in Beryl and Jenkins' Lumber yard and had worked in the town hall as the reliable and conscientious bailiff for the county court. He had just happened to be around the right place at the right time when the old police chief retired and headed down to Florida. Mayor Pierpont saw an opportunity and had immediately asked the energetic young bailiff in the courthouse how he felt about being the new police chief.

When the old chief had left, there were three police officers already on the Brown Bear Junction Police force. Those three had been squabbling for months before the police chief actually retired over who was going to be promoted to be the next police chief. Sergeant Gordy Makum was old, grizzled, had a sharp tongue and had offended at least half the citizens of Brown bear Junction at one point or another. Jeremiah Adkins and Fritz Zimmerman were both good average officers, but, truth be told, neither of them had much gumption or horse sense.

Mayor Pierpont had worked several times with the young county court bailiff and knew that Tinker not only had common sense and a sharp mind, but that the young man had higher goals and ambitions for his life.

Although the three officers had bristled angrily when they first heard of Tinker's appointment, over the past few months they had come to appreciate the new chief for the abundance of varied skills that he brought to the job.

Turning into the back alley behind Becca's Bar and grill, Tinker began to carefully pick through the rubbish and garbage cans, checking for signs that raccoons had indeed been there foraging.

As the Chief of Police moved quietly around the back alley, he heard something coming toward him on the other side of the fence. Tinker simply edged his way to the back wall and then stood stock still, waiting for what might appear.

After a few moments of snuffling and movement outside the alley, Tinker watched as a yellow Labrador and a black Labrador both with tags on their collars padded quietly through the open gate headed toward the garbage cans. Tinker stood motionless as he watched the two labs nudge over the garbage cans, spilling their contents all over the frozen ground. Quickly moving to the open door the dogs had entered through, Tinker closed and latched the door. The two dogs glanced up at Tinker, but gave him little notice, as they continued to forage through the spilled garbage from the restaurant.

Walking over to the back of the bar and grill, Tinker pounded heavily several times on the service door. A few moments later, Rebecca Meyers swung open the door, a disgruntled frown gracing her sixty-year-old face.

As soon as Rebecca spied Tinker, her frown lifted and turned to a curious stare, "Hello Chief! It's about time you got here..."

About that time, Rebecca caught sight of the two labs snuffling through the spilled garbage and a look of true surprise flashed across her wrinkled features, "Bert and Ernie! How did they get in here? Did you let them in Chief?"

"Apparently, someone leaves the gate door open, Miss Rebecca," Tinker smiled with secret delight while trying to maintain a professional demeanor. "And it seems that the stealthy raccoon raiders turned out to be two foraging dogs. And they're your own dogs to boot, Miss Rebecca."

With a tip of his hat, Tinker started to walk away, then turned and added, "If I were you, Miss Rebecca, I'd make sure of two things. First, have the cook and dishwashers make sure they securely shut and bolt the door to the fence after they bring out the garbage. Second, since we do have a leash law here in Brown Bear Junction, I'd make sure my dogs were either in their own yard behind that nice, new white picket fence you put up two years ago, or on a leash. Otherwise, unfortunately, my officers and I just might have to give you a ticket and call Lance Yamhill's animal control truck to pick them up. Today, it'll just be a warning, because you're such a fine upstanding citizen. Hope you have a nice day, Miss Rebecca!"

Opening the door to the alleyway and glancing back at Rebecca, Tinker saw with satisfaction that her face was now as beet red as could be, and she was about ready to grab onto the offending canines and haul them off home. He imagined the trip would not be all that pleasant for the two garbage hounds.

As he ambled through the snow and ice back toward the police station, Tinker began to smile. He even began to whistle. It was going to be a wonderful day after all.

Chapter 12

Doc Stone walked through the front door of Treasured Memories, his smile as bright as the day was chilly. He glanced at both Wendy and Mandy and doffed his winter hat, "Morning ladies! And a beautiful morning it is!"

Wendy smiled and stood up, her feather duster in her hand, turning toward Doc, "Good morning yourself, Doc! It's been over a month since we've seen you come looking for little treasures for that beautiful wife of yours! Good to see you back!"

Mandy walked around from in back of the counter and gave Doc a big hug, "Doc's been coming here for years. At first he came here getting little presents for his mother and aunts. Now, he's turned into a connoisseur of antique art and jewelry to please his sweet Missus!"

Doc chuckled and glanced around the shop with a practiced eye, "Well, picking up the occasional little knick-knacks and jewelry boxes for mom and her sisters was a bit less expensive than buying my sweet wife beautiful things, that's for sure!"

Mandy laughed, her eyebrows raised naughtily, "Well, Doc, that's the price of having a gorgeous wife who likes beautiful things! Gotta' keep her happy!"

Doc's eyes stopped on the collection of porcelain dolls and he strode over to get a closer look, "These are beautiful, Wendy, Mandy. They are really quite exquisite. How much?" His fingers carefully touched the porcelain and silk dresses, admiring the workmanship and costly materials. Then his eyes settled on a particularly beautiful doll and he smiled. The doll was absolutely stunning. Long red hair, emerald green eyes and an hourglass figure, just like Jordan.

Wendy stepped closer and gazed closely at the handsome doctor. In his eyes, she could easily spot the immense love and caring that he held for Jordan. For a moment, she felt a touch of sadness and regret. She was only thirty-six, but somehow at times she felt sixty, as if the world had passed her by while she had been taking good care of her younger brother. She had spent her last seventeen years with one goal in mind: raise Andy, feed him, cloth him, and give him whatever he needed to be successful in life. Now, what did she have to show for it? Well, it certainly wasn't a wonderful husband like Malcolm Stone.

Shaking her head to clear it, Wendy smiled at Doc, "Now Doc, we've always had a good time haggling over items, but these dolls, well, they are unique. There are only a few of this quality still around. The cost will be dear, but then you do understand that, don't you?"

"Ah, but my dear Wendy," Doc winked and tilted his head to the side, his eyes staring directly into Wendy's, "that's the fun part, isn't it? Deciding just what that price might be?"

Mandy, standing off to the side, grinned as she settled down to watch. There was nothing she liked any better than a spirited exchange between two experienced hands at negotiating prices.

Twenty minutes later, Doc walked eagerly and contentedly out of Treasured Memories, an exquisite wooden box containing the beautiful redheaded porcelain doll under his arm and a large smile on his face.

Mandy continued cleaning the jewelry shelf as she glanced over at Wendy standing behind the cash register, a crooked smile on her weathered face, "I'd say that was a win-win, boss! You got a good price and he got a beautiful treasure."

Wendy smiled back with a twinkle in her eye, "Most enjoyment I've had in awhile. Doc is fun to haggle with! It brings out the best in him and in us!"

Mandy nodded, "On that I would agree. And it's the first time I've really seen you smile in several days, boss."

Mandy glanced over at Wendy, correctly assessing her boss' mood, and spoke quietly, "I'm here you know, if you want to talk about it. Whatever it is."

Wendy glanced up quickly, caught unaware. Her face was whiter than usual, and although her eyes looked a bit puffy and red, like she'd been secretly crying, her eyes narrowed and turned irate and on edge for a moment. Then, as quickly as it came, Wendy covered up her raw feelings with a pleasant smile and a shrug, "Thanks, Mandy. I appreciate the offer. But it's just some stuff I've got to wade through. You know, sometimes life sucks."

Mandy glanced back at her boss thoughtfully, peering through the jewelry display case as she continued to clean, "I know. Life isn't fair and it comes with no darned instruction manual. But, it just seems like whatever it is that's bothering you is tougher than normal. I just thought maybe it would help to talk about it."

For a moment, Wendy considered telling Mandy all

about her issues with Andy, his new girl friend, and her worries about where her life was headed. Then she coughed and responded, "I'm okay. Just 'off my feed' as my granddaddy would say."

A smile flashed across Wendy's face, "You know, we got a really good price for the porcelain doll, thanks to our friend Doc. What do you say we close the shop for a few minutes and run over to the bakery! I've been smelling their apple turnovers for the last hour! How does a hot apple turnover and a cup of Al's cappuccino sound?"

Within two minutes, the sign on the front door had been changed from OPEN to CLOSED and the two women were laughing and hurrying across the snow and ice-covered street to Al's Bakery.

***

Anne Marie Thompson and Olivia Savaadra peered intently into the glass display case at Jeb and Zeke's super video game store. Their friend Jennifer Wilson kept an anxious watch out the front window for the middle school bus. The bus stopped for several students on the corner right outside the video store and it was due within the next five minutes.

"I don't see it!" Anne Marie's voice was two octaves higher than her regular tone and her nimble fingers tapped the glass display irritably.

"I don't either," Olivia chimed in as she moved to the next large display case, her eyes scanning the titles and video games hurriedly. "We're never going to find it before old Mr. Peavey gets here!"

Jeb and Zeke, opening several boxes of newly arrived video games glanced at each other and grinned. Zeke picked a brand new game out of one of the boxes and sauntered over to where the two girls were furiously checking out the games on display.

"Would you by any chance be looking for this?" Zeke asked, holding the new game up so the two girls could see it properly. Zeke, like Jeb, knew their clientele well and had a pretty good idea what they might be looking for.

"Look! Look! Cheerleaders V! In 3D!" screamed out Olivia, startling three other customers in the shop.

"Oh, thank you Mr. Peters! That's exactly what we were looking for!" exclaimed Anne Marie, clapping her hands and jumping up and down. "We'll be the first girls in middle school to get to play it! Awesome!"

As Olivia paid for the game, Jennifer called out urgently, "Mr. Peavey's comin' down the street! We've got to go! I don't want any more detentions for being late! My dad will ground me for the rest of my life!" With that, Jennifer ran to the door and swung it open wide, looking back at her best friends anxiously.

Zeke handed the game to Olivia with a grin, winked and called out, "You girls better get on that bus! We don't want to get in trouble from keeping you from a proper education! Have a great day!"

"Run, girls! And enjoy the game! Let us know how you like it!" called out Jeb from back of the counter. Then he grinned and watched the three girls high stepping it energetically through the snow and ice until they boarded the old yellow bus along with eight other middle school kids.

As the bus closed its creaky door, turned off its caution lights and started grumbling and groaning down the street in the freezing early morning temperatures, Zeke turned to Jeb and chuckled.

"Sure glad we don't still go to school! I never did like all that sittin' around in classes and bein' quiet and all those rules!" Zeke shook his head as he got back to sorting out the games they had gotten in.

Jeb glanced up at his old friend, with a mischievous twinkle in his eye, "Do you remember the time we put the principal's desk up on the flat roof of the school?"

Zeke stared back at Jeb, shook his head and laughed, "Haven't thought of that stunt in quite a while. Took us most of the night as I remember. Good thing the old high school didn't have a security system!"

"Yeah, I twisted my ankle and you broke two fingers, but we got that old monstrosity up there! It took the fire department and their ladder truck four hours to get it down," Jeb mused, as he applied sales tags to the bottom of the video game cases.

"We wouldn't have been caught if old Stanley Munger, the night custodian, hadn't seen your daddy's old green truck sittin' out in back that night," Zeke chuckled, shaking his head.

"Yeah, well, three months of detention and a hundred hours of pickin' up and cleanin' bathrooms was still worth it!" Jeb replied firmly, his jaw set from past inflexibility on the issue. "Old Principal McKenzie was a mean spirited, cantankerous old fart!"

"Now, Jeb. You shouldn't speak ill of the dead. 'Member our daddy's taught us that?" Zeke replied with a straight face, then winked and added, "Even if he was!"

As the two old friends chuckled and continued to check off video games on the invoice and add price stickers, the front door to the video game store opened and closed, letting in some frigid February wind.

Standing before them was a six foot eight inch man who weighed in the rough vicinity of two hundred and seventy pounds. He was dressed in a heavy green parka, a green wool hunting hat and work boots. His intense blue eyes were focused directly on the two old friends. To say that the tall man had Zeke and Jeb's undivided attention would be an understatement. His size alone demanded attention in no uncertain terms.

Jeb and Zeke had seen the man around from time to time, and knew who he was, but had never been formally introduced. Jeb reached out his hand over the counter somewhat hesitatingly and stared up into the cool blue eyes of the big man.

"Mr. Shanks, I presume?" Jeb declared, a bit louder than needed. "Good to make your acquaintance, sir."

C.R. Shanks glanced down at the two old men in front of him and smiled. He nodded to both men, shook their hands and responded, almost in a low, deep whisper, "Good morning, gentlemen. I am indeed C.R. Shanks. Pleasure to make your acquaintance Jeb," he nodded at Jebediah, "and Zeke," he turned and nodded as well toward Ezekiel.

The big man glanced around the shop at the other customers who seemed to be taking no notice of their conversation and then glanced back at the two shop owners. "I would truly appreciate your help with something, gentlemen."

Jeb and Zeke glanced at each other with surprise. What on earth could they do to help this massive young man? Turning their attention back to the man, they could see he was holding up a small picture, obviously pulled off a printer.

"This man, Tinmouth Pritchard, is a person of interest in a case I'm working on. I'm a private investigator." C.R. showed them his P.I. badge and credentials, then held the picture back up for them to get another glimpse of, "I'm led to believe that the two of you know Mr. Pritchard and might know where he lives."

Jeb and Zeke glanced at each other again. If there was one thing they were not, it was stool pigeons. Over their seventy odd years, they had done a number of things that hovered around and were even at times outside the lines of the law. They knew many friends and colleagues who had stepped outside the law as well. But they had never informed on anyone, and weren't about to at this late date.

Zeke stared up into the vivid blue eyes of C.R. Shanks, his smile gone, "Mr. Shanks, we do know old Tinmouth. But to be very honest, we have a real hard time informing on anyone, let alone someone we have known for over fifty years."

"That's just not the way we treat folks, sir, and we hope they will do the same for us. We hope you understand," added Jeb, a slight frown creasing his brow. Unconsciously, Jeb had balled up his fists and was standing very rigidly as he stared up at the big man.

C.R. nodded in understanding, then continued in his soft, low voice, "I do understand and I can appreciate your loyalty. I wouldn't be asking if it weren't really important that I find the man."

The private investigator eyed the two old men, as if deciding how much to tell them, then he leaned over the counter, and with a great deal of sincerity whispered, "This man assaulted a young woman outside her work in Brown bear Junction. Her name is Elizabeth Fallon, daughter of the late Benjamin Fallon. We believe Mr. Pritchard has a vendetta to settle with her. He threatened her, gentlemen."

Jeb and Zeke look startled for a moment, then Jeb responded, "Ben Fallon's daughter? Little Elizabeth?"

Zeke interjected, "Ben Fallon was our good friend when we worked in the lumber business. We supplied him with a lot of quality hardwood to use in his woodworking shop."

Jeb continued, his face a bit whiter, "We went to his funeral just a few days ago. Told Elizabeth how sorry we were. She seemed devastated by his death."

Both Jeb and Zeke took a moment, glancing at each other. They let their thoughts run back to their relationships with Ben Fallon and his daughter. Then both old friends nodded to each other and they gazed up at the big man who had been waiting patiently.

"We can't abide with any man manhandling a woman. It's just not right," Jeb muttered, low and with a hint of anger.

"We had no idea Tinmouth had gotten to be like that," Zeke explained, shaking his head slowly, "and as much as we hate giving out information on people we know..."

Zeke cut in, "We will in this case. We'll do it to help out an old friend's daughter. Poor girl, she doesn't need that kind of problem right after her dad up and dies."

Jeb declared, "Tinmouth has been living in a vacated hunting cabin up in the woods about a mile and a half from here. Least that's the last place we know of, Mr. Shanks. We can draw you a simple map that'll get you there."

A few minutes later, the tall private investigator tipped his hat in appreciation and strode purposefully out of the video store. Both Jeb and Zeke watched him go. Zeke whistled out one long, low note and whispered, "I don't think I'd want to be in Tinmouth Pritchard's shoes."

Jeb nodded his agreement, wondering what would

come of the information they had just given.

***

Miles Perry stood in front of the counter in the sheriff's office, wool hunting hat in hand, the wet snow dripping off his large work boots onto the hardwood floor. He stared down at Darlene and smiled, "'Morning Miss Darlene. I come for my dog."

Darlene peered over her half glasses at the farmer and her brows furrowed, "Your dog, Miles Perry? Really? Why was your dog holed up in back of the Turnbull Mystik's packing plant? Why wasn't she home having her pups on your farm? How do you explain that?"

From the back room, a low, rumbling growl began at the sound of Miles Perry's voice. Darlene turned her head in the direction of the growl and then turned back to stare at Miles, her eyes deeply suspicious, "Sounds like that poor old dog doesn't want anything to do with you, Miles. Can you explain that?"

Miles' face flushed for a moment, then his smile vanished for a moment and his eyes turned mean, "Now see here Miss Darlene, that dog's mine. She used to be a stray, no doubt turned out by some unfeelin' family. I was kind enough to let her stay in my barn and she was there the last three years. Then along about December she vanished. I bin lookin' for her. When I heard about the dog what the sheriff brung in, I knew it was her. I come to claim what's mine."

Just as quickly as it had come the meanness left his eyes and the smile returned. He continued in a softer, kinder tone, "I figure that old dog has finally earned her food and keep. Those puppies will fetch a handsome price. Like I said I come to claim what's mine."

Darlene stared at the farmer, as her thoughts raced

around her head. She had never cared much for Miles Perry. Right now, she cared even less. After a momentary hesitation she stood and stared Miles right in the eye. "The vet's comin' to look over the mother and puppies. He's gonna' give them their shots and check to see if they're healthy. They're staying right here until after that, then we'll see. You understand, Miles Perry?"

Miles' face reddened again and he was about to respond when Horace Scofield strode determinedly over to the front desk, a dark frown on his own usually happy face, as he stared balefully at the farmer, "I think you heard Miss Darlene, Mr. Perry. That's the way it is. Now, is there anything else, or can I show you out?"

Miles Perry scowled unhappily and then glanced at both Darlene and Horace, "I know my own way out, thank you, Deputy!"

As he swung opened the door, he turned back and added with finality, "I intend to have my dog and her litter. I'll be back after the vet's been here. You can count on it."

With a loud thud, the door closed behind him, and Darlene and Horace watched as the peeved farmer strode down the steps and climbed quickly into his old truck.

Darlene turned and stared at Horace, secretly proud of how the deputy had supported her and stood up to Miles Perry. But instead of smiling and thanking him, she did what she always did, "Best get a move on and take care of those troublesome pups, Deputy Scofield! I'd better not see or smell anything that resembles puppy doo in there!"

Horace, knowing Darlene only too well, grinned and nodded, heading back toward the back room, "Yes,

Ma'am, Miss Darlene, I'll be doin' just that!"

As Darlene settled back down in her chair, eyes on the computer screen, she hoped against hope that there was a way that old Miles Perry would be thwarted in his claim to the poor, bedraggled mother dog and her five cute pups. Darlene frowned. The man just didn't deserve them. That's all there was to it.

Chapter 13

Father O'Flaherty looked across the table in their booth at Tina's Diner at Marcus Templeton and Theo Dunham. He hungrily shoveled another forkful of eggs over easy in his mouth while he glanced back and forth between his two oldest friends, "You say I went and got the key out of the desk in the study? Humph! That's pretty smart if I do say so myself!"

Both ministers nodded. They each had a headache and they were somewhat sleep deprived from their eventful night watching over the village priest. Theo yawned and took another long swig of steaming hot coffee, "Then you went to the church, just like you did before."

"Only we had taken the sacramental wine out of the fridge and hidden it," Marcus declared, shaking his head.

"So, then I went back to bed?" inquired Flynn O'Flaherty, eyeing his two colleagues while taking another bite of buttermilk pancakes with syrup. "That was it?"

Again, both ministers sighed and nodded wearily.

"Well then," Father O'Flaherty declared animatedly, his eyes widening, and his right eyebrow rising up. "There is one thing I can't figure out. I'd like to know which one of you geniuses thought that me sleeping with a stuffed bunny rabbit would keep me from sleepwalking? What good did you think that would do? Honestly!" Father O'Flaherty rolled his eyes and wolfed down another forkful of eggs.

Marcus Templeton and Theo Dunham simply glanced at each other and sighed. Helping Father O'Flaherty with his sleepwalking was getting to be a bit more than they had bargained for.

***

Jordan Smith-Stone was up on a footstool restocking her pharmacy's shelves when Doc came striding energetically through the pharmacy's front door. As the beautiful pharmacist glanced down at her enthused and animated mate, she couldn't help but laugh out loud. Doc was obviously bursting with some extraordinary news he wanted to share with her, his eyes twinkling, his smile broad and his demeanor nothing sort of delighted.

"Okay! I give up! What's up?" Jordan inquired as she stepped down off the stepstool and placed the box of prescription drugs on the countertop. "I can see that whatever it is, it's eating you up! So give!"

Jordan reached out and pulled Doc close, kissing him deeply and then gazing up into his eyes. Then she noticed that one of Doc's arms was hidden behind him. Arching her eyebrows she grinned and whispered, "What do have there, Dr. Stone? Could it be something for my birthday tomorrow?"

Doc chuckled and shook his head, then he brought a beautiful ornate wooden box out from behind his back, his eyes lighting up eagerly as he handed it to his adored wife, "I can't wait! I just have to give this to you now. Okay?" His face looked just like an excited little boy who has picked a bouquet of flowers from his mother's garden to give to her on Mother's Day, thought Jordan. So sweet, so innocent, he never fails to touch my heart deeply.

"Well, Doc," Jordan raised an eyebrow, acting like she was considering whether giving her an early present would be okay, "I don't know. Formality indicates…"

"Stuff formality, convention and rules, woman! Open it!" declared Doc, his grin as wide as she had ever seen it. "Don't keep me in suspense! Open it Sweetheart!"

Doc laid the box carefully on the counter and Jordan, enjoying the moment, took her time caressing the beautiful workmanship of the box, itself. "It is a beautiful box, Sweetheart! Thank you so much!" Jordan gushed, reaching out and hugging her husband.

Doc shook his head and laughed, "Stop teasing me, Jordan! You know your present is inside the box, you wily enchantress, you!" It was obvious that Doc could hardly contain himself.

Jordan slowly slipped off the wooden lid and stared in astonishment down at the charming porcelain doll. She became very quiet for a moment, gazing at the beautiful figure, then glanced back up at Doc, hugged him tightly and whispered, "It's perfect. I love it. Thank you so much!"

While he hugged her, Doc could feel Jordan sobbing, and his face turned white, his smile gone, suddenly truly concerned. He hesitated for a moment and then whispered, "What's wrong? Don't you like it?"

After a few moments, Jordan pulled away, her eyes red and still filled with tears. She reached up and caressed Doc's cheek gently and smiled through her tears, "No, Sweetheart. I love it. You couldn't have given me anything I would love more."

Jordan reached into the pocket of her pharmacy lab

coat and brought out a tissue, "Many, many years ago, my dear mother collected porcelain dolls. She had started when she was a little girl. She loved them dearly. Mother would show them to me when I was just a little girl and spend hours telling me the stories behind all the dolls. It was a special time that I shared with her and I loved it."

Jordan wiped her eyes and reached out to caress the doll, "They were all destroyed in a fire when I was eight. My mother said it didn't matter, that all that mattered was that no one was hurt. But despite what she said, she never seemed the same ever again. It was like she had lost some piece of her. And she and I never again spent time together like we had with the dolls. I missed that so."

Jordan reached down, picking the porcelain doll up tenderly and smiled, "Now, this is the start of my collection. You and I will add to it over the years."

She glanced up almost shyly at Doc and whispered, "And when we have children, I will spend time with them, telling them the stories of my dolls."

Doc stood motionless, watching his usually independent and strong wife, realizing that inside her, there was still a shy and sensitive little girl who loved and needed him as much as he knew he loved and needed her. That was perhaps the best gift that Doc had ever received. He leaned down and kissed her softly on the forehead and simply smiled.

***

Tinmouth Pritchard was trudging silently through the snow and forest back toward his cabin. He was cradling his bow in one hand and in the other he carried two large, field dressed rabbits. The rabbits would make a wonderful stew, and Tinmouth surely did love his stews.

He thought of the forest and the small nearby lake as his grocery store. Whenever he needed food, he just went out and picked some up.

As he approached the abandoned cabin he had been living in for the past three or four years, he saw a man waiting on the front step. Actually, as he looked closer, there were two men. One of the men was very tall and big shouldered, and initially he had blocked Tinmouth's view of the smaller man. To his advantage, the men had not yet seen Tinmouth.

Immediately Tinmouth's guard went up. Strangers waiting outside his cabin could mean only bad things. They weren't wearing fish and game uniforms. That meant they weren't there to confiscate the game he had stored away in the small shed and give him a summons to appear in court for illegal hunting. They could be there to evict him for illegally staying there, or they could be bill collectors, although he thought he had outfoxed most of them. Another possibility crossed Tinmouth's mind. Maybe they were here about his little talk with Elizabeth Fallon last night. It really didn't matter which one, all of the possibilities spelled out one thing. T-r-o-u-b-l-e. And Tinmouth didn't like trouble when it was directed at him.

Tinmouth slipped the rabbits into the game pouch in the back of his jacket and raised his bow, reaching quickly for a hunting arrow. The arrows he used were deadly, three razor sharp blades set in a perfect triangle around the metal core. They were not only deeply penetrating, but they tended to make sure the target he shot bled out very quickly.

Holding the bow out and notching the arrow all in one fluid motion, he moved closer to the men still standing at his front door. As he approached he deftly slipped behind the thick growth of trees that surrounded the cabin on all four sides. The wind was right and he could hear the two men, so he stopped behind a large pine for a moment and just listened.

"This is the right place, it has to be," the shorter man with the fancy clothes stated, glancing around in every direction. The man obviously was not a hunter or at home in the wilderness. The man kept rubbing his hands and moving his feet as if they were really cold.

The big man though was at ease. He had a long, heavy parka on and old work boots. From the bulge under his coat, Tinmouth guessed the big man was carrying. Probably just a handgun, but one never knew anymore. People did strange things, and Tinmouth had seen a lot of things in his lifetime.

Just then, the tall man turned and listened carefully. All of a sudden he stiffened a bit and spoke out loudly, his eyes scanning intently across the landscape, "Tinmouth Pritchard, we're here to talk to you. I know you're out there. Step out where we can see you."

The tall man's voice was deep and commanding. It had a tone to it that made Tinmouth not want to disregard it. Although he didn't like giving up his position to the two men, he decided that he might be best advised to listen to what the tall man said. Tinmouth hadn't lived to be this old without a certain amount of self-preservation instincts.

"Who wants to talk to me, and why?" Tinmouth's words sounded sharp and cutting on the cold breeze that swayed the branches of the nearby trees. Tinmouth moved slightly out from behind the tree, his bow now up, the feathers of the arrow barely resting against his cheek.

The tall man raised his hands slightly, and stared at

Tinmouth, a crooked grin flashing across his mouth. Tinmouth wasn't watching the man's body or face however. He was staring at the man's eyes. The tall man's eyes were deadly serious, as he watched him, evaluating him.

"My name is C.R. Shanks. I'm a private detective. This here is Andy Morrison. He's a lawyer over in Brown Bear Junction. We've come to talk to you. Put down the bow, Tinmouth Pritchard. That is your name, isn't it?" The big man was now staring straight at Tinmouth, his hand not more than a few inches away from the bulge under his coat.

Now Tinmouth Pritchard was an excellent marksman with a bow, but as it had been said many times, many ways, he knew well enough not to bring a knife to a gunfight. He lowered the bow but kept it notched. Then he walked a few feet closer, studying both men.

"What do you want with me, mister?" Tinmouth called out, his aggravation beginning to show now that he realized that his secret little world had been invaded.

"Actually, Mr. Pritchard," the lawyer declared, still looking pretty cold, "we're here to discuss the incident that happened between you and Elizabeth Fallon last night. Could we come into your cabin and talk?"

Tinmouth glanced at the tall man, ignoring the lawyer for a moment, "You say you're here to just talk. Is that true? On your honor?"

The private investigator nodded slightly, adding in a soft but deep rumbling voice, "Unless you get other ideas, Mr. Prichard." His eyes gleamed with a certain iciness that Tinmouth could not mistake. With a sigh, Tinmouth lowered his bow, tromped up to the door of the cabin, shoved open the door and walked inside.

Once inside the men peeled off their coats as

Tinmouth added more wood to the fire. Andy sat on a trunk by the door and C. R. stood leaning casually against the side of the fireplace, where he could see everything in the small, dilapidated cabin. With the P.I.'s coat off, Tinmouth could see the big handgun at his waist. From the looks of it in its holster, Tinmouth was pretty certain that it was a .357 magnum.

After he had purposely taken his time poking the fire and adding more wood, Tinmouth sat back in the worn old rocker by the fire and glared back and forth at the two intruders.

"Say what you gotta' say. Then I'll be askin' you to leave," Tinmouth's tone had an edge and was to the point.

C.R. nodded to Andy. The young lawyer stared at the old hunter and began, his voice firm and without any pretense of hospitality, "Elizabeth Fallon works in my law firm. I know that you used to work for her father Benjamin."

Tinmouth spat suddenly into the fire, catching the lawyer off guard, his eyes already filled with disrespect and anger.

Andy glanced hesitantly up at C.R. who showed no concern and then continued, "I understand that you feel Mr. Fallon wronged you, cheated you out of money."

Tinmouth spat again, turning away from the lawyer but still listening carefully.

"Last night, you grabbed Elizabeth in the parking lot by our office and tried to intimidate her, Mr. Pritchard," Andy's voice had risen, as he was obviously beginning to get sick of both Tinmouth's attitude and his utter disregard for him as a person.

"Do you realize that you committed several crimes,

Mr. Pritchard? Crimes that might end up with you in jail, serving time?" Andy's eyes had narrowed, the hero beginning to peek out of him. The need to protect Elizabeth and bring justice to an unfair situation was strengthening and driving him now. That was one of the strongest reasons he had become a lawyer. To protect the innocent and bring justice to the world, at least where and when he could.

Tinmouth Pritchard turned toward the lawyer, his yellowed eyes narrowing as well, "And what about the money I'm due, counselor? What about the house I lost because I couldn't pay my bills? What about the wife and kids that left me, never wanting to see me again? What about those things, Mr. Fancy Pant's attorney? What about them?" As Tinmouth spoke, his tone grew louder and more furious. The spittle flew from his mouth and he stood up and walked slowly over to Andy.

Andy, sensing the fury, the white hot hate in Tinmouth's words, leaned back, his own eyes growing large and wide in shock at the vehemence of the ragged old woodsman.

Almost involuntarily, C.R. Shanks stepped between the two men, the palm of his hand resting on the butt of the big handgun, his eyes cold and intense.

"If I were you, Mr. Pritchard, I would sit back down. Now." The private investigator's words weren't a request. That was obvious to Tinmouth. They were a verbal command that if not obeyed immediately, would be followed by a physical action that would be nothing short of overpowering.

Tinmouth turned and stared warily at the private eye, as he slowly withdrew back to his rocking chair.

"I understand that you have a grievance, which I will be looking into, Mr. Pritchard," a much-relieved Andy

Morrison continued, "but there will be no more intimidation. There will be no more threats. I have already taken out a restraining order in Miss Fallon's name against you, Mr. Pritchard. If you come anywhere within fifty feet of her, you will be violating that order and be immediately sought out and placed in jail. Do you understand that, Mr. Pritchard?" Andy had regained his composure and was back into hero mode once again. He stared directly at Tinmouth, his eyes demanding a response to his question.

"I understand, Mr. Lawyer," growled Tinmouth. "But you understand this. This ain't over 'til I say it's over. Do you understand that, counselor?" Tinmouth's look was filled with hate and the overwhelming need to avenge all the terrible things in life that had befallen him.

Andy stood up and pulled on his expensive wool jacket and walked to the door, "I will get back to you, Mr. Pritchard with whatever information I find concerning the wages that you feel you are owed. But just you remember," Andy pointed his finger at Tinmouth Pritchard as he and C.R opened the door of the drafty cabin, "leave Elizabeth Fallon alone. Good day to you, Mr. Pritchard."

C.R. followed Andy out the door and the two of them walked quickly away from the cabin. Andy let out a deep sigh and glanced a bit guiltily over at C.R., "I sure am glad you were with me today. Thanks. Now I just hope that crazy old man leaves Elizabeth alone."

C.R. Shanks, keeping a wary eye on the cabin as they walked away, simply whispered softly, "I've seen a lot of fellas in my day, Andy. But that man doesn't appear to be playing with anywhere near a full deck. He blames Miss Fallon for everything bad that's happened in his life."

Shanks turned and stared at Andy for a moment as they stomped through the snow and ice, "And now, I think all that hate and revenge just might be focused on you, my friend."

As Andy pushed himself to keep up with C.R.'s long strides, he began to have a sinking feeling in the pit of his stomach. For a moment, he wondered if this was the way that all heroes felt.

Chapter 14

Old Doc Wentworth shuffled out from the back room at the sheriff's office, peeling off examination gloves and tossing them into the biohazard garbage receptacle in the far corner. His face was calm and unruffled as always, his old greenish eyes filled with what Cash always described as the 'wisdom of experience'.

"Well, Darlene, all the pups now have their shots and I've dosed 'em for tics and fleas. Dosed the momma and gave her a couple of shots with vitamins and nutrients as well. She's pretty run down. She needs lots of food and plenty of water."

Doc Wentworth rolled down his sleeves and put on his ancient topcoat, glancing back to where he'd been working on the pups and their mom, "She's dehydrated and severely malnourished, but with some love and care, she should make it."

He turned and faced Cash and Yamato, his craggy eyebrows lowering as his eyes narrowed. "But that's not the worst of it. That dog has been mistreated. I found marks where she'd been whipped, and a couple of purple and yellow bruises where somebody, not too long ago either, hit her or threw something at her."

Doc's face reddened as he talked, getting more and more animated, "I'd like to know who did that to her, sheriff! If I had a name I'd call the SPCA and the county Humane Society. It would serve the cruel SOB right!"

Cash and Yamato exchanged glances, and then glanced back at Doc Wentworth, "We appreciate knowing, Doc. That will make our decision of what to do with the dogs a lot easier."

"Darn right it will!" Darlene declared angrily, almost coming out of her chair. "Those poor dogs! You don't worry, Doc, we'll make sure it never happens again!" Almost instantly, Darlene reverted to form, sitting ramrod straight behind her desk, all visual signs of her anger and fury swept away, vanished and contained.

Cash turned his surprised gaze from his secretary back to the vet, "Darlene's right, Doc. Those dogs will never go back to their last owner. That's a promise."

Doc Wentworth pulled on his overcoat with a little help from Yamato, and then turned, a strange look on his wizened face. "That reminds me. I could swear that the female used to be owned by Tom and Sally Ustinov. Remember, they lived at the old Franklin house for a few years? Then Tom got a good job up in Silver Pines Crossing? At the foundry up there?"

Yamato interjected, "Yeah! I remember them! They had that little boy, Danny I think was his name."

She turned quickly to Cash, her beautiful dark eyes animated, "You remember boss! We helped them find Danny when he got lost and was roaming around in the woods?"

"Oh, yeah," Cash smiled and nodded. "Sure, I remember, the Ustinov's."

Cash turned and glanced at Doc Wentworth, his mind racing. "I wonder. You think that dog might have gotten lost when they moved? Seen it happen a bunch of times. You wouldn't happen to know where they live now, would you, Doc?"

Doc Wentworth nodded, as he pulled on his galoshes and headed toward the door, "I'd say the dog gettin' lost is just about right. Female's about six, and they moved away three, four years ago. If I were you, I'd call Francine Muldoon, secretary at the Silver Pines Crossing town hall. Tell her I said 'Hey!'"

As Doc Wentworth climbed slowly down the steps of the sheriff's office and shuffled through the snow to his old restored Hudson, Cash and Yamato waved goodbye and closed the door after him. As Cash turned around, Darlene caught his eye with a stern stare.

"You're not going to let that old Miles Perry have those dogs are you? You meant what you said to Doc Wentworth, didn't you? Tell me true, Cash Green!" Although the rest of her body didn't give away her intense feelings, Darlene's eyes were determined and uncompromising.

Cash stopped for a moment, slightly surprised yet not astonished by the passion of Darlene's words and stare, "Darlene, have you ever, in all the years you've known me, seen me go back on my word?" He said it quietly, but with great feeling.

For a moment, Darlene blushed and looked down at her desk. Then her gaze came back up to meet his, "I'm sorry I questioned you, sheriff. I know you to be a man of your word..."

As she went back to typing without glancing over at the sheriff or Yamato, she added, "Even if you are a bit stubborn and bull headed at times."

Cash and Yamato glanced at each other and as they went into the back room to check out the pups and their mom, they exchanged a wide grin and a silent chuckle. That was Darlene. She always got in the last word.

As they knelt by the mother dog, the puppies came tumbling out of their makeshift bed to eagerly greet them. Cash glanced down at the half-starved and abused mother dog. She stared back up into his piercing gray eyes with a gaze that was filled with trust, affection and growing hope.

***

Elizabeth Fallon stood in Andy Morrison's office, listening to the young lawyer finish up his update concerning Tinmouth Pritchard. "So, this afternoon he will officially get served the restraining order I got from Judge Curmudgeon. I have C.R. Shanks bringing the court document over to that shack he's holed up in."

Andy was obviously excited and invigorated, as he paced around his office, his eyes gleaming animatedly, "I believe Mr. Pritchard got the message we meant him to get this morning when we visited him. If he knows what's good for him, he'll just leave you alone."

Andy stopped pacing for a moment and stood directly in front of Elizabeth, his face suddenly serious. "But I did tell him that I would look into his claim about your father owing him money. I intend to do that, Elizabeth. I'm going to need to look at your father's financial records going back quite a few years. Are you okay with that?"

Elizabeth shrugged and nodded, "I guess. Dad has all his records boxed up by the year in the old shed out back of the house. I've never actually looked at them, but he was pretty good at keeping an accurate account of things."

Elizabeth frowned slightly, hesitated and then asked, "But what if you find that my dad owed him money? Will that mean that I'll have to pay Tinmouth what he owed him?" Her eyes looked worried and anxious.

Andy glanced at her, and nodded, "Yes, I'm afraid it would. But we'll deal with that when and if we have to. But don't worry, I'll work it out with you. There are lots of ways to handle it. Let me figure that out, okay?"

Andy's grin came back as he continued pacing around his office once again, his adrenaline kicking back in from his brush with danger that morning. He obviously was feeling good about taking physical action and championing Elizabeth. To say he was on a high at that moment would have been an understatement.

On the other hand, Elizabeth Fallon looked worried. As she turned her gaze from the rapidly talking young lawyer, and glanced out the window at the snow, ice and cold, her eyes were troubled. Troubled and distressed. She had felt for a few brief days as though things might turn out to be all right. Now, with the possibility of more bad debts added to her already overburdened life, she was starting to sink back into a stifling despair and hopelessness. It was a hopelessness that seemed to leave her no way out.

Meanwhile, in the woods several miles away, Tinmouth Pritchard was packing up. He knew enough to move away from the dilapidated cabin before more trouble found him. From experience he knew that once people knew where you were, bad things invariably happened.

He tenderly packed his guns and bows in their leather cases, making sure that they were safe and sound before stowing them in the back of his battered old Dodge pickup. After packing up a couple of boxes of meat and food along with a duffle bag full of clothes and odds and ends, he was ready to go. He carefully looked around, wanting to leave nothing he would have to come back for later.

As the old truck rumbled noisily along the old logging road, Tinmouth sat stiffly behind the wheel, his face a reddened and angry grimace. He already had made his mind up where he was going. It was a place he had held in reserve, should he ever need it. Up almost on the top of the next mountain over, there was a basic A frame shelter, built by loggers sixty or seventy years ago. It had been used as shelter from storms and a place to sleep at night while they were logging around the clock. No one had stayed in the shelter for over fifty years and hardly anyone ever hiked by there. But, for now, it would serve his purposes well.

As Tinmouth drove, he kept rehashing the confrontational meeting with the lawyer and the tall private eye that morning. Each time he thought it through, he got angrier and angrier. The gall of that young butinski to serve a restraining order on him! All he was doing was trying to see that justice was done! Ben Fallon owed him money. Ben was dead so that meant that Ben's daughter owed him money. It was plain as the nose on your face! Now the simpering girl had gone and gotten that interfering lawyer involved.

Tinmouth ground the gears angrily in the old truck as he turned off and started up the rut of a logging road toward the top of the mountain. The more he thought about his problems, the more they came to rest on the shoulders of the young lawyer who had been so haughty and demanding to him that morning. It was as C.R. Shanks had predicted. Tinmouth Pritchard now had transferred all his anger, rage and retribution to Andy Morrison.

To Tinmouth, his path was clear. Eliminate the young lawyer and his problems would go away. Without the lawyer, things would go back to as they were. He could then easily deal with Ben Fallon's daughter and get his money back. Once he had his money, he could start a new life, somewhere new. Somewhere nobody knew him. He desperately needed a fresh start.

The old truck's motor growled and grumbled as it slowly climbed up the snow and ice filled path. As he drove onward, Tinmouth Pritchard's thin lips curved upward in a smile. It was a smile that contained no warmth or love or happiness. It was a smile that meant no good to anyone. It was a smile of reckoning.

***

Wendy Morrison was livid. Andy had just called her, bursting to share with her the news of his confrontation that morning with Tinmouth Pritchard. She was in the storeroom behind her shop. As she opened newly received boxes and unwrapped the inventory from inside them, she fumed. As she fumed her mind raced. The more she thought, the more she fumed.

She was beside herself with worry and anxiety. Why had Andy placed himself in harm's way for this new paralegal? Wendy shook her head as she unpacked. Andy seemed fixated on helping this young girl. Through her motherly apprehension and concern, all Wendy could see was that the girl was obviously penniless, and had a less than desirable past. Andy had not only befriended her, but he had given her a job, and now it seemed that he was spending a good deal of his time protecting her.

Wendy shook her head in frustration once more and frowned as she dug into the next box. There wasn't anything she could do to make Andy realize that this girl, this Elizabeth Fallon, wasn't worth his time and effort. Her younger brother, the brother she had raised for seventeen years, was now a grown man and had a mind of his own. No matter how she tried to subtly suggest to him that he should take it easy and be careful in his relationship with this girl, he didn't seem to get it. Girls like Elizabeth were always looking for handsome, wealthy young men like her Andy.

Suddenly, Wendy's eyes went vacant for a moment. Then, a moment later, there was a steel hard glint that flashed coldly from her narrowed eyes. It was almost as if she wasn't herself anymore. Whoever the new person was, they were in complete control.

Taking off her apron, Wendy called out to Mandy who was in the salesroom of Treasured Memories, "Hey, Mandy, I've got to go out for a few minutes. I won't be long." Her voice was calm and firm.

Mandy's happy and contented voice rang out, "Got it boss! Been pretty slow in here anyway today! Be careful. That dusting of snow on top of the ice on the roads can be treacherous. See you soon!"

Five minutes later, Wendy was standing at the massive front desk of Lesner, Malkowitz, Freedman and Lister. She smiled at the receptionist, who had just gotten off the phone.

"Good morning, Miss Morrison! How are you this morning?" Anita, the receptionist asked Wendy. The receptionist's smile and makeup were perfect, yet slightly understated. "I'll tell your brother you're here!"

"No, thank you, Anita," replied Wendy quietly, resolutely, "I'm here to see Elizabeth Fallon if I may."

"Oh!" Anita's face lost the perfect smile for a moment and her expression became somewhat quizzical. But the smile was quickly back as the receptionist buzzed an extension, quickly and efficiently relayed Wendy's message, then glanced back up at

Andy's older sister.

"She'll be right out, Miss Morrison," Anita declared with a slight nod of her head. "You can have a seat in the waiting area until she gets here if you'd like."

"No, thanks," Wendy replied. "I think I'll just wait here, if you don't mind."

Walking a few feet away from the main desk, Wendy gazed around at the large, plush waiting room of the well-established law firm. Beautiful brand name furniture, elaborate coffee and cappuccino machines as well as a counter with muffins, Danish and small, exquisite snacks made the waiting area feel at once comfy and homey while being relatively lavish and luxurious.

"Miss Morrison?" came a quiet, almost timid voice from behind her.

Wendy turned and there stood a thin, obviously self-conscious young woman. The young woman's eyes were wide and innocent, but also filled with a myriad of anxieties and fears. Her mannerisms were of a person who was overburdened by worldly cares and worries. Far too many woes and concerns for her tender years.

Wendy had come to have a confrontation with the woman, to tell her to leave her naïve brother alone. Instead, although she had no rhyme or reason to do so, Wendy's heart suddenly went out to the shy young woman.

"You wanted to talk with me, Ma'am?" whispered Elizabeth, staring curiously into Wendy's eyes, clearly trying to figure out what Mr. Morrison's sister could possibly want with a mere fledgling paralegal.

Wendy walked over to the young woman, clasped her hand on Elizabeth's forearm, smiled and whispered quietly, "Could I persuade you to have a cup of Al's cappuccino with me this morning?"

For a moment, Elizabeth simply stood there, wondering what was happening. Then, she smiled shyly back and replied, "I have a break in fifteen minutes. Could I meet you there, Miss Morrison? If that isn't too much trouble?"

"Sounds great! See you there," Wendy declared and with a wave, she turned and walked briskly back through the entrance.

For a moment, Elizabeth Fallon simply stood there watching Wendy leave, trying to figure out was what happening. Then, with a slight shake of her head, she walked back to her cubical and settled down to scan through the law book she was searching for previous legal precedents.

She glanced at the clock on the wall, checking to see when her break was, not wanting to be late to meet with Andy's sister. Although the whole incident seemed a bit curious to her, Elizabeth didn't question it. She was determined to do her job, fit in and create a new life for herself, one way or another.

Chapter 15

Tom Ustinov didn't get two steps inside the sheriff's office before the mangy mother dog in the back room came bounding out, overjoyed to see her long lost master. It was easy to see that the dog and the man had a long, happy history together. Her tail was wagging happily, her tongue was out and she raced over and buried herself in his loving arms as he quickly knelt down to greet her.

"Whoa, there, girl!" Tom chuckled as he tried to hug the wiggling and excited dog that couldn't get enough of him. Then his chuckle halted abruptly as he took a closer look at his reunited companion. His fingers gently probed the still raised and discolored welts on her back and legs and he felt her thin sides, carefully touching her protruding ribs and bones.

"Sheriff," Tom Ustinov's face was flushed and angry as he stood up, staring at Cash, "who's mistreated her?" Tom's eyes were obviously filled with a great deal of sudden anger and indignation.

Cash walked over and shook Tom's hand, a smile on his face, "I understand your concern. But I think the important thing, right now, Mr. Ustinov, is that she's back with her owner and will be well taken care of..."

Cash's explanation was interrupted by the tumbling, barking and enthusiastic invasion of five small puppies as they ran out to find their mother from the back room.

Tom Ustinov's frown vanished, his eyes widening in surprise at the sight of the rollicking pups. The man knelt back down and eagerly started petting and talking animatedly to the lively puppies, while the mother dog simply watched while leaning lovingly against her old master with contentment and joy.

Sitting behind the counter and joyfully peering over at the happy scene in front of her, Darlene Pitts did the almost unimaginable: she smiled. Her eyes were moist with unshed emotional tears and she was clasping and unclasping her hands together as she watched, unaware that both Cash and Yamato had seen her. As quickly as the sheriff and deputy noticed, however, they looked away, giving Darlene her private moment undisturbed.

The joyful and heartwarming scene was rudely interrupted, however, when Miles Perry opened the front door of the sheriff's office and barged in out of the cold February day.

Miles face was set in a determined scowl as he entered. Then he glanced down at the dog and Tom Ustinov, his eyes widening as he exclaimed in a self-important, blustery manner, "Hey, mister! That's my dog!"

Tom Ustinov turned to peer at where the gruff exclamation came from, staring up at the thickset farmer. Then his eyes narrowed.

Cash Green is a very quick and intuitive man, but even he couldn't reach Tom Ustinov before Tom had swiftly stood up and smashed a hard right hand into Miles Perry's flabbergasted face. The farmer dropped like a load of bricks with a loud thud on the hardwood floor, and simply sat there staring up at Tom in astonishment.

"That's for abusing my dog," declared Tom, his eyes flashing with anger and undisguised loathing at Miles Perry. Beside Tom, the abused dog was eyeing Miles furiously, a deep, low growl rumbling in her throat.

Cash quickly stepped between Tom and the shell-shocked Miles, glancing back and forth between the two men. His gray eyes were narrowed and unwavering and his manner all business, letting both men know wordlessly that there would be no more fisticuffs that day.

"Miles, I do believe the rightful owner of this dog and her pups has come along." Cash reached down and with one hand quickly brought the farmer to his feet. "And as far as I am concerned," Cash glanced back meaningfully at Tom, "this matter is closed. Isn't that correct Tom?"

Although Tom was still furious at the beatings that the farmer had inflicted on his lost dog, he stared into the sheriff's fierce gray eyes and saw that there was only one correct answer to that question. "I guess that's right, sheriff. The matter is closed."

Cash turned and stared at Miles, gray eyes flashing, his hands on his hips, "I believe you were just going. Is that right Miles?"

Miles simply rubbed his sore jaw and nodded. With one last resentful, but respectful, stare at Tom, the completely deflated farmer turned, opened the front door of the sheriff's office and stepped out into the freezing temperatures. As soon as the farmer had left, the dog's growls halted.

As the front door closed, Tom grinned somewhat apologetically and shrugged, "Sorry Sheriff Green. I'm not normally a violent man."

Tom knelt down and gave the mother dog a long hug, while the puppies continued to clamber happily over his knees and onto the back of their long-suffering mother.

"I know that Tom," Cash spoke quietly, with a small grin playing around his lips. "Violence is rarely the best solution to any matter."

Yamato's dark eyes twinkled as she stared at Tom Ustinov playing with his dogs and then glanced back over at her boss. "But sometimes, there is the right time and place for it," she chuckled.

"Amen to that!" declared Darlene as she nodded her head vigorously and turned back to her typing.

***

C.R. Shanks stood by the front door of the old hunting cabin where he and Andy Morrison had found Tinmouth Pritchard, his cell phone to his ear. The cabin was empty. All of Tinmouth's guns, bows, and camping equipment were gone. The doors and windows had purposely been left open and there was already a coating of snow and ice forming over the inside of the cabin.

"I have no idea where he might have gone," he spoke loudly, to enable his voice to be heard over the chilly February wind. "His tire tracks are visible for awhile, but then they get lost in the other tire tracks on the crisscross of logging roads up here. Lots of hunters and outdoorsmen drive around the area. We just have to accept the fact that he's gone."

On the other end of the phone, the private eye could hear Andy hesitating, trying to come up with something they could do to make sure Tinmouth Pritchard was legally served the restraining order. Realistically, however, as long as he wanted to remain hidden, there was enough dense woods and wilderness to allow him to do that, at least for awhile.

"Okay, come on back," replied Andy, suddenly deflated and disappointed. "We'll just have to keep a good eye on Elizabeth and make sure the old rascal doesn't pop up again and harass her. Thanks, C.R."

The line went dead. C.R. stuffed his phone back into his jacket pocket and pulled his broad collar up around his neck, as the wind whistled around the bare trees and made complex little whirlwinds in the snow.

The private investigator took one last look around and climbed into his Jeep Wrangler. The tall man settled into the driver's seat and frowned. Something about all this didn't feel right. C.R. had a gut feeling and like Cash's gut feelings, his were pretty much on target. C.R. didn't think this was over. He had a nagging feeling that wherever Tinmouth was, the old reprobate was not going to let the matter drop quite so easily.

Back at Lesner, Malkowitz, Freedman and Lister, Andy Morrison was already on the office intercom with his secretary Jennifer Allen, "Hey, Jen, I need to see Elizabeth Fallon, buzz her for me, would you? Thanks."

Andy sat at his desk, staring out into the icy, white February landscape, trying to rationalize to himself that not being able to serve Tinmouth Pritchard with the restraining order was no big deal. He did so, because he needed to make it sound believable to himself before he tried making it sound believable to Elizabeth. Unfortunately, Andy wasn't sure that truly was the case. He remembered the anger on the old man's face when they had confronted him. Somehow, Andy didn't believe Tinmouth was going to give up his quest for financial compensation that he honestly felt was due him, at least not this easily.

Momentarily, the intercom buzzed back, and Andy hit the button, "Sorry, Mr. Morrison, Miss Fallon stepped out for her break." Jennifer's voice was calm and professional.

Then came a hesitation and his secretary added, in somewhat more personal tone, "It seems she was going to meet your sister at Al's Diner, Mr. Morrison."

"Thanks Jen," replied Andy, as he hit the intercom button and turned to stare at the picture of his sister that he always kept on his desktop. His brow knitted slightly as he stared at Wendy's photograph. Staring at the picture, he whispered in a soft inquisitive tone, "And just what did you want to see Elizabeth about, sister dear?"

***

Two streets over, in a booth at Al's Diner, Elizabeth Fallon and Wendy Morrison were just sitting down in a booth. Elizabeth had no idea why she was there, while Wendy had a definite agenda.

Elizabeth smiled uncertainly and adjusted her necklace and the collar of her dress uneasily. She glanced briefly from time to time at the older, but still youthful looking woman across the booth from her as she pretended to study the diner's menu.

Wendy Morrison looked up from her own menu. "Well, I've heard so many things from my brother about you, it's nice to finally meet you," declared Wendy, her eyes studying the young woman, a warm smile spreading across her lips.

"Oh?" managed Elizabeth, curiously, "Mr. Morrison told you about me?" The young woman seemed honestly surprised, thought Wendy.

"Yes," Wendy responded, as she pulled her paper napkin across her lap, "He mentioned that he was the legal counsel and executor for your late father. More recently he apprised me of the incident when you were assaulted as you went to your car, and how he visited that gentleman and made out a restraining order against him."

"Oh," Elizabeth's cheeks flushed and she glanced down at her menu again, obviously in some discomfort and embarrassment over the whole situation.

Wendy reached over and placed her hand on Elizabeth's. At first, Elizabeth began to pull her hand away, but then she hesitated and finally allowed Wendy to grasp her small hand tightly. Elizabeth's eyes met Wendy's.

"I'm very sorry about your father, my dear," whispered Wendy firmly. "Andy and I lost our parents when we were teenagers. We understand how hard the loss can be."

Elizabeth saw the honest care and empathy in Wendy's eyes and she tried to relax a little, "Thank you, Miss Morrison. It has been hard."

As the two women chatted a bit more animatedly, ordered coffee and a pastry, and got to know each other a bit better, they didn't bother to glance out the window. If they had, they most probably would have seen a dilapidated old truck parked across the street. Inside the old truck was Tinmouth Prichard, and Tinmouth wasn't smiling.

***

Tinker LaGrange glanced up from the seemingly endless pile of papers stacked in a rather random and spiraling fashion on his desk as the front door to the Brown Bear Junction Police Station swung open. In strode Cash Green and Ericka Yamato.

"Hey Chief!" called out Cash, dusting the light

covering of snow off his hat and coat as he walked toward the police chief's desk. "How is the world treating you today?"

Cash winked and smiled at Tinker warmly. Ever since Tinker had taken over as the Chief of Brown Bear Junction, Cash and Yamato had been valuable resources and become fast friends with the young police chief. Their insight and experience had come in handy more than once for young Tinker.

Tinker smiled back, sighing and pushing himself away from the pile of papers on his desk, "The world is being rather good to me today, Sheriff Green! And just how is it treating you and your beautiful deputy this morning?"

Yamato, despite all her experience and independence, blushed slightly at the compliment, as Cash declared firmly, "We just happen to be tip top, Chief LaGrange!"

Yamato glanced around the police office, which was twice the size of their sheriff's office back in The Falls, grinning and commenting, "What do you do with all this space, Tinker? You could park your police cars in here and still have enough room for a few desks and a waiting area."

From the front desk Myrna Lynn Jones looked up from her typing and raised her eyebrows ominously. Myrna Lynn had been the secretary and dispatcher for the police station for the last eon or so and everything in it had been bought, decorated or arranged by her. The police station may have had chiefs come and go, but Myrna Lynn was a permanent fixture.

Yamato noticed Myna Lynn's immediate displeasure at her comment and quickly added, "But it certainly is beautifully arranged, Chief LaGrange!"

Myna Lynn nodded her head once, as if in

confirmation of the compliment and briskly went back to her typing. Yamato glanced at Cash and raised her eyebrows slightly, as if she had just managed to barely avoid an icy, treacherous corner on a mountain road. Cash winked and glanced back at Tinker.

"You said that you had a case you wanted to get our opinion on, Chief?" Cash settled down in the chair nearest Tinker.

"Yes, I do, Cash," Tinker stood up and pulled on his heavy parka emblazoned with the Brown Bear Junction Police Department emblem and logo. "But knowing the two of you," Tinker pulled his Glock out of the desk and placed it in his shoulder holster, "I figured we would do our consulting over Al's fresh baked apple pie and a cup of coffee. What do you say?"

"Ah! Our fee for the consultation, right?" Yamato quipped with a wink and a smile.

"Indeed!" Tinker responded immediately, gesturing toward the front door and smiling warmly.

"Well, Yamato," Cash chuckled as he stood up and followed the young police chief out the door, "he has our priorities pegged alright. He drives a shrewd bargain, does he not?"

Yamato simply chuckled and shook her head as she followed her boss, "Your priorities, Cash Green! You're the one that has the love handles starting to develop!"

The police chief declared over his shoulder as he stepped down onto the wide front porch of the police station, "I'm afraid I have to agree with your deputy there, Sheriff."

Tinker gave Cash a mischievous wink and commented, "'Cause Miss Ericka's figure is somewhere in the 'amazing to fabulous' category!"

Moments later, the police chief staggered forward

into the snowy street as Yamato gave him a discreet but friendly little shove. When the police chief turned around and glanced at the deputy, she had a prim smile on her face, but a mischievous glint in her dark eyes, and was walking step for step with her obviously amused boss.

"Gotta watch that first step," Cash casually whispered to the chief, stifling a chuckle.

I can see that," replied Tinker, glancing back at Yamato with a big grin on his face, "It can be, as they often say, a real doosie!"

Chapter 16

Tinmouth Pritchard sat in the driver's seat of his old truck, the well-worn motor idling roughly. He rubbed his bare hands together for warmth and then blew hot air on them more from habit than need.

He watched the two women in the diner window, impatient to have a private word with Benjamin Fallon's daughter. She had turned out to be more of a thorn in his side than he had imagined when he first came up with the plan to recover the wages he felt he was due. Tinmouth frowned, his craggy eyebrows knitting together in one deep, shaggy brow. He wasn't about to allow that uppity young thing to come between himself and his rightfully earned cash.

Tinmouth's thoughts narrowed to the task at hand. He glanced over at the passenger side seat. There was his Pa's old .38-55 lever action with the old octagonal barrel leaning peacefully up against the seat. Next to it was his old recurved bow. He had other, more modern, compound bows, but he preferred his old faithful standby. It had killed nearly fifty deer over the years, and it simply felt right in his hand as he released the arrow. Tinmouth Pritchard liked the tried and true, whether it be oatmeal for breakfast, long wool underwear in the winter or a time honored weapon.

Hopefully, he wouldn't have to use either of the

weapons. With any luck, he could intimidate the young woman enough to get his money without need of their services. But if he didn't...

Tinmouth suddenly spotted The Junction's young chief of police in his rear view mirror. He was walking across the snowy street toward the diner. Not only that, but Tinmouth recognized that the Chief was walking and talking with that nosey sheriff from The Falls and his deputy. Tinmouth's frown deepened and he let out a soft, angry grunt of displeasure.

Shifting the old truck into first, Tinmouth slowly crept away from the curb and was soon rumbling down Main Street, headed out of town. As he drove, careful to keep to the speed limit and not attract attention, Tinmouth cursed irritably to himself. He would have to find another time when he could have a private talk with Benjamin's daughter. Then he smiled. But it wasn't a kind or happy smile. He smiled because he knew he would find that time. He would find it very soon.

As Tinker, Cash and Yamato entered the diner, brushing off the thin dusting of snow on their jackets and hats, Wendy Morrison and Elizabeth Fallon were well into their pastry.

"So, Elizabeth," began Wendy, sipping from her steaming cup, "you plan on making a career at my brother's law offices?" Wendy's eyes were inquisitive and intent. She was leaning slightly forward, eager to hear the young paralegal's answer.

Elizabeth smiled shyly, glancing up from her pastry, "Honestly, I don't know, Miss Morrison. All I know at the moment is that I need this job."

Elizabeth glanced out the window, her eyes becoming sad and wistful for a moment, "My father left me with a lot of bills. I really need to make some money. Once I get the bills paid off, I really don't know what will come next in my life."

The young woman turned her gaze back to Wendy, her face a bit weary, but her eyes earnest and frank, "I feel like there's a huge weight on my back, Miss Morrison. I just want to get it off and then see where my life might lead me."

Wendy stared at the young woman attentively, nodding slowly as she listened, "I understand, Elizabeth. It sounds like you are trying your best to take care of things in your life. I applaud you for that."

Wendy then frowned slightly, considering her next words carefully. Her eyes glazed over for a moment, and then they came back into focus. Her dark eyes narrowed. She hesitated, stared into the young paralegal's eyes and continued almost in a whisper, "You seem like a sweet, bright young woman. As such, I suppose it's only natural that my brother is rather taken with you."

Elizabeth's eyes widened in surprise, and she leaned back, placing her cup down abruptly. A small splatter of coffee flew up over the rim and onto the booth's shiny tabletop. Elizabeth's hand instinctively flew to her mouth as she gazed in shock at Wendy Morrison.

"Taken with me?" Elizabeth managed in a shrill whisper as her hand moved to her throat. "You must be mistaken, Miss Morrison! We hardly know each other!"

Elizabeth started to rise from the table, then sat back down again, hard, her mouth open, her thoughts racing. "Miss Morrison, that can't be true! He has indeed been kind to me. He helped me refinance my father's debts and he helped me get the job at the law firm. But we've never been close or intimate in any way!"

As Wendy watched the embarrassment and shock of the young woman, she began to doubt that Elizabeth was anything but what she seemed: a poor young woman who was struggling to deal with the life she had been dealt.

Wendy placed a hand firmly over Elizabeth's, and stared straight into the young woman's eyes, "Elizabeth, please calm down. I don't mean to insinuate that there is anything underhanded or bad by disclosing my brother's feelings."

Wendy patted Elizabeth's hand kindly and continued to speak in hushed tones after glancing around the diner to see who might be listening to their conversation, "I merely wanted to bring it to your attention."

Elizabeth relaxed slightly, still staring uneasily at Wendy. Discovering the mess she had made on the tabletop, she hastily mopped up the coffee with her napkin and turned her gaze back to Andy's sister.

Wendy spoke slowly, almost as silent as a whisper. "You see, I have raised Andy ever since our parents were killed in an accident when he was thirteen. He hasn't had many people in his life other than me. We worked hard to get him through college and law school. I worked two jobs and he worked at night to help with the expenses."

"Once he had become a lawyer he was totally focused and intent on making a name for himself in his profession. We live together, Elizabeth. I wash his clothes, make his meals and I am his best friend. I have made his success the main goal of my life, you see, and he is sheltered and quite naïve. Although it's true that Andy is a wonderful, caring and intelligent young man, he has little or no experience with relationships and in dealing with the fairer sex." Wendy smiled and patted Elizabeth's hand in a manner she felt was reassuring once again.

Elizabeth sat quietly, listening to Wendy, her face pale, her emotions deeply hidden.

"So, in helping you, in defending you from that man who tried to harass you the other night, in taking care of you, he has come to think of himself as your champion. Your hero, and perhaps," Wendy tilted her head gazing into Elizabeth's eyes thoughtfully, "much more."

Elizabeth frowned uncomfortably and stared down at her plate, "I assure you Miss Morrison, I have done nothing to lead Mr. Morrison on in any way. I know that I'm not good enough for such a wonderful man..."

Wendy interrupted with a soft whisper, her eyes gazing deep into Elizabeth's, "I'm sure you haven't Elizabeth. I simply felt you should know what he's feeling. After all that's only fair to you, isn't it?"

Elizabeth suddenly glanced at her watch distractedly, and stood up, awkwardly grabbing her coat and purse from the seat beside her, "I'm terribly sorry, Miss Morrison. I'm late. I have to run. I don't want to get in trouble."

As Elizabeth walked quickly away, she turned and smiled slightly, "Thank you for the coffee and Danish. Thank you for everything. I shall keep it in mind. Good day, Miss Morrison."

Wendy watched the young paralegal pay at the cash register and then walk briskly across the street toward the law offices of Lesner, Malkowitz, Freedman and Lister. Elizabeth's head was down and she was obviously still embarrassed and ill at ease from her meeting with Wendy.

Wendy turned back to her coffee and took a long, slow sip. She wasn't exactly sure how she felt about the meeting, but at least she had planted a seed in the young woman's mind. Perhaps that was enough to keep her own world exactly as it was for the time being.

Placing her cup down gently and glancing up, she noticed young Tinker LaGrange for the first time. The young chief was smiling and waving at her from a table three booths away. Wendy smiled broadly and waved enthusiastically at the fledgling chief of police.

***

Sean Frasier peered out at the rapidly increasing snowfall. It was nearly recess time for the younger students and he had to make a decision. He had to either keep them in or send them out to play in the snow. On one hand, if he sent them out to play, the kids would have a great time in the snow. But, they would probably come in with wet snowsuits, hats, boots and mittens, causing their teachers an additional amount of time and effort to hang the garments out to dry in the coatrooms. There was also the hard reality that the duty teachers would roll their eyes and complain about standing outside in the falling snow. It was a fact that most of his teachers, especially the veteran ones, detested outside duty when it was raining or snowing.

On the other hand, if Sean kept the kids in, the teachers would have to stay in with them, which meant they wouldn't get a break. A teacher's breaks were sacred. They considered them essential allowing them to go to the bathroom, get a cup of coffee, work in their rooms, and get a break from their 'little darlings'. Teachers religiously guarded their breaks with a jealousy and protectiveness that was akin to the ferocity of a mother bear protecting her cubs.

THE FALLS: Cupid's Arrow

Sean glanced over at his secretary, Angie Banker, to see if she might have an opinion. But Angie held up her hand in a 'stop' motion and looked away. Angie had been school secretary for the past three principals at the West Sugar Shack Falls Elementary School and she had long ago learned to stay out of the decision-making and politics that went along with being the leader of the school.

Sean chuckled to himself. Good for Angie. Then he turned his gaze back to the falling snow and made his decision. He walked over and grabbed the microphone from the school wide broadcasting station.

"We will be having recess today at the tone of the bell," he spoke clearly and slowly into the microphone, waiting a moment for effect. He could hear the students' shouts of joy from several nearby classrooms. Then he continued, with a clever twinkle in his eye, "I will be taking recess duty, so all other duty teachers may remain indoors."

Even though he couldn't hear them, he knew that several duty teachers were having their own silent shouts of joy, and he grinned at the thought. Grabbing up his coat, hat and gloves and slipping on his heavy galoshes, Sean made his way toward the door of the office. Angie Banker turned as he went past her for a moment, winked and whispered, "Always the hero, right, Mr. F?"

Sean grinned even larger, shrugged semi-apologetically and hustled out through the hallway to the playground where the kids were pouring out onto the cold, frozen, white playground. He was greeted by shouts of excitement and pure delight as the kids were running around trying to catch snowflakes on their tongues and simply reveling in the falling snow.

Sean took a deep breath of icy air and breathed out a cloud of mist, smiling and waving to the kids. The students and the principal had a well-understood relationship. He loved them, and they loved him. Sean had no children of his own, so they were essentially 'his kids'. As for the students, he was their dad, or grandpa or caring big brother while they were at school. He was, at once, a commanding figure to admire and respect, and someone who was just as likely to play and have fun with them as any of their other friends.

One of the side doors opened just then and Nancy Sturgis, one of his first grade teachers, stepped outside. She was all bundled up for the snow and the cold and she smiled when she saw Sean, "Thought you could use a helping hand, Mr. Frasier. It's hard to watch several hundred kids at each end of the playground, although if anyone could do it, it would be you."

Nancy hesitated and then added in a conspiratorial whisper, "And I'm not one of the teachers who think they'll melt if they get wet!"

Sean and Nancy shared a chuckle as they rubbed their hands and their eyes instinctively started scanning the kids and the playground, keeping good track of where and what the students were doing.

"I kind of like these snowy days," Sean stated, nodding to himself. "It reminds me of when my brother William and I used to play on this playground. Good memories."

Nancy nodded as well, "I can remember playing with my brother Daniel back in Florida when we were kids. 'Course there was no snow."

The young teacher glanced over at her principal, and grinned, "But we had plenty of lizards, frogs and snakes to play with!"

Sean watched Bobby Mason and Mary McDonough enthusiastically rolling a snowball across the snow-covered playground, the ball growing larger and larger until it was the size needed for the bottom of a large snowman.

"I went down to Florida once," Seam declared, turning his gaze onto several of the first graders who were eating handfuls of freshly fallen snow, "but I couldn't get used to the heat. We went to one of the botanical gardens in July and I thought I was going to die from the humidity!"

Nancy grinned, "Yup, that'll do it! You were doing the tourist thing though. Floridians never go to those places in the summer. They're pretty nice in the winter."

"I came out of that place wheezing and my clothes were completely soaked. My mom thought I was having a seizure of some kind!" Sean chuckled as he watched Emily Jordan and Stephanie Bridges making snow angels over by the teeter-totters.

Sean turned and winked at Nancy, "But at least she bought William and I huge ice cream cones to make us feel better!"

Nancy shook her head, "As far as I'm concerned, ice cream is its own food group. I simply have to have some everyday. My favorites are Moose Tracks, Carmel Ripple and Mango Madness, all from The Scoop, of course." Nancy sighed even thinking about the delicious flavors she had mentioned.

Sean nodded, "Ice cream is a staple of mine as well. But I'm simple, old fashioned I guess you could say. Chocolate, coffee, and French vanilla are my standbys. All from The Scoop as well, of course."

Sean suddenly had an inspiration, his eyes lit up and

he declared delightedly, "We should definitely have an ice cream social at the end of the year for the whole school! Bring in Norma and Trish and serve everyone great big sundaes before they go home for the summer!"

Nancy's eyes twinkled and she chimed in eagerly, "Hold it on the last day! Just before we let the kids go! Have their last memory of the school year be a sweet and delicious one!"

As the snow fell, and the children played delightedly, the principal and the teacher animatedly planned out the year-end ice cream celebration on an icy playground in the middle of a snowstorm in February.

***

"So, do you remember Burton Phelps? The old guy who runs Brown Bear Hardware and Farm Equipment?" Tinker emptied three packs of sugar substitute into his coffee and poured in a generous helping of cream. "Well, we've got this kind of feud going on between him and the other Main Street merchants."

"Sure," Cash replied, glancing up at Tinker as he forked up a bite of warm apple pie. "He's been a fixture here in The Junction for decades. What about him?"

"Well, Burton used to have an empty lot down at the end of Main Street where he would display his larger farm equipment. You know, like full sized tractors, cultivators, haying machines, commercial roto-tillers. Stuff like that." Tinker took a long deep sip from his steaming mug.

Yamato and Cash glanced at each other curiously, waiting for Tinker to continue.

"Seems that when the town council and mayor raised the property taxes and changed the zoning of the vacant lot from agricultural to commercial, Burt had a hissy fit. He declared that he wasn't going to pay the higher taxes on an old, empty property and sold it immediately." Tinker glanced appraisingly back and forth from Cash to Yamato.

"And...?" Yamato interjected, leaning forward.

Tinker took another swallow of coffee, shrugged and continued, "So he put as many of those big pieces of farm equipment as he could on the front, side and back lots of his hardware store. They are packed in there like sardines! I've never seen anything like it! It looks like a hoarder's nightmare come true!"

"Ah! I see where you're going. I expect the good merchants of the Junction have frowned upon what they deem as an eyesore and petitioned you to do something about it, correct, Chief?" Yamato grinned, a mischievous twinkle in her eyes.

Cash had broken out into a smile as well, but he was politely covering it with his hand.

Tinker flushed slightly, but doggedly continued, "Exactly right. The mayor, the town council, and several of the merchants have privately visited me in the police station to discuss what can be done. They don't want to start a war with old man Phelps, but they want the mess around the hardware store cleaned up. I have been given a directive. I have to get the equipment off there by Valentine's Day or the town council will go to the county court to have it done legally."

Tinker stared at Cash and Yamato, his face now pale, his eyes uneasy. "Hey, it may seem funny, but either way, I'm behind the eight ball. If I can't get old man Phelps to move the equipment of his own free will, I'll have to go in and move it legally. Burt Phelps has lots of family and friends in town. If I move him without his permission, I'll alienate half the town. If I don't get the job done to the mayor and the town council's satisfaction, I'll alienate the other half. It's almost like I can't win, one way or the other."

Yamato reached out and patted Tinker's arm, her grin turned to a soft and kindly smile. "Hey, Chief, it's not the end of the world. Honest. This job brings you all sorts of fun situations. You can't let them get you down. Right, boss?" Yamato turned and glanced at Cash.

Cash nodded and leaned forward, "She's right, Chief. There's got to be a way to work it all out. But most importantly, you have to always do what you think is right. A good officer of the law has to follow their heart."

"And your gut," Yamato added with a wink.

Cash smiled at the somewhat relieved young police chief and whispered low as he took another bite of warm apple pie, "Tell you what. Let's finish this delicious pie and take a walk down the street to the hardware store, what do you say?"

Tinker managed a slight smile and nodded enthusiastically. Starting to recover his appetite, the chief of police dug into his slice of pie and exhaled a deeply thankful sigh.

As the three law officers enjoyed their mid-morning snack, Wendy Morrison stepped out the front door of the diner and walked briskly and happily along Main Street. It was high time she got back to Treasured Memories. Mandy had been holding the fort for an hour now, and her employee would be more than ready for her own break.

Wendy picked her way through the snow and ice as she traveled the short distance to the shop. While she walked, Wendy ran down through her list of 'to do's' for the day. With the issue of Elizabeth Fallon off her list, she could get on to more mundane matters.

Just as she reached the front steps of the shop, Andy's car pulled up alongside her and he quickly opened the car door and climbed out. Wendy could see that he was scowling and his face was rather red. Staring at him, she wondered what could be wrong with him. She really had no idea.

"Andy? What on earth is wrong..." she began, staring at her brother as he charged up the steps toward her.

"How could you?!" he shouted loudly, his eyes narrowed and furious, "How could you be so cruel to Elizabeth?!"

Wendy reached out a hand to calm her younger brother but he pushed it firmly away, "Whatever do you mean, Andy? How could I do what?" She was having a difficult time trying to figure out just what she had done wrong.

Could it have been her meeting with Elizabeth? In her mind she went through their discussion. She had met with Elizabeth for coffee, set the young woman straight about the life that Wendy had made for herself and Andy and tried to be honest with the poor girl. What was the harm in that?

Andy was beside himself, "Elizabeth has resigned! She wouldn't tell me why. Just that you and she had met and that she couldn't work at the law firm anymore!"

Wendy shook her head and again reached out to her brother in an attempt to calm his obviously wild attitude. "Andy, slow down! I haven't done anything. If the poor girl finally realized that she wasn't right for you, what does that have to do with..."

"Not right for me?! What do you mean not right for me?" Andy's eyes hardened and he leaned forward and grabbed his sister by the arm. "What did you say to her? Tell me!"

Wendy pulled away from his firm grip and backed up a step, her eyes narrowing and her face becoming stern, "Really, Andy! I don't see why you are accusing me of doing anything to that girl. I was just having an honest conversation with her. I inquired if she was after your money. I asked if she knew that you were interested in her…"

"You did what?!" Andy's eyes instantly widened with shock and surprise. He staggered back as if he had been slapped.

After a moment's hesitation, the young lawyer turned and ran back to the driver's side of the car, opening and then slamming the door closed forcefully. In a flash, he was gone, his car slewing wildly down the icy street.

The shop door opened and Mandy leaned out, catching sight of Andy's car as he sped hurriedly away. Then the older woman turned and stared at Wendy, her eyes widening in apprehension as she whispered with deep concern, "Oh, Wendy. What have you done?"

Chapter 17

Burt Phelps was just closing his old fashioned manual cash register and bidding Elvira Picket a very good morning as she walked out of the hardware store with her new living room blinds, when Cash, Yamato and Tinker entered the front door. The front door bell jangled furiously as each of the three law officers entered the shop, nodding politely to Elvira as she nodded in tacit acknowledgement and left.

Burt's eyes spied Tinker, and narrowed automatically. The smile from his face vanished as well as he came around the counter to meet the chief of police.

"I already told you, Tinker LaGrange, I ain't movin' my equipment," huffed Burt, crossing his arms resolutely and staring at the young lawman with exasperation. "A man's got to make a livin' and to do that, I got to display my farm equipment. Ain't no use askin' again. You'll get the same answer as last time."

Tinker glanced back uneasily at Cash, who stepped around the chief of police and extended his hand with an easy smile to the shopkeeper, "Good morning, Mr. Phelps. Remember me?"

For a moment, Burt Phelps squinted thoughtfully at the sheriff, then a large grin spread across his weathered face, and he declared loudly, "Well I'll be jiggered if it ain't little Cash Green, Stew and Leana's son! How are you son?"

Cash shook Burt's hand heartily, and nodded, looking the old shopkeeper straight in the eye, "I haven't been called little in quite awhile, Mr. Phelps, but it's certainly good to see you again."

Burt Phelps shook his head, gazing at Cash, animated and obviously delighted to see him, "I'll bet I haven't seen you for almost twenty years, Cash! Your dad and I used to do business all the time."

Burt suddenly sobered up and his eyes showed a mix of compassion and remorse, "I miss your dad, son. I went to his funeral and paid my respects. He was always as honest as the day is long and he was a good friend."

Burt glanced into Cash's gray eyes, "I hear you're a lot like him. That's good. The world can use more honest and caring men. Men you can count on to do the right thing." Burt looked over meaningfully at Tinker, his scowl returning for a moment.

Cash nodded kind-heartedly, "My dad always counted you as a good friend as well, Mr. Phelps. I heard him speak of you often when I was younger."

Burt turned his attention to Yamato, and his smile sprang back into action, as he reached out a hand and inquired, "And who is this lovely young lady?"

Yamato shook the shopkeeper's hand enthusiastically, with a twinkle in her eye and a lopsided grin on her face. "Good to meet you, Mr. Phelps! I'm Ericka Yamato, Cash's deputy from The Falls."

Ericka glanced around the old fashioned hardware store and remarked, "Great store, Mr. Phelps! I love that you kept it just as it was decades ago. Really gives a wonderful atmosphere to it."

Burt preened slightly, his chest swelling up a bit and

he smiled graciously, "Good of you to say, Miss Yamato. I've tried to keep it just like my daddy would have been proud of. It's my pride and joy."

Cash leaned against the counter and tipped his hat back, staring carefully at the old shopkeeper, "Mr. Phelps. I know you respect the truth and a man who tells you the truth so I'll get right down to why we're here."

Old Bert Phelps glanced from Tinker to Yamato and back to Cash again, his thoughts racing, his face impassive, patiently waiting to hear what the sheriff of The Falls had to say.

"I understand how proud you are of your store and the tradition that's gone into it," Cash began, glancing around appreciatively at the well-kept country hardware store. "My dad was the same way. He always took great pride in his own store. His shop was always neat, clean and he always tried to give the community the best goods and service he possibly could."

Cash nodded and glanced back at Bert Phelps, "My dad would be proud of what you've done here, Mr. Phelps."

Bert Phelps' eyes welled up with unshed tears as he tried to maintain his composure.

Cash continued, quietly, respectfully, "But it seems that there's about to be a problem, Mr. Phelps." Cash was staring into the old man's eyes.

Bert Phelps' eyes narrowed and bit and he replied, "What kind of a problem, son?"

"The town council and the mayor have ordered the chief to persuade you to move the large pieces of farm equipment on your property. If he can't do that, they told him they would do it legally."

Cash continued to hold the old man's gaze, his gray

eyes open and honest, "The merchants on Main Street have all complained that the farm equipment is creating an unsightly nuisance and interfering with their businesses."

Cash continued to hold the old man's gaze, "Now, Chief of Police LaGrange doesn't want to do this. He respects your property rights and your God given freedoms. But he has no choice in the matter. It's his job."

Bert started fidgeting, glancing back and forth between Cash and Tinker, his thoughts unsettled as he continued to listen.

"But the chief asked Yamato and I if there was anything we could do to help, which was very smart of him." Cash glanced back at Tinker with a concealed wink, then gazed back at Bert, a smile starting to creep across his lips. His eyes twinkled as he continued, with a bit more enthusiasm, "I think I may have a solution."

Burt stared at Cash, unsure if he should stubbornly start bellowing about his freedoms or if he should hear the sheriff out. He decided to do the latter.

"Kasmir and Ivan Rostov have a piece of land with a large well constructed barn about a mile out of Brown Bear Junction that's been deserted for over five years. They used it to house beef cattle, but then moved the cattle to another one of their barns up north a few years ago. That lot is closer, and more accessible to the railroad."

Cash smiled broadly at the old shopkeeper whose eyes were filling with understanding, as he finally realized where Cash was going with his conversation, "Anyway, I talked to Kasmir and they are looking around to rent out the property, at a fair rate," Cash winked at Burt, "and they're quite anxious to do so. In fact, Mr.

Phelps, I'd be willing to bet they'd jump at an opportunity to rent it out."

Burt smiled as well, nodding his head, finally beginning to enjoy the discussion, "Well! That sounds like just the thing! I'd much rather have all the big machinery out where customers could walk around and really get a good look at it. I'll admit that. It's been pretty crowded in my yard and I've lost more than one sale from customers not being able to see the goods they're interested in as well as they like."

Burton Phelps paced back and forth, rubbing his scruffy chin, "Yes! That could work. Now if I could get the phone number of..."

Cash held out a slip of paper with Kasmir and Ivan's cell phones, handing it with a smile and a wink to the now enthusiastic storeowner.

As Cash and Burt Phelps shook hands heartily, a look of unconcealed relief swept across Tinker LaGrange's face. Yamato had to stifle a grin as she and Tinker stepped forward to shake hands with the delighted shopkeeper as well.

"No hard feelings, chief?" Burton Phelps asked with a broad smile as he squeezed Tinker's hand and pumped it energetically.

"Absolutely not, Mr. Phelps!" chuckled the chief of police, "I'm just glad we could find a happy solution to everything!" Tinker glanced back at Cash and Yamato, his gratitude evident.

"Well then, chief," declared Burt as he walked back behind the counter, the phone numbers in his hand, "don't be a stranger around here! Have a great day!"

Burton stopped for a moment and turned his gaze onto Cash, and spoke in a low, quiet, almost reverent tone, "And Cash Green, I do believe your daddy would be proud of who you are and what you're doin'."

Cash nodded gratefully, his eyes filled with unspoken appreciation, as he turned quietly and walked toward the door.

"And Miss Yamato? It's always wonderful to have such a beautiful lady come and visit! Don't let it be the last time, you hear?" Burton Phelps winked bodaciously and grinned at the beautiful deputy. Yamato laughed delightedly and just as bodaciously returned the wink.

***

Andy Morrison squealed the tires of his car on the wet, icy pavement as he came to a sudden stop outside the home of Elizabeth Fallon. The house was about a mile and a half outside Brown Bear Junction, about halfway between The Junction and The Falls on a five acre piece of land. The property was somewhat rundown and had three buildings on it. There was the main rambling farmhouse, a large shed that Benjamin Fallon had used for a woodworking shop, and a medium sized barn where Benjamin had stored his inventory of handmade wood furniture. At the moment, snow and ice covered the landscape, with a few small, narrow paths shoveled out to enable Elizabeth to come and go between the three buildings.

As Andy rushed up the sidewalk, his heart pounding, he had enough sense to hesitate a moment, attempting to calm himself down on the front porch before he knocked.

The young lawyer, taking a deep breath and not wanting to seem too emotional, knocked three times in rapid succession. No answer. He waited a few moments and then knocked again. Still no answer.

Andy peeked through the small windowpane in the front door and saw nothing but a few indistinct shapes of furniture in the semi-gloom of the interior. He moved toward the side of the porch and stared in the window, his hands cupping his face to enable him to see inside a little better. He now had a good view of the living room and the kitchen beyond that, but still could see no lights or any sign of Elizabeth. Beginning to be a little more concerned about Elizabeth's welfare, Andy decided to check around back.

The young lawyer moved quickly down a narrow, shoveled path. The snow banks on either side of the path were easily up to his waist. As he walked quickly around to the rear of the building, he spotted the back door. Next to the door were the garbage bins and then, three or four paces directly across from the back door was the entry to the large woodworking shop.

As Andy uneasily climbed the rickety steps to the back porch, his mind began to come up with every terrible scenario possible. Could Tinmouth Pritchard have followed Elizabeth and kidnapped her? What if her car had broken down out on a little used rural road? What if she had come home in despair after his sister's visit with her, shot herself, and was lying on the floor inside the house, bleeding out as he knocked helplessly on her door?

He knocked with more urgency on the old back door. He noticed the peeling paint on the doorframe and the general lack of maintenance around the whole house and yard. In his precise, ordered head, he was already creating a plan to get Elizabeth's house repaired and brought up to snuff when he hear a sharp twang from the direction of the shed.

Suddenly, he felt as though had had been struck sharply with a fist in the middle of his back. Glancing down, his eyes widened in shock as he saw the sharp head of an arrow sticking out of his body. Almost in slow motion, he reached out to tentatively brush the sharp edges of the arrowhead with his finger. There was blood on the arrowhead. Suddenly the realization that it was his blood made him feel weak in the knees.

He crumpled in sections, first his knees giving way until he was kneeling. Then he slowly pitched forward, turning awkwardly as he fell, finally landing on his side. As he lay there, he felt his heart pumping wildly. He desperately tried to dig his cell phone out of his pocket. As his fingers shakily tried to dial 911, his vision clouded over and vanished. Finally, feeling very drowsy and sensing the beginnings of a deep ache in his chest and back, he lay still, his blood darkening the snow covered walk.

Andy didn't hear the quiet footsteps going away, nor did he hear the car entering the driveway a minute or two later. His face relaxed and his fingers opened, releasing the cell phone into the snow.

"Emergency hotline," came a distant voice muffled in the covering of white. "How can we help you?"

***

"Many thanks for today," grinned Tinker, hoisting a cup of coffee and saluting Cash and Yamato, "you sure as heck saved my butt!"

Cash smiled back, standing next to the old wood stove in the police station, "No problem, my friend, we just happened to know someone who could supply what Burton Phelps wanted: a place to sell his farm equipment where there wasn't a problem attached."

Yamato walked over to the front window and gazed up and down Main Street, "Now all the merchants, the town council, the mayor, Burton Phelps and you can be happy. A real win-win, Chief."

"Which reminds me, boss," Yamato turned and glanced at Cash, "we left Horace holding down the fort and by now he's probably getting a bit fidgety because we're not there."

Cash sighed and reached for his heavy winter coat, "That's true, Yamato. We'd best be going Chief. Thanks for the coffee and pie."

Tinker nodded, stood up and moved toward the front door, walking along with Cash and Yamato, glancing at both of them earnestly, "Just remember, if I can ever be of any help to you, all you have to do is call. Thanks again. I really appreciate it."

The phone rang and a moment later Myrna Lynn Jones called out from her desk behind the front counter, "Chief, just got a 911 call, but no one was on the other end of the line."

All three of the law officers stopped in their tracks and stared at Myrna. "Can you trace the call, Myrna?" asked Tinker, walking briskly toward her desk.

"Well, I suppose we could try, but I'll have to call it in to the state police and see what they can do. Then again it could take forever, boss. It ain't as easy as the crime dramas on TV make it out to be, y'know." Myrna stared cynically at her young boss over her glasses, waiting for his response.

"Call 'em, Myrna," Tinker nodded affirmatively, "tell them it's a priority."

Myrna shook her head, sulkily punching in the numbers for the state police mobile crime lab, all the while grumbling, "It's just as likely old Mable Humphreys calling in a 911 about the stray toms after her precious Angora pussycat, Maybelline, again!"

Before Myrna could finish dialing, the phone rang again. Myrna answered it, and glanced meaningfully over at Tinker, who was staring intently at his dispatcher.

"It's Elizabeth Fallon, out on Route 271A. She's calling in a shooting," Myrna relayed the message, pausing at times between words.

Cash, Yamato and Tinker all were in high gear. Tinker grabbed his coat and weapon as he blurted out, "Route 271A. That's a shared jurisdiction between The Junction and The Falls."

Cash called out over his shoulder as he raced out the front door, Yamato close behind him, "Figured we'd handle it together, Chief! See you there! Myrna, call Doc Stone and have him meet us there and call out The Junction's EMTs. Thanks Myrna!"

As the door sung shut leaving Myrna alone in the office, she glanced up wide-eyed from the phone and called out to no one in particular, "But the shooting wasn't done with a gun! It was with a bow and arrow!"

Chapter 18

Doc Stone stood in the cold winter air, his breath coming out in a light mist as he stared at the EMTs hurriedly carrying Andy Morrison toward their rescue vehicle. His glove-covered hands were covered in blood. The blood had spattered up onto his parka as well as he had worked feverishly to remove the arrow and stop the bleeding. After a moment, he turned and glanced at his friend, Cash Green, his eyes wide with agitation.

"I can't believe it. Andy was just at our house for dinner. He seemed so happy and at ease. And now this..." Doc stripped the gloves off his hands and disgustedly shoved them in a biohazard bag. His face was pale and it was obvious that the attack on his young friend had truly disturbed him.

Cash moved a little closer to Doc, glancing back at Yamato and Tinker LaGrange as they continued to tape off and work the crime scene. Elizabeth Fallon stood on her back porch, her eyes wide and unfocused. She was staring anxiously at the metal stretcher that was being carefully stowed inside the emergency vehicle. Elizabeth was tightly clutching her parka around her, shivering noticeably. Cash assessed correctly that her shivering was more shock induced than cold related.

Dr. Meg Monroe was busy supervising the EMTs as they secured the patient in the vehicle. It was obvious from her intense focus and the way she curtly admonished the EMTs when they didn't get everything just so in their treatment of the unconscious lawyer that she was in a slight state of shock herself.

"Doc, it's never easy," Cash spoke quietly and calmly to his longtime friend, "but when it's a friend or a relative, our emotions simply go off the charts. It's natural to feel that way."

Doc turned and stared at Cash for a moment, hesitated and then nodded, "It gets harder every year to deal with people we know and care about, Cash. I guess I'm just getting soft." Doc's voice trailed away as he glanced down at the medical bag he was packing up.

Cash reached out and placed his hand on Doc's shoulder, "No, Doc," the sheriff whispered fiercely, "you're getting better. You care that much more. That's the way it should be."

Cash's gray eyes flashed with emotion as he continued, "I'm proud of you, Doc. You are one of the few people I truly respect, trust and care about. And that's as good as it gets."

With a hearty pat on the back, Cash caught Doc's eyes for a moment and gave him a quick, meaningful nod. As the sheriff of The Falls moved off to consult with Tinker and Yamato, Doc Stone stared after him for a moment. Then he nodded to himself, a little strength creeping back into his eyes. With a slight smile playing around his chapped lips, Doc Stone hurried off toward the old hospital van.

"There are footprints in the snow," Yamato was telling Tinker as Cash approached the two of them, "that head off toward the woods. Tough to tell, but they appear to be average size, looks like work boots of some kind. There are some other footprints around the back building and to and from the road, but they look as though they are small, a woman's. They're probably Elizabeth Fallon's." She took several more digital photos of the prints.

"These woods are on the edge of the forest that heads on up toward the mountain," Brown Bear Junction's police chief replied thoughtfully, as he stared toward the tall mountain that lay halfway between The Junction and The Falls.

Cash interjected, "And there are lots of old ramshackle lean-tos and cabins where somebody experienced in the woods could hide out." The sheriff stared expressively at both Yamato and Tinker. "That means we've got some tracking to do. I've called Sergeant McNealy of the Vermont State Police and asked him to meet us here with one of his canine units to help us trail whoever did this."

"I think I know who that might be, sheriff," a soft, deep voice came from in back of the three law officers. They turned and there stood C.R. Shanks.

"I believe I have information that could help your investigation, sheriff, chief," the tall private investigator nodded politely at Yamato and then to Cash and Tinker. "I heard the call on the police scanner," C.R. added, as he noticed each of the law officers staring at him dubiously, "and thought I might be of some use."

By the time Sergeant McNealy and the canine unit had arrived, C. R. had briefed Cash, Yamato and Tinker on the events involving Elizabeth Fallon, Andy Morrison and Tinmouth Pritchard. The sheriff, deputy and chief of police had asked enough questions to alleviate their skepticism towards the intent and sincerity of the tall private investigator and Cash had even requested C.R.'s help in tracking the attacker.

"Seems like we're always meeting under solemn circumstances, sheriff," puffed Sergeant McNealy as he hefted a backpack out of the back of his state police cruiser and shook Cash's hand firmly.

"That's the truth, sergeant," replied Cash, nodding in agreement. Then he stared into the burly sergeant's eyes and added, "But I'm always grateful that you're there, McNealy. You know how much I appreciate your help. Good to see you."

A curt but friendly nod was McNealy's standard response. The muscular sergeant turned and called out, "Duffy! C'mon over here."

"This is Corporal Duffy and this," McNealy smiled and knelt down on one knee to greet the canine unit, his chest puffing up with pride, "is the best nose in the business! Stanley, meet Sheriff Green, Deputy Yamato and Chief LaGrange!" McNealy stroked the dog's broad shoulders tenderly, glancing proudly up at the three law officers.

Taking his cue from the sergeant, Cash knelt down and ruffled the bloodhound's ears gently, staring at the shiny coat and intelligent gaze in the deep brown eyes, "Good to meet you Stanley."

"Good to meet you Sergeant. I gotta' ask about the dog's name. Why Stanley?" asked Tinker curiously, obviously cautiously admiring the bloodhound from a few feet away.

Corporal Duffy spoke up, "He's named after the British adventurer who found Dr. Livingston, of course sir." When a blank look appeared on Tinker's face, Duffy grinned and added, "You know Chief, as in 'Doctor Livingston, I presume?'"

As Tinker shook his head, still blissfully unaware of the reference, Cash smiled and stood up. In the meantime, Yamato had hurriedly retrieved an emergency first aid kit from the back of her cruiser and had rejoined the group. "We're ready to go when you are, boss," she announced, her dark eyes set and determined.

For the first hour and a half, Stanley guided the group through wooded snowdrifts and snow covered fields, busily sniffing and snuffling as they headed closer and closer to the base of the mountain. The footprints came and went in the blustery wind, shifting snow, ice and forest debris, but the bloodhound's focus never wavered.

Stopping for a well-needed five-minute rest, Cash sidled closer to where C.R. Shanks was leaning against the trunk of a tall pine. The sheriff took a deep swig from his canteen and offered it to C.R. who accepted it gratefully.

"So, you think the animosity between Morrison and Pritchard could be strong enough for him to take this drastic an action?" Cash asked quietly, his intelligent gray eyes observing the tall Private eye carefully.

Shanks swallowed and shrugged, "I'm not much of a betting man, Sheriff Green, but I'd say that Tinmouth Pritchard was a very spiteful, determined man. The fact that he would try and intimidate Elizabeth Fallon and then get furious with Morrison and me when we went to talk to him shows me two things. First, that the man is capable of physical violence. Second, he has focused all the trouble and bad luck in his life into one incident: his loss of wages from Benjamin Fallon. In his mind, he figures that's the root of all the evil in his life. Elizabeth Fallon and then Andy Morrison stood between him and getting his money. That, to me, makes him a dangerous man."

Cash stared at the big man for a moment, and then pulled out his cell phone, a look of concern spreading across his face, "Darlene? It's me, Cash. Please have Horace go over and pick up Elizabeth Fallon immediately. He's to make sure she stays at the sheriff's office until we get back. Yup, it's urgent. Thanks, Darlene."

Yamato had been listening attentively, "What's up boss?" she asked leaning over toward him. Her dark eyes were filled with unknown apprehension, just from the sensations she was picking up from Cash.

"Elizabeth Fallon is alone at her house, Yamato," Cash whispered earnestly. "What if we're wrong, and Pritchard doubles back and..."

"Got it, boss," Yamato nodded, a frown creasing her smooth brow. "You want me to go back? I can make it back there in about forty, forty-five minutes?"

Cash considered for a moment and then slowly shook his head no. If Tinmouth Pritchard was on his way back to Elizabeth's house, forty minutes would be too late.

***

Andy Morrison's face was pale and drained. The truth was that his face was only two or three shades darker than the sterile white sheets on his hospital bed. He was lying motionless in the critical care unit of the West Sugar Shack Regional Medical Facility.

Clustered around the side of his bed were several medical monitors and displays. There was everything from machines displaying basic monitoring of oxygen level and blood pressure to an ECG and an EEG. Numerous tubes and wires twisted out from the machines and ended up in or on Andy as he lay unconscious.

Standing next to the young lawyer was Meg Monroe. She had worked feverishly on the young man and now kept returning to his room every few minutes to check up on him. After listening to his heart for the twentieth time since the young lawyer had been admitted, she took the stethoscope away from her ears and wrapped it automatically around her neck once again.

Meg stared down at the motionless Andy Morrison in the hospital bed and painfully remembered the charming, young, and delightful young man at the dinner party at Jordan's a few night before. Meg frowned. She remembered the kiss on her cheek at the end of the wonderful evening. She frowned deeper. From that scene her memory immediately shifted to how disappointed and rejected Andy had sounded on the phone when she had told him that their relationship was not to be. Meg kept returning guiltily to the fact that she had, although innocently and inadvertently, hurt the young man emotionally. For caring, compassionate Meg, that was a heavy burden to bear.

Meg shook her head, frowning even deeper, blaming herself for hurting the young lawyer. On some level, she even wondered if she might have helped cause him to be here now, on this bed, in critical condition. She knew that it was a crazy thought, but somehow, seeing him lying there, she couldn't help feeling it.

Meg shook her head again, her stubbornness and determination winning out over her guilt and remorse for past actions. She reached out and touched the young man's shoulder, needing for a moment to grab onto something real. Then, with a determined but resigned set to her jaw, she strode purposely out of the critical care ward and picked up one of the hospital wall phones.

The phone rang in Treasured Memories. Mandy was out in the back room, restocking some of the small items that usually sold quickly in the shop. Wendy Morrison had just returned to the shop after running over to the post office to pick up the mail. She placed the amount for one more sale down in accounts receivable and then turned from her accounting ledger and picked up the phone.

"Treasured Memories. What treasure can we help you find today?" Wendy spoke cheerfully, a smile brightening her face.

As Wendy listened, her smile vanished and the twinkle in her eyes suddenly went out. Wendy staggered against the counter, reaching out with her free hand to grip the shelf tightly as her knees buckled and her stomach flipped wildly over.

Sitting down awkwardly in the chair behind the counter, she grasped the phone with both hands, her breath coming in short gasps. She managed to answer questions that she was asked from time to time, but with short, staccato monosyllables. When the call was over, she sat holding the phone in a death grip as the busy signal rang across the shop, over and over again.

Finally, Mandy came back in, carrying a box filled with replacement treasures. It only took one glance to know that something very wrong was happening to her boss and friend.

"Wendy! What is it?" Mandy asked loudly, placing the overloaded box carelessly on the counter. Several small items on the top cascaded out of the box and landed on the glass counter with a shrill ping.

Racing around the corner of the counter as fast as possible, Mandy grabbed the phone from Wendy, heard the busy signal and hung up. Then she pulled Wendy to her feet and held her gently in her strong, caring arms.

"Wendy, what is it? What's wrong? Talk to me!" Mandy whispered hoarsely, staring anxiously at her boss.

Wendy's eyes focused for a moment as she turned and stared wide-eyed at her friend and employee, uttering a rasping, horrified whisper, "Andy's in the hospital. He's been shot!"

***

Horace Scofield was having a bad day. He had stayed up late, disregarding his wife's admonitions to come to bed, in order to watch a suspenseful mystery on TV. Staggering wearily to his bedroom, he found two of his kids snuggled in with his wife and no room for him anywhere in the bed. Grabbing a blanket from the linen closet, he headed back to the living room where he twisted and turned on the couch for several hours trying to get to sleep, only to have his seven-year-old son come and delightedly jump on him with great gusto an hour before sunrise.

With less than an hour's worth of real sleep, his eyes red and his back sore, Horace desperately tried to get back into his wife's good graces by volunteering to make school lunches for all the kids. As they grabbed their lunches and headed out the door, his kids glanced curiously into their brown paper bags and raised their eyebrows. Their father had packed them lunches that were very different from their mom's usual homey style.

Each bag contained a bag of chips, a sandwich made of two pieces of white bread and a slab of leftover meatloaf with no condiments, a juice box and a large hunk of extra sharp cheddar cheese from Rostov's Dairy. Each of them was perhaps an adequate lunch for

Horace, but not a lunch that any of his kids would be begging to consume. Thankfully, to his children's credit, they only stared at each other for a moment, quietly thanked their dad and went on their way to catch the bus.

Glancing at the clock, Horace realized that not only would he be late to work, but that he would have to skip breakfast, his favorite meal of the day. Then, once he was at work, Horace had gotten the message that he was to 'hold the fort' while Cash and Yamato were off gallivanting over in Brown Bear Junction. His stomach complaining loudly, he had to handle not only Widow Campbell's complaint about raccoons raiding her birdfeeder, but Viola Brigham's rant concerning the teenagers who had been smoking in back of her barn and left cigarette butts all over the place.

A disgruntled Darlene had then put him to work cleaning up the pile of unfinished reports he had stacked on his desk, knowing that no matter how he tried, he could never get his reports to meet Darlene's lofty standards.

On top of that, Cash's urgent call had come in for him to race over and pick up Elizabeth Fallon as quickly as possible. Horace had grabbed a cold cup of coffee and jumped in the car, doing his best to follow Cash's orders. But halfway there, he swerved to miss a rabbit in the road and spilled half of the cold coffee all over the front of his deputy's parka.

As he drove the last half-mile to the Fallon's place he glanced up from trying to wipe up the mess only to find his cruiser halfway over into the other lane of the snow covered road. To make matters worse, an old rattletrap of a truck was heading straight toward him. His eyes widening with surprise and alarm, the deputy swerved violently back to his side of the road. In the process he successfully managed to spill the rest of the coffee in his mug all over the passenger's side seat.

The old rattletrap truck rumbled by on the other side of the road as Horace simply sighed and gave up. It was finally evident to him that no matter what he did, or how he did it, today was a total calamity in every way. Resigning himself to the inevitability of the situation, Horace pulled into the Fallon's driveway. After a brief attempt to at least clean off the passenger's side seat so Elizabeth could sit down, Horace climbed out of his cruiser and walked up to the front porch.

Several knocks on the front door brought no answer, so Horace tentatively tried the doorknob. It was unlocked. Horace opened the door slowly calling out, "Miss Fallon? It's Deputy Scofield from The Falls' Sheriff's Department. Hello?"

No one answered him back so he walked inside, and tried again, "Miss Fallon? Elizabeth Fallon? It's Deputy Scofield and I'm supposed to pick you up and bring you to the sheriff's office. Are you here? Miss Fallon?"

A quick but thorough search of the house revealed nothing and no one. Horace glanced out the window. There was a car in the back driveway, presumably Elizabeth Fallon's. He walked briskly out to the cruiser and called the license number in, quickly finding out that it was indeed hers.

Horace took stock of the situation and did the only thing he could. He called Cash.

"Boss? I'm at Elizabeth Fallon's house, and there's no one here. Her car is in the driveway, I ran the plates. The house is unlocked." Horace waited and listened intently.

"Did you check outside?" came back Cash's winded

voice.

"Affirmative, Boss, nothing," replied the deputy.

"Did you see anybody near the house on your way in?" Cash asked breathing as though he had been running hard through the snow.

"Nope, just a rabbit. I swerved to miss it and spilled my coffee. Then I was trying to clean my jacket and..." as Horace recounted the incident, a light bulb went on in Horace's sleep deprived brain.

"Wait! There was an old truck that went by going the other way!" Horace's tone raised an octave as it often did when he was excited or stressed.

"Yeah! The truck was about a half a mile from the house," Horace was already jogging back out of the house toward his cruiser, "That happened about ten minutes ago!"

"Did you see who was in it?" Cash asked, his voice quieter and obviously more intense.

"No boss I honestly didn't. You see, I was, um, t-t-trying to keep from hitting the truck," Horace stammered guiltily. "I was trying to clean up the coffee spill. And..."

Suddenly realizing that Cash didn't really want to hear about anything but the facts, Horace stopped and began again, "No, I didn't get a look at anyone inside the truck, boss."

Horace hesitated slightly and earnestly added, "I'm sorry boss."

Cash spoke calmly and quietly, "That doesn't matter now, Horace. Get on the road. Go as fast as you can safely, but don't use the lights and siren. No use spooking Tinmouth Pritchard if that indeed is his truck."

"Tinmouth Pritchard?" replied Horace inquisitively as he quickly climbed into the cruiser and pulled out into the snowy road, "Isn't that the old guy who shacks up in deserted hunting cabins out in the woods?"

"That's him Horace. He may very well have Elizabeth Fallon with him. If you find them, don't try and apprehend them, just keep watch and stay with them. Check in with me every five minutes, understood?"

Cash sounded like he was running again, "We'll catch up with you in about fifteen minutes if we're lucky. Horace, this is important. Tinmouth may have taken the Fallon girl against her will. She may be in danger." Cash's voice was deep and solemn as he continued, "He might be the one who shot Andy Morrison, Horace. Take all precautions. Understand?"

Horace gulped audibly and then his jaw set with pride and determination, "Understood sheriff. I'll take all precautions. Deputy Scofield, Over and out."

Chapter 19

Wendy Morrison sat in the waiting room at the hospital, her hands were motionless in her lap and her head bowed over. Her eyes were shut and teardrops were slowly falling down her cheeks and landing silently on her hands. Beside her sat Mandy Wagner. Mandy kept glancing over at the door to the critical care unit whenever she allowed her eyes to move away from her friend and boss.

Dr. Meg Monroe had met with the two women when they first had arrived at the West Sugar Shack Falls Regional Medical Facility. Dr. Monroe had been brief and to the point, explaining to Wendy and Mandy that her main concern at the moment was to keep close watch on Andy. The doctor had told Wendy that her brother was in critical condition and that although the arrowhead had almost miraculously missed Andy's heart, it had nicked or cut several major arteries and organs.

Mandy had noticed how worried and intense the young doctor was and had remained relatively quiet, letting Wendy talk to the doctor during the short time she had met with them.

Now, Mandy couldn't help but feel that Wendy was near the edge of her sanity. Wendy had almost completely shut down after the young doctor left. It had been all Mandy could do to get Wendy over to a chair before she slumped over and closed her eyes. Mandy had come to the decision that she needed to talk with the young doctor the very next time she walked briskly by, monitoring Andy's condition. In Mandy's opinion, Wendy needed emotional help, soon.

In the critical care wing, Meg was on the speakerphone with Cash, her eyes staring through the heavy glass window into the next room where Andy Morrison lay unconscious. Doc Stone stood by her side, leaning up against the desk, alternately glancing in at Andy and attentively listening to his young colleague.

"Yes, missed the heart but nicked several other blood vessels and organs. We had to suture up several other arteries and veins, and the blades of the broadhead arrow did a massive amount of damage to the surrounding tissue," Meg frowned slightly, tying to catch most of Cash's words as his voice wavered in and out. The sheriff was obviously in an area with poor cell phone coverage.

Doc joined in, "Cash, the arrows were specially made. They weren't store bought, but handmade by using various handpicked components. I've had a little experience with archery. Both my brothers hunt with bows, make their own arrows and are nuts about making them very precisely. Many real bow hunters are."

"Can you tell me anything about the arrow you took out of Andy? Something that might be helpful for identification purposes when we catch up with the person who shot Andy, Doc?" The phone crackled and faded in and out as Cash spoke.

Doc glanced at Meg, then down at the arrow they had cut and removed from Andy. It lay on the desk in a plastic evidence bag. "Sure. The fletching is made from Turkey feathers. The arrowhead is a fixed four blade broadhead."

"Fixed?" came back Cash's reply.

"Yes. Broadheads can either be fixed, which means they are stationary, or they can be mechanical. In mechanical arrowheads, the blades lie almost flat to the shaft of the arrow until they hit something. Then the blades expand violently into the quarry once it hits its target, doing a great deal of damage. That type of head doesn't penetrate as far as a fixed broadhead, but they almost always kill what they hit. Andy's probably lucky this arrow wasn't mechanical."

Doc continued, "The shaft is a carbon fiber outer with an aluminum core. This particular shaft has medium stiffness, medium 'spine'. That means it's flexible, but still fairly stiff. The brand name on the shaft is Tru-Flight, which is used a lot here in New England. The model is an 'Elite' and it's a dark green color."

"Doc, I had no idea what a font of information you were on archery," Cash's voice sounded very far away.

"Well, you listen to your hunting crazed brothers go on and on for twenty years, you're bound to pick up something," Doc responded with a wry smile.

"Meg, Doc?" came back Cash's voice a bit stronger now.

"Yes?" Meg responded quietly, her eyes still staring through the heavy glass at the pale body on the hospital bed. She looked worn and spent, as if she had aged ten years.

Cash's voice was suddenly low and apprehensive, "How's he doing?" Doc glanced down at the phone as he listened. Doc had known Cash so many years he could actually visualize the look in his friend's piercing gray eyes as he asked that vital question.

Meg hesitated and spoke calmly, professionally, "Critical, not quite stable. The next few hours should tell us a lot. I'm checking him every few minutes. Doc is helping me with the other patients in the hospital so I can be there to watch any changes. We'll let you know as we go along. No promises, Cash. That arrow did a lot of damage."

Cash hesitated a moment and then replied, "Thanks. Keep me posted."

Meg's eyes flashed with anger and an unspoken fury for a moment as she leaned over and whispered into the phone, "Make sure you get the person who did this Cash. Frankly, I'd like to see whoever it is brought back in a body bag."

Doc Stone's eyes widened in shock and surprise as he stared over at his unerringly caring, thoughtful, and tender colleague. Quickly deciding that now was not the best time to broach the subject of why her change of heart, Doc simply coughed and turned away. As he did so, he glanced out into the waiting room.

It was empty.

***

Newt Anderson and Remy Renquist were walking briskly up West Street toward the town square. They were bundled up in their new cold weather gear. Since Newt and Remy had lived most of their lives in England and Scotland, they were still relative neophytes to the frozen, snow-covered winters in New England. They tended to severely overdress, just in case. They each had a goose down parka, fluffy earmuffs, thick ski hats and their parka hoods pulled up over their heads. In addition, they wore ski pants over their jeans, tall thermal boots and sported specially designed gloves that were intended to keep your hands warm at a minus fifty degrees Fahrenheit.

Although they were as snug and warm as a bug in a rug, the locals had taken to smiling and shaking their heads at the overdressed Brits. Many older New Englanders made it a point of pride to wear as little as possible, to show their disdain and determination not to let their frigid winter weather get the best of them. Needless to say, there were more than a few witty comments whispered about Newt and Remy's getups. But the simple fact was the townsfolk loved the two Brits so dearly, they had never once been teased or joshed about their outerwear to their faces.

Remy and Newt had left Dream Rides a few minutes earlier, and were trudging along in the snow toward Tina's Diner for a late lunch. Dream Rides was the creative masterpiece of the two Brits and their partner, Drake McKiernan. The huge store was split in two by an absolutely magnificent manmade stream and waterfall. On one side, Drake sold Harleys. On the other, Newt and Remy sold hot air balloons, parts and rides. Together, the store sold adventures and their catchy slogan was "Where the Adventure of a lifetime begins!"

"It's still bloody cold!" complained Remy, glancing over at his chum, peering through the front of his parka hood. "You'd think it would at least thaw a bit for Valentine's Day!"

Newt chuckled, and shook his head, "I don't think it works that way, me Bucko! Winter's here for awhile yet."

"Since the bloody squirrel saw his shadow that means there's six more weeks of winter, right?" Remy plodded on, his tone obviously dismal.

"That's what Jeb and Zeke told us. Remember they

had that party at the video game store and everyone watched Punxsutawney Phil come out of his den on TV? Phil saw his shadow. That means six more weeks of winter." Newt turned and watched several cars go by, as he smiled and waved.

"And it's a groundhog," Newt added.

"What's a groundhog?" Remy replied, turning to stare at his friend with a quizzical look on his face.

"Phil is a groundhog, not a squirrel," explained Newt patiently.

"Squirrel! Groundhog! All I know is its going to be bloody cold and snowy for six more weeks!" Remy huffed as he shook his head and resolutely kicked a piece of ice left over from someone's shoveling. The piece of ice went skittering out into the road just as an old rattletrap truck rumbled by, heading down West Street toward Route 4 and the interstate.

The hunk of ice was crushed immediately beneath the nearest front tire of the well-worn truck. Instinctively, both Newt and Remy glanced up at the driver of the old truck. Remy wanted to wave a 'sorry!' gesture about the ice chunk to the driver, Newt looked simply out of natural curiosity.

The driver was an old man with a camouflage hunting jacket on. In the passenger seat there was a young woman, her face pale and obviously frightened. In the driver's right hand he held a handgun and it was pointed directly at the young woman's face. The image only lasted a second or two, but it was dramatically imprinted on both Brits. They turned and stared at the old truck as it went by, then glanced at each other. The intense cold and the wintry weather were immediately forgotten.

"Bollocks! Did you see the same thing I did?" asked

Remy, his eyes wide in shock, the words tumbling quickly out of his mouth.

"A girl with a bloody gun to her head? I certainly did!" declared Newt as he pulled his cell phone out of his pocket, ripped off his glove and punched in 911.

Remy stared after the fast disappearing truck as Newt spoke into his phone, his voice firm and loud, "Yes, Miss Darlene? It's Newt here, dear. Yes, I'm quite well, thank you. But Darlene, Remy and I want to report a truck headed out toward Route 4."

Newt listened for a second, shook his head and continued, "No, the truck's not the issue, Dear Lady. There's a girl being held hostage in it! The old guy driving had a bloomin' gun to her head! Yes Ma'am, a handgun. She was white as a sheet!"

Remy turned back to his friend, his eyes twinkling, and announced proudly, "Tell her I got the bloody license plate as well, chum!"

***

Tinmouth Pritchard was focused on one thing. Getting what was due to him. Well, in essence what had been due to him for all these years. Each year that had gone by since he left his job with Ben Fallon, he had gotten more and more bitter about it. Each year he had gotten a little more determined to get even and get the money he felt he was owed. At this point, after so many years of living alone in the woods, drifting from one deserted hunting cabin to the next, living by his wits and hunting skills, it was his only focus, his only goal in life. Nothing else mattered.

He glanced over at Ben Fallon's daughter as she sat shivering and terrified in his passenger seat. He had gotten around that upstart lawyer who had tried to keep him from dealing properly with Fallon's daughter.

Now, it was time to deal with the girl. Time to get what was rightfully his.

Tinmouth glanced in the rearview mirror. He spotted two men in parkas as they turned and stared in surprise and shock at his truck as it left town. He saw one of the men pull out a cell phone as he continued to stare at the rapidly disappearing vehicle.

Tinmouth glanced down at the old Ruger P89 pistol that he had bought back in 1993 and a buzzer went off in his head. Tinmouth frowned, realizing the two men must have seen the gun. That was the reason they were staring. It had to be. His mind raced. If they saw the gun, then they probably called someone. But who? He shook his head and then nodded once, affirming his thoughts. If the men had seen the gun then they probably just called the sheriff's office. That meant he had only a few minutes to get out of sight before the sheriff and his deputies would be out looking for him.

Tinmouth glanced down at the Ruger once more. It still was in pristine condition. If there was one thing that Tinmouth Pritchard was, it was being thorough and precise about taking good care of his weapons. They were his livelihood. He depended on them to eat and survive. For once, one of his dependable weapons had let him down. He slowly lowered the Ruger below the line of sight if anyone else looked in the window.

Tinmouth searched his mind hastily, searching for someplace where he could go to hide, to talk to Fallon's daughter, to work out how to get what was owed him. Suddenly, the perfect place came to him and he smiled. He would take her to the place where he had always felt the safest. He turned to Elizabeth Fallon and grinned, showing her his yellowed, tobacco stained teeth. Elizabeth stared at the grinning old man, glancing with terror and confusion at the gun he still had pointed at her and she buried her head in her hands and wept. She wept silently, agonizingly.

For some reason, Tinmouth's dirty, stained teeth and his leering grin had been the final straw. It had put her over the edge. She could control her shocked and terrified emotions no longer.

In reality, Tinmouth Pritchard's grin was horrible. The old woodsman hadn't been to a proper dentist in over fifteen years. If he got a toothache, he pulled the offending tooth out. He brushed his teeth with tree bark and he smoked and chewed tobacco several hours a day. He ate large quantities of meat and very few vegetables. His face was weathered, wizened and lined well beyond his years. Add to that his disgusting habit of snorting phlegm from both his nose and throat every few minutes and you had a pretty disgusting spectacle.

As Elizabeth wept, she wept not only for herself but for Andy Morrison. She had found Andy collapsed in a snow bank by her back door, his burgundy red blood spreading rapidly across the pristine whiteness of the snow. She had stood, transfixed, for several moments when she first found him, her eyes wide and disbelieving. Then she had knelt down beside Andy, searching for a pulse. Once she found one, even though it was slight, she had urgently called 911 and stayed by Andy's side applying pressure to his wound until Dr. Monroe, Doc Stone and the EMTs had arrived. As they desperately worked on him, she had stood on her back porch, watching as the medical personnel fought to save Andy's life. She grieved, wept, and felt as though it was her fault that the kind young man had been so brutally attacked.

Doc Stone had taken a quick look at Elizabeth, and

tried to get her to go in and rest. But she couldn't, and she wouldn't. In Elizabeth's heart and mind it was her fault that Andy was so badly wounded. She had no doubt about that.

Once the doctors had secured Andy and headed off to the hospital and the sheriff and his posse began to follow the tracks that could only be those of Tinmouth Pritchard, Elizabeth Fallon had sat down listlessly on the steps to her back porch, heedless of the time or the weather.

That was where Tinmouth Pritchard had found her. She had been still sitting on the back porch, shivering, nearly frostbitten, terribly disoriented. She hadn't tried to run, but he had grabbed her roughly and shoved her into his truck without a word. And now, he was most likely going to kill her.

That really didn't matter to her now. What did matter was Andy Morrison. He had tried to help her. He had tried to save her. Now he was lying in the hospital. She didn't even know if he was still alive.

As suddenly as they started, her tears stopped. She picked her head up and stared at Tinmouth Pritchard. She was no longer afraid.

Chapter 20

Wendy Morrison was on a mission. She sat tensely behind the wheel of her late model SUV, hands gripping the steering wheel tightly, hurtling down the street, slewing precariously around corners on the snow and ice covered roadway. As she drove she was focused on one thing and one thing only. She was intent on reaching that self-centered young woman who had caused the catastrophe that had left her poor brother unconscious and in the hospital, hanging onto his life by a mere thread. She was going to make sure that Elizabeth Fallon never had anything to do with her brother ever again.

Skidding and squealing around a corner, the snow and ice sent her tires sliding across the road at a ninety-degree angle. As Wendy fought the wheel, barely stopping the skid before hitting the guardrail, Mandy Wagner gasped loudly, hanging onto the door grip for dear life and exclaimed, "What are you doing, Wendy!? Where on earth are we going, and can you please slow down so we can get there in one piece?"

Wendy never took her eyes off the road or her concentration from what she knew she had to do. She had to save her brother from the troubles and pain this interfering Fallon woman was inflicting on him. She would accomplish that, one way or another.

Mandy stared with disbelief at her friend and boss. She had never seen Wendy like this. She knew that Wendy had her moods and that her boss could have times where she was preoccupied with her thoughts for hours at a time. But she had never seen anything like what she now saw in Wendy Morrison. Frankly, it scared her. Deeply.

As Mandy turned and stared anxiously out the windshield, she tried to figure out where they were headed. They were now driving on a one-lane road heading away from The Falls and back toward Brown Bear Junction. Mandy was sure that she didn't know anyone who lived along this strip of road.

Glancing back once more with great unease at Wendy, she tried to figure out where her friend might be taking them. Perhaps she was headed to their shop, Treasured Memories? Or Wendy and Andy's home? Andy's law firm? Where?

Suddenly stomping on the brakes, Wendy whipped the creaking and whining SUV into a long driveway. Gunning the car once more, Wendy hurtled the car forward down the lightly snow-covered drive and then stomped on the brakes with all her might once again. The car slid to a stop not three feet in front of the white picket fence surrounding the back of the house.

Jumping out of the car, Wendy Morrison raced through the well-shoveled path, burst through the yellow crime scene tape, and began banging with her closed fist on the back door of Elizabeth Fallon's house.

Nauseous and disoriented after their unbelievable journey, Mandy swung the car's passenger side door open and promptly vomited her lunch onto a pristine white snow bank. As Mandy wiped her mouth with a tissue she had found crumpled in her pocket, her head continuing to throb, Mandy heard Wendy pounding ferociously on the back door. Only now, she could hear her yelling over the pounding as well.

"Get out here, you vile homewreaker!" Wendy was shouting, her voice rising in tone and vehemence as she continued, "I know you're in here! You can't fool me! Open this door!"

Mandy stumbled awkwardly out of the car and attempted to stand without the world spinning around or shaking from one side to the other. Finally gaining her 'sea legs', Mandy walked slowly and carefully around to where Wendy was pounding on the back door.

"Stop it!" Mandy shouted with all of her strength.

Wendy did stop. She turned and stared at her friend, her cheeks were flushed, her eyes wide, and her hand frozen in the act of pounding on the door. Her knuckles were red and raw, and her eyes were bloodshot.

Mandy stared into the brutal, vicious eyes of Wendy Morrison, "What are you doing?" she yelled loudly, trying to get through Wendy's intense focus. "What's wrong with you, Wendy?"

Suddenly, Wendy Morrison's eyes unfocused and she literally caved in. It was as if the raging fire inside her went out, and she slumped down, dropping awkwardly onto the back steps. Then, Wendy began to cry. As she cried, she rocked herself back and forth, slowly, rhythmically, holding onto herself tightly.

Mandy hesitated for a moment, unsure of what to do. Then she slowly walked over and sat down next to her friend, leaning over and placing her arm comfortingly around Wendy's slumping shoulders.

Mandy stared off into the woods, in the direction where Tinmouth Pritchard had supposedly come, holding her weeping and grieving friend. She knew only one thing at that very moment. She was worn out and unsure of what was real and what wasn't anymore.

***

The old rattletrap truck slowly turned down the snow-covered dirt road. It drove past the grove of snow-covered pine trees and the leafless stand of oaks and maples, bumping and rumbling along the deeply rutted, little used road.

Finally, Tinmouth Pritchard pulled into a side path that was clogged with snow up to the tire wells and stopped. He nimbly climbed down out of the truck, crossed over to the passenger side and opened the passenger side door.

"Get out," Tinmouth waved the Ruger P89, gesturing impatiently for Elizabeth to get down out of the truck. As the young woman did so, she glanced all around, wondering where on earth Pritchard had taken her.

They had driven for a few miles on Interstate Route 4, then pulled off at the Silver Birch Crossing exit. But at the exit from the interstate, Tinmouth had turned east instead of west toward Silver Pines Crossing. Now here they were four or five miles and several twists and turns later, each turn taking them deeper into the woods. They were stopped in a small clearing. There were two houses that she could see. One was two stories high, an old colonial style, at least a century old and fairly rundown. The other, sitting next to the large house was a small cottage which was also noticeably vacant, but in much better condition.

Tinmouth Pritchard was staring at the small house, his eyes somehow unfocused and his thoughts far away. Then he snapped back to his usual cantankerous and belligerent self. "Over there. Get moving Missy!" he growled menacingly at Elizabeth. He motioned toward the small cottage's front door.

The day had turned into one of those cloudy, gray days that stalk New England winters. The wind had begun to whip up and the intense cold was increasing. Elizabeth suddenly began shaking, her fingers and toes nearing frostbite. Elizabeth's reeling thoughts somehow focused on the surreal notion that the vast clouds of warm air they were expelling as they breathed were turning to crystalline mist that truly looked like they were both smoking cigars.

The door to the cottage was open and they went in. The house was even colder than it was outside, if that was indeed possible. But the house itself looked like someone had lived there not too long ago. Tinmouth went straight to the wood stove and built a fire with the paper, kindling and logs already laid out neatly nearby.

As Tinmouth busied himself, his back was turned to Elizabeth. She might have tried to get away, but instead, she found herself drawn to looking around the small but neat rooms, staring at the little odds and ends that make a house a home. There were family pictures everywhere. The house had obviously been owned by a family with two children, both boys. She could see photographs of the boys at various ages. In several of the pictures there was a father or a mother. Glancing closer at the father, Elizabeth found herself surprised to see the striking resemblance of a younger Tinmouth Pritchard.

As if on cue, Tinmouth turned from feeding the fire, scowled and pointed to the rocking chair a few feet away from the stove. "Sit down," came his gruff, terse exclamation.

Elizabeth did. But she continued to stare inquisitively

around the room. It was obvious to her now. This was where Tinmouth and his family had lived in better, happier days. This was where Tinmouth had felt most at home. Elizabeth thought about the situation she found herself in at the moment. She knew how upset and stressed she was. It only made sense to assume that Tinmouth must be just as tense and anxious. Her brain, putting two and two together, told her that it would only make sense for Tinmouth to retreat to somewhere he felt at home. Safe. As she continued to stare around the small home, she decided that this place must still be Tinmouth's place of refuge, a place to get out of harm's way.

Finishing the chore of loading and starting the fire, Tinmouth closed the door to the stove and stood up, glancing around the room himself for a few seconds. Then his gaze fell back upon Elizabeth. He walked over, grabbed a wooden straight back chair from the simple table on the other side of the room and sat the chair down just a few feet away from her. Sitting down heavily in the chair, with an almost audible sense of relief, Tinmouth Pritchard stared intently over at the young woman sitting in the rocking chair. Suddenly, in his own minds eye, he once again beheld the focus of his rage and resentment. He saw Benjamin Fallon's daughter.

Ben Fallon, the man who had withheld wages from him from years. Fallon had done so in order to give their customers good, well made furniture at an affordable price. It didn't matter to Tinmouth that Fallon had withheld even more wages from his own personal paycheck. He could do that if he wanted, after all he was the boss. But Fallon had cheated him, Tinmouth silently reasoned once again. It was now time to recoup his losses, with interest.

A malicious grin spread across Tinmouth Pritchard's face, his eyes twinkling with trouble. He leaned forward and stared straight into Elizabeth's face. He was so close that Elizabeth could smell his stale breath.

"Now it's time for us to talk, Missy," Tinmouth's voice was calm but firm, definitely in control.

Tinmouth tilted his head to one side and the smile vanished, as his eyes narrowed meanly, "Your father owes me for work that I did. Good, hard, honest work. I figure he owes me almost ten thousand dollars stretched out over the years I worked for him."

Elizabeth swallowed hard and blinked. It was first time she had heard a figure and she wasn't sure how to respond. She had no idea what might set the man off, or what would infuriate him. She also knew that there was no one around to save her this time. No one knew where they were. Whatever happened here, it was her wits against his.

Before she could think of an answer, Tinmouth leaned closer still and whispered harshly, "And that money's been owed over a number of years, Missy. That means I'm owed it, plus interest. A lot of interest, Missy!" Tinmouth's eyes gleamed and he grinned a yellow, toothy grin once more.

Elizabeth took a deep breath and replied in her calmest, quietest tone, "I understand what you want, Mr. Pritchard. I wish I had the money to give you. But I don't. My father died a penniless man, owing tens of thousands of dollars."

She continued on quickly, not allowing Tinmouth the time to respond until she was done with what she needed to say, "Right now, I owe over fifty thousand dollars to the bank and to several outstanding creditors.

I'm in debt up to my eyeballs and I just lost my job. I have nothing, Mr. Pritchard. Absolutely nothing."

For a long moment, Tinmouth Pritchard sat there, his brain attempting to assimilate what he had just been told. It had never entered his thoughts that the girl didn't inherit money from her father. He had never even considered that she was as broke as he was. Now that reality shattered his thoughts.

He jerked back in his chair, as though he had been slapped. Hard. Then his eyes went from wide-open shock and surprise to scowling and narrow, filled with anger and distrust, "You're lying, Missy!"

He stood up, violently, knocking over the chair and pulled out the Ruger P89 from his belt, pointed it right at the face of Elizabeth Fallon and bellowed out furiously, "You're lying! Tell me you're lying, Missy! Tell me right now!"

***

Jebediah Able Smith and Ezekiel Morton Peters were having a semi-amazing day. The two old friends and business partners sat on wooden folding chairs in their toasty fishing shanty out on Lake Pumpkinseed. Their miniature pellet stove was sending out pleasurable waves of heat, keeping the inside of the shanty toasty and cheerful. The two small windows on either side of the shanty let in enough light to be able to watch the weather, without having to experience the wind and snow firsthand. The solid wooden floor had two wide openings to ice fish from and their power auger had made short work of the four and a half feet of ice directly below them.

At the edge of the two perfectly circular holes were two tip-ups for each of the old men. They were new, aluminum tip-ups which alerted the fisherman of any bites and then set the hook automatically when the fish pulled down hard enough. On each tip-up was a reel with a long length of twenty-pound monofilament fishing line.

Jeb had brought a cooler stocked with beer and bottled ice tea and a large thermos of steaming hot coffee while Zeke had finagled his daughter, Emily, to fix them up a Tupperware bowl of leftover fried chicken as well as a bag full of assorted cookies and crackers. They had even set up a transistor radio on one of the built-in shelves and were listening to country music.

They were having merely a semi-amazing day because they had only caught one small perch and two pumpkinseeds over the two hours they had been fishing. But as Zeke's daddy had always told the two boys when they were younger: sometimes it wasn't where you got, but how you got there that mattered.

Zeke took a long swig of hot coffee and stared out the window, "Hey! Looky there, Jeb! There's the Burman boy and his cousin headed this way!"

Jeb leaned forward and craned his neck, peering out toward where Zeke was pointing. There were Jeremy and Parnell Burman trudging through the foot and a half of snow on the frozen lake, pulling a flexible flyer sled behind them. The wind was blowing and whirling around them, and their cheeks and noses were getting bright red from the cold. The boys seemed cheerful enough, with a box of fishing gear, a bait container, and their grandpa's old seven foot long ice spud bouncing along on the old sled as they grew closer to the shanty.

Jeb and Zeke poked their heads out the door to the shanty and called out, "Hey! Jeremy! Parnell! Come on in and warm yourselves up!"

The two boys waved their acknowledgement and

dragged the sled over to an area a few yards away from the shanty. They quickly scraped the snow off a small circular part of the ice and then jogged eagerly over to the shanty, slipping through the door and closing it quickly behind them.

"Hey Mr. Peters, Mr. Smith!" Jeremy smiled and nodded gratefully to Jeb and Zeke. "Thanks for the chance to warm up. We thought we might try our luck today! Saturday's about the only day we have to go fishin'! School's on all week and church is Sunday..."

"...So here we are! But it sure is cold out there, ain't it?!" Parnell grinned, his cheeks looking as red as the new red pumper truck safely parked out of the elements in The Falls firehouse.

Jeb glanced with pride around their cozy, well equipped shanty, "Yup, I can remember when I was a kid coming down with my dad and choppin' out holes in the ice. We'd fish for a couple of hours and then go home, frozen like so much meat in a storage locker, right Zeke?"

Zeke nodded at the memory, "Yup, I remember it just like it was yesterday. Lots of fun, but it took us hours to warm up once we got home."

"Our mothers would make a royal fuss over us when we got back. They'd make us strip down in the living room. Then they'd scoot us in to take hot baths while they scolded our dads for keeping us out in the cold too long," chuckled Jeb, shaking his head. Those were fond memories.

"Well, we better get back out there. Those holes aren't gonna' make themselves," Jeremy grinned and stood by the door, waiting for Parnell who had been warming his hands at the pellet stove.

"Want us to cut your holes with the power auger?"

Zeke offered, half standing up.

"No thanks, Mr. Peters," Jeremy waved a hand, "my grandpa says a man should cut his own holes if he's gonna' go ice fishing. Part of the process, he says. Guess he means we'll appreciate the fish that we catch more."

Zeke nodded and then turned and glanced at Jeb, "Well you're grandpa's probably right. But the fish don't seem to be bitin' too much today anyway."

Parnell grinned and winked mischievously at Zeke, "Maybe they've just been waitin' for us, Mr. Peters!"

Zeke just chuckled as the boys closed the door behind them and quickly shuffled out to begin chipping out their holes. Jeb glanced at Zeke and grinned as well, "Who knows? Maybe those two sprouts will have better luck than us."

Half an hour later, Jeremy and Parnell had two small holes cut out of the ice and were placing their live minnows on their hooks. Instead of tip-ups the two boys had a length of fishing line wrapped around a stick. Jeb and Zeke smiled and watched the two boys through the shanty window as they fixed their bait and lowered their lines.

Zeke whispered with a somewhat wistful look on his face, "Don't that just remind you of when we was kids?"

"Yeah, it does, old friend. I sure does," Jeb nodded, sipping hot coffee and watching the boys unroll the fishing line as their hooks went further and further down into the icy waters of Lake Pumpkinseed.

Suddenly, Parnell's line jerked his hands down almost into the water. The boy's eyes widened with surprise and excitement as he set the hook and began pulling up his prize. Jeremy had no sooner stopped gazing down into the dark slate colored water of his small fishing hole to look and see what was going on with his cousin, than his own hands jerked down toward the freezing water.

Within a minute, each boy had hauled out a huge fish. Parnell's was a two-foot pike, and Jeremy's was a deep-gutted small mouth bass. The boys then literally danced around on the ice and snow, exuberantly holding up their trophies for Zeke and Jeb to see.

Jeb and Zeke opened the door to the shanty and hollered out, "Alright! Great fish, boys!"

The boys kept pulling out fish after fish for the next hour while Zeke and Jeb looked on in stunned amazement. By the time the boys had packed up, warmed themselves by the pellet stove and taken off across the lake toward home, they had caught several bass, three pikes, a musky and several large perch.

As Zeke and Jeb watched the boys trudging happily through the snow back the way they had come, they glanced forlornly over at their fish bucket. Three small perch and two little pumpkinseeds were all they had to show for the day. Feeling just a bit dejected, Jeb glanced at Zeke and sighed, "Those boys just happened to hit it right. Maybe it will be us next time."

Zeke hesitated thoughtfully, and then nodded solemnly, "Well maybe so, old friend. But one thing I do know. I ain't gonna' have to take any hot bath when I get back 'cause we're fishin' in the lap of luxury!"

Then Zeke's face cracked open into a toothy grin, and he winked delightedly at his old friend. Jeb, finally getting into the spirit, chuckled and clinked beer bottles with his best friend and fishing buddy.

He was reminded once more of Zeke's daddy's saying. Sometimes it wasn't where you got, but how you got there that mattered.

***

Cash Green glanced in the rear view mirror. Directly in back of him was Chief of Police Tinker LaGrange in his Brown Bear Junction police car and a few car lengths back of Tinker was State Trooper McNealy in his green and yellow state police cruiser. The three law enforcement cruisers had finally joined up heading down the interstate after spending fifteen minutes splitting up and checking out every logging road or side road that was headed out of town.

After Newt and Remy had called in their sighting of an old truck with a man threatening a young woman with a handgun, it had only been a matter of minutes before Cash and his posse had arrived on the scene.

Cash glanced over at Yamato in the passenger seat, his eyes sharp and piercing as they usually were when he was hot on the trail, "Makes sense that he didn't stay around town, although we had to spend the time checking out the side roads, just in case."

"Tinmouth Prichard is many things," Yamato spoke quietly, her eyes scanning the road and landscape up ahead intently, "but he is no fool. He knew we were going to spread out and cover any of his usual hangouts. He knew when to move on. Now…"

Yamato hesitated, turning to gaze carefully into a grove of trees as they went past, "…we just have to figure out where he went."

The two-way radio crackled and Darlene's firm, loud monotone could be heard, "Base to Falls One, Base to Falls One…come in."

Yamato responded, "Falls One to Base. Whatcha' got, Darlene?"

Darlene spoke up, a bit more hesitantly, "Well, I don't usually interfere, but I thought you and the sheriff should be aware of something. Don't know if anything will come of it, but figured you should know anyway. 'Bout fifteen years ago, Tinmouth Pritchard used to live up by Silver Birch Landing. He and his wife and kids, two boys, now grown men, used to live in a little grove of trees about three miles west from the interstate exit for Silver Birch Landing."

Darlene was silent for a moment then added in a softer, quieter voice that sounded nothing like Darlene, "He used to be a decent man. Nice wife, good, polite kids. He was a fair to middling woodworker as well. After he left Fallon's Woodworking Shop, things just sorta' went downhill. Wife tried to help him, but she finally left after awhile, taking the kids with her. They moved upstate around Winooski, from what I hear."

Cash glanced at Yamato, and then spoke into the two-way, "So what are you saying, Darlene?"

The voice on the other end became firmer, more like herself, "Just that he's got some basic goodness somewhere, Sheriff. Be a shame to shoot the man after all he's gone through in his life. Base out."

The exit sign for Silver Birch Landing came into view as Cash and Yamato glanced at each other. Turning on his blinker, Cash checked the rear view mirror again. Sure enough both cruisers following him turned on their directional lights as well.

Five minutes later, Cash pulled his Jeep Liberty up slowly and quietly, stopping on the dead end road. A hundred yards farther on was a grove of trees. Just visible through those trees were two buildings. Cash climbed out of the Jeep and closed the door with barely a click. He motioned to Tinker and McNealy to join them.

"This looks like it might be Tinmouth's last real home," Cash whispered as he glanced over at the two buildings. The smaller house had smoke lazing out the chimney, and there was an old rattletrap truck sitting near the front door.

"Sure looks like somebody's home," Tinker whispered back, his eyes intently scanning the area around the house. "And I'm guessing by the snow drifts on the driveway and walkway that haven't been shoveled, that whoever is in there, just got there."

"Those are fresh tracks in the snow," Yamato added, pointing toward the thigh deep tracks running from the truck to the front door.

McNealy glanced at Cash, and without a word, Cash knew what he was asking. "No, let's not get any backup just yet," Cash whispered, remembering Darlene's unusual conversation on the two-way a few minutes before. "Let's get a little closer and see what we have here. Agreed?"

Cash glanced thoughtfully at both the Brown Bear Chief of Police and the Vermont State Trooper, his eyebrows up, asking for their input. Tinker and McNealy glanced at each other for a moment, then turned and nodded in the affirmative back at Cash.

"Alright then. Let's take two teams, one goes to the back door, one goes to the front window. Let's do it real quiet and find out what's going on in there before we do anything. Agreed?" Cash glanced openly at Yamato, Tinker and McNealy.

With a nod, all of them started forward, Yamato teaming up with Cash and heading toward the front window, while Tinker and McNealy made a circuitous route toward the back of the house, moving quietly but quickly through the heavy drifts of snow.

The snowdrifts, icy crust, stinging wind and freezing temperatures made navigating the hundred yards more of a gauntlet than a walk in the park, but after a heart pounding five minutes, the two teams were in position. Cash and Yamato were crouched down in the snow below, and to each side, of the big front window while McNealy and Tinker were hunkered down below the back porch guns out, ready and waiting in the snow and swirling wind.

Cash glanced at Yamato and nodded. Yamato slowly stood up and peered into the front window, being careful to keep out of sight. She looked around the room attentively. Although she saw a hunting cap and some gloves, she saw no one. Returning to her original crouch, she shook her head and pointed at Cash.

As the sheriff slowly rose up, peeking into the window carefully, from his vantage point he saw Tinmouth Pritchard standing over a very pale and wide-eyed young woman. Tinmouth's back was to him, but the young woman saw him almost immediately. Her eyes widened even more and her hand involuntarily flew to her mouth. Cash immediately dropped down and motioned to Yamato that he had seen the two of them. He pointed urgently toward the front door and drew his Glock 9mm. Yamato got the drift right away.

Silently, the two of them crawled over to the front porch and began to climb the stairs. Step by step they moved toward the front door. But as Cash placed his full weight on the last snow-covered step, it groaned loudly.

Yamato and Cash stared at each other uneasily and then they both automatically turned and pointed their Glocks at the front door.

Chapter 21

Mandy Wagner brought a cup of hot coffee back from the hospital waiting room vending machine, only to find Wendy Morrison just as she had left her. Wendy's head was down, her hands folded submissively in her lap and her breathing was so shallow that Mandy could hardly notice it at all.

"Here, drink this," Mandy tried to keep her voice calm but firm, hoping that Wendy would respond. Wendy hadn't said much since Mandy had helped her into the car at Elizabeth Fallon's place and then drove her friend back to the hospital waiting area.

Wendy didn't seem to respond, so Mandy touched her shoulder hopefully, gently squeezing it. In response to her touch, Wendy glanced up at her friend. Her eyes were filled with anguish and heartache. But she reached out her hands and gratefully took the paper coffee cup.

As Wendy sipped the coffee, Mandy turned and glanced toward the critical care ward. She saw Dr. Monroe in Andy's room, checking the readings on several machines, and then turning to leave. Before the young doctor did so, however, she stopped and stared down at the unconscious body of the young lawyer. It was easy to see that Meg was very concerned about the condition of her patient. It was also easy to see that the emotion she was feeling was more than just professional. The young doctor seemed personally concerned for her critically ill patient as well.

As Dr. Monroe left Andy's room, she noticed Wendy and Mandy in the waiting area and quickly made her way toward them. As she approached the two women, Meg smiled slightly and glanced back and forth between them, "Miss Morrison, Miss Wagner, I wish that I could tell you more, but right now, I don't know much more than I did an hour and a half ago."

Meg turned and stared at Wendy, "Your brother's condition hasn't changed. One good thing is that the repair work we did on his organs and blood vessels seems to be working. There's no sign of internal bleeding. That's a very good thing. His vital signs remain weak, at best. But the main thing right now is that his condition hasn't worsened."

Meg looked tired and worn all of a sudden as she gamely tried to smile and convey her professional confidence and composure. When Wendy did not respond, Meg glanced at Mandy. Her expression, changing to one of concern, the young doctor asked quietly, "Is everything alright?"

Mandy glanced down at her friend, sitting in the hospital waiting room chair, sipping coffee and slowly rocking back and forth and sadly shook her head. "No, I don't think everything is alright, Doctor." Mandy glanced expressively at Meg and with her head gestured slightly down toward Wendy.

"Do you think Dr. Messina, our on-call therapist, could be of help?" Meg asked quietly, studying the slowly rocking form of Wendy Morrison.

Mandy nodded firmly and then bit her lip, trying not to shed any tears. It broke her heart to see her friend so emotionally overwrought. Mandy, as most old

Vermonters, found it hard to believe that a psychiatrist was the best 'medicine'. It was hard for her to admit that her friend wasn't strong enough mentally to deal with difficult issues and problems.

Meg nodded reassuringly at Mandy and spoke quietly but firmly to Wendy Morrison, "Miss Morrison, I can see that you're not feeling well. Why don't you just let me take you to a quiet room where you can lie down for awhile? Miss Wagner can come with you. If there's any news about your brother, I'll come and get you right away, Okay?"

As she spoke, Meg motioned for Tom Foley, one of the hospital orderlies, to come and help her with Wendy. As Meg firmly took hold of Wendy's arm, easing her up and out of the chair, Tom quickly brought a wheelchair over. Meg glanced up at Mandy and whispered, "You'll stay with her for awhile, 'til Dr. Messina gets here?"

Mandy nodded and took a firm hold of Wendy's other arm, as she and the young doctor lowered the still emotionless woman into the wheelchair. In less than five minutes, the orderly had carefully wheeled Wendy into a private room and, with Mandy's help, had placed the distraught shopkeeper onto the bed. As soon as Wendy's head hit the pillow, she closed her eyes and lay still.

Nodding her thanks to Tom Foley, Mandy closed the door to the room and sat in the chair by the window. Listening to the steady breathing of her friend, and beginning to relax, Mandy stared blankly out into the frozen world of February in New England. The swirling, icy wind blew snowflakes around the side lawn of the hospital, and into almost a myriad of rhythmic patterns. The sight of it somehow relaxed Mandy even more.

Mandy sighed deeply, and concentrated on trying to simply relax, knowing that her friend would now be getting the best of care. Not surprisingly, letting her tension and stress go for at least a little while, everything hit an exhausted Mandy all at once. She felt truly worn out and drowsy. Within five minutes, her eyes had slipped closed and she had fallen asleep, her head resting gently against the pristine white wall of the hospital room.

***

"Get away from that door!" bellowed the muffled but loud, angry voice of Tinmouth Pritchard.

Cash and Yamato stood motionless, each of them only a step or two from the front door. They glanced at each other and Cash made an immediate hand gesture, slowly bring his open hand down several times, conveying to his deputy that they needed to deescalate the situation.

"It's Sheriff Cash Green, Tinmouth," Cash leaned toward the door, making sure not to stand in front of the door or the doorframe. "I'm not going to lie to you. You know why we're here."

Cash glanced at Yamato, motioning for her to try and get in position where she could see in through the small window on the other side of the door without being seen herself. Yamato nodded in understanding. She moved quietly, carefully, crawling under the window and then carefully crouching to look inside. When she had a clear view of the two people inside the cottage, she leaned back slowly and nodded to Cash.

"Tinmouth, we're not going away. We have the house surrounded. You need to talk to me about what's going on," Cash's voice was firm, deliberate and calm. He knelt down by the front door and listened for a response.

Several moments later, Tinmouth called out, "This ain't nobody's business but me and Ben Fallon's kid. It's just between us. You need to leave, Sheriff. You're trespassin'!"

Cash listened carefully, hesitated and then responded, "Tinmouth, if you were sitting in Tina's Diner, discussing business over a cup of coffee and a piece of pie, I'd agree with you. But you're not. You've got Elizabeth Fallon in there against her will. You've got a gun, Tinmouth. All of that says that it's now officially my business. Are you alright, Elizabeth?"

A hushed, obviously uneasy voice came back faintly, "I'm okay, sheriff. Mr. Pritchard hasn't hurt me. He just made a fire so we could get warm."

Cash called out a little louder, "Good, Elizabeth. Tinmouth, not only is it my business, but Deputy Yamato, Chief LaGrange and Sergeant McNealy of the Vermont State Police are here as well."

From the back of the house came Tinker's strong, determined voice, "The sheriff's right, Mr. Pritchard. We're all involved now and we're not going away until this is settled. We need to talk."

There was some noise inside the house and Cash glanced over to Yamato. She glanced in and then whispered, "He's pulled Elizabeth up out of her chair and into a corner toward the back of the house. He's holding her in front of him, like a hostage." Yamato's eyes narrowed with concern.

"Ain't nobody coming in here!" yelled Tinmouth, his voice now beginning to crack with strain and stress.

"That's fine, for now," Cash called out in return. "But we are going to talk, Tinmouth. Starting right now. If you don't talk, then you will leave us little choice.

Understood?"

Cash stood, getting himself right next to the front door, should he have to rush in quickly if the discussion became too intense, "Tell me why you felt you had to take Elizabeth here, Tinmouth?"

It took a few moments, but Tinmouth responded, his voice lower, with a touch of weariness, "I had to talk to the girl. I had to make her see that I was owed that money, fair and square. That blasted lawyer was getting' a restrainin' order! He wasn't going to let me see her! He butted right in! Him and that tall private eye!" Tinmouth stopped for a moment, his voice resonating with fury and his own brand of righteous indignation.

"Then I come up with a way to talk to Ben's daughter. Get her away. Explain everything to her. Show her beyond a shadow of a doubt that I was honestly owed that money." Tinmouth's voice was quieter, focused, as if he was reasoning it out to himself as well as to the sheriff and his posse.

There was silence for a few moments, then Tinmouth's voice was heard again, "This wasn't the way it was supposed to be. Ben and me used to be friends. I liked workin' for Ben. But he was so soft hearted, he gave the wood working we done away for such a cheap price. Everybody knew he was a soft touch..."

Another shaky, but strengthening voice from inside interrupted Tinmouth, "My father cared about people, Mr. Pritchard. That's why he reduced the prices. He did it so everyone could afford beautiful, handmade furniture. He loved what he did, and he wanted to share it with others. Didn't you want to share your skill and talent with others too, Mr. Pritchard?"

Tinmouth replied softly, "Yeah, I liked to have people

use the furniture I created. 'Course it made me feel good. But I needed money for my own family..."

Yamato whispered to Cash that Tinmouth had moved away from Elizabeth and that the old man had picked up an old picture of his family and was staring at it remorsefully.

"...and the low prices he was selling our handmade furniture for was keeping me from doing right by them." Pritchard's voice trailed off and Cash could hear the man slowly pacing the floor inside.

Cash glanced at Yamato. She was crouched beside the window, ready to follow any instructions he gave. His heart warmed as he thought of all the years they had served together, as colleagues and as friends. He trusted Yamato with his life. He had for a long time. The Sheriff of West Sugar Shack Falls turned back to the door and quickly made a decision.

"Tinmouth, I understand. I do. But you need to come and open the door and let us in. That's the only way this can end without someone being hurt. Come to the door and let me in." Cash slowly laid his gun down in front of the door and continued, "I've put my gun down, Tinmouth. I'm trusting you. Now come and let me in."

Yamato's eyes widened with surprise, but she never hesitated, making her way quickly and silently over to the doorway, her gun raised and ready.

The old man stopped pacing and stood staring at the door. Then he glanced at the tears cascading down Elizabeth's face and made a decision. He turned, pointing his Ruger deliberately at the middle of the front entrance, walked to the door and opened it.

Cash stood there, hands out to his sides, quiet and composed as he stared into Tinmouth's red and bloodshot eyes. "Tinmouth, let's sit down. Let's talk this out." The sheriff's voice was calm and low, his eyes open and filled with trust and honest compassion.

Somehow, Tinmouth Pritchard could sense that if anyone could work through the difficult situation he now found himself in, it was the man who stood before him. Tinmouth Pritchard lowered his Ruger and hesitantly motioned the sheriff inside.

***

Meg Monroe stood quietly by the bedside of Andy Morrison. Her eyes were closed for just a moment as she whispered a little silent prayer for his recovery. She did the same for every patient she was worried about. In all honesty, however, she acknowledged to herself that this little appeal was a bit more passionate than usual. The young doctor still was feeling guilty about turning Andy's affectionate inquiries down a few days before.

Suddenly, she heard a painful gasp right next to her. She turned and was shocked to find that she was staring down into the open eyes of the young lawyer.

"Andy!" Meg whispered eagerly, as she quickly reached out her hand to feel the pulse in his wrist. "Tell me how you're feeling!"

Andy's eyes flashed a look of both pain and surprise, then narrowed and shut for a moment as he grimaced, obviously in a great deal of pain. His hand moved shakily toward his chest, and Meg caught it and kept it from touching all the bandages, wires and tubing that now were attached to him.

Meg stared at the machines that were hooked up to Andy, satisfying her need to personally check his vital signs, as she continued to hold his hand tightly and speak in a soft, but calm, firm voice, "Andy. This is Dr. Monroe. Meg Monroe. You've been shot. You're in the hospital. Talk to me."

A soft moan came from Andy's lips as he arched backward in the bed, pain obviously wracking his wounded body. Satisfied that his vital signs were all improving, Meg instinctively glanced out into the waiting area. Then she remembered that Andy's sister had been placed in a private room an hour or more before, waiting for Dr. Serafina Messina, the town's only psychiatrist, to come and speak to her.

At that moment, Andy's eyes opened wide once again and he groaned once more, his body stiffening to deal with the intense pain shooting through him. "Meg..." Andy's voice was hoarse and low, barely audible.

"Yes, Andy, I'm here," Meg squeezed the young lawyer's hand reassuringly, staring into his eyes. "What is it, Andy?"

Andy's brow wrinkled as he tried to hold the pain in check, and he stared at Meg, his eyes wide, a look of shock and realization overwhelming his pale face. His words came out as an incredulous exclamation, "She shot me!"

Meg stared at Andy for a moment, processing his words. Then Meg leaned down close to Andy and asked, "You mean he shot you, don't you?"

Andy struggled to maintain consciousness as wave after wave of pain hit him. He grabbed Meg's shoulder and with great intensity and deliberation, he enunciated each word carefully, as he whispered as loudly as he could, "No. She shot me! I can't believe she shot me! I don't understand! Why did she..."

As Andy slid back into unconsciousness, all the pain and tension lines in his face softened. His fingers relaxed their grip on Meg's lab coat and slid to the white sheets of his bed.

Meg stared down at the now unconscious young man and once again involuntarily checked his vital signs as her brain sought to fully grasp what Andy had been trying to tell her. She shot him? Who could the 'she' be? For a moment, Meg shuffled through the possibilities in her thoughts. Then it suddenly came to her.

The young doctor ran out of the critical care ward and down the corridor. Bursting through the door of a private room, she found Mandy Wagner fast asleep, slumped rather uncomfortably in a hospital chair, her head leaning up against the wall. Small little snores rose up from her as she slept. Turning toward the bed where Wendy Morrison had been placed just an hour ago, Meg's eyes widened.

Pulling her cell phone out of her pocket, she dialed 911. Darlene Pitts answered in her usual monotone, "Sheriff's Office, how may we help you?"

"Oh, thank goodness I got you! Darlene, it's Meg," the young doctor spoke quickly, urgently. "You've got to let Cash know that the person who shot Andy Morrison wasn't Tinmouth Pritchard!"

***

The three hunters were no more than seventy-five yards apart, each settled behind a fallen tree or a boulder in the deep ravine that ran up and down the steep mountainside. The early morning mist in the air swirled around them, as the eastern sky began to lighten. It was a bitter cold and the sharp wind swept down the mountainside, rustling the thick covering of fallen leaves that covered the forest floor along with a few traces of a late night snowfall.

It was the first weekend of white tail deer hunting in November and the mountains, fields and woods of

Vermont were teaming with hunters. The three hunters had already heard several other hunters pass by on their way up the mountain, and they had seen two others quietly making their way along the ridge just above them. There had been no sharp, echoing shots yet this morning, but all that would change very soon as the sun began to rise and the eastern mountains began to have a faint rosy, orange glow around them.

The young hunter in the middle of the ravine sat behind a fallen log, his eyes wide, scanning the bottom of the slash where there were numerous dead pines and hardwoods, making the area a perfect place for deer to hide.

His heart was beating fast, as he nervously felt the weight of his grandfather's old Winchester .38-55 on his lap and in his hands. It was a rifle that his grandfather had proudly passed down to his father, and now, just in time for his first deer hunt, it was being passed down to him. His dad had jokingly told him that the old rifle's bullet speed wasn't much faster than what a grown man could throw, but, he added, if the slug hit something, that something stayed hit.

His dad was to his right and his brother-in-law was to his left, just at the edges of the ravine. The ravine had three levels, with ridges running across those levels. It was the perfect place to sit in the morning and let the deer come to them. His dad had explained that most of the deer went down into the fields and low lands to sleep, and then, come first light, they would quietly, slowly make their way up the mountain to feed and to hide in the thick groves of trees.

The young hunter had thoroughly enjoyed the huge breakfast they had eaten at home long before dawn. They had consumed great quantities of scrambled eggs, bacon, pancakes and fried potatoes. Then they had driven to the mountain and hiked quickly up to the ravine in the pitch dark. The young hunter remembered with embarrassment slipping and falling several times on the way up, landing in the heavy coating of fallen, dead leaves and the small drifts of freshly fallen snow.

Now that they were stationed in their places, he was determined to make his father and brother-in-law proud. He scanned back and forth over the dark, shadowy landscape below him, striving to see as much as he could in the predawn gloom.

He could just barely see his dad and he knew about where his brother-in-law was, but he couldn't quite see him. The young man was beginning to feel his muscles stiffen up. He had been keeping very still, worrying nervously about moving around too much, not wanting to scare any approaching deer away.

He noticed the glow around the edges of the eastern mountains was brightening. At the same time, he began to feel even colder. He was dressed in long underwear, wool pants and shirt, wool socks and a heavy wool hunting jacket with a wool hunting cap and shooting gloves. His outfit was basically camouflage, with several stripes of bright orange to make sure other hunters didn't mistake him for a deer. At that moment, however, he felt like someone had poured ice cubes into his boots and gloves and his body was not only feeling stiff, but frozen as well.

He rolled his eyes and thought, what else? Within a few seconds, he knew what else. He had to pee. Badly. Glancing guiltily around at where his father and brother-in-law lay in wait, he stood up quietly, unzipping the front of his heavy wool pants and leaned against the fallen tree.

As he waited for relief, he saw the doe. In the first light from the rays of the sun streaming over the mountains, a small, beautiful, dainty female picked her way up the ravine. Her ears twitched from one side to the other, listening intently as she grazed on leaves, plants and anything she could forage on. Her large, light brown eyes moved rapidly across the ravine, glancing here and there, as she picked her way cautiously, silently through the underbrush.

His need to evacuate vanished in the excitement of the moment and he quietly zipped up his pants and sat back down, attempting to remain unseen and unheard by the approaching deer. He glanced to his right, where he saw his father watching the doe intently. As the small female made her way up the ravine, gliding gracefully between trees and shrubs, he could just barely hear her footsteps in the leaves and snow.

He watched his first live deer in the woods, captivated by her charm and beauty. Suddenly, he felt the weight of his grandpa's rifle in his hands again. He looked down at the cold steel of the barrel and then back toward the delicate, stunning charm of the young female. For the first time, the realization set in: he was here to kill a deer.

As his thoughts raced, two more does slipped up the ravine and caught up with the lead female. The three deer then took their time grazing and moving slowly along the slash, as if they didn't have a care in the world.

Suddenly, the young man caught a glimpse of movement up above him on the first ridge that ran across the ravine. He turned carefully and there, gliding quickly and silently through the trees at the top of the slash, was a huge buck. The young man quickly counted the horns, almost unable to believe his astonished eyes. It was a ten pointer. The deer was in just the right location so that he knew that neither his father nor his brother-in-law could see it.

The big buck stopped for just a moment, and stood motionless, staring down toward the young man. His chest was thrust out, his horns glinting in the morning sun as he held his noble head high.

Jeremy slowly picked up the heavy rifle and brought it up to his right shoulder, his right eye aiming down the open sights. Jeremy felt the trigger with his index finger, placed the bead on the end of the barrel in the middle of the magnificent buck's chest and he drew a deep breath, just like his father had taught him. Letting half of the breath out, he steadied his aim. At that moment, the big buck turned its proud head and stared directly at the sixteen-year-old.

Jeremy froze, gazing at the deer in his sights. As the boy stared, he couldn't help but be totally in awe of the splendid creature standing so proudly, so freely, so amazingly there before him. In that instant, Jeremy made a decision. He lowered the .38-55. Jeremy smiled and let out his breath slowly, relieved and delighted with his own choice.

The buck tipped his head slightly to the side, as if thanking the boy and his proud brown eyes glinted in the first rays of sunlight. Then, the next moment, he was gone, vanished into the hardwoods and pines farther up the ravine.

The young man slowly turned back to watch the three doe, who now had begun to move more quickly, and surely up the slash toward where the buck had disappeared. It was as if their mission of distraction was done and they were off to scout another ravine, another part of the mountain to protect their leader.

Jeremy's emotions were jumbled. On one hand, he wanted his dad and brother-in-law to be proud of him. On the other, he felt unable to shoot the magnificent deer without bring down upon himself what he knew would have been a huge gnawing regret.

Glancing back to each side of him, he could see that neither his dad nor his brother-in-law had noticed the trophy buck pass above them. He breathed a sigh of relief and smiled to himself as he settled himself back down to wait and watch.

"Okay! Time out!" Jeb's voice broke the scenario as he stood up from the gaming chair and stretched, "I call potty break! That sensation of cold when the sun came over the mountain was way too realistic! Made me have to go!"

As Jeb sprinted off toward the video store bathroom, Zeke put down his controller, took off his headset and stood up as well. He turned to Jeremy Burman, grinning and winking, "That's a really realistic hunting game isn't it? Just like bein' in the woods with my dad!"

Jeremy stood up, glancing at the paused landscape on the 3D triple HD screen and stood up as well. Then he glanced back at Zeke who was pouring himself a cup of coffee from the back shelf of the store. In the back of his mind, Jeremy wondered how much Jeb and Zeke knew of what his character had just gone through. In his own mind, he made a decision: he wasn't going to tell his hunting buddies that he had let a trophy buck get by him. Plain and simple, that fact was only on a 'need to know' basis. And nobody really needed to know but him.

Jeremy grinned, walked briskly over to where Zeke was standing, opened the refrigerator and pulled out a cold soda, "Yup! It's a great game all right, Mr. Peters! Seeing it on the triple screen and in 3D is awesome! I'm really glad you asked me if I wanted to play! It's as good as being there!"

Chapter 22

Wendy Morrison stood in the living room of her home. She was staring at the mantel and the built-in bookshelves, glancing from one picture to another. The pictures were all of Andy and her at different ages. There was the one at their parent's funeral. Andy was sobbing and clutching desperately onto his big sister. Andy had been thirteen and she had been eighteen. She had been about to enter college that fall. That was the first of her own dreams she had given up so she could take good care of her brother.

Next was the picture of his soccer squad in middle school as they held up the trophy for the district championship. She had taken that photo. She didn't even want to guess how many soccer games she had gone to over several years. She had always been there for him, always cheering him on.

She turned her gaze to Andy's high school graduation photo in his cap and gown. He was all smiles, waving at her from the stage in the auditorium. She had taken that one too. She remembered how hard she had worked with him for two summers to get his grades up so he could go to a good college.

The next picture was of the trip they had taken to Yellowstone during the summer of his sophomore year in college. They had rafted the white water, ridden burros and hiked miles and miles of trails. She smiled sentimentally and a tear slipped down her cheek. It had been one of the few vacations where he hadn't gone off having a good time with his friends while she stayed home and worked two jobs in order to pay all the bills.

Then there was his college graduation picture. He was proudly displaying his degree. The smile faded from Wendy's face. She would never have a degree, even though she had been Valedictorian of her high school graduating class. She stared at Andy's broad smile, his sparkling eyes, his pride in graduating.

On the wall next to his college degree was his law school degree. It was written in gold, flourishing text. It was the ultimate symbol of his becoming a lawyer, something that Wendy had badly wanted to become, once upon a time, before the death of her parents cut her dreams short.

There was one last photograph. It was of Andy and her as he handed the key to Treasured Memories to his sister, both of them standing beside the front door, just after he had bought it for her. His face showed his delight. Hers was a bit more subdued. She remembered feeling like the store was a consolation prize he had bought her to make up for all she had lost, all she had given him. Somehow, it didn't equal out in her mind or in her heart.

Wendy turned and stared out the window at the drifts of snow and lightly swirling wind. It was beginning to snow again and she didn't have much time.

She walked decisively out of the living room, up the stairs and to her own small bedroom at the top of the stairs. She opened the door and entered. This room was really the only thing she could call her own. Wendy smiled understanding full well the irony involved in that idea. It was the only thing that was hers and yet it was located in his house, bought by his money.

On her bed stand was a photo of her parents and her before Andy had been born. It was the picture she treasured most. It always made her wistful for that time back again. She gazed at the old picture, wondering, if there had never been an Andy, how different her life would have been.

On the wall next to her bed were two bows and archery equipment. She reached out and gently touched one of the bows, glancing up at the picture hanging next to it. It was a photograph of her on the varsity archery team in high school. Wendy had been the captain of the team both her junior and senior years. She had been state individual champion two years in a row, and carried her otherwise lackluster team to second place in the state tournament her senior year. She glanced down on the bookshelf where six different archery trophies stood. The trophies were well polished and obviously cherished.

Wendy glanced out the window into the large fenced in back yard. There were two archery targets set up. Wendy religiously took a few minutes after cleaning up the supper dishes, even in the freezing temperatures and snow blown climate of a New England winter, to go out and shoot several quivers of arrows each evening. Feeling the power of the bow in her hand, the fletching close to her cheek, somehow comforted her, made her feel that the private inside part of her wasn't dead quite yet.

Shaking her head and pushing away the disturbing memories that kept trying to crowd it, she grabbed her favorite bow. She selected several arrows, the ones with the fixed three bladed broadheads, metallic blue shafts and the four fletchings made out of turkey feathers. The same bow and arrows she had used earlier at Elizabeth Fallon's house.

That was where she needed to go now. She was convinced that Elizabeth Fallon had finally been the one that had torn Andy away from her. Of course, deep down inside, Wendy had known that was going to happen sooner or later. Andy needed her less and less these days. No matter how much she did for him or hard she tried to make him happy, Andy was slowly but surely growing away from her.

Wendy's thoughts flitted back to the scene at Elizabeth Fallon's earlier that day. After Andy had been so upset with her, yelled at her and driven away in a rush to comfort Elizabeth, Wendy had decided she had no other choice. It was time to get rid of Elizabeth Fallon. Then Andy's attentions would come back to her, at least for a while. She had told Mandy that she needed to leave the shop for a few minutes, stopped off at home and picked up her archery equipment, then quickly driven to the old Fallon place.

When she reached the Fallon house, Wendy had parked up the road a ways, trudging through the snow until she was near the back door. To her surprise, Andy was sitting on the back porch, looking sad and remorseful. When he looked up and saw her standing there, holding her bow with an arrow already nocked, his eyes had grown wide with surprise and alarm. He had asked her what she was doing there and why she had her bow with her. Wendy hadn't answered. She had simply stared at her brother, watching him grow more and more angry at her. He began shouting at her, furious with her, ordering her to put the bow away and go home. Wendy didn't respond, because deep inside,

Wendy knew that all her brother's anger and hurtful words were all the doing of that tramp, that Elizabeth.

Wendy made a decision. She did the only thing she could. She was determined to save her brother from himself, and from that tramp. When he turned away for just a moment, she pulled up her bow and in a quick, fluid, practiced motion, loosed the arrow. As Andy lay on the ground, his blood staining the snow drift where he fallen, she stared into his startled eyes. She could see the pain and the agony within him. But she knew that what she had done was needed to purge his thoughtless and sinful feelings for Elizabeth. As her brother reached a shaking hand out to her and hoarsely uttered her name, Wendy had turned and left.

Her mind slipped back to the present. It was time to go. It was time to finish what she had started. Wendy pulled on her winter boots, slipped on her warm camouflage parka, picked her bow and gear back up and headed downstairs. Her head ached horribly. Her head was crammed with too many thoughts, too many feelings and conflicting emotions. She had to wash them all away and go and do what needed to be done. She needed to make sure that Elizabeth Fallon never bothered her or Andy again. Maybe then Andy would come to his senses. That was of course, if he lived.

Wendy slipped out the door and moved quickly, lithely to her compact car. She placed her bow in the trunk and opened the driver's side door. Elizabeth Fallon's house was only ten minutes away. After she dealt with that meddling tramp, she would return to the hospital to comfort her brother. Being badly injured, he would finally need her again. Truly need her. Need her to take care of him, cook for him, wash him, and read to him. And she would be there to do those things and more, just like before when he was thirteen.

Wendy Morrison smiled a beautiful, sweet smile as she started up her car and pulled out slowly into the snow-covered street. It would be just like when their parents had died. Andy would need her, in every way and she was going to be there for him.

***

Cash stood in the doorway, his Glock 9mm on the floor of the porch, his hands out where Tinmouth Pritchard could see them. Cash glanced over at Elizabeth Fallon, checking quickly to see if she was okay, then his gaze turned back to the man in front of him. Tinmouth had lowered his Ruger, but still held it, ready if needed.

"You know why we're here, Tinmouth," Cash declared, loud enough for Tinker and McNealy outside the back door to hear him.

The old man nodded wearily, as he stared into Cash's piercing gray eyes, "I reckon. You want the girl back."

Cash nodded slowly, making no quick motions to upset the old woodsman, "That's part of it, Tinmouth."

The old man's eyebrows furrowed and he frowned, as the Ruger came halfway back up toward the sheriff, "Part of it, sheriff? What's the rest of it, then?" Tinmouth glanced curiously back at Elizabeth who was still seated in the chair by the fire.

"You know the other part," Cash declared quietly, staring at the grizzled old man, his eyes betraying nothing, just calm and unafraid.

Just then, Cash's two-way crackled. "Base to Falls One...come in." He glanced down at it, frowning. What could Darlene want at this moment that couldn't wait until all this was over, he thought to himself.

Tinmouth stared at the two-way and then glanced back up at Cash, "No, Sheriff Green, I ain't got no idea what 'the other part' is! So why don't you tell me?!" Tinmouth's face had turned hard, his eyes were narrowed and the Ruger was now pointing at the middle of Cash's chest.

Outside the front door, Yamato had her Glock pointed directly at Tinmouth Pritchard, her finger lightly squeezing the trigger, her face tense and rigid, when her own two-way came to life, "Base to Falls Two...come in Yamato! It's important!"

Her eyes and her Glock remaining trained on her target, Yamato reached slowly and quietly for the radio, whispering curtly, "Darlene, this better be good."

Cash quickly decided to take another tack. He took a step farther inside and turned to Elizabeth, his voice quiet and calm, "Miss Fallon, are you alright?"

Elizabeth Fallon glanced uneasily back and forth between Cash and Tinmouth, obviously in distress over the situation, but seemingly with most of her wits about her. "Yes, sheriff, I'm ok. I'm not hurt in any way, thank you for asking." Her voice was calmer than Cash had anticipated, but still a bit shaky. Her cheeks were flushed and she was sitting ramrod straight in the chair, as if she were cautious of moving and upsetting Tinmouth Pritchard.

"Well, sheriff, are you gonna' tell me what in blazes you're talkin' about or not?" Tinmouth's voice rose in both volume and intensity, as he walked between Elizabeth and Cash, purposely placing himself where Cash had to look at and deal with him. The old man's eyes were tinged with growing suspicion and distrust.

Cash gazed into Tinmouth's eyes, his hands coming to rest at his sides. His muscles were at full attention while his feet were planted firmly on the floor, ready to move in whatever direction needed. "Andy Morrison," was all that Cash stated, his tone firm and direct.

Tinmouth stared suspiciously at Cash for a moment, his eyebrows rising dramatically, "What about that young buttinski?"

For a couple of rather long moments, Cash studied Tinmouth's body language and face. Something he was particularly good at doing. Cash Green could usually tell when someone was lying, or concealing something. In his gut, Cash felt certain that Tinmouth Pritchard was doing neither of those things.

Cash relaxed a bit, and rubbed his chin. Rubbing his chin meant only one thing: Cash was thinking. He was making all the pieces fit together in the puzzle he had spread out before him.

"You don't know what happened to Andy?" Cash asked quietly, his eyes sizing up the old man again.

Tinmouth sneered and snorted with contempt as he shook his head, "Does it look like I care what happened to that interfering shyster?"

At this, Elizabeth suddenly stood up, causing Tinmouth to jump back with alarm, quickly attempting to keep both her and the sheriff in his line of sight. Elizabeth Fallon stared at Tinmouth, her eyes wide with anger, hot tears beginning to roll down her red cheeks, as she spit out, "How can you say that! After you shot him? How can you be so heartless?!"

As Elizabeth began to weep, her hands covering her eyes, Tinmouth Pritchard lowered the Ruger halfway and burst out with a solemn declaration, "See here! I never hurt that little meddlesome whippersnapper! Sure, I would have liked to, but I didn't! Last I saw of him, he and that tall drink of water private eye broke into my cabin and told me he was slappin' a restrainin' order on me!"

Tinmouth Pritchard suddenly had a look of pure innocence flash across his face, which was quickly replaced by a scowl and an angry sneer. "So you're tryin' to pin that on me too, huh, Sheriff Green?! Well, I done a lot of things in my life, but I never shot no one! Never! Felt like it a bunch, but I never did it! No sir!"

Yamato's voice could be heard from outside the door, causing Tinmouth to crouch down and quickly bring up the Ruger, pointing it at the open door, "Boss, something you need to hear. Darlene got word straight from Meg. Andy woke up for a minute and told her. Tinmouth is telling the truth. He didn't shoot him."

Tinmouth turned and stared at the sheriff, his face plastered with the most outlandish smirk Cash had ever seen. Cash couldn't help but think that Tinmouth's yellowed and decaying teeth were truly a sight to behold.

Cash held up his hands in submission, "Okay, Tinmouth. Then we only have one thing to discuss." Cash's eyes glanced over at Elizabeth who was still sobbing, leaning against the side of the blazing fireplace, and then back to the old man.

Tinmouth sized up the sheriff. From what he knew of him, the Sheriff of The Falls was honest, hard working, decent and reasonable. He also knew that the sheriff was said to be tough as nails and no one to be trifled with. With a sigh of mixed regret and relief, Tinmouth lowered the Ruger and set it on the table.

As Tinmouth plopped himself with obvious acceptance and resignation into a chair, Yamato, as well as Tinker and McNealy, who had been watching through the back windows, stepped slowly and carefully into the cottage, guns out but lowered. Yamato walked quickly over and handed Cash his Glock, whispering confidentially into his ear, "Boss, Meg also told me that Andy blurted out 'she shot me' before he fell unconscious again."

Immediately, both Cash and Yamato turned and stared intently at Elizabeth Fallon who was still sobbing by the fireplace.

***

Louisa May McFadden held her end of the bright red and pink sash exactly to the mark that Danny had penciled in earlier on the wall. On the other side of the main arch in the entryway of the art gallery and museum, Danny was invisibly attaching the opposite end of the sash using eyehooks and wire. They each stood on the next to highest rung of two eight-foot stepladders.

"Does that look about even?" Danny called out, trying to crane his neck backwards and check on how the sash looked. He squinted a bit, and then peered over his glasses, looking through one eye and then the other, trying to gauge the height on each side.

"All I know is, if you don't hurry up and fasten my end, I'm going to have to drop it!" Louisa May burst out, grimacing at the ache in her arm and shoulder muscles, as she stared over at her husband of over fifty years imploringly. "Please, Danny! I can't hold it any longer!"

At that, Danny stopped fussing over the wire he was using to hold up the sash and climbed down his stepladder, quickly moving it over so that his ladder stood right next to Louisa May's.

In less than a minute and a half, Louisa May's end was fastened securely to her side of the entryway arch. Louisa May was now standing on the floor, looking up and proudly admiring the beautiful Valentine's Day decorations that she and Danny had placed all around the gallery.

Louisa May massaged her still sore shoulders as she slowly walked around the stunning art gallery, making sure they had properly decorated it for their upcoming Valentine's Day Extravaganza.

During their two day Valentine's Day Celebration, just as last year, all the artwork in the gallery was going to be on sale for twenty-five percent off. There were several heart-shaped signs all around the gallery stating that fact, as well as a program that could be picked up at the door on pink paper. The program listed each piece of art, the artist who had created it, the original price and then what it would cost with twenty-five percent off.

The program also listed the gallery website and home page where there were detailed descriptions of each piece of art. There were even two computers with touch screens set up to display the website on stands at the side of the lobby. Guests could use these to find out more about any piece of artwork they were interested in.

On the table by the entrance, there was also a stunningly beautiful fountain, itself a work of art by one of the gallery's artistes. Floating in the fountain, there were at least twenty, small intricately carved swans. Every hour on the hour during the Extravaganza two swans would be picked out of the water. On the bottom of each of those swans were numbers, that when placed together in the order chosen, corresponded to the listing of a piece of art on the gallery's website. That particular piece of artwork would then be on sale for fifty percent off for the next hour only. Considering the price tags on many of the pieces of art in the gallery, it was a huge saving. Both Mona and Louisa May were sure that the drawing would be a big hit with the devoted and enthusiastic attendees.

"It all looks great, Sweetheart," called out Danny as he put away his tools and placed the two stepladders carefully away in the storage closet. "Looks prettier than a speckled trout just pulled out of a brook, Darlin'!" Danny grinned and nodded his head emphatically.

"Mona's gonna' be de-lighted!" added Danny as he walked briskly away toward the kitchen area, his stomach telling him that it was done decorating time and well nigh on to snackin' time! He whistled happily as he strode off.

"And what's this that Mona's going to be de-lighted about?" came an enthusiastic voice as Mona Castillo swung open one of the huge front doors, letting in a swirl of snow and bitterly cold air. Mona was carrying a large box with tiny but exquisite Valentine's Day gifts in little red bags that were to be given out to anyone who attended their Valentine's Day sale, whether they bought any artwork or not.

Louisa May chuckled and walked quickly over to her benefactress and the owner of the art gallery, taking the large box away from Mona and placing it on the large mahogany table by the entrance. "Hopefully, about the way the place looks, all ready for our Extravaganza," replied Louisa May, winking at Mona and gesturing all around the gallery.

Mona glanced appraisingly at all the decorations around the main viewing area and then glanced along the balcony of the second floor, where another lengthy red and pink sash looped its way gracefully all along the long railing. She gazed at the large red and pink bows set along each wall between paintings, sculptures and pieces of artwork. Then she walked over and gently touched the huge red heart in the middle of the downstairs lobby which was adorned with large pink and white ribbons and a large cupid sculpture, donated by none other than the famous Spanish sculptor Don Diego Cervantes himself.

Mona turned back to Louisa May, her eyebrows lifted, her face impassive. For just a moment, Louisa May held her breath and her heart skipped a beat, afraid that Mona did not approve of the lavish decorations, although she had been the one to suggest them. Then, Mona's lips turned upward, her eyes twinkled merrily and she let out a joyful laugh, rushing over to embrace her handpicked art museum curator.

Louisa May soon joined in the laughter and shook her head at Mona, as Mona winked and continued to laugh and stare at the beautiful decorations.

As the two women's laughter finally petered out, Danny happened to saunter back into the main lobby, one hand holding a hefty roast beef sandwich, the other hand holding a napkin. His mouth was stuffed to overflowing. One glance at the two women and Danny swallowed. Glancing back and forth inquisitively between the two still chuckling women, Danny finally asked what he was thinking, "Is everything okay, Miss Mona?"

Mona and Louisa May glanced at each other, exchanged knowing winks and Mona declared loudly, "Why Danny! Miss Mona is De-lighted!"

As the two women began their laughter all over again, Danny raised an eyebrow, scratched the back of his head in bewilderment, then shrugged and walked away. He continued to relish his sandwich rather than trying to figure out what was so gosh-darn funny.

At that, Louisa May and Mona laughed only harder.

Chapter 23

"You're sure you want to do this?" asked Chief Tinker LaGrange once again, gazing at Elizabeth Fallon attentively. "You were kidnapped at gunpoint and taken somewhere against your will. You don't have to do this. You understand this, right?" Tinker glanced curiously over at Cash and Yamato, then back to Elizabeth.

Elizabeth Fallon placed her steaming teacup on the table in the sheriff's office back in The Falls, and nodded with a determined conviction as she glanced around the room at Cash, Yamato, Sergeant McNealy and finally back to Chief LaGrange.

"Yes, I understand, Chief LaGrange. I know that I have the right to press charges against Mr. Pritchard. I simply prefer not to." Elizabeth glanced over at Tinmouth Pritchard, sitting in one of the holding cells on the other side of the room. Tinmouth's bluster and aggressiveness was long gone. Once he had surrendered his Ruger at his old house, Tinmouth had slumped into a chair and been almost unresponsive ever since. In Elizabeth's eyes, there shone a real sense of kindhearted compassion.

"Could I talk to Mr. Pritchard for a moment, Sheriff Green?" Elizabeth asked, standing up and turning toward Cash hopefully.

"Of course, Elizabeth," Cash answered quietly with

a slight smile. He gestured approvingly toward the holding cell and nodded.

Tinker turned to Cash as Elizabeth made her way over to the cell, his obviously puzzled face displaying a slight frown. "What do you suppose she wants to say to him?" he whispered.

Yamato glanced at Cash, her dark eyes twinkling, and then smiled as well, "My bet is that she knows how much he's gone through and she wants to try and make things right."

"But he kidnapped her! He took her away at gunpoint..." Tinker started to mutter back quietly, until he was cut off by Yamato's gently shushing gesture. Yamato pointed toward the holding cell and all three law officers watched and listened as attentively to the scene that was playing out before them as they could without being too intrusive.

Elizabeth stood outside the holding cell, gazing down on Tinmouth Pritchard, her voice was soft, but firm and shaded with not only kindness but understanding, "Mr. Pritchard, you and I are a lot alike."

Tinmouth glanced up, his face weary and defeated, his bloodshot eyes studying the young woman in amazement for a moment before he answered, "How in Heaven's name are you and I anything alike?"

Elizabeth's answer came immediately, as if she had thought about the relationship between the two of them for quite awhile, "You have lost the people in your life that you loved the most, just as I have. You and I both have been given some difficulties to deal with in our lives. Neither of us has any money and we both need to find a way out of the situations we find ourselves now in." Elisabeth's eyes were wide and sincere, her attitude open, determined and accepting.

Tinmouth Pritchard's eyes widened as he considered what she had said. He suddenly leaned back as though appreciating for the first time that he and his old bosses' daughter were alike in more ways that he had realized. As he gazed up at the young woman, it was obvious that his attitude toward her was slowly changing. Instead of seeing her as a means to getting back something he felt he was owed, he was beginning to see her as a real person.

"I'm not pressing charges, Mr. Pritchard," Elizabeth said quietly, looking the old man straight in his eyes. "I can understand why you did what you did. You couldn't think of any other way to get what you needed and wanted."

Tinmouth Pritchard leaned forward again, a slight frown creasing his forehead, "Miss Fallon, I don't know what to say…" His voice trailed off as he stared at the young woman, bewildered but genuinely grateful of her generous gesture.

"There is one thing I'd like you to do, however," Elizabeth broke in and declared,

Tinmouth's eyes narrowed with suspicion, as if he was beginning to see the hidden agenda behind her kindness, "Oh? And what might that be?"

"I'd like you to come and work for me. I'm going to start my father's woodworking shop back up. All the tools are there, and there's been no end of townsfolk requesting pieces of handmade furniture, in hopes that my father's shop would continue on at some point." Elizabeth stared down at the flabbergasted Tinmouth, "My father said you were one of the best woodworkers and craftsmen he ever worked with. I want you to help me start my father's shop up again."

Tinmouth Pritchard simply sat on the cot in the

holding cell, his eyes wide, his mouth hanging open, completely blown away by Elizabeth Fallon's offer. He simply stared at the young woman who was by now getting up a full head of steam.

"We'll need one more woodworker, but dad said that you and he knew several good ones out in nearby communities. That would be your job, to find one who could work well with the two of us." Elizabeth started pacing back and forth in front of the holding cell. She not only had Tinmouth Pritchard staring and listening to her, but Cash, Yamato, Tinker and Sergeant McNealy were completely captivated as well.

"There's an old apartment up over the woodworking shop. It has a bedroom, a small kitchen, a bathroom and a sitting room. It has a wood stove upstairs and one down in the wood shop. It should be a perfectly good place for you to live as soon as we give it a good cleaning out. I won't ask for rent as long as you work with me."

"I know that you still have some things to work out with Sheriff Green and Chief LaGrange, but I'll wait for you if you need to serve some time in jail. While I'm waiting I'll hire whoever you think would best fit in with us, get the woodworking shop ready to run and get your apartment ready."

Elizabeth stopped pacing and turned to stare at Tinmouth Pritchard. Her voice was a bit shaky, but determined and her eyes were wide and imploring. "Mr. Pritchard, this really works out best for both of us. I hope you can see that. I have a lot of debts to pay, and I am determined to pay them. I've made my mind up about that. I will share the profits from the shop in a three-way split. You, me, and whoever else you feel we should hire to work with us in the business."

Elizabeth Fallon walked over to the holding cell, stuck her small arm and hand inside and asked determinedly, "What do you say, Mr. Pritchard? Do we have a deal?" Elizabeth suddenly looked small and frail, but unwavering and resolute.

Tinmouth Pritchard didn't move for several moments. Then, he slowly stood up, walked over to where Elizabeth was standing and shook her hand. He shook her hand hesitantly at first, but then with much more vigor and affirmation. The look on his old wizened face suddenly transformed from one of despair and anguish to one filled with hope and gratitude.

"I will work with you, Miss Fallon," Tinmouth Prichard muttered thankfully. "I will! And we'll make the old shop just as good as the one your daddy ran. I promise!"

In moments, both Tinmouth and Elizabeth had tears of joy running down their cheeks, crying shamelessly in front of their law enforcement audience.

A short time later, Yamato sat at the interview table with Elizabeth Fallon. Cash, Tinker and Sergeant McNealy stood leaning against the wall, watching and listening closely.

"Elizabeth, I understand you've been through a lot today, but there are some questions we need to ask. Understood?" Yamato's dark, intelligent eyes searched Elizabeth's as she spoke.

Elizabeth nodded. It was obvious she was physically weary and emotionally worn out as well, but she smiled slightly and nodded, "Yes, Deputy Yamato, I understand."

Yamato glanced back at Cash and began, "Meg Monroe was with Andy Morrison when he suddenly became conscious..."

Elizabeth leaned forward, obviously concerned but delighted, "Mr. Morrison's awake! How wonderful! Is he going to be all right? I was so worried!" The relief on Elizabeth's face made the next question even harder for Yamato to ask.

"Miss Fallon," Yamato asked quietly, her eyes ready to assess Elizabeth's reaction, "were you the one who shot Mr. Morrison with an arrow?"

Elizabeth Fallon jerked backward, a gasp escaping her throat, her eyes wide and incredulous, "Me? Are you serious? I would never hurt Mr. Morrison! He gave me a job! He helped me plan out how to pay off my father's debts! He was so wonderful to me! Why would I ever do anything to hurt him! He was like my own guardian angel!" Elizabeth burst out in tears, but unlike her tears with Tinmouth, these were tears of sadness and embarrassment.

Yamato nodded and glanced back at Cash. It was more than evident that Elizabeth Fallon wasn't the 'she' that had shot him. That left only one person that had any motive and opportunity to kill Andy Morrison.

As Yamato comforted Elizabeth as best she could, Cash slipped aside and whispered privately to Chief LaGrange and Sergeant McNealy, "Okay, we need to mobilize our three agencies and begin a search for the one person who's left as a suspect."

Tinker LaGrange and Sergeant McNealy both nodded decisively, grabbing their coats and hats and heading toward the door as they answered together in unison, "Wendy Morrison!"

***

Jeremy Burman burst through the classroom door, anxious to leave behind his third period English class. As the students streamed out of the class into the high school hallway all around him, he experienced a large allotment of relief and a delightful sense of freedom. Mr. Milford, his sophomore English teacher, meant well but his one hour and fifteen minute class was about one hour and ten minutes too long for most of his students. Jeffrey Milford went on and on about sonnets, seventeenth century English writers and he simply loved to read Chaucer's Canterbury Tales to his uninspired and painfully disinterested students.

His students had given Mr. Milford the name of Sir Geoffrey Milquetoast. The 'Sir' was due to his adoration of English literature. 'Geoffrey', since Chaucer's first name was Geoffrey, which was much like Mr. Milford's given name of Jeffrey. 'Milquetoast', primarily because their teacher constantly went on and on in such a glowing, long-winded fashion about early English literature to his students that they had begin to truly detest it rather than love it, as was his fondest hope.

As Jeremy hurried through the crowded hallway, adjusting his backpack as he went, he glanced up and came to a complete and sudden stop. There not ten feet in front of him was Matilda the Hun. Matilda Rodriquez, Dean of Students at West Mount High, the union high school that included The Falls, Brown Bear Junction and fifteen more small towns, was a commanding force. She was aggressive, authoritative and zeroed in on students who, she thought, needed her help, whether they wanted it or not.

Jeremy had surfaced on her radar toward the end of his freshman year. Jeremy's test scores were off the charts, he was a wizard with a computer and he was creative as the day was long. But, in his classrooms, he hardly ever joined in any discussion, purposely shied away from his teachers and stayed on the edge of the social crowd.

The basic truth was that Jeremy was very intelligent and more than capable, but he didn't enjoy the limelight. He much preferred listening and watching to talking and participating in class. For Matilda the Hun, however, he had become a challenge. She wanted to 'mold him' into a more rounded, complete high school student. She wanted Jeremy to share and give back to his teachers and classmates through his interaction with them. In short, Matilda wanted Jeremy to become a productive member of West Mount High.

"Weren't you supposed to come and see me yesterday afternoon, young man?" Matilda asked icily, her narrowed eyes staring at Jeremy, hands on her solidly built hips.

"Yes, Ma'am, I was," Jeremy answered honestly, as he began to sweat even though the temperature in the hallway was cool if not downright chilly. The chill in the air was primarily due to the fact that the outside doors were being held open as students changed classrooms. "I was headed there, but Mr. Forester saw me in the hall and asked me to stop by his classroom. He wanted to go over some math problems with me." Jeremy grimaced at the thought.

Ichabod Forester was a demanding, anal math teacher who seemed to take particular pride in hounding the brighter students in his classes to constantly improve and advance their knowledge in math. If you were a student of The Headless Mathman, as the students had dubbed Ichabod, and had a good grasp of math, you were likely one of the lucky few who found themselves prodded, poked and pushed by the fanatical math instructor to increase your mathematical awareness.

Matilda the Hun squinted at her quarry, hesitating for a moment and then finally accepting Jeremy's answer as the truth. There was one thing that Matilda was very good at. She could look you in the eye and tell if you were lying to her. If you did lie to her, she would thoroughly and delightedly dismantle your falsehood without a second thought about child abuse ordinances or any fear whatsoever of Child Protective Services.

"I understand that you're still sitting in the back rows of Mrs. Morgan's history class. Is that true?" Matilda's eyes grew narrower, as she studied her victim.

"Well, Ma'am," Jeremy swallowed loudly, "you told me not to sit in the back row in her class anymore. I'm not. I'm in the next to the back row." Jeremy's eyes were still wide and uneasy, but filled with the absolute truth and Matilda tilted her head and expelled air, which sounded quite similar to the hissing of an old steam train stopping to pick up passengers.

"Let's move up to either the first or second row, shall we?" Matilda smiled, showing her perfect, white teeth. Jeremy had decided that he liked Matilda Rodriguez a lot better when she didn't smile than when she did. Her smile somehow made him think of a pack of wolves showing their teeth just before they ate you.

"Yes Ma'am," mumbled Jeremy, glancing uncomfortably away from the sight of Matilda's perfect set of teeth. As he did so, he happened to notice who was coming down the hall toward him.

Most of the high school students had already entered their fourth period classrooms, with only a few stragglers rushing by, trying to make sure they weren't late to their classes. Being late probably meant a detention. Most kids loathed detentions because it meant they had to stay in school longer than they

THE FALLS: Cupid's Arrow

already were scheduled to. Most teachers loathed giving them, because then the students would sulk and act depressed for the rest of the period. Jeremy didn't think detentions worked, but he wasn't about to sound off on the subject.

Sylvia Jean Jones was hurrying along, trying to stuff her books into a small backpack. She had obviously gone to her locker to change her morning textbooks out for her afternoon ones. As she rushed along, she wasn't really looking where she was going. If she took three more steps, striding the direction she was headed, she would run smack dab into the back of Matilda the Hun.

Now for the past year and a half, Jeremy Burman had been totally charmed and captivated by and in total awe of Sylvia Jean Jones. Jeremy thought she was the most beautiful, most amazing and most desirable girl on the face of the planet. He had adored her from afar. But, he had never spoken to her. He was quite sure that if he spoke to her, or if she, by chance were to say something to him, he would faint dead away on that spot.

The closest Jeremy had come to Sylvia Jean was walking behind her in the hallway. Sometimes, if he was lucky enough, he would get close enough to smell her. She smelled like soap or vanilla, he couldn't decide which.

Jeremy had a mere two seconds to make a life-changing decision. He could either save Sylvia jean Jones from walking right into Matilda the Hun, which would mean that Matilda would make Sylvia Jean's high school years anxious and horrid at best, or he could simply watch the collision happen and slink away as Matilda turned and started in on the unsuspecting young lady.

Jeremy took the high road. He leaned forward, acting like he had tripped over his own feet, which wasn't exactly a stretch, and bumped directly into Matilda the Hun. Matilda's eyes opened wide with surprise and shock as she let out a bloodcurdling scream. She staggered slightly at the force of Jeremy's weight suddenly bumping into her, but her stocky physique was up to the task. In fact, Jeremy bounced off Miss Rodriguez and sprawled head over teakettle on the hallway floor.

Matilda's piercing screech made everyone else in the hallway come to a complete and sudden stop, including Sylvia Jean Jones. Sylvia Jean's eyes widened with astonishment as she glanced first at how close she was to Matilda and then down at Jeremy who was sprawled on the tiled floor, staring up at her in complete and abject embarrassment. Sylvia Jean was an intelligent young lady. It didn't take her long to figure out what had just happened. With a quick, easy grin, she mouthed the words, "Thank you!" and continued on her hurried way down the corridor.

Jeremy suddenly was washed over by the warmest, most wonderful feeling. As he stood and listened half-heartedly as Matilda the Hun went up one side of him and down the other, he snuck a glance at the rapidly disappearing Sylvia Jean Jones.

During the next five minutes, as Matilda Rodriguez loudly lectured Jeremy, scolded him, berated him and finally rolled her eyes, gave up and walked away from him, Jeremy could only think of one thing. Sylvia Jean Jones had smiled and spoken to him!

***

As Elizabeth Fallon sat in the passenger seat of the cruiser that had pulled over by the shoveled out walkway in front of her house, she smiled wearily. She sat motionlessly beside him as Deputy Horace Scofield slowly drove the Jeep Liberty down her long driveway, parking just behind her small little subcompact. Elizabeth shook her head, suddenly realizing how much her ordeal of being held hostage had actually taken out of her. She had been running on pure adrenaline for some time now, and she could feel her energy starting to spiral down, getting ready to crash.

Horace closed the driver's door of the cruiser with a thud and trudged quickly through the snowdrifts to open the front door of the cruiser for her. It wasn't more than a minute before they both stood at the door of her house. Horace reached out and the door swung open. His smile was open and earnest, "Here you go, Miss Fallon! Bet you're glad to be home."

After helping Elizabeth through the door, Horace took her hat and coat and pointed to a rocker in the front room, "Cash told me to get you home, get you comfortable and get some food into you."

Horace grinned as he checked out Elizabeth's refrigerator, "I see just the thing! Sliced deli meat, cheese and a tomato! I'll make us some sandwiches!" Horace hefted the teakettle and placed it on the gas stove, turning up the burner as he searched the cupboards for mugs and plates.

"The boss said you'd most likely be pretty tired, Miss Fallon. So as soon as we get some food into you, a little nap will be just what the sheriff ordered!" Horace chuckled at his witty turn of phrase, congratulating himself for cleverly substituting sheriff for doctor in the old adage.

As Horace chatted along and bustled merrily about the kitchen, Elizabeth found that the longer she sat quietly in the rocker, the sleepier she felt. Soon, Horace's ramblings, the smell of the fresh sandwiches and the teakettle beginning to whistle faintly had lulled her to sleep.

As Elizabeth Fallon slept, she dreamed. Flashes of scenes rushed through her thoughts. Her father's funeral. Meeting Andy Morrison at his office for the first time. The two scary encounters with Tinmouth Pritchard. Tinmouth's grinning yellow stained teeth. Meeting Wendy Morrison for coffee. Finding Andy Morrison's bloody body in the snow with an arrow stuck deep in his chest. Talking with Tinmouth Pritchard at the jail. Being asked at her interrogation if she had shot Andy Morrison. Her dreams careened along, faster and faster, until she woke herself, sitting up with a jolt.

Staring around in the last few rays of sunlight, she saw Horace Scofield reading the paper over on her couch. He glanced up when he heard her awaken and smiled at her.

"Ready for the tea and sandwich now, Miss Fallon?" Horace stood up and gestured cheerfully toward the small kitchen table where he had placed a plate with a sandwich and had an empty teacup ready to be filled. The very table where she and her father had eaten most of their meals over the course of her life, thought Elizabeth.

Elizabeth stood up slowly and walked over to the place Horace had set. As she passed the living room window, she glanced out at the deputy's cruiser. She turned away, but then, with sudden realization, she turned back to stare at the cruiser once again. On the side of Horace's car was one word, spray-painted over the law enforcement shield of the West Sugar Shack Falls Sheriff's emblem. The word was: Tramp.

Elizabeth's eyes widened in shock and alarm as she turned and called out quietly, fearfully, to the deputy, "Deputy Scofield! Come here, quick!"

Horace Scofield was at her side in moments, his gun drawn, his face pale and stern. He stared uneasily at the writing on the car. Then he noticed with a quickly growing foreboding that both tires on this side of his cruiser were flat. The ominous thought that they couldn't get away, even if they wanted to, raced through Horace's head. A shaken Horace Scofield pulled Elizabeth away from the windows. Placing her in a windowless corner of the kitchen, Horace stood in front of her, his gun out, his eyes scanning the windows and doors intently as he grabbed his two-way and spoke urgently into it.

"Falls Three to Base! Falls Three to Base! Come in Darlene!" Horace's voice was quiet but intense. As he spoke, his eyes wandered back and forth across the rooms on the first floor of Elizabeth's home. The last rays of light were casting shadows everywhere. On most calm, serene evenings in February the growing shadows would give the rooms and the yard a charming ethereal quality. But on this particular evening in February, fearful things seemed to lurk in every shadow.

"This is Base...over," came the reply that Horace was so counting on. "What's wrong, Deputy Scofield?" Darlene's voice had lost its usual monotone, and a certain urgency had replaced it.

"We need backup!" Horace whispered hoarsely, his head felt like it was on a swivel as he continued to scan the growing darkness within the old house. Horace hated the darkness, he had ever since he had been a child, although he didn't like to admit it. But he knew that if he turned on the lights, he and Elizabeth would be much easier targets to see, and to harm.

"My cruiser's tires have been punctured and someone has spray-painted the word 'tramp' on the side of it. Miss Fallon and I are in the kitchen, in a corner away from the windows. We're both okay so far. I don't know what's going on, but we've got a real issue here!"

The two-way sputtered once and then there were a few moments of silence. Horace glanced at the two-way with a growing sense of impending doom. What if the radio had gone out before Darlene heard his message? What would he do? Finally Darlene's voice crackled to life, "The sheriff knows. He's on his way. He says to hunker down and hold tight."

Horace took a deep breath, "Roger that, Darlene. Thanks."

Darlene's voice came back once more, tinged with a little more concern and caring, "Sheriff says he believes in you, Horace, and..."

There was a momentary pause and then Darlene finished her thought, her voice more quiet and compassionate than Horace had ever heard her, "...and I do too. Over and out."

Horace stared at the two-way for a moment and then a warm grin spread over his face. Darlene cared about him. She really cared about him! Horace took a deep breath and enjoyed the feeling for a second longer. Then the smile vanished and he spoke quietly and calmly to Elizabeth Fallon.

"We're going to head over to the stairs. If we can make it up those, then we can find a place to watch the stairwell. That will be the only way anyone can reach us. Understood? Are you up for it?" Horace stared intently at the shaken young woman behind him in the corner.

Elizabeth Fallon nodded her head quickly as two tears slipped down her hot cheeks. To Elizabeth, it was Tinmouth Pritchard abducting her all over again. The nightmare had returned.

Chapter 24

Meg Monroe walked briskly back from her rounds in the general ward of the hospital, glancing out the window at the last rays of daylight. She thought to herself, winter days are so short! Late sunrises, early sunsets, and gray skies most of the time. Then when the sun does shine, it has no real warmth.

Staring at the sunset as she strode along, she almost ran into Peggy Pendergast, a relatively new candy striper at West Sugar Shack Regional Medical Facility.

"Oh! Good afternoon, Dr. Monroe!" squeaked Peggy as she glanced into Meg's eyes anxiously, while the bottles of medical supplies, all neatly placed in order on the tray she was carrying, all shifted around precariously.

"Sorry!" Meg glanced at Peggy's new candy striper name tag, "Sorry, Peggy! I wasn't watching where I was going. Are you all right?" Meg smiled reassuringly at the high schooler and patted her gently on the arm.

"I'm fine, Dr. Monroe," Peggy smiled shyly and then her eyes widened as she remembered what nurse Flora Henriksen had told her to do. "Oh! Miss Flora told me to let you know that Mr. Morrison is awake. She said to tell you…"

By this time, Meg was jogging off down the corridor. She turned and called out over her shoulder, "Thank you, Peggy! Have a good evening!"

Peggy Pendergast glanced after the rapidly disappearing doctor and then down at her tray. The medical supply bottles she was supposed to deliver from Head Nurse Flora to the duty nurse in the private ward of the hospital were all rolling around freely on her tray. With a resigned sigh, Peggy Pendergast slowly turned around and headed back to Miss Flora, knowing that there would most likely be a long lecture involved about doing a job correctly.

By the time Meg Monroe reached Andy Morrison's private room in the critical care ward, he was already awkwardly thrashing around. It was obvious that he was in great discomfort, and that his wound might well need attention.

"Andy!" Meg declared as she raced into his room and gently but firmly made him lie back on the bed. She noticed he must be very weak, since it took very little strength to tenderly push him back down. "You need to stay quiet! You'll rip out the sutures and start bleeding again, perhaps internally. Do you hear me?" Meg's insistent eyes caught and held Andy's and he nodded weakly in response.

"Meg...it hurts so bad..." Andy's low, feeble voice trailed off as he grimaced in extreme pain and agony. A tear slipped down his cheek as he moaned softly.

"I know, I know," Meg replied as she quickly worked to increase the dosage of his pain medication drip. She rapidly checked his vital signs on all the machines he was hooked up to, while she intently examined his bandages for signs of bleeding, "You've been through quite an ordeal."

Andy suddenly twisted his face around, his eyes wide, as he remembered. "Meg!" he whispered hoarsely. "My sister! My sister shot me!" Andy's eyes glanced down incredulously at the tubes and bandages on his chest, then he glanced back up into Meg's eyes once more.

"Why?" he whispered, his eyes now filled with tears. As he lay there, shaking from pain and sorrow, one strangled sob shook his entire body. "Why would she shoot me?"

Meg's kind heart went out to the young man lying before her. He turned his face away and clenched his fists, trying his best to fight the pain and despair that was overwhelming him. She reached down and firmly grabbed his arm, squeezing it tightly. She had no answers to ease his distress or his anguish. Andy Morrison swallowed hard and looked back up at her, his eyes red and already swollen. No words were spoken, but he nodded as if to acknowledge her wish to comfort him in some small way.

Out in the waiting room, Serafina Messina was speaking intently with Mandy Wagner. Mandy was glancing back and forth between Dr. Messina and the touching scene inside Andy's critical care room.

"She has seemed preoccupied and quiet for some time now," Mandy sighed, trying her best to remember any clues that Wendy Morrison might have given that something was dramatically wrong.

"Wendy was always a very private person," Mandy stated, her thoughts racing back over the last few months, "and she took things to heart a lot more than most. Small little things that didn't amount to much, you know?"

Serafina watched the older woman carefully, "Did Wendy ever seem violent to you, in any way?"

"Lands, no!" Mandy turned and stared at the

psychiatrist, her eyes widening dramatically. "Although she seemed more and more edgy at times, even a bit disjointed in what she said and did. Funny..." Mandy hesitated and looked away.

Serafina peered at the older woman, a frown appearing on her forehead, "Funny what?"

Mandy sighed and relented, "Well, I was going to mention this when I talked to you, doctor, and I know it sounds crazy. But sometimes it seemed like she was two different women, ya' know?" Mandy turned and gazed into Serafina's eyes, obviously troubled at 'tattling' on her employer and friend, but seeing no other solution.

"Once moment she would be happy and joking. Then, a minute or so later, I would turn back around and start talking with her again and she would be just as cold, bitter and angry as can be. Ten minutes later, the happy, funny Wendy would be back."

"Did you ever notice when these switches would occur?" Serafina asked Mandy, picking up her notebook and writing notes in it.

"Well," puzzled Mandy, her eyebrows lowering as she thought, "at times it would be when we talked about Mr. Andy, her brother. Other times it was when she talked about her future or her brother's future." Mandy shrugged and stared at Serafina, then turned away and watched Andy and Meg in his hospital room.

"It sure looks like he's in real pain, doesn't it, Dr. Messina?" Mandy sounded compassionate, her voice showing the wear and tear of the terrible events of the last few days. She was wringing a tissue around her fingers, her body stiff and obviously ill at ease.

"Thank you, Miss Wagner," Serafina replied, touching Mandy's arm comfortingly as she stood up. "Perhaps I could be of help to Andy right now," she turned and explained over her shoulder as she walked toward the critical care unit.

Meg Monroe saw Serafina coming and motioned with a look of relief for her to come into the room.

"Andy," Meg leaned over and spoke quietly to the injured lawyer, "this is Serafina Messina. Dr. Messina. She's a really good psychiatrist here in The Falls. She's a pretty nice lady as well. Her husband is William Frasier. You know, you met him. He's the writer."

Meg was talking very quickly, hardly taking time to breathe. Serafina could see that the whole incident, plus too many twelve and fourteen hour days and nights with not enough sleep were beginning to take their toll on the young and usually energetic doctor.

"Why don't you let Mr. Morrison and I talk while you take a break, Dr. Monroe," Serafina gazed meaningfully at Meg, subtly nodding her head toward the door.

Meg understood and silently, gratefully accepted. Checking Andy's vital signs once more, Meg smiled and patted Andy on the arm, "Dr. Messina will take good care of you while I'm gone."

As Meg slipped away toward the doctor's break room and the distinct possibility of a strong cup of coffee with her feet up, Serafina came and stood by the side of Andy's bed. It was easy for anyone to see how much pain the young lawyer was in physically. But what she was mostly interested in at this point was what kind of pain he was feeling emotionally.

"Andy, I know you're in a lot of pain right now. But I really need to ask you some questions. Just do the best you can, ok?" Andy looked up into the beautiful woman's eyes and nodded with resignation. Andy knew all too well what she was about to ask him, and he knew as much as he wanted to protect his big sister, his honest answers could help his sister more than hurt her.

"Andy, tell me about your sister, please," Serafina whispered, leaning toward the stricken lawyer.

Andy grimaced with a wave of pain as he tried to find a comfortable position. When he realized there was none, he hesitantly began, his voice weak but clear, "My sister is everything to me, Dr. Messina. She has been ever since my parents died when I was thirteen. I love her with all my heart."

For fifteen minutes, Mandy Wagner watched the physiatrist and the lawyer talking animatedly in the critical care room a few yards away. The tears fell down her cheeks as she thought of her best friend, Wendy, out there somewhere, alone and hunted. Mandy shook her head slowly and couldn't help but wonder, how had things gone so wrong so suddenly?

***

There was a large maple tree that stood a few feet away from the Fallon's family home. It was a gnarled and twisted old maple, with several large and sturdy branches reaching up to the dark, cloudy, February night sky. Where those large branches came together in a knotty crotch and then branched off separately, Wendy Morrison waited patiently.

The skin on Wendy's face was nearly frozen, but she didn't even notice. Her sharp eyes were intent and obsessive, as they watched Deputy Horace Scofield and Elizabeth Fallon kneeling by the head of the stairs. From her chosen place of hiding, Wendy could easily look into the second story windows. She was no more than twenty feet from the deputy and the tramp. Wendy could see them staring expectantly down the staircase, Horace with his gun out, the tramp leaning against the wall, her face a mask of terror and fear.

Wendy smiled. She was glad that the tramp was frightened. She deserved to be. Soon the tramp would be dead and then Wendy could go back to being the nice Wendy. She could go and comfort her dear brother Andy over Elizabeth Fallon's death and help him recuperate from his injury. Good Wendy would enjoy being needed again. She would enjoy that very much.

But right now, she was the tough Wendy. The tough Wendy came out whenever there were difficult things to deal with. She had first appeared when her parents had died and she had to give up her dream of going to college, take care of her brother, feed them both and make enough money so they didn't lose their home. All of that occurring at eighteen years of age. Tough Wendy had been her way of coping with the hard realities of life. From then on there had always been two Wendy's. One to take care of and love her brother and one to deal with the hardships the world had to offer.

Each year, the two Wendy's had grown farther and farther apart. The hard Wendy, who preferred to think of herself as Adelaide, which was her given middle name, got more and more unfeeling and became more cynical and ruthless. All the while good Wendy became kinder and more gracious, choosing to blot out Adelaide from her consciousness more and more as each year rolled around. At this point, Wendy didn't even realize that Adelaide existed. But when things got tough, when stress levels rose, Wendy submerged into her subconscious and Adelaide took over and surfaced.

Adelaide tilted her head and wiped the swirling snowflakes away from her eyes as she stared in the window, fascinated by how the two pitiful humans thought they were safe, hidden away up the stairs. They obviously expected her to crash through a downstairs window or door. Then Deputy Scofield would predictably try and shoot her as she stormed up the stairs after them.

Adelaide smiled once more. In her pocket she had a fairly large rock. Her plan, at this point, was to throw the rock at the window. In the confusion and shock that followed, she would have time to get off one, maybe two arrows. The first arrow would be for the deputy. The second arrow would be for the tramp. Then she would climb down, walk the quarter mile to her hidden car and drive back to her house, where she would change back into her regular clothes and dutifully go to the hospital. With any luck she would get to the regional medical facility before Andy regained consciousness.

Adelaide reached into her pocket and grasped the rock, moving slightly to the right to get into the best shooting position. She took a deep breath and brought the rock out of her pocket. She pulled an arrow from her quiver and made ready. Then the hand holding the rock drew back and aimed as the other hand gripped her bow, ready to nock the arrow, aim and shoot.

Bright headlights of three cars broke the silky darkness. The cars were traveling fast, and they turned into the driveway just below her. The cars slewed to a weaving, skidding halt, swerving almost uncontrollably on the ice and snow in the driveway. Adelaide's eyes narrowed, her mouth contorted into what might have been an angry snarl and she placed the stone back in her pocket. She quickly brought the bow back behind the limbs of the tree and pressed her body tightly to the trunk so she could not be seen.

Adelaide watched intently as Sheriff Cash Green and

Deputy Yamato jumped out of the first car and ran toward the front door, handguns drawn. Chief LaGrange and an older state trooper slammed the doors to their own cruisers and warily jogged around the house to the back door, scanning attentively all around the yard, their guns weaving back and forth, glinting in the patchy moonlight as they ran.

Suddenly, the sheriff called out loudly and moments later, the lights flashed on from within the house. The front door was thrown open. Moments after that, the police chief and trooper were let in the back door. Adelaide didn't hesitate. There was no time to lose. She turned and nimbly dropped down into the snowdrift just below the tree. Glancing back over her shoulder, she moved swiftly and silently away from the house, through the shadows and the falling snowflakes. In moments, she was gone.

***

"Have you seen her?" were Cash's first words as he strode through the front door of the Fallon's homestead. Yamato moved quickly to the back door to let in Tinker and Sergeant McNealy, while Cash crouched in the entranceway of the house. His eyes and Glock rapidly moved along all the windows on that side of the house.

"No! Nothing!" answered Horace, with Elizabeth standing right behind him. Horace's face was white and drawn, and Elizabeth's eyes were red and wet once again.

Horace had just enough time to blurt out his reply before Cash glanced over at Yamato, Tinker and McNealy, shaking his head purposefully. The sheriff swiftly dashed back out the front door, barking out an order to Horace as he went, "Stay here! Get Miss Fallon to a sheltered corner away from the windows. Now!"

Horace pointed to a corner of the room where they couldn't be seen and, taking Elizabeth firmly by the arm, he determinedly secured her away from sight. Horace could hear Elizabeth's fast, shallow breathing and could almost feel Elizabeth's pulse racing as he stood in front of her, handgun out and ready.

Cash and Yamato circled the side yard, using their small but powerful LED flashlights to carefully search the drifts of snow for signs of Wendy Morrison. At the same time, Tinker rummaged cautiously around the back yard and the outbuildings while Sergeant McNealy quickly but professionally searched the front yard for recent footsteps.

Almost immediately, the beam of Yamato's LED flashed across the fresh, deep imprints beneath the maple tree next to the house. The small footprints angled off toward the road while still making use of the shadows of the nearby trees and shrubs.

Cash glanced at Yamato and then stared back at the house. He seemed to be struggling with his priorities. Then he whistled long and low, which immediately called over the chief of police and state trooper.

Cash's eyes flashed with determination and urgency as he stood regarding his posse, "We need to do two things. First and foremost, get Elizabeth back to the Brown Bear Junction Police Station where she'll be as safe as we can make her. I believe you have two officers on at night, correct Chief LaGrange?"

Tinker turned and glanced at Cash, "You know I do." Tinker nodded quickly, his eyes intent, his lower jaw jutting out.

Cash nodded, "Good. Horace will take my cruiser and drive Elizabeth there immediately, if that's okay with you, of course, Chief?" Tinker nodded immediately.

Cash turned to Sergeant McNealy, his eyebrows lowered, his face taunt. As Tinker pulled out his cell phone and walked a step or two away to contact his men, Cash, whispered solemnly to the weathered state policeman.

"I need roadblocks, McNealy, roadblocks on every highway going in and out of this area as quickly as possible. We need to contain her here so…" he hesitated a moment, then gritted his teeth and continued, "…so we can hunt her down."

Sergeant McNealy's eyes were unwavering as he nodded once. The big trooper trotted back through the snow to his cruiser, ready to call in for backup.

Yamato gazed intently at Cash, reaching out and touching his arm, her eyes dark and thoughtful, "Hey boss. What's wrong? You're usually the one who is positive and upbeat, no matter the circumstances. I gotta' tell you, you look pretty grim."

Cash stared off into the winter night for a moment and then stared directly into Yamato's eyes, his voice barely above a whisper, "I just got a text message from Dr. Messina. She thinks that Wendy Morrison has a split personality."

Yamato frowned and responded with surprise, "Truly a split personality? So, what does that…"

Cash finished her sentence, his tone low and tense, "It means that if we catch up to Wendy and the nasty Wendy is in control," Cash glanced away for a moment a weary, somber expression spreading across his handsome features, "it probably won't be a happy ending."

Yamato took a long hard look at her boss, drew in a deep breath and nodded. Yamato knew how important it was to Cash to bring their suspects in alive. She was also well aware that if Dr. Messina was right, in this instance, they might not have a choice.

Together, Cash and Yamato headed quickly back into the house to escort Horace and Elizabeth out to Cash's cruiser and get them on their way to safety.

Chapter 25

Mallard Hornsworth and his sister Alice sat by the roaring fireplace in their large, renovated cottage on lake Pumpkinseed. All around the cottage, the wild February winds swirled and howled from time to time, whipping up the freshly fallen snow and creating miniature snow tornados that could be seen from the specially developed, double-pane and insulated windows.

Mallard and Alice each had a manuscript in one hand and a cup of steaming Earl Grey tea in the other and it was obvious from the look in their eyes that they were lost in thought as they read the literary draft quickly but thoroughly. The two literary agents were busily engaged in reading and evaluating the latest novel from Windermere Peacock, one of their most recent clients. Windermere specialized in suspense dramas with an exotic twist in the plot near the end.

When assessing a manuscript's worth and appeal, the two literary agents preferred to read the submitted work together, finishing it in as close as possible to one or two sittings. That gave them twice the insight and expertise to deal with what positive characteristics the book had, what it lacked and what they could do to help their client sell the piece to just the right publisher.

The gray classic tabby in the corner near the

fireplace, stood up, stretched and lazily but purposely walked out to the kitchen. It was past his suppertime, and he had been waiting patiently for his two people to remember to feed him, but his tummy was now beginning to growl. As he nosed around his empty dish and lifted his nose to sniff at the various smells emanating throughout the kitchen area, Alice happened to notice him out of the corner of her eye.

"Oh, my! Poor, dear Basil! I'm so sorry!" Alice sputtered, immediately deposited the manuscript onto the mahogany table next to her and quickly shuffled out to the kitchen in her fluffy slippers.

Opening the fridge, Alice got out Basil's favorite winter supper: a small piece of freshly cooked haddock. Placing the fish in the cat's dish, Alice added a little dried cat food off to the side and one of Basil's favorite chewy treats. After placing the dish down on the floor as Basil softly mewed his delight and thanks, Alice poured a small amount of milk in the other cat bowl and placed it beside the fish.

As Basil Rathbone, or more accurately Phillip St. John Basil Rathbone, named after the English actor whose most famous role was that of Sherlock Holmes in numerous films, heartily indulged himself in his dinner, the grandfather clock, and several other clocks around the cottage chimed eight o'clock.

Mallard glanced up at the sound of the chime, checking his own pocket watch and then glanced over to where Alice was standing and watching their pet thoroughly enjoy his meal. His own stomach was rumbling as well. As he set down his tea cup and unfinished manuscript, Mallard pushed himself up out of the overstuffed armchair and called out to his dear sister.

"I say! Alice my dear! Don't you think it's about time that we joined old Basil in an evening repast?" Mallard smiled hopefully, making a point to dramatically check his pocket watch once again.

Alice chuckled with affection and amusement, glancing over at her older brother. Mallard was always hungry, she thought. It didn't matter if it was before dawn; the middle of the day or late at night, Mallard Hornsworth always had room for 'a little something' as he liked to call it.

"Yes, Ducks! I was just about to get us some supper," Alice called out as she turned toward the fridge, preparing to check out what might taste particularly good that evening.

Mallard had already shuffled over to the window of their office, staring out toward Lake Pumpkinseed. During the summer, Mallard would be out on the forty-foot long dock a dozen times a day. He would go out to feed his precious ducks (thus the 'Ducks' nickname given to him affectionately by the locals), or readying one of their boats to go out for a sail or spin, or sometimes just to simply enjoy the beautiful landscape around them. That's what he was imagining at that very instant. During the dead of winter though, the lake was coated over with several feet of ice and snow, while the drifting snow, icicles and freezing temperatures that kept Ducks and Puddles housebound most of the time, surrounded their house.

Yes, they went out to get the mail, thought Mallard, to shovel their walk and for the occasional walk in the beautiful, but chilling environment, but for the most part, they were house bound for several months each year. Several friends would stop by from time to time, but their winters were endured in near-seclusion and, consequently, were the best time of year for them to get their work done.

Even Basil Rathbone wasn't much for going outside once the snow banks had reached up over his head, and Basil was a long, tall cat indeed. During the spring, summer and fall, Basil was a whirlwind of activity, chasing mice, birds and the occasional squirrel. He often stayed out late and could be heard mewing loudly at the back door during the wee hours of the morning. Alice would let him in at those times, but she would also thoroughly chastise Basil for his late night activities and thoughtless behavior.

Mallard sighed and turned away from the darkened windows, as his nose began to smell the beginnings of a hearty meat pie! Alice was an excellent cook and made him all manner of British pastries, main dishes and baked goods. Over the years since Alice had come to stay with Mallard, he had steadily put on a little more weight each year. Now, he had found, most embarrassingly, that nearly all of his pants were a bit too snug around the waist. Alice had recently told him that they would be going on a diet come summertime, so Mallard was bound and determined to stock up on all the delicious goodies he could now.

"Meat pie, my love?" sniffed Mallard as he shuffled into the large, completely renovated chef's kitchen. The huge, gleaming appliances always made him feel extraordinarily comforted and well taken care of as he stood back and contentedly surveyed the beautiful kitchen area.

Alice chuckled and glanced meaningfully at her brother, a twinkle in her eye, "Best eat well now, my darling Ducks! Because spring is coming, and with it," Alice winked mischievously at her staring brother, "comes The Diet!"

The words themselves caused Mallard to recoil deep within, but he did his best not to show his reaction, choosing to downplay the emotions he felt. Best not to give Alice too much fodder for her remarks about the impending diet, he thought wisely.

Basil wound himself in a figure eight around Mallard's ankles, purring noisily as he did so. Alice glanced down and shook her head, feigning disgust, "Hey now! I'm the one that feeds you, Mr. Rathbone! Not him! Best be giving me some of that loving, old chap!"

As if on cue, the big tabby promptly left Mallard and began rubbing his chin up against Alice's legs, his purr reverberating around the kitchen area. Reaching down, Alice lovingly scratched the tabby's chin and neck, then turned back to tend to the juicy, succulent meat pie she was about ready to pop in the oversized, commercial oven.

"Where did you leave off in Windermere's novel?" asked Mallard, picking fitfully at a bowl of grapes that were sitting on the counter. He glanced up at Alice as she closed the oven door and placed the protective hand mitten on the shelf next to the stove.

"Ah, I was just to the point where the power had gone dead and the housekeeper was heading out to the garage to see if she needed to change a fuse..." began Alice, leaning back against the gleaming French doors of the huge refrigerator.

""Ah! So you haven't gotten to the part about the..." blurted out Mallard, his eyes wide with excitement.

"No! Don't tell me! You know I hate that!" Alice interrupted, placing her hands quickly over her ears, glaring at her brother. Her brother, as with most older siblings, delighting in telling her what was going to happen next whenever he got a chance.

Mallard simply popped a grape in his mouth and grinned smugly as a content and well fed Basil padded his way back to lie down on his warm, comfy bed by the side of the roaring fireplace. Perhaps he would dream of springtime and chasing a furry little mouse, or a colorful, elusive butterfly. Then again, perhaps he would simply take a catnap while listening to his two favorite humans.

***

The night was cold. Corporal James Anderson of the Vermont State Police stood behind the luminously painted sawhorses and orange cones strung across Owl Creek Road just below the deserted old Putnam place. He rubbed his cold hands together and blew his semi-warm breath into them, while squinting up the road into the darkness.

"There's nobody out there, Stace," he called out to Corporal Stacy Vermeil as he stomped his heavy winter boots on the pavement, hoping to warm up the other end of his extremities as well. He didn't mean the remark to come out as sounding whiny, but he regretfully realized that it had.

Standing by the driver's side door of their cruiser, Stacy reached in and pulled out the two-way. She glanced out into the darkness and then clicked down the send button, "Cruiser 34 to dispatcher. Come in dispatcher."

Almost immediately the voice of the calm and even voice of the night dispatcher on duty came back, "This is the dispatcher. Over."

Stacy turned and glanced at her partner, who had finished stomping his feet for the moment and was listening to her conversation attentively, and replied, "Any further info or instructions on the road blocks around The Falls?"

There was a slight hesitation, as if the dispatcher had checked in with her supervisor, then the answer came back, "Negative. No new information. How about on your end?"

"Negative. Thanks. Over." Stacy returned the two-way to its cradle in the car and stood back up, softly closing the car door and walking over to where her partner had started his ineffective 'need for warmth' dance once more.

"Nothing new," she said under her breath, looking around the empty stretch of road they were patrolling. Her eyes squinted as she stared intensely, as if that would make her able to see farther in the dark.

"I heard," James muttered, now blowing on his cold hands and stamping his even colder feet both at once. In the treetops on the side of the road, an owl hooted. The sound echoed around the empty area, making their station seem even more desolate.

Funny, thought Stacy, even though I know we're only a little more than a half a mile from the town square of The Falls, this feels like we're a million miles from nowhere. It must be because of the dark, the freezing temperatures, the towering snow banks all around us and the softly falling snow that muffles every sound and blurs your vision. And maybe, just maybe, because I watched that thriller on late night TV last night as well, she added candidly to herself. Stacy was twenty-eight, her partner twenty-five and neither of them had been on roadblock detail before. But then, there's a first time for everything, Stacy rationalized, pulling her heavy official state trooper jacket closer around her.

Suddenly almost blinding headlights came around the bend up the road and they could hear the faint whirr and ping of a car motor in need of a tune-up. Stacy glanced at James and nodded, as she pulled the safety strap off her Glock 9mm and left it sitting loosely in its holster. James quickly moved out in front of the cones and sawhorses, holding up his hand and waiting for the car to stop. Both troopers had their powerful flashlights out, pointing them up the road at the small subcompact that was slowly coming to a stop a few yards away.

In reality, their flashlights didn't help them see much, since the beams of the now stopped car were on high. The snowflakes that were now beginning to fall heavier were lit up and beautifully illuminated by the bright, piercing twin beams of light. James hesitated a moment and then took two steps toward the car, his hand now attempting to shield his eyes from the bright glare from the headlights.

"Sir, uh...Sir, or Ma'am, could you please click onto your low beams," James was starting to call out, as he turned his head slightly to try and see into the car through the windshield.

Suddenly, as if in slow motion, James was thrown back violently against one of the sawhorses knocking it and two adjacent orange cones over before coming to rest on his back on the pavement. A bright blue shaft of an arrow protruded from James' stomach and his eyes were glassy and terrified. His badly shaking hands immediately reached out and held onto the shaft, as his jacket and hands instantly began to be covered with his own oozing, spurting blood. A low moan arose out of his half opened mouth as he stared down at his midsection in complete disbelief and horror.

After one startled glance at her partner, Stacy automatically reached for her Glock. She had it halfway out of the holster when a clear, calm, shrill voice declared loudly, "If you draw that gun, you're as good as dead, officer."

Something about the voice dredged up and set off an ominous alarm deep within Corporal Vermeil. Some innate sense told her that the voice meant what it said. Disgusted with the necessity for her own self-preservation taking priority over capturing this criminal, she slowly slid the gun back into its holster and raised her hands. As she did so, her eyes desperately tried to make out who the figure was that was walking toward her. The silhouette of the person approached swiftly. The silhouette was surrounded by the overwhelming glare and halo effect of the car headlights and the softly falling snow.

Several minutes later, Stacy's eyes opened and she immediately winced painfully. She had one searingly painful headache and it took several moments for her eyes and equilibrium to adjust enough so she could even sit up and look around. She immediately found that her hands were tied tightly behind her back and her gun was gone. With sudden realization, Stacy quickly turned and stared down at James Anderson.

The pavement under the fallen trooper was covered in a mass of blood. He was motionless. His unseeing eyes were open, his face pale and drawn, his lips were blue, and at first glance Stacy was deathly afraid he wasn't breathing.

As she struggled to get out of the rope that bound her hands behind her, the corporal tried to come to terms with what had happened and what she now needed to do. The road had been cleared on one side of the roadblock, an opening large enough to let a small car through. She could see the tire tracks of a subcompact on the pavement in the gathering snow. As her eyes scanned across the scene, she could also see the trunk of their cruiser was wide open.

Stubbornly shaking her head as she worked uncomfortably through the sharp pain in her head and neck, she struggled to her feet. As she did, a few drips of warm liquid rolled down her cheek and into her mouth. Stacy came to the sudden realization that her forehead was slick and wet. Suddenly, the trooper could smell and taste her own blood from where she had been struck and knocked unconscious. Stumbling over to the cruiser's trunk, she stared inside, hoping against hope that what she most feared would not become a reality.

Her hopes were dashed as she stared inside the trunk. The shotgun and box of shotgun shells that they always carried in the trunk were missing. So was one of their flak jackets. Hers. One of the smoke bomb canisters was gone as well.

She groaned with pain as she awkwardly moved her bound hands over to her left back pocket and worked feverishly to pull out the small jackknife she always carried. The jackknife her dad had given her when she was twelve and she had proudly taken away to Girl Scout camp for the first time. He had always told her never to go anywhere without a knife in her pocket. Good old dad. He'd been right. But, the agonizing process of reaching it, pulling it out and opening it with her tightly bound fingers seemed to take forever.

Once her bindings were cut off, she knelt down and gently checked Corporal Anderson's pulse. There was none. She placed the blade of the jackknife under his nostrils in hopes that she might see at least a trace of breath coming from his lungs. Again, she came up empty.

With a determined set to her jaw, she raced around to the driver's side of the cruiser. There were no keys in the ignition, and the keys weren't in her pocket. They wouldn't be in James' pocket, because she drove. Always. She was a much better driver than he was, although he had often argued that she was not.

She stared down at James, lying on the pavement and realized with an abrupt, sharp heartache that caught her off guard that he would never argue with her again. Whoever had assaulted them had most likely thrown the keys to the cruiser off into a snow bank somewhere. Frustrated, but not beaten, Darcy sat down in the driver's seat and spoke sharply, resolutely into the two-way.

As she quickly but carefully gave the dispatcher the details of what had happened, the owl in the nearby tree hooted once again. The snow continued to fall even harder, almost as if it's pure, pristine white crystals were trying hard to cover up the violence, death and horror of the scene.

Five minutes later, Sergeant McNealy's cruiser pulled up with a screech of its tires by the roadblock. He climbed quickly out of his car and found Corporal Vermeil sitting on the pavement, her partner's head in her lap. Her own head was bare and she had a bloody gash with congealed blood covering half of her head and her pale, cold face. Her eyes were filled with tears, but she stared boldly up into the eyes of her superior and declared, "I'm not going to the hospital until we catch her, Sergeant. I want to be there. I want to make sure she gets what's coming to her. I owe it to him, and to me."

Stacy's eyes were red but filled with a strong resolve and purpose. Sergeant McNealy didn't even argue with her. He knew the book stipulated that a wounded trooper had to be sent to the emergency room and then sent home to recuperate. But he also knew how he would feel if he had been in Corporal Vermeil's shoes. She had just lost a partner, most of her weapons and the use of her car. She had been outsmarted, embarrassed and abused. There was no way that if he were in the same situation he wouldn't demand the very same thing.

He stared down at the trooper, a dark frown on his forehead, his sharp eyes carefully assessing her. Then, with one quick nod, he agreed.

***

Kent Armstrong stood on the steps of the West Sugar Shack Falls Regional Medical Center and stared up into the falling snow. He glanced over at Brittany Stearns and she gave him the 'thumbs up' sign. Kent nodded at the cameraman and took a deep, calming breath.

The cameraman panned across the nearby town square and then moved the eye of the camera along the outside of the brightly lit up hospital, finally stopping on the two figures, bundled up and standing on the front steps. He zoomed in on Kent Armstrong's handsome, compassionate face.

"We are coming to you tonight from West Sugar Shack Falls, Vermont. In the past few days this small town has seen two brutal attacks with a bow and arrow. Andy Morrison, a successful young lawyer from the law offices of Lesner, Malkowitz, Freedman and Lister of Brown Bear Junction, was shot and is now in critical but stable condition in this very hospital."

Brittany took over, in perfect synch with her partner, "The second victim was Vermont State Corporal James Anderson who was viciously shot down while trying to man a road block that was being utilized to contain the person behind these atrocious crimes."

Brittany turned and pointed up to the second story of the hospital, then glanced back into the camera, her eyes concerned and sympathetic. "Hopefully, now that Andy Morrison has become conscious, he has been able to alert the Sheriff's Office here in The Falls, the Police Chief of Brown Bear Junction, Chief Tinker LaGrange, and Sergeant McNealy of the Vermont State Police who the actual attacker is. That would explain the road blocks and would also mean that the three law enforcement agencies, working in concert, are closing in on this fiend."

The camera switched over to Kent as he glanced from Brittany to the camera's blinking red eye, "At this moment, the three law enforcement agencies that we named continue their urgent manhunt for the person who badly wounded Andy Morrison and killed Corporal James Anderson. Our prayers and sincere condolences go out to the victims' families." Kent stopped for a moment, slightly bowing his head, his face filled with solemn empathy and sorrow.

The camera shifted back over to Brittany, who raised her own head from her private moment of silence and stared into the eye of the camera, her voice low and intense, "If whoever has committed these vile attacks is out there listening to this broadcast, we have this to say to you. You will be caught and you will be brought to justice. Unfortunately, Vermont has not had a death penalty since 1965, so you will not receive the punishment that best fits your crime. But you will have a lifetime to think about what you have done and the pain and sorrow you have caused the families of your victims. Shame on you, whoever you are."

Two tears rolled slowly down Brittany's perfectly made up cheeks, as she finished her statement to the attacker. She appeared genuinely overwhelmed with the brutality and ruthlessness of the crimes. The camera lingered on her face for a moment, and then turned to Kent, who was staring with genuine compassion at his partner. Kent immediately picked up the strand and completed their live report.

"It's only three days until Valentine's Day and since these assaults have been committed with a bow and arrow, the local community has begun calling these crimes the Cupid's Arrow attacks. At this time of year, we are used to celebrating love and friendship and giving gifts to the ones we love most. Unfortunately, this is a Valentine's Day that The Falls and the surrounding communities will not soon forget."

"This is Kent Armstrong, with my partner Brittany Stearns from the West Sugar Shack Falls Regional Facility for Channel 3 WCAX News. We will be standing by to bring you the next live episode in this harrowing chain of events. Now, back to your regularly scheduled programming."

As the camera light flashed off, Kent turned to Brittany and held out his handkerchief. Her eyes glistening, she accepted the handkerchief and nodded her thanks, then, without a word, she walked slowly off toward the side of the medical facility.

Kent watched her go, tilting his head to one side. The tears on camera were a side of Brittany he had never seen before. True, in the past, she had been all about getting her stories in the limelight and ruthlessly following a story until she got what she wanted. But as of the last year or so, Brittany had been a totally different person. She had become kind, hard working, and a team player.

As Kent tried to figure it all out, he turned and went back to the news van, bringing his wireless microphone back and checking on transmission of the live feed. Brittany, on the other hand, walked away from the news van, a sly smile surfacing on her beautiful face.

She could only begin to imagine how the hearts of her loyal fans had reached out to her, as her tears cascaded down her beautiful cheeks on live TV. Brittany could hardly wait to see the tape from the live feed and see how wonderfully compassionate and selfless she had been. Brittany almost chuckled to herself. The statement to the criminal had been tactically brilliant on her part, she commended herself. It had made her seem heroic, empathetic and kindhearted all at the same time. It couldn't have gone better.

Brittany walked a bit farther in the snow, smiling, her eyes glistening with clever schemes and ideas to turn her into the most adored and acclaimed roving reporter ever. And after that, perhaps an anchor chair was waiting. Who knew how far she could go?

As the snow fell on her perfectly coifed hair, she hummed a little tune to herself and continued to congratulate herself for her outstanding performance.

Chapter 26

The two gangsters slipped out of the gleaming new 1929 DeSoto and glanced vigilantly all around the front of the restaurant. Their long, bulging jackets concealed .45 caliber Thompson submachine guns, commonly known as Tommy guns. After making sure the front of the café was clear, they motioned to their boss, Frank Delvineri.

It was 1929 in the heart of North Chicago. Every day was a brutal struggle between the different mobs and the city police. The mob's control was at his zenith, and they gripped the city in a steel vice.

Delvineri, known to his friends and family as Frankie D., adjusted the heavy, expensive topcoat over his shoulders. With his dark eyes staring straight ahead, he strode swiftly into the restaurant. He was dressed in an expensive tailor-made suit with a stylish fedora tilted jauntily on top of his slicked back hair. The patrons in the front of the bistro glanced up in surprise at the mob boss, froze for a moment, then hurriedly scrambled for the exits knowing all too well what was about to occur.

As Delvineri walked quickly and quietly toward the back room, he nonchalantly shrugged off his topcoat onto the black and white vinyl floor, exposing two gleaming Tommy guns with wooden stocks and grips, one in each hand. The two soldatos or soldiers still following the boss of their family, their capofamiglia, glanced apprehensively at each other. They simultaneously cocked their weapons, readying themselves for anything. They both frowned slightly and respectfully nodded to each other, knowing full well that this could be end of one or both of them.

Frankie D. burst through the small door to the private back room, Tommy guns leveled, his passionate eyes filled with fury and determination. There were three tables in the small room. At the table farthest in the back was seated Delbert "Dutch" Moran, the half-brother of The Godfather, "Bugs" Moran. Moran was the mob boss of this branch of the notorious North Side Irish Gang. Deep in discussions with him sat his consigliore, hardened Irish mobster, Paddy O'Neal. At the other two tables sat several low level soldiers, busily and greedily immersed in savoring the restaurant's heartiest cuisine.

A few blocks away, the soon to become infamous Valentine's Day Massacre was occurring at a dismal garage located at 2122 North Clark Street. Frankie D. had been honored by his own Godfather, Al Capone, with the privileged task of carrying out the second phase of the hit. Frankie D. was to kill Dutch and his men and then join up with the main part of their mob later.

Frankie D.'s guns blazed as he took out the three soldiers seated at the right hand table. The three men never even had time to drop their food-covered knives and forks or hastily wipe the smeared food off their greedy lips and mouths. Just as the three mobsters realized what was about to happen their eyes grew large and one, the heaviest man, even started to choke on a particularly large bite of meat pie.

Frankie's two henchmen, carefully noting where their boss was aiming, immediately dispensed with the two soldiers seated at the left hand table. Several of their bullets destroyed a whole shelf stacked with unopened wine bottles that were standing behind the two unfortunate men. As the soldiers' bodies slipped lifelessly to the floor, the two men were covered not only with their own blood and the food from their table, but also with the streaming vino from dozens of broken wine bottles just behind them.

As the smoke from the Tommy guns cleared slightly, Dutch Moran and Paddy O'Neal coolly regarded Frankie D. as he stood before them, a huge grin spread across his jubilant face.

"Well, Frankie," quipped Dutch as though they were merely sitting down for a friendly drink, "what brings you here on such a cold and gray day?"

Paddy O'Neal's hand had quietly disappeared into his jacket pocket, a move which both of Frankie D's soldiers had noticed. Observing the narrowing of the two soldiers' eyes, Paddy removed his hand slowly, smiling and raising his hands high in the air. "Gentlemen," Paddy spoke softly with his rich Irish brogue, "let's not be hasty now. We're all friends, now aren't we?"

Paddy winked slyly at the two mobsters, as they returned a glowering stare, their fingers tight on the triggers of their submachine guns that were leveled at his chest.

"So Frankie, what's the bottom line?" Dutch ventured almost in a whisper, leaning forward and tapping the ashes from the massive cigar between his fingers. His eyes had narrowed to slits and he was carefully observing his adversary, watching for a sign to tell him what to do next.

Frankie tilted his head and stared down at the trapped mob leader, savoring every moment of his victory. He aimed his two Tommy guns straight at Dutch's head and replied...

The picture on the three, sixty-inch 3D screens froze to the frustrated groans of two of the four game players.

Zeke jumped up, his face mirroring his embarrassment, as he awkwardly scuttled off in the direction of the bathroom at the back of the video store, "I'm sorry! If I don't take a break I'm going to wet my pants! Sorry! Be right back!"

William and Sean Frasier glanced over at each other and stretched, as they watched Zeke hustle off, "I guess I could go for a cup of tea, as long as we're pausing for a moment," Sean sighed.

Jeb stood up and walked over to where the hot water dispenser stood on the back counter, quickly opening the cupboards to pull out four cups and tea bags, "Sounds good to me, too, Mr. Principal!" Jeb glanced over at Sean, and he grinned and winked.

As William stood, stretched and walked over by the back window, he called out, "If Zeke hadn't conveniently needed to evacuate, I'm thinking that you and he might be pushing up daisies right about now." Then he turned and stared at Jeb, his eyebrows raised, obviously expecting a retort of some kind.

Sean chuckled as no response was forthcoming, "William, my dear brother, the reason Zeke paused the Valentine's Day Massacre: Chapter II was simple." Sean gazed at Jeb, who was busily engaged in making tea for all of them, completely trying to ignore the two Frasier brothers at this point.

"Shall I tell him or will you, Jeb?" Sean chuckled to himself, obviously enjoying the situation Jeb had been placed in.

Jeb turned for a moment, a slight smile on his face, his eyes twinkling, and replied, "Oh, by all means, Mr. Principal. Please be my guest!"

Sean shook his head, still chuckling and turned to his brother, "Zeke took a break so Jeb, or should I say Dutch Moran, and his consigliere, better known as his old friend Zeke, could come up with a strategy to turn the tables on Frankie D. and us," Sean bowed dramatically, "his two Tommy gun toting henchmen!"

As Zeke returned, the four serious gamers stepped up to the counter and each picked up a steaming cup of Earl Grey. While William stood guard between the two video store owners, convinced that they were going to try and work out a secret plan to win the game, Sean simply grinned and stared out the back window into the dark, snowy February night.

Suddenly, bright lights flashed, temporarily illuminating the shadowy, snow-covered street as a light colored subcompact swerved dramatically around the corner almost losing control. As Sean stared out into the night, he watched the car finally correct its skid and then speed toward the Town Square and Falls Avenue.

Sean frowned and stared out the window. Who could be out there at this time of night, driving like a maniac? Sean hesitated a moment, wondering if he should alert Cash or Yamato. Glancing over at the late hour, he shook his head and decided against it. Let Cash and his deputies get some rest. They were in the middle of a case and they probably needed to get some sleep.

"Hey, Mr. Principal!" called out Jeb, already back in his gaming chair, "we're ready to go! Unless you want to concede, that is?" Jeb's face was lit up with a sly, clever look that certainly promised some surprises to come.

Sean grinned and strode to his chair, draining his tea mug and sitting down, glancing confidently over at his brother, and with a wink turned and replied, "Concede, Jeb? Why, it never entered my mind. Of course if you want to, we would be more than happy to consider it!"

***

Adelaide struggled through the tall snowdrifts at the back of the hospital. She had ditched Wendy's puny little subcompact a block from the regional medical facility. She sneered disgustedly as she shook her head at the thought of the small, boxy hybrid car her alter ego had purchased. If she, Adelaide, had been in charge when choosing a vehicle, she would have gravitated to a much larger, more powerful vehicle. Perhaps she would have purchased a rugged truck or an SUV capable of expertly handling the logging roads around the area in the dead of winter.

Adelaide glanced into the well-lit windows of the facility, knowing that she really didn't have to worry about anyone inside the building spotting her. The back lot of the hospital was heavily wooded and had few overhead lights. She moved stealthily and quickly, tromping through the snow, feeling her strong legs warm to the task.

Up ahead, she spotted the critical care unit on the second floor of the hospital. From Wendy's being there before, Adelaide knew where Andy was. All she had to do was to get inside and get to her brother. Then she would take him far, far away. She would take care of him and nurse him back to health. Once he was back on his feet, their life would get back to normal, she had convinced herself of it.

But first, she must get her brother away from all the intruders and meddlers that stood between them. It was as if time had slipped back to when she was eighteen and Andy was thirteen. She needed to reinvent their lives once again. She needed to take care of Andy and start their lives over. How, she wasn't sure. But that really didn't matter now. All that mattered was rescuing Andy and taking him away.

Adelaide spotted a low porch roof just below the critical care windows. If she could get up onto that roof, she should be able to climb up to the window of her brother's room. Adelaide grinned confidently. That shouldn't be much of a challenge. After all the survival courses she had participated in and excelled at over the years, that should be an easy task indeed.

Inside the hospital, Mandy Wagner sat in the waiting room outside of the critical care unit, her eyes dry but red and weary. She sat bolt upright, her eyes staring in at the critical care unit. Next to her sat Serafina Messina. Serafina's face was a bit pale and drawn. The two women would glance at each other from time to time, but no words were exchanged. It was as if they were waiting. Waiting for something to happen. From time to time, they would glance toward the front doors of the hospital, but their eyes would soon turn back to the still figure in the bed in the critical care ward.

There was only one patient in the critical care unit. That one patient was covered by a sheet and lying quite still. Meg Monroe was inside the unit at the moment, checking the vital care monitors and then turning to stare down at the man in the bed. After a few seconds, she walked wearily out of the room and glanced over at Mandy and Serafina. With a quick wave of her hand and a slight nervous smile, Meg turned and walked slowly toward the nurse's station, prepared to do her normal hospital rounds.

Outside, the snow swirled fitfully as the winter wind blew in concentric circles around the base of the medical facility. On the roof of the low porch, Adelaide quickly and expertly began to climb up to the window ledge just above her. Over one shoulder was slung the state trooper's shotgun. She carried her bow over the other shoulder. Tucked in the back of her pants was the Glock 9mm that she had taken from Stacy Vermeil.

In three quick moves, Adelaide had reached the window ledge and stared cautiously inside. There was the bed she had seen her brother in, and the sheet was pulled up around him. Peering in, she couldn't see his face because he was turned away from the window, but that didn't matter. If she could get in and get him on a gurney, she could steal an emergency vehicle and be gone within three to four minutes. But she really needed those three or four minutes.

Staring through the brightly lit window, Adelaide's eyes widened with anticipation as she spotted a metal gurney in the corridor, just outside of the critical care ward. Quickly scanning the waiting room, she noticed Mandy sitting with Dr. Messina. Adelaide's eyes narrowed. Neither of the women should give her any trouble, but if they did, she would have no problem getting rid of them. Neither meant anything to her. Less than nothing.

Her eyes traveled quickly to the nurse's station. There was an old nurse sitting there. Adelaide promptly dismissed her. The older nurse would be of no concern to Adelaide as she quickly moved her brother out of the ward and down the hall to the emergency exit. There were no doctors or orderlies anywhere around. And no law enforcement officers stationed to hold her brother prisoner. That was a stroke of luck all in itself. Adelaide grinned to herself. The sheriff, the chief of police and the state troopers had badly underestimated her, and she would take full advantage of it.

In most hospitals, the windows in patient's rooms don't open, for a variety of logical reasons. However, the windows in some older hospitals, such as the West Sugar Shack Falls Regional Medical Facility had been built before those particular reasons were a concern. Adelaide carefully pushed the window open, going no farther than necessary, and quietly slipped over the windowsill into the critical care room.

Quickly unslinging her bow and nocking an arrow, she rolled over once and came to a crouch next to the hospital bed. Glancing quickly out to the waiting room and checking and re-checking carefully to see that neither Mandy nor Dr. Messina had noticed her, Adelaide turned her intense attention to the hospital bed and the man within it. Lifting the sheet back carefully, she whispered softly but urgently, "Andy! Wake up! We're going to get out of here!"

The calm, resolute face and piercing, steel gray eyes of Sheriff Cash Green caught Adelaide unaware. She suddenly jerked backwards, as if she had been slapped with a strong backhand. Her eyes were wide and in momentary shock.

"I don't think so, Wendy. I don't think so," declared the Sheriff of West Sugar Shack Falls.

***

Mandy Wagner and Serafina Messina moved quickly, purposefully, as they ran the thirty-five feet from where they were sitting in the waiting room to the door of the doctor's lounge. Once inside, Meg Monroe locked the heavy door and the three of them stood well to the side and toward the back of the room. They stared at the door expectantly. Their hearts were racing like trip hammers and they strained to hear anything that might give them a clue as to what was going on out in the main part of the hospital.

At the same time, Tinker LaGrange and Ericka Yamato raced up the steps to the second floor from the lower corridor where they had been waiting, in case Wendy had decided to storm the front door. Their handguns were drawn, as they crouched and moved closer and closer to their quarry. They both zeroed in on Wendy as she stood in the critical care room, stunned and staring down at the man in the bed.

"If need be, you take the head shot, I'll go for the body," Yamato whispered urgently as they pressed forward, now not more than forty feet from the critical care room. A swift nod from Tinker was all the response she got.

Yamato's eyes stared at the diminutive figure standing over Cash. In her heart, she knew that she would not risk Cash's life. He had instructed them to shoot only as a last resort, but Yamato had already decided that any threat from Wendy Morrison toward Cash, and she would not hesitate to pull the trigger.

The thick metal double doors at the end of the long corridor that led to the emergency vehicles burst open and Sergeant McNealy and Corporal Stacy Vermeil came charging up the ramp. McNealy was quick, but Vermeil was quicker. Part of her head still glistening with her own blood, she raced up the corridor, turned the corner and found herself standing not more than twenty feet and a plate glass window away from the woman who had killed her partner and rendered her unconscious.

The first thing that Vermeil noticed was the state trooper issue shotgun slung over Wendy's shoulder. Her eyes narrowed even more with white-hot anger and the need for revenge. She tightly held her handgun straight and true, aimed directly at Wendy's head. As she stood there the thoughts of her partner, Corporal James Anderson, lying lifeless on the snowy pavement, the dark pool of his blood reaching out in every direction, ravaged her mind. Stacy felt a strong urge to pull the trigger without waiting. But she also was a loyal, caring and disciplined trooper. She stood there, grimacing, ready to follow her orders to the letter. She just hoped that her emotions didn't cloud her judgment.

Sergeant McNealy quietly moved to her side, his voice low and barely audible, "I know what your heart wants you to do, Corporal. I understand. I've been there, several times. But you're too good a state trooper for that. Stand tall and make me proud."

Stacy bit her lip hard enough to draw blood and took a deep breath, feeling the calming presence of McNealy, and not wanting to let him down. She moved the aim of her Glock to Wendy Morrison's thigh and simply waited.

Quicker than anyone anticipated, Adelaide was in control of her emotions once again. In her hand was the Glock 9mm, pointed directly at Cash as she swiftly used her peripheral vision to assess her situation. She saw the chief and the deputy in the waiting room, as well the two troopers just outside the critical care unit. All of them with their guns trained upon her. Mandy and the psychiatrist had vanished and there were no doctors or nurses within sight.

There were only two options, Adelaide thought.

Surrender or use the sheriff as a human shield. And surrender was not really an option as far as Adelaide was concerned. She smiled scornfully. Weak little Wendy would have jumped on that option, without a doubt.

"Get up, sheriff," her voice was calm but demanding as she stared down at the man in the bed. "If you value the lives of your friends as well as your own, get up and turn toward them."

Her hand grabbed Cash's arm and pulled him quite violently halfway out of bed. At that move, Adelaide upped the ante. Everyone in the next room attempted to find their best position and angle for a kill shot.

Realizing that Wendy had aggressively forced his hand, Cash knew that he needed to play along, at least for the moment. The tall sheriff awkwardly climbed the rest of the way out of bed and stood facing the four law enforcement officers in the next room. He raised his hands up as well, showing Wendy that he was not going to resist. She quickly pulled him roughly to her, and stripped his Glock from his holster, tossing it into the farthest corner of the room.

Cash stood at least ten inches taller than Wendy Morrison. Adelaide had already planned to use that to her advantage. She pushed him forward, growling quietly and furiously, "We're going out that door, Sheriff Green. If you try and crouch, duck or slip out of the way, the first shot will be to your gut. The second shot will hit," Adelaide chuckled nastily, "that pretty little deputy in her head."

"Do you understand?" Her voice was low and harsh, filled with rage and resolve. From the tone, Cash had no doubt that the woman meant what she said.

"I understand, Wendy," he replied in a calm, mild

voice.

"Wendy's not here, sheriff," came the mocking reply, "that whiny wimp hasn't been around for quite awhile when there's decisions to be made. She can't deal with the hard stuff. You'll just have to deal with me."

Cash almost turned and stared at the small but physically powerful woman pushing him toward the door. Wendy wasn't here? Then who did she think she was? Ever the tactician, Cash realized that fact might somehow help him diffuse the situation, even now.

"Whom am I speaking to, if you're not Wendy?" His voice was flat, unemotional. He stopped and dug in his heels. As she continued to try and push him forward, he stood where he was, refusing to let Wendy move him any further until he got an answer.

Feeling Cash tighten up and resist her attempts to move him forward, Wendy grimaced in frustration and declared, "I'm Adelaide, you meddlesome sheriff. You're dealing with Adelaide!"

Cash frowned and half turned, glancing over his shoulder, his piercing gray eyes staring down at the diminutive woman. As an instantaneous and brutal answer to his not following her commands, Adelaide promptly reached up and cracked the back of his head violently with the butt of the gun. Then she poked him viciously in the back with the gun barrel and snarled, "I don't have all day, cop. You move, or you die. Choose."

Cash jerked forward with the sheer pain and the force of the blow to his head. Stumbling forward, he hit the wall just on the other side of the door, falling to his knees. In his already weakened condition, he struggled to maintain consciousness. Adelaide instinctively crouched and swiftly moved forward, sensing the momentary loss of her human shield.

A lone shot rang out. The plate glass door to the critical care unit exploded into a million pieces. The next moment, Adelaide reached down with all her strength and roughly pulled Cash to her, wrenching him upward. Cash, still woozy from the concussive blow to his head was in no condition to resist. Within moments Adelaide was secured behind the tall sheriff once more.

There was, however, one difference. A 9mm slug had completely passed through Adelaide's thigh. She winced at the agonizing, nearly dehibilitating pain and watched blood streaming down her leg to the floor. Adelaide knew that the longer she stood there, the worse she would feel and the weaker she would be. She knew that she had no time to lose.

Her eyes narrowed and filled with frustrated fury. Adelaide shoved Cash out through the smashed door of the critical care unit. Her Glock was pressed up against his spinal cord, and she shouted out so everyone in the whole hospital could hear. "If anyone, and I mean anyone, tries anything heroic or stupid, depending on your viewpoint, the sheriff's a dead man. Best case scenario, he'll live and never walk again. Do you all understand?"

Her relentless gaze flashed around the waiting room, staring deep into the eyes of the assembled law enforcement officers. From the hate and rage in her glance, each of them knew that she would execute what she had said, even if they were lucky enough to shoot and kill her instantly.

Cash held up his hands as the blood trickled from the gash on his head down his neck and onto his uniform. He shook his head as he glanced at Yamato, McNealy, Vermeil and LaGrange. They all knew what he wanted, what he was telling them to do. He had just nonverbally ordered them to 'stand down' and let Wendy Morrison take him where she wanted.

Adelaide shoved the sheriff forward and he responded, moving as quickly as he could in the direction she chose. She moved him quickly down the hospital stairs, heading for the front door. Each step that she took, she left a fair sized spattering of her own blood.

Finally, as she stopped Cash at the front door, she muttered, "Stay there!" She grabbed a wool scarf from the coat tree and tied it as tightly as possible around her thigh, grimacing, sucking in air and moaning slightly as she pulled it even tighter.

"Nobody follows us! Understood?" she snarled desperately, her voice beginning to lose some of its pure fury. Cash glanced at each of them, lifting his eyebrows and using his hands to gesture for them all to stay put.

Yamato stared at Cash, shaking her head slowly, subtly. He raised his eyebrows further and nodded, requesting her to wait. To stay put. Cash knew that what he was asking was the hardest thing in the world for his deputy and friend. She was not a patient person when it came to someone's safety, especially his.

Finally Yamato nodded almost imperceptibly, as Adelaide pushed the wounded sheriff out the door and into the snowy, winter night.

Adelaide shoved Cash forward once more, her leg now throbbing painfully as the loss of blood began to take effect. Four, five, six steps down the front stairs and they turned onto the cleanly shoveled sidewalk.

As she shoved the sheriff forward, her sense of urgency growing, Cash spoke quietly, calmly once again, "You need to have a doctor take care of that Adelaide.

You don't have long. From the looks of the blood flow, the bullet must have hit a main artery or vein..."

"Don't you think I know that, sheriff?" came back the sarcastic reply. Adelaide seemed out of breath by now, her shoves becoming increasingly weaker. Cash turned back carefully to look in the direction of the hospital. He could no longer see the front doors and they had walked at least a hundred yards down the sidewalk, getting close to the town square.

Luckily, for once, there were no other citizens out on the streets. They were all probably at home, watching the late night news, getting ready for bed. Cash silently uttered a short, passionate prayer that no one felt a need to walk their dog for the next few minutes.

"Adelaide?" Cash asked as he walked along, heading toward the town park. "Do you want me to see if I can try and stop that blood? I've been around Doc and Meg so long that I kind of know what to..."

"No! I don't want you to stop the blood, you fool!" Adelaide snarled angrily, her eyes overflowing with contempt and anger. "But you can tell me one thing."

Cash glanced back and replied over his shoulder, "What Adelaide?" He noticed that her pants were drenched in her blood and that there was a long, easily spotted trail of blood all along the sidewalk. They would be easy to trail, he thought as he glanced around at the neighboring bushes and trees, wondering where Yamato and her posse might be at this moment. He had no illusion that she would have stayed at the hospital after he and Adelaide left.

"Where's Andy?" sounded a small, lost little voice.

Cash stopped abruptly and turned around. There where Adelaide had been a moment before, was Wendy. She glanced up at the tall sheriff and almost apologetically handed him the Glock, shucking off the shotgun into the snow. She still held tightly onto her own bow, cradling it protectively in her hands.

Cash tentatively reached out, and after realizing that it was okay with her, he picked Wendy up in his arms, bow and all. He immediately started back toward the hospital, his long strides traveling quickly over the freshly shoveled sidewalks.

"Andy's going to be okay, Wendy," Cash whispered as he noticed the massive quantities of blood still pouring out of Wendy. Fearing the worst, he immediately started to jog toward the hospital and was relieved to see Doc Stone and Meg running toward him. Yamato gently took the woman from his arms and stared up into his still woozy and blurred vision.

"I got it from here, boss," she whispered.

Wendy's eyes had closed. She had slipped off. Her pale face and shallow breathing spoke to her critical condition. But on her face now was the calm, kind expression that most folks would recognize as Wendy Morrison, owner of Treasured Memories.

Within twenty minutes, Wendy was in a private room. She was getting massive amounts of plasma and was in critical but stable condition. As soon as she had been given enough of a transfusion to make surgery possible, they would operate on her gunshot wound. Both Doc and Meg had agreed that she had a better than average chance of recovery.

The mood of the hospital's emergency room was lighthearted and relieved. They had gotten through a dangerous situation without any more loss of life. Wendy was in a private room, with Horace and one of Tinker's deputies standing guard. Everyone was so thankful and cheerful, even though they had lost

Trooper Anderson, that none of them wanted to get up and leave. They had all gathered in the emergency room while Doc had quickly and efficiently taken care of Stacy's head wound and was now working on Cash.

Cash was sitting stiffly on an examination table as Doc Stone was sewing up the fairly long gash in his head. Doc Stone was rather enjoying the fact that Cash had to sit still and listen to him for once.

"You really should have just let us capture her as she entered the hospital," Yamato was asserting passionately as she watched Doc stitching away on a wincing Cash. She gave her boss a stern glance, pointing her finger at him, her dark eyes flashing, and added, "You deliberately put yourself in danger! That's not acceptable!"

Cash winced again and glanced over at Yamato, patiently countering, "Honestly Yamato, it was the only way I could see to keep it from ending up as a 'Gunfight at the OK Corral' type scenario."

Tinker, leaning against the wall and intently studying the model of a backbone hung from the wall, interjected noncommittally, "Yamato is right in one way, but you're right too, Cash. Just depends on what you wanted to accomplish, I guess."

Both Cash and Yamato glanced over at Tinker and raised their eyebrows. He glanced at both of them and then just grinned, winking and adding, "Or not!"

Serafina Messina walked into the emergency room, and stared at Cash, wincing for him as she watched Doc pull one stitch tight and begin the next.

"Once Wendy has recovered a bit I'll spend some time with her. Try and get to understand her. I know you will be picking her up as soon as she's ready to travel, Sergeant McNealy, but I'll do what I can to begin working through her emotional and psychological issues before she leaves. That way the psychiatrist at whatever institution she ends up at will have a starting point for her treatment."

McNealy, never known for his loquaciousness, simply smiled, nodded and tipped his trooper hat in appreciation. Next to him stood a despondent Corporal Stacy Vermeil. She had a bulky white bandage around her head and was staring out the large window of the emergency room into the blustery night. It had been a bullet from her gun that had shattered the plate glass door and wounded Wendy Morrison in the thigh. She was having a difficult time with her emotions.

On one hand, she had shot the person who killed her partner, in effect bringing the hostage situation with the sheriff to a swift close. On the other, she had not meant to shoot the woman. It had been simple instinct. Stacy had been cold and weary, slowed by her head wound and emotionally distraught by the death of her partner. It had been a perfect storm of a situation.

McNealy, noticing her staring distractedly out the window of the emergency room reached over and squeezed her shoulder. When she turned and stared back at him, he simply smiled and mouthed the words, "I'm proud of you."

As Stacy Vermeil smiled wearily back, she nodded, acknowledging and accepting his gracious praise. The Sergeant was not one to hand out compliments willy-nilly. You had to earn them. She knew that, and treasured it even more.

Meg Monroe stepped into the emergency room and called out cheerfully to Doc, "Hey, there, Doc! Time for us to go and patch up our first dual personality patient! You ready?" Meg quickly and efficiently stripped off her examination gloves that were covered in blood and dropped them in the Hazmat disposal canister.

"The correct term, Doctor Monroe, would be a multiple personality disorder caused by stress, if you please!" Serafina chuckled and winked at Meg, who curtsied grandly to the therapist, in effect, lightheartedly bowing to her expertise.

"Be that as it may, we have a date in the operating room, Doctor Stone! Don't be late!" Meg replied, in obvious good spirits.

As Meg smiled and disappeared through the swinging doors, Yamato glanced over at Doc and chuckled, "Best get a move on Doc! Or Meg's apt to come back in here and call you Malcolm!" Yamato, relieved enough to be joking around, turned and winked at Cash. The sheriff glanced at his deputy, returned the wink and grinned slightly. He was just glad to see that Yamato was feeling better about the whole episode and was beginning to relax.

Doc Stone, finished with Cash's wound, turned and glanced at the nurse who was in attendance and announced in a firm tone of voice, "Beatrice, he's all yours. Make sure you put on the ointment that stings a lot. Just so it will remind him not to do this again!"

As Doc winked at Cash, he turned and strode out the swinging doors on his way to the operating room. He called back over his shoulder, "I'll have you know, Deputy Ericka Anastasia Yamato, that only my dear mother and my darling wife gets to call me Malcolm!" With that he was gone.

Cash turned and stared at Yamato who had quickly gotten up and was striding purposefully toward the exit. He lifted his right eyebrow, an action that caused his stitches to pull and sent a wave of pain down his face.

He persevered, "Anastasia? Did I hear Doc right, Yamato? Your middle name is..."

The slam of the exit door cut his sentence short, but Cash was already chuckling. Anastasia. Yamato had never told him. He could hardly wait to catch up with her!

Chapter 27

Serafina Messina stood beside Andy's hospital bed, gazing down at him. He was conscious but still listed as critical. Andy was in a private room in the regular ward. Cash had moved him from critical care just after he and Yamato had arrived at the hospital earlier that night. At that point, Cash had no idea where Wendy was, but all the evidence seemed to point to her showing up at the hospital, sooner or later. And her reason for coming would be her brother.

"She's in surgery right now," Serafina's voice was quiet and calm, as she watched Andy's reaction to the news about his sister. "You have to try and understand, Andy, that when your parents died, she had to take on a great deal of responsibility. Developing a tough side, a part of her personality that could withstand all the bad things that happened, was your sister's way of coping with the vast change in your lives."

Andy nodded thoughtfully, and then stared out the window into the snow filled winter night. "I just can't believe it. How could I have lived with her all those years and never have had any idea that there were two distinct people inside her? How is that possible?" He turned back and stared at Serafina, desperately searching for answers.

"When she was with you, she was Wendy," Serafina

whispered, her eyes honestly meeting the questioning stare of the young lawyer. "When there was a problem, she dealt with it as Adelaide. Adelaide became stronger and stronger as she grew older and dealt with more and more of her life."

Mandy Wagner, leaning against the wall in the back corner of the room, stepped forward, resting her hand on Andy's arm, her eyes wet with unshed tears. "I saw some of it Andy. I wondered at times how she could be so kind and patient and caring one moment and hard, direct and impersonal the next. I guess I just assumed that was the way she handled things."

"You can't blame yourself, Andy," Mandy continued, "we all saw what we wanted to see. She had us all fooled. She was quite good at hiding Adelaide. I'm sorry that I didn't see it coming, Andy. I'm so sorry."

The hot tears suddenly began rolling down her weathered cheeks. Mandy sobbed once, squeezed Andy's arm and then stepped quickly away from his bed stopping by the window, gazing out into the darkness.

"Mandy, I don't blame you," Andy called out weakly. "Not at all. If I didn't see it after being with her for all these years, how could you?" His gaze shifted back to Dr. Messina.

"What's going to happen to her, Dr. Messina?" His question was almost a whisper, his face filled not only with a wracking pain from his wound, but the genuine fear and uncertainty of what was going to happen to the one person he had left in his immediate family.

"Well, I'm not the sheriff, or a judge and jury, but she killed a Vermont State Trooper, as well as almost killing you. She attacked Corporal Vermeil and Sheriff Green. She has a number of other minor charges to deal with as well. The serious issues she had with her mental health will also need to be factored in."

Serafina drew a deep breath, kept eye contact with Andy and continued, calmly and with compassion, "Vermont repealed the death penalty back in the 60's. That probably means that she'll spend the rest of her life in mental institutions and in prison, Andy. I can't envision a point where she'll really ever be free to live a normal life again. I'm sorry." As she finished, Serafina searched deep in the eyes of Andy Morrison, hoping to find the strength that he would need to deal with what she believed to be the truth.

Andy mulled it over for a few moments, and then his eyes filled with resignation and tears. He nodded with understanding, reaching out and squeezing Serafina's hand. "Thank you, Dr. Messina, I appreciate you telling me the truth."

At that moment, Elizabeth Fallon cautiously opened the door to Andy's room and peered in. Her eyes were anxious and she immediately smiled tentatively when she spotted Andy. "I'm so sorry. Am I interrupting anything?"

At the sound of Elizabeth's soft voice, Andy glanced eagerly over at the doorway as his eyes widened with surprise and pleasure. It was obvious that he had been very worried about Elizabeth and was now overjoyed to see her. For the first time since he had been shot, Andy Morrison smiled weakly. Serafina even noticed that his hand lifted slightly, trying to gesture to Elizabeth.

"No, not at all, please, come in," Serafina smiled and motioned eagerly for Elizabeth to enter the room. The psychiatrist turned quickly to Andy and smiled warmly, "I'm going to leave you two so you can catch up. I'm figuring that each of you has lots of questions about what's been happening to the other."

Serafina squeezed Andy's arm encouragingly and turned toward the door, glancing meaningfully over at Mandy as she did so. Fortunately, Mandy quickly understood and took Serafina's clue, stepping up and planting a gentle kiss on Andy's cheek.

"I'm going to go with the doctor. I am desperately in need of a good cup of coffee!" Mandy smiled and quickly followed Serafina toward the door, smiling invitingly at Elizabeth as she passed by her.

"I don't know if we can find a good cup of coffee at this hour, Mandy," Serafina joked, "but we'll certainly give it a try! Any coffee is better than no coffee."

With a quick wave to Elizabeth, Serafina and Mandy slipped out into the hospital corridor. Once outside the room with the door securely closed behind them, Serafina began walking slowly down the hallway toward the doctors' lounge, a delighted smile spreading across her face. She turned and glanced at Mandy, her eyes twinkling a bit, "I think, right now, that young lady might be the best medicine for him."

Mandy smiled perceptively and nodded back.

Together the two exhausted women breathed deep sighs and headed toward that cup of coffee, good, bad or mediocre, wherever they might find it.

***

The next morning dawned a good deal warmer, with clear skies and a bright blue sky. The snow was beginning to soften and thaw, at least for the moment, and the roadways and sidewalks were wet with melting snow. It was the very beginning of the fabled February thaw. The thaw that signaled the best maple sap run of the winter.

Up on the mountain, Herbert Rockford stood near the collection shack in the West Sugar Shack Falls Maple

Syrup Incorporated compound and stared out at his workers. They were already busily at work collecting sap over the entire maple sugar grove. Herbert was overjoyed. It was going to be a perfect sap day. Cold night, warm day, and the maple sap would be running freely, filling the plastic collection lines with the sweet, sticky liquid.

Cash and Yamato were just arriving at the sheriff's office as the first rays of sunlight burst over the mountains to the east and filtered down through the valley where The Falls was located. Yamato hesitated for a moment before she entered the office and turned, eagerly raising her face and closing her eyes to feel the first real warmth that she could remember from sunlight in several months.

Cash walked over to the back shelf to begin his daily ritual of making the first pot of coffee. He moved gingerly, his muscles sore from two long treks through the woods and snow drifts over the past twenty-four hours. He had stood for at least a half an hour under a hot shower when he finally had arrived home early that morning. After four hours of sleep, he was not at his best, but certainly less tired than he had been after his run-in with, and little gift from, Adelaide.

Thinking of her gift to him, Cash tentatively reached up and touched the back of his head, where the gauze from his bandage was slightly wet. His head felt like it was two sizes bigger, and he had not been able to wear his hat this morning for two different reasons. First, his head hurt too much when he put the hat on. Second, his hat didn't really fit with the large lump and the dressing Doc had put on his head.

With a sigh, which was partly from relief and partly from weariness, Cash concentrated on the task at hand, making some strong coffee. Yamato, on the other hand, seemed perky and cheerful.

"Hey Boss," she called out as she settled at her desk, enthusiastically booting up her system and swiftly checking her email, "there's a message from the Vermont State Police. Seems Tinmouth Pritchard won't be seeing too much jail time. He may be out in a few months, due to Elizabeth Fallon's support and assistance."

Cash nodded, declaring quietly, "That sounds about right. Tinmouth and Elizabeth should make a good, if unexpected, team to re-start Ben Fallon's woodworking business up again. I heard that several of the merchants in the area are simply delighted to know they can plan on some locally made furniture available for them to sell in their stores."

Yamato glanced over at Cash, a small frown momentarily denting her perfect forehead, "Is Horace still over at the hospital? Still on guard duty?"

Cash nodded without glancing over at his deputy, "Yup. He'll be relieved at nine this morning. The Vermont State Police are taking over the case, for several reasons. First, the attacks occurred in an area that was between The Falls and Brown Bear Junction, not really our jurisdiction or Tinker's. Second, of course, would be the death of Corporal Anderson."

Cash glanced expressively over at Yamato, his face long, his gray eyes saddened. "We take care of our own, Yamato. Like I've always said, we take care of our own."

Yamato nodded in silent agreement, returning Cash's glance.

Then her mood lightened once again and she stood up, her eyes twinkling, "Hey Boss, how about I go over to Tina's and buy us a real breakfast? I sure could go for something warm and tasty. Something that would stick to our ribs! What do you say?"

Cash smiled and shook his head, chuckling slightly, "You know what Yamato? You like to eat even more than I do! The darn shame is, you never gain an ounce and I have to work forever to get rid of my love-handles!"

As a grinning Yamato grabbed her coat and opened the front door, she met Darlene Pitts on her way into the office.

"'Morning, Darlene!" Yamato declared, giving Darlene a warm smile and a wink. "Breakfast is my treat today! Anything you'd especially fancy this beautiful morning?" Yamato hesitated a moment to give Darlene the time to think it over.

The wait was a small one. Darlene glanced over at Yamato and promptly announced, "Been hankering for some buttermilk flapjacks with real Vermont Grade A maple syrup, Deputy, if you really want to know."

Darlene neatly hung up her hat, muffler and overcoat on the coat hooks by the door, adjusted the collar of her blouse and continued speaking as she made her way over to her desk. "Started to make some up this morning and then I had to answer the phone. By the time I got back, Moses' old no-account coon hound Gabrielle had knocked the mixing bowl off the table and was licking it clean."

Cash turned and stared at Darlene, then glanced at Yamato as a grin crept across his face, "Am I to presume that Gabrielle is still alive?"

Darlene never looked up as she arranged her desk, ready to start the day, a look of haughty impatience crossing her weathered face, "Not that he deserves to be. Moses fell all over himself apologizing for the foolish beast. Then he grabbed his coat, pushed Gabrielle out the door and made tracks faster than a rabbit with a skulk of foxes on his trail."

"Skulk of foxes?" Yamato grinned and glanced at Cash, "never heard that one."

"Well some people use earth, others use lead and a few still continue to call it a leash. I have always preferred the term skulk, because to me, that's what foxes do. They skulk." With that, Darlene uncovered her typewriter, and inserted her first three-ply work order of the day, done explaining her morning.

Yamato winked at Cash and was out the door. Cash turned back and slowly made his way to his desk. Darlene, with her excellent peripheral vision noticed him wincing as he took a moment to sit down.

"I suppose going home and taking the day off is unimaginable?" Darlene declared in her low monotone, never taking her eyes off the work order.

Cash winced a bit as he moved his head and sighed. Then he responded patiently to his dispatcher, "I'll be okay. Just need some coffee and a few minutes to loosen up the muscles."

Then, on second thought, he turned and faced his dispatcher, staring at her thoughtfully for a moment, "You know, I'm not as young as I used to be, Darlene."

Darlene immediately halted her typing and stared at Cash, her eyes unwavering and annoyed, her eyebrows raised and her mouth pursed up tightly, "Cash Green, did you just tell me that you were getting older? Really?"

Cash stared back at Darlene, not sure what button he had pushed, but, typical man that he was, he decided to try and bull his way through the discussion, "Yeah. I'm almost forty Darlene. Law enforcement is a young man's game."

Darlene just glared at Cash, her skinny arms folded tightly over her chest. The longer she stared, the more uneasy and uncomfortable Cash became.

Finally, Darlene spoke, her tone low and firm, but with a hint of real emotion running through it, "Cash Green, I have been the secretary and dispatcher at this office for the past thirty-five years. I have had to break in three new sheriffs. I do not ever want to have to go through that unsettling, frustrating experience again. Don't you ever think about retiring. Do you hear me? Am I making myself perfectly clear?"

Cash nodded solemnly, staring at Darlene as she struggled mightily to maintain her composure. For once he found himself speechless.

Darlene adjusted her eyeglasses and stared over them at her boss for a moment, hesitating, pale, and unsure as to whether she should add to her stern orders. Then her eyes watered up for a moment and she relented, her voice soft and barely audible, "You are the best sheriff I have ever worked with. You are strong and tough when you need to be, smart as a whip, and you really care about the people of our town."

Cash simply stared at Darlene. He had never heard her speak like that to anyone, and it had deeply touched him. Again unsure how to respond, he replied with what he knew would not embarrass or offend his exacting and persnickety secretary, "Thank you, Darlene. I appreciate your sentiments."

The color was returning to her face and her voice was much stronger now, nearly back to her old self as she added with finality, "Now, enough of this 'old' nonsense. You're just tired and worn out. Heaven knows, that can happen to any of us."

Cash glanced over at Darlene, partially amused, partially curious to see what might come next, as she typed and sniffed huffily, "Even me, for heaven's sake! I'm more than twenty years older than you, Cash Green, and I'm fit as a fiddle!"

At that moment, Yamato burst through the door carrying several bags and a large serving tray. She was so loaded down and her smile was so infectious, that Cash and Darlene immediately stood up and walked over to help her.

As they were filling their plates with hot, savory goodies, Cash glanced over at Darlene, only to have her stop from piling flapjacks on her plate, stare up over her eyeglasses at him in her usual proud and haughty manner. He simply turned away, shook his head and turned back to piling eggs and bacon on his plate. He reminded himself that although you might see a crack in Darlene's armor once in awhile, that moment didn't last long and it would soon vanish before your very eyes.

***

With only one day left before Valentine's Day, Bert Westin and Milo Shapiro were at work before the crack of dawn, trying to coordinate all the finishing touches for the town's Valentine's Day celebration. It was a great chance to bring in some money for the town's businesses as well as providing an opportunity to celebrate 'the beginning of the end' to a typical Northeast winter. Although winter could linger well on into May, with even the rare ice storm at the beginning of June, the citizens of The Falls could at least begin to see the light at the end of the proverbial tunnel.

Alma Stewart, the town council's hard working and efficient secretary was bustling around the place, running back and forth between the two councilman's offices. She was copying off the flyers they were going to post up all over town later on that day with the schedule of all the activities planned to celebrate Cupid and love in general. The two selectmen were running her ragged, worrying about things she had already taken care of. She was about at the end of her proverbial rope.

Alma shook her head and took a deep breath, as she made coffee, dialed up the newspaper to remind them to place the ad in The Falls Gazette for tomorrow morning, and listened to both Bert and Milo calling impatiently to her from their offices. Finally, she glanced in the direction of the first and second councilmen and raised her eyebrows. With great determination, the little town hall secretary marched over and stood between their two offices and shoved her small, but strong fists on her ample hips.

"Now, listen up!" she bellowed. Her little frame seemed to grow taller and shone with robust resolve and willpower as she spoke. For the first time in the last hour, the town hall was so silent you could actually hear a pin drop. Bert and Milo's stunned faces could be seen peering around the edge of their desks, their eyes wide, their mouths wide open and staring at their secretary with rapt attention.

"Contrary to popular belief, I am only one person! I cannot listen to each of you pontificate on and on about how you want to change this or that after we have already settled and arranged on how preparations for the festival will be done! Everything is in place, gentlemen! What is done, is done and can't be undone! I can't ask merchants, townsfolk and town workers to change everything simply because each of you got a burr under your saddle about some insignificant detail here and there!"

Alma drew in a deep breath of air and swiftly continued, her eyes flashing with righteous fury, "We have been working on this celebration for the past two months and it is going to be wonderful! Absolutely wonderful! Am I making myself clear?"

Both Bert and Milo nodded dutifully, their eyes still glazed over from the shock of Alma's tirade. As swiftly as the vehement outburst had appeared, it suddenly dissipated and was gone.

"Now, I will get back to running off the brochures, gentleman, if you don't mind," announced Alma as she marched back toward the main office and the copying machine center. As she strode purposefully along, she turned, smiled and called back over her shoulder, "Your coffee Bert, and your tea Milo, will be on your desks in three shakes of a lamb's tail, along with a few of those little sugar pastries from Federman' Bakery you each like so well!"

As Alma marched off, humming softly to herself, Milo Shapiro and Bert Westin timidly stepped out of their offices for a moment and stared at each other.

"What do you suppose that was all about?" Bert whispered quietly, immediately checking anxiously to see if Alma had heard him. His whole being was uncertain and hesitant as he gazed down on the diminutive second councilman.

Milo glanced in the direction of the town secretary who was busily preparing their coffee and tea and shook his old head in bewilderment, "You're asking me to explain what a woman does, Bert Westin?"

Milo turned and limped back into his office. Leaning heavily on his cane, he had returned to his curmudgeonly self, "Better to ask me which came first, the chicken or the egg! Bah!"

Bert watched Milo shuffle back to his desk and settle himself slowly into his office chair. Then he turned back and stared out at the fast approaching Alma Stewart.

"Time for your coffee, Mr. First Councilman!" chirped the now cheery tones of the town secretary. Her green eyes were twinkling with good humor and a droll little smile was occupying her face.

"Sit down! Sit down! Time for a little something to keep up your spirits and your constitution!" Alma shooed Bert back into his office and set his coffee cup, a creamer of half-and-half and three packets of artificial sweeteners on his desk along with a delicious smelling plate of warm pastries.

"There you are! Eat up! Enjoy!" Alma happily cajoled, winking at Bert as she hustled out the door of his office and into Milo's. Bert Westin watched Alma go, a befuddled look stuck on his slightly pudgy face. Then, he sighed and smiled indulgently as he began to prepare his coffee.

"Here you are Mr. Second Selectman! Hot Irish tea, just like you prefer! And a plate of warm pastries to boot!" Alma clucked like a mother hen as she arranged the tea and baked goods in front of Milo, taking great care to place them close enough so he didn't have to strain any old muscles to reach them.

"Honey?" grumbled Milo as he inspected the teacup and then glanced up irritably at Alma.

"Pure clover!" responded Alma, holding her hands together in front of her, completely attentive and smiling.

"Two squeezes and no more?" Milo muttered, stirring the mixture in the teacup.

"Two squeezes, no more, no less," replied Alma

quickly, her smile unwavering.

Milo raised a craggy eyebrow, and peered up at Alma, "Hot water poured over the leaves?"

Alma nodded efficiently, "As always, Mr. Second Selectman."

Milo poked the pastries, growling out, "Cheese in the middle and not that horrid strawberry?"

"Absolutely, Mr. Second Selectman", responded Alma with a quick nod of her head.

As Milo sighed and sipped his first taste of tea, Alma was already hustling back to her desk with a large contented smile on her face. There, she thought, the nonsense is over for the day and they'll let me alone so I can get my work done. It's all in knowing how to handle them, it really is.

Alma sipped her own coffee as she stood by the copier watching the papers flip through the machine, piling up at the discharge chute. It was going to be a delightful day, she thought to herself as she chuckled silently. Absolutely delightful and productive, now.

Chapter 28

Jeremy Burman sat in his homeroom, trying to study for the Chemistry test that was scheduled for his fourth period class. Trying was certainly the operative word. Six rows in front of him, Sylvia Jean Jones was seated, animatedly whispering with one of her friends, Millie Montrose.

Jeremy stared at Sylvia Jean and sighed. He wanted to walk up to her, introduce himself and begin a relationship with the beautiful, popular sophomore. Just then, Sylvia Jean glanced up from her conversation and Jeremy quickly stared down intently at his chemistry text, anxiously trying to hide himself in the formulas and definitions.

Jeremy was staring determinedly at the page, but his mind was anywhere but on chemistry. Well, he thought, that's not entirely true. I'm kind of thinking about chemistry, but the relationship kind, not the substances you mixed up in beakers in the classroom. Jeremy was so shy that he hardly ever talked to girls. When he did, his tongue felt like it was tied in a knot, his palms began to sweat and his words came out sounding like a foreign language.

His sister, Lorraine, had tried to tell him that girls usually felt the same way, and that a simple smile and a warm "Hi!" went along way in getting to know them.

But Jeremy somehow doubted that. Lorraine had always been positive, cheerful and everybody loved her. She went out of her way to make people feel special. Jeremy, on the other hand, was a loner, not even in any one particular group at school.

He wasn't a jock, even though he was good at baseball and basketball. He wasn't exactly a nerd, although he was probably the smartest kid in his class. He certainly wasn't one of the popular crowd. You actually had to laugh and smile and mingle with other kids to be one of those. He definitely wasn't one of the tough, mean kids who secretly smoked out back of the school and were always giving teachers' grief. He was simply Jeremy. He was one of a kind.

Jeremy hesitantly glanced back up from his chemistry text and looked straight into the eyes of Sylvia Jean Jones! She was staring at him! She had a big smile on her face and her friends were staring at Jeremy as well. Jeremy cringed inwardly, dropped his gaze and stared even harder at the open page of the chemistry text. He could feel that he was beginning to blush.

He closed his eyes tight and immediately began to sweat. He knew that his heart rate had just doubled. Sylvia Jean had stared at him! Then his lack of self-confidence reared its ugly head. What if Sylvia and her friends were talking about him? Laughing at him because they'd caught him staring their way? His stomach rolled violently. Feeling beads of sweat rolling down his chest and back, Jeremy wished fervently that he could shrivel up into a ball and roll quietly away.

"Hi," there came a voice from just beside him. Jeremy opened his eyes and stared up to find Sylvia Jean Jones standing there, smiling, her beautiful eyes sparkling, hands behind her back, swaying slightly as she stared down at him.

"Uh, Hi!" stammered Jeremy, his heart moving up and sitting right in the middle of his throat. Miraculously, he managed a lopsided smile and hoped she didn't notice that he hadn't used his mouthwash that morning.

"Billy Joe, Nadia and I just happened to notice you were studying for your chemistry quiz today," Sylvia Jean's voice rang out melodiously like a chorus of angels, or at least what Jeremy thought a chorus of angels would sound like.

"Yeah?" Jeremy stared down at his chemistry book. Of course you're studying chemistry, dunderhead, he thought.

"Oh! Yeah, I was," he quickly amended, staring up and immediately losing himself in those beautiful green eyes.

"Well," Sylvia Jean blushed slightly, "we were wondering if we could study with you? You're the smartest person in the class, and none of us really gets chemistry, you know?"

Jeremy sat looking up at the beautiful sophomore in stunned shock. Sylvia Jean Jones stood swaying slightly not three feet away from him, asking him if he could help them study. She was asking him for a favor! Him!

"Sure!" Jeremy declared, a little too assertively, standing up and smiling at Sylvia Jean. "That would be great! I could use some study pals as well!"

As soon as the words came out of his mouth he winced inwardly and scolded himself. Study pals! Did you actually say study pals to the coolest girl in school!

"Great! I'll tell my friends! We've still got twenty minutes before first period! I'm sure Miss Winston will let us use the table at the back of the room to study together!" Jeremy glanced back at their homeroom teacher, Minerva Winston. This was Miss Winston's second year teaching and she was still trying to be a 'friend' to all her students. So Jeremy was pretty certain she would let the four of them study at the back table.

As Sylvia Jean almost danced delightfully up the rows of seats to whisper excitedly to her friends, pointing at Jeremy and at the back table, Jeremy simply stared, overwhelmed and filled with pure joy. The biggest smile he had ever smiled in his life crept across his face and it would last until he got off the bus from school late that afternoon.

***

Elizabeth Fallon stood self-consciously beside the bedside of Andy Morrison. Her eyes were wide and tinged with a shy uneasiness as she gazed down at the bandages covering his chest wound, and all the medical equipment that Andy was still hooked up to.

"Oh, Mr. Morrison! I'm so sorry…" Elizabeth began, her eyes tearing up as she stared at Andy's pale, worn face.

"No, please," interrupted the young lawyer sincerely, instinctively reaching out and grasping Elizabeth's hand, "don't say you're sorry. You have nothing to be sorry for. I'm the one that should be apologizing." Andy's voice was weak, but filled with determination and passion.

Elizabeth frowned slightly and shook her head, "You? Apologizing for what? All you've ever done is tried to help me!"

Andy shook his head ruefully, "That and I inadvertently made my sister," Andy choked back a sob and then continued, "try to kill you."

Elizabeth reached over and placed her hand on

Andy's, giving it an encouraging squeeze, "That wasn't you. That was your sister. Just like I inherited my father's debts. That wasn't me. But now I have to deal with them, just as you have to deal with your sister's actions."

"Speaking of my sister, do you know what they've done with her? I think everyone's afraid to talk about her around me right now." Andy struggled for a moment to sit up, but the searing pain radiating from his chest forced him to fall back on the bed.

Elizabeth shuffled her feet for a moment, unsure what to say and what not to, but she found herself unable to keep the truth from the critically ill young man on the bed in front of her. For some reason, all her defenses came down around the young lawyer. Simply put, she trusted and respected him.

"Well, after they captured her she was brought back to the hospital," Elizabeth peered compassionately into Andy's eyes, "and after the surgery..."

"Surgery? What surgery? What happened?" Andy's eyes became gravely concerned, as he stared up at the young woman.

"Your sister took Sheriff Green captive and forced him to be her shield. Then she tried to escape. But she was wounded when she hit the sheriff over the head with her weapon. One of the state troopers," Elizabeth hesitated, then realized that it was best to tell Andy the truth, "shot her in the leg. It was the partner of the trooper your sister killed at the road block who shot her."

Elizabeth stopped for a moment, staring worriedly down at Andy, wondering how much bad news he could take. Andy stared out the window for a moment, trying to digest the news, his face filled with a pain and sorrow unrelated to his chest wound. Then he turned back to Elizabeth and nodded slightly, as if to tell her to continue.

"She and the sheriff made it out of the hospital. The sheriff told the other law enforcement officers to let your sister take him. He wanted to prevent anyone from being hurt further, I believe. But they only got a little ways down the street before the loss of blood from her wound caused her to pass out. The sheriff started carrying her back here as fast as he could. Doc Stone and Dr. Monroe reached him and stopped the bleeding. But she needed an operation to repair the damaged blood vessels and close up the wound." Elizabeth had spoken quickly, wanting to get it all out at once, not wanting to linger over the story, wishing to spare the young lawyer any emotional pain that she could.

Andy frowned as he considered the actions of the night before. He didn't doubt the truth of what Elizabeth has said. But, deep down inside, he still had difficulty with the ultimate realization that his sweet older sister, the sister who had spent most of her life taking care of him, had actually shot him and turned out to be a murderer.

Andy turned back to stare up into Elizabeth's kind and compassionate eyes, "What happened? Is she…is she…? I mean…is she okay?" Tears rolled down his pale cheeks as he waited to hear whether his sister had survived. In the back of his head, he had been secretly dreading that Wendy might have eventually died and they weren't telling him due to the severity of his own condition.

Elizabeth, realizing his overriding fear, quickly responded, "She's still unconscious. The operation was a success. But it will take quite some time before she's strong enough to start any rehabilitation. She nearly died from loss of blood."

Andy wiped his eyes self-consciously and shook his head, taking a deep breath. Then he glanced back up at Elizabeth, another frown passing across his pale face, "Do you know anything about what is going to happen to her? Legally, I mean?"

Elizabeth shook her head slowly and shrugged, "All I know is that when she's well enough she will be transferred to a state institution where she can get the help she needs with her mental disorder. After that, she will have to deal with the criminal charges. I guess that's a question best asked the sheriff."

Andy nodded, understanding only too well from what Elizabeth had told him the long road that his older sister had before her. It would take years, decades, for Wendy to get better emotionally and pay off her debt to society. Compounding that would be the death of a state trooper. That always became an especially difficult legal issue. At least, because Vermont had no death penalty, he didn't have to worry about that possibility.

Deep down inside, Andy knew that as a lawyer, he would do everything he could to help his sister get through the ordeals that lay ahead of her. And, as her brother, he would be there to help in any way he could emotionally as well.

Elizabeth watched Andy struggling to come to grips with the events of the past few days. She understood as well how terrible it could be to lose someone near and dear. She missed her beloved father terribly. So, she could relate with what the young lawyer was going through at the moment.

"Would you like it if I stayed and we talked for awhile?" Elizabeth asked it hopefully but quietly, not sure Andy would want her around with everything else on his mind.

But Andy's face brightened and his eyes lit up, a shy smile flickering around his lips, "Oh, please! I would really like that, if I'm not keeping you from anything," Andy replied happily.

Elizabeth pulled over a chair and sat down next to the young lawyer. They talked animatedly, with shy smiles and a great deal of relief, not about Andy's sister, nor about Elizabeth's father. They talked about everything else but.

***

The archer took a deep breath, let half of it out and stood very still, concentrating on the shot. There was a slight breeze from left to right, and she had done well gauging its effect on the flight of her arrows during her previous shots. As she let the arrow fly, she remained almost motionless, focusing in on the path of the arrow, unwaveringly willing it to the center of the target.

As the arrow struck, deep within the center circle, a huge smile broke out across her face and she jumped for joy. All around her the spectators let out a loud, enthusiastic cheer and ran to congratulate her. As she was hugged, praised and applauded, she laughed and enjoyed it all, feeling good about her attempt and the outcome.

A beaming Jeb and Zeke both stepped forward, Jeb shaking Lorraine Burman's hand and Zeke quieting down the noisy, energized crowd standing around in Smith and Peters' Super Video Store. The huge seventy-inch HDTV screen dimmed a bit as Jeb paused the video game and turned back to the assembled crowd.

"Great job, Lorraine! Seems as though she's got a real chance at winning the Valentine's Day 'Shoot Like

Cupid' contest!" Jeb declared loudly, gesturing at the slightly embarrassed but excited Lorraine. This, of course set off another chorus of cheers and applause.

After an appropriate pause to allow their customers and the other contestants for the 'Cupid's Challenge' contest to express their enthusiasm, Zeke raised his hand and waited for relative quiet.

"As you all know, this is the second day of our little video archery contest! Contestants have until noon tomorrow, Valentine's Day, to qualify and post a score. As you all know, the scores are tabulated on fifteen arrows over three distances. Top score wins a brand new XBPSIV video system with wireless controllers, motion sensor control and Dolby sound! The same cutting edge system we are using today!"

Again the crowd cheered lustily.

Zeke continued, "The second place contestant will win a sixty-inch LED HDTV!"

Once more the building shook with applause and excited cheers.

Zeke raised his hand once more, and finished with, "Third place will entitle that contestant to any six video games they desire from our fully stocked video shelves!"

Again, the room echoed with the cheering and stamping of feet from enthusiastic and excited contestants. Jeb and Zeke glanced at each other, satisfied grins spreading across their weathered faces as they turned back and stared around the room.

Over one hundred and sixty three contestants had already stepped up and tried their luck at the video game. It was free to enter and a wonderful goodwill PR move by the cagey old friends. It was also a heartwarming and generous gesture from two men who had already given back to their community time and time again. It betrayed the secret kind and caring hearts of The Falls' two biggest scallywags.

At that moment, William Frasier and his beautiful wife Serafina Messina Frasier stepped in out of the February thaw and glanced around at the dozens of citizens who were now starting to disperse. As the crowd browsed around the video store, eagerly checking out the new video systems, peripherals and games, a curious William walked over to where Jeb and Zeke were congratulating Lorraine on her astonishingly good performance in the archery contest.

"Hey Jeb, Zeke and Lorraine! What's going on?" William asked inquisitively, glancing from Lorraine and the video storeowners to the paused video game on the wide screen TV.

Jeb and Zeke exchanged winks and chuckled as they watched William's curiosity get the better of him. "Well, well, if it isn't one of our favorite customers!" Jeb replied.

Zeke tipped his head to the side and chuckled, "We wondered when you and your super competitive brother would show up!" Zeke gestured toward the big screen HDTV.

Jeb drew himself up proudly and spoke softly but with great enthusiasm, "This is the brand new Archery 3.0 videogame. It isn't even available in video game stores yet. This is a Beta testing version for us to try out and send back our comments and feedback to the video game company. We happen to know two of the designers that developed it, and they thought," Jeb glanced over proudly at his buddy Zeke and then continued a bit smugly, "that we would be the perfect testers for their newest version!"

"And to do that, we could think of no better way than to have a Valentine's Day archery shooting contest!" interjected Zeke, bursting with pride and enthusiasm as well.

Zeke pointed to one of several large signs on the back wall that promoted and explained in detail the rules and prizes of the contest. William studied the poster for a few seconds, a large smile spreading slowly across his handsome face.

"Well, then," William announced, glancing back and forth from Jeb to Zeke to Lorraine, "you can count on Sean and I to enter as soon as he gets out of school this afternoon!"

Serafina walked up behind her husband, slipped her arm through his, and shook her head as she chuckled at his eagerness and intensity when it came to any videogame, anywhere, anytime.

"So, I'm assuming dinner might be a little late tonight, dearest?" Serafina gazed innocently up into her husband's eyes and smiled to herself as she saw him squirm a bit uncomfortably, his eyes widening.

"Oh! We were going to have a quiet dinner tonight! I forgot!" William's face went a bit pale, as he hurriedly tried to remediate the situation.

Serafina reached up on tiptoe, kissed his cheek playfully and giggled, then shook her head and replied, "No, its okay. I'm just 'pulling your chain' as you and your brother like to say! Come and take part, enjoy the contest. Then tomorrow night, Valentine's day..." Serafina's eyes flashed meaningfully.

"I will take you wherever you want to go to dinner and there will be absolutely no video games! You have my promise!" blurted out a relieved and excited William. He leaned down and kissed his beautiful wife gratefully and lovingly.

Zeke and Jeb simply stood by and grinned. Lorraine smiled and then glanced back over at the video storeowners. "Well, I guess I'll be going! Always so much stuff to do up at the maple syrup compound! But I'm glad I came by. Jeremy had made me promise I would. He knows I like archery and used to be pretty good at it."

Lorraine blushed a bit, but smiled and continued sweetly, "He had entered the contest and was adamant that I should as well. He teased me unmercifully until I gave in!"

"Thanks! It was fun! I hope you get lots of contestants! Have a great day!" Lorraine reached up on tiptoe, kissed both Jeb and Zeke tenderly on their stubbly cheeks and then walked briskly and cheerfully toward the door ready to get on with her day. Both Jeb and Zeke touched their cheeks gently afterwards and gazed tenderly after the sweet young woman as she walked away.

William turned and called out to Lorraine as she was almost out the door, his tone encouraging and positive, "Good luck, Lorraine! I hope you do well!"

Lorraine turned, her eyes twinkling as she called out over her shoulder, "Good luck to you, too, Mr. Frasier! But I know you won't need it!"

Jeb and Zeke watched the sweet granddaughter of Grandma and Grandpa Burman leave and then turned to William, their eyes twinkling as well, "She surprised us. We've never seen her play a video game before. She had an amazing score. She had perfect form and the motion sensitive controller seemed to love her aim and release. 'Course we can't give out scores to anyone until the contest is over, but let's just say that right now, she's in the running for a prize."

William took in the information, nodded and smiled, "Well good for her! I've always thought Lorraine was a very special young lady." Then he turned and started gazing eagerly at the video screen.

"Do you think I could take a few practice shots?" he gazed at Jeb and Zeke his eyebrows up, obviously seriously intrigued and unable to wait until that afternoon to get his hands on the game.

"Sorry," replied Zeke, as he unpaused the system, then saved the game and shut it down for the moment, "but everyone gets three practice shots just before they start their turn. It's in the rules." Zeke pointed up at the small print in the poster on the back wall.

"Oh, yeah, I see," William declared staring once more intently at the poster. He turned with a big grin to face Jeb and Zeke.

"Alright then, we have a date later this afternoon, gentlemen," declared the author, winking and smiling at the two video storeowners. Shaking Jeb and Zeke's hands as if sealing the deal, William reached out, took Serafina's arm and cheerfully walked out the front door with a slight wave over his head.

Jeb and Zeke watched the happy couple walk out into the warming February thaw. Then they glanced back at each other, each sporting a large grin. Things were starting to get interesting!

***

Christian Reynard Shanks strode at a regular, brisk pace along the logging road about halfway up the mountain. He unbuttoned his heavy winter coat and threw it over his shoulder, glancing up into the sky, and smiling at the balmy, fickle winter sun that had finally decided to warm up this frozen part of the world.

He was on his way up to a log cabin that he had built several years ago. It was small, but it was a place that was secluded and well out of the way. It was a place to spend a few days at a time away from the cares, hustle, bustle and deadlines of the work-a-day world. It was his oasis, his sanctuary. After the mess with Tinmouth Pritchard, Elizabeth Fallon, Wendy Morrison and her brother Andy, he was more than ready to spend a few days tromping the woods, cooking over the fireplace and spending time communing with nature.

Truth be told, C.R. Shanks liked the silence and beauty of the woods much better than his private eye business and his home on the outskirts of Brown Bear Junction. It seemed as if more and more people wanted to hire him for more and more outlandish and often distasteful reasons. He thought of some of the more prevalent examples he had been hired to deal with over the past few years. Following an errant husband or wife to get proof of their infidelity was up thirty percent in the last ten years. Serving subpoenas and other legal papers had risen a good forty percent during the same time period. Not to mention his least favorite job, being a personal bodyguard for a certain amount of time. That part of his business had doubled in business over that time as well.

Shanks took in the beauty of the forest, the icicles that were dripping from the branches of the trees, the snow, beginning to turn to slush in places, and the deer track that would soon disappear with the melting snow. He knew that in a day or two or three, the cruel, freezing winter wind would begin to bluster and blow all over again and the landscape would be frozen once more for weeks at a time. But he still loved and waited for the February thaw every year. It gave hope of a bountiful spring and sultry summer to come.

C.R. spotted the small cabin just up the trail and smiled to himself. He would settle in and then find a nice rabbit or two to make rabbit stew in the big, black pot hanging over the roaring fire he would soon make in the ample fireplace. That brought another smile to his ruggedly handsome face.

As he reached the cabin, he unlocked the door and began to air it out from a month or two of sitting empty. Glancing around, he noticed that he hadn't filled up the wood box the last time he was there, so he decided that gathering up enough wood for two or three days would be his first real chore.

As he cleaned out the cabin, opening windows, sweeping out the dust and insects that tend to move in when the humans move out, the tall man couldn't help but go over in his mind the next job he had waiting for him when he went back to his regular life. He had promised a new friend that he would help them find a lost loved one. It would probably entail some travel, possibly as far as California. He really had no idea where the trail might lead him, but compared to some of the jobs he took on, it sounded like a real breath of fresh air.

Speaking of fresh cold air, he thought shivering involuntarily from a chill in the clammy cabin, it's time to gather that wood. Hoisting up the canvas carrier to place the wood that he scoured the nearby forest for, he headed off toward a hardwood grove that always had plenty of wood for him to use. He usually didn't even have to cut any trees or branches down. This far up in the mountains, there was plenty of useable firewood just lying around to keep his fire blazing for the short time he was there.

His thoughts slipped back to the person who had commissioned him to find their lost family member. He had met Meg Monroe just a few days ago when he had been working with Andy Morrison. Shanks smiled to himself. She was a beautiful young woman, but he wasn't really sure that she was his type. He chuckled. On the other hand, he was very sure that he wasn't her type.

Meg Monroe was independent, strong and always cheerful and positive. There was very little about her not to like. But he knew from experience that most strong, independent women liked to have their men around when they wanted them. They also wanted their companions to be independent but predictable and smart enough to stay out of their way when they were busy with something they deemed important.

Picking up a snow-covered piece of maple and shoving it in the carrier, C.R. grinned. He knew himself. He was a good, kind and caring guy. But he loved his freedom, and was what most women termed a 'loner'. He knew that it would take a very special kind of woman to be willing to take him and his own special lifestyle on for any length of time.

As he tromped through the melting snow toward the cabin, he thought about what Meg Monroe had asked him to do. He still remembered how pretty she looked when they had talked, and how good she had smelled. Shaking his head, C.R. grinned again and brought himself back to the point he was thinking about.

Meg Monroe had never known her father. Or to be specific, she didn't remember her biological father. Her mother had told Meg that her father had left when she only three. Meg loved her mother, and had a wonderful, caring childhood. She had a strong and caring relationship with her stepfather and loved him dearly. But now, as she came closer and closer to the thirty-year milestone, Meg wanted to know more. She wanted to know if her real father was still alive, and if he was, who he was and where she might find him, should she so choose.

Meg had made one thing perfectly clear. If Shanks found her father, he was not to let the man know anything about her. He was to bring the information back to her, along with pictures and C.R.'s personal estimation of the man. Then Meg would decide what to do next.

Reaching the cabin, Shanks dumped the wood in the wood box and picked his Winchester lever action rifle up off the bed. It was time to find a rabbit warren or two. Shanks smiled and licked his lips impatiently as he headed for the door. Rabbit stew, with little potatoes, carrots and onions! All washed down with a pot of strong coffee as he watched the stars. He could hardly wait.

Chapter 29

The mysterious plastic storage container sat on the lunch table in the high school lunchroom. Jeremy Burman had just pulled it out of his brown paper lunch bag. He stared down at it for several seconds, studying it, considering the possibilities.

He always packed his own lunch. It was always the same, a sandwich, a bag of chips and a piece of fruit. But here it was, an unexplained plastic container sitting on the lunch table before him. Either his grandma or mom had probably packed him a treat of some kind.

"Hey, Jeremy!" Jamison Ewing, one of his friends at the union high school, grinned, leaned over and poked the container playfully with the tip of his finger. "What's in the box?"

Jamison had more freckles than any kid Jeremy had ever seen. He also had a wry sense of humor and was a master at keeping himself out of trouble. No matter what mischief Jamison got into, the effects seemed to slide right off him just like he was made of Teflon. Jamison was also very curious, and wasn't at all shy about prying into people's thoughts and actions.

"Hey, Jeremy," Jamison repeated louder and more persistent when Jeremy didn't respond. "Didn't you hear me? I said, what's in the plastic tub?"

"Darned if I know," Jeremy finally replied, glancing

up at his friend and smiling. "Probably something my grandma or mom baked."

Jamison attacked his apple, biting off almost a quarter of it in one, mammoth mouthful. With his mouth full, he glanced around the lunchroom and hummed softly to himself. Jamison was always doing something, usually several things at once.

As Jamison dug around inside his own lunch bag, looking for more food, Jeremy carefully opened the top of the container sitting in front of him. Inside there were two beautiful cupcakes. Each had a bright pink frosting. On the top of each was a large red candy heart. The wording on the hearts read Happy Valentine's Day!

Jeremy grinned. They were from Lorraine. Lorraine had spent hours in the family kitchen last night making dozens of Valentine's Day cupcakes to hand out to all the maple sugar workers tomorrow. She had also put a few away for their family to share as well. Obviously she had managed to save a couple out just for him.

Jeremy and his Grandpa Burman had each tried to steal one last night, they looked so delicious, but she had caught them both. Lorraine had laughed and taken the cupcakes back, slapping their hands playfully and telling them that they had to wait until Valentine's Day, just like everybody else. Obviously, Lorraine had softened and secretly sent two of the cupcakes with him to school.

Jeremy looked down into the container thoughtfully. Two cupcakes. He could be a pig and eat them both, or he could share. He glanced up at Jamison who was currently engaged in trying to stick a spoon on his nose for the amusement of the rest of their friends. Jeremy grinned and shook his head.

Glancing up, Jeremy saw Sylvia Jean Jones walking

straight toward him. Jeremy's eyes widened and he felt his heart beat speed up rapidly. His palms turned sweaty once again and he gulped as he watched the beautiful young sophomore almost bounce effortlessly over to his table.

"Hi, Jeremy!" Sylvia Jean exclaimed, her eyes sparkling and her mouth bowed up in a beautifully animated smile. Sylvia Jean agilely slipped onto the bench across from him, staring him straight in the eyes.

"I just wanted to tell you how much my friends and I appreciated you helping us study for the chemistry exam!" Sylvia Jean's hair cascaded down into a charming ponytail and there were little ringlets by each ear. "You were a lifesaver! We just didn't get all that stuff he was trying to teach us in class! But you made it seem interesting and fun!"

Jeremy was certain that his face was turning a brilliant shade of red. Not only that, but Jamison's full and rapt attention was now turned toward Jeremy and Sylvia Jean. Jeremy could see Jamison's eyes light up as he watched the pretty sophomore speaking to his friend. Jeremy hoped against hope that Jamison would simply keep still and not cause him any further discomfort.

That was not to be.

"Hey, Jeremy! Introduce me to your new friend!" Jamison grinned and elbowed Jeremy in his side. Sylvia Jean turned her attention to Jamison for a moment, smiled and then replied.

"I'm Sylvia Jean. Sylvia Jean Jones, nice to meet you." She nodded in a polite way, watching Jamison carefully.

"Sylvia Jean, this is my friend Jamison," Jeremy managed to get out, his voice an octave higher than usual as he fought through a slight wave of shyness and embarrassment.

"Nice to meet you, Jamison," Sylvia Jean responded, then she turned back to Jeremy, her eyes filled with delight and thoughtfulness.

"Anyway, I just wanted to tell you how much that meant to us, to me," Sylvia Jean blushed slightly, and then smiled shyly as she added, "and I wondered if..."

"If what, Sylvia Jean?" quickly asked Jamison, winking at Jeremy and then staring at the beautiful young girl. Jamison was obviously enjoying the somewhat extraordinary and slightly awkward interaction between Jeremy and Sylvia Jean, unable to keep from snooping and prying just a bit.

Jeremy suddenly turned and glared at Jamison, speaking in a very low, deep and commanding tone, "Didn't you have to run over to English class and bring back the paper you edited to Miss Canfield during lunch today?" Jeremy's stare left no room for alternatives; he was definitely telling Jamison to "bug off".

Jamison, for once, amazingly took the hint. Jeremy wasn't sure if it was because Jeremy's eyes were glowing with rage, or if Jamison realized that this was a bridge he best not cross, or if Jamison was simply helping him out by heading out to bring his paper back. Fortunately, at that precise moment, the reason really didn't matter.

As Jamison strode away from the table with his backpack jauntily slung over his shoulder, he grinned broadly, winked subtly at Jeremy and waved a cheerful goodbye to Sylvia Jean.

Jeremy, a ton of relief coming out in a small sigh, turned back to Sylvia Jean and smiled shyly, "You were saying, Sylvia Jean?"

Sylvia Jean smiled again, and then, just before she spoke, she happened to stare down into the plastic container at the beautiful cupcakes.

"Oh, wow! What gorgeous cupcakes! Who made them?" Sylvia Jean's eyes were wide with true amazement and delight.

Jeremy proudly replied, "My sister Lorraine made them. She's really good at baking! Everybody says she could work at Federman's bakery, her creations are so good!"

Sylvia Jean's look slowly turned from amazement to wistfulness. Jeremy instantly could tell that Sylvia Jean was yearning for one of Lorraine's cupcakes. Jeremy's basic thoughtfulness and consideration came out. Without thinking about it, he reached down and very carefully picked one of the cupcakes up, placing it down in front of Sylvia Jean.

"Here, please have this one. I have two," Jeremy smiled and nodded at Sylvia Jean.

Sylvia Jean's eyes widened even more as she glanced from the beautiful cupcake to Jeremy. Her blush reddened and she smiled with delight.

"Thank you, Jeremy! That's awesome!" she managed to whisper as she reached out and accepted the gift. Then she looked up into Jeremy's eyes and her gaze softened as she added, "I was wondering if you'd like to walk me back to my next class? Maybe we could talk?"

Jeremy gazed at Sylvia Jean as she took off the wrapper on the cupcake and took her first scrumptious bite. The question she had asked was simple enough. But what did it mean? Did it mean "Will you walk me to class so I don't have to carry my books?" or "Will you just walk me to class so I don't have to walk alone?" or, and he began to redden even more as he thought of this possibility, "Will you walk me to class because I'd like to see about being boyfriend and girlfriend?"

Sylvia Jean stood up, smiling happily and eating her cupcake and motioned Jeremy to come with her. He decided he would deal with the 'what if's' later. As he walked over beside her, and they walked out of the lunchroom, eating their delicious cupcakes, he suddenly realized what had happened.

For the first time ever, he had given a girl, other than his family members, a Valentine's Day present!

***

As the shadows grew longer and the dusk approached that warm day during the February thaw, the two Frasier brothers opened the door to Smith and Peter's Super Video Game Store and strode inside. There was already a large gathering of video-gamers, talking excitedly, laughing and robustly cheering on the contestants for Jeb and Zeke's Valentine's Day Archery Contest, glibly named "Cupid's Challenge" on all the posters around the store.

"Well, there seems to be quite a turnout," Sean whispered to his brother, as he glanced appreciatively around the store. "Kind of neat to see who is a video-gamer and who isn't!"

William nodded, smiling and intrigued himself as he stared around the shop, checking out who was in attendance. There were probably twenty-five people, ranging in age from eleven or twelve to the late sixties, eagerly watching and evaluating the shots of the contestant that was just finishing up her turn.

Meg Monroe mimicked the moves of shooting her last arrow and watched the arrow thud solidly into the center of the target. Zeke who nodded his head in appreciation as the young doctor stepped back away from the shooting zone. Meg immediately noticed Sean and William and stepped toward them through the delighted crowd, accepting handshakes and fist bumps from the appreciative onlookers as she went.

As she reached the two brothers, she was smiling, her eyes twinkling, obviously excited and pleased with her recent performance. "Hey guys! I'm not surprised to see you here!" Meg declared.

"Well, I can't say the feeling is mutual!" William responded with a chuckle, his eyes twinkling with good humor, "I had no idea you were a video-gamer, Dr. Monroe!"

Meg laughed, wiping a few beads of sweat off her forehead, obtained during her shooting round, "Well, I'm not, usually. But during medical school and as a resident, we had long shifts and sometimes, we would get into video games just to keep us awake! I got so I was pretty good! I could beat most of the guys!"

She turned her head and glanced back at Donald Morganstein's brother, Aldo, as he was gearing himself up to begin his practice round. Zeke and Jeb were patiently pointing out the basics of the game and patting Aldo encouragingly on his shoulder.

Meg giggled and shook her head, "I came because Doc Stone told me what the prizes were. I thought that I might be able to win a big TV or a gaming system that we could set up at the hospital." Her eyes were expressive as she smiled a bit shyly, "You know, it would be neat to have something like that for the kids and the patients. It might just take their minds off their problems and help them get better quicker."

Meg shrugged rather self-consciously, glancing back and forth at the two brothers, "Just thought it was worth a shot!"

Both William and Sean glanced at each other guiltily. They both were here to win prizes to heighten their own gaming pleasures. Meg was here to give whatever she won to the hospital. All of a sudden they both felt very selfish and inconsiderate. They turned their gazes back to the young doctor.

"That's really sweet of you, Meg," Sean replied quietly, his eyes kind, thoughtful and sincere. "I hope you win something. Really." Sean leaned over and hugged Meg gently without warning, surprising Meg a little.

"Thanks, Sean," Meg responded, her eyes a bit curious at the principal's sudden generosity, but taking it in stride, smiling warmly. "I hope I do too!"

William reached out and shook Meg's hand. His emotions had also been touched by Meg's selfless reason for entering. "Good luck, Meg. I really hope you do well. Winning the equipment for the hospital is really thoughtful. It's a great idea. How do you think you did, anyway?" he asked.

Meg shrugged as she picked up her coat, getting ready to return to the hospital, as her eyebrows rose in uncertainty, "I don't really know. I did pretty well, I think. But Jeb said I was the two hundred and forty-first participant. That's a lot of people! Odds aren't very good!" Meg grinned cheerfully as she pulled on her coat and headed toward the door.

"Got to do rounds, then paperwork, then work in the lab on some cultures, then..." Meg hesitated and glanced back at the two Frasier brothers. "Did I mention eating in there anywhere?" She laughed at her own self and then waved cheerfully as she hurried out the door.

"Bye! Good luck, guys!" Meg shouted out to the brothers as she stepped out into the gathering darkness.

"Bye Meg!" Sean and William sang out in unison as they watched the diminutive but vivacious young doctor rush off out the door and down the street toward the medical facility.

Then the Frasier brothers turned to each other, a determined look in their eyes, each pretty sure what the other was thinking. Their eyes gleaming with a new competitive fire, they strode resolutely over to where Jeb and Zeke were cheering Aldo Morganstein on as he strained, his concentration intent, to hit the target with his video arrow.

***

Meg Monroe walked briskly down the corridor of the hospital, the small brown teddy bear sitting in the crook of her arm. The little bear's soft, smiling furry face was turned toward her, and his dark brown eyes twinkled brightly. Meg smiled slightly as she looked down at the bear.

Not more than fifteen minutes ago Meg had stopped off at the hospital's little gift shop. She was still feeling troubled and saddened for everything that had befallen Andy Morrison. Truth be told, she was even feeling a little guilty. It seemed to her that ever since she had politely but firmly rebuffed Andy's advances, he'd had nothing but bad luck.

When she had been on rounds a few minutes earlier, she had stopped at Andy's private room and glanced in through the glass in his door. Andy had been lying quietly, staring out the window at the sunrise, one single tear rolling down his flushed cheek. It had touched her caring heart. Even though she had gathered her emotions and then swept into the room, all cheerful and full of positive energy, she hadn't been able to forget the way he had looked.

Today was Valentine's Day and Andy's only immediate family was in the critical care unit, the Vermont State Police stationed at her door. His sister, Wendy, would serve a long time in a mental institution, working through her dual personality disorder. She would serve an even longer sentence in a prison for killing a trooper and wounding her own brother.

Andy's world had literally been turned upside down, and Meg was determined to at least make his Valentine's Day a little bit brighter. Her kind heart and caring personality went out to the wounded young lawyer, and being the champion that she was for people who were suffering or in need, she could do no less.

Meg glanced down at the little bear, who had a darling little red bow around his neck and came with a small, cheerful little card that shouted out in bright red and pink letters, "Happy Valentine's Day! Have a beary, beary wonderful day!" Her smile grew a little. She knew the little bear and his cheery greeting wouldn't make up for the disaster in his life, but at least, she hoped, it was a start.

As Meg passed by the nurse's desk, Flora Henriksen glanced up from her reports and stared over her half-rim reading glasses at Meg.

"Just going to check up on Andy Morrison," declared Meg, smiling and shifting the little bear to the arm away from Flora, trying to hide him away so she wouldn't have to explain why she was carrying him. But the head nurse's quick eyes saw the little bear, and her eyebrows rose slightly. Then Flora stared back up at Meg, studying her carefully.

Flora simply nodded and glanced back down at her reports, replying in her normal professional tone, "I see,

THE FALLS: Cupid's Arrow

Dr. Monroe. Well, it's true that young man could do with some cheerin' up, I suppose."

As Meg continued down the corridor, she stopped just before Andy's room, trying to figure out exactly what she would say to him as she gave him the bear. She didn't want to embarrass him any more than she had when she rebuffed his advances, but she also didn't want him thinking that she had any intentions of getting involved with him. That wouldn't do at all. She sighed and figured that she would come up with something on the spur of the moment.

As she stood there, she heard quiet voices coming from Andy's room. Puzzled at first, she turned around thinking the voices might be coming from another room. But no, there were the voices again, and one of them definitely sounded like Andy Morrison. Growing more and more curious, she quietly peeked in through the small panel of glass in the door.

There was Andy Morrison lying in his hospital bed. Next to him sat Elizabeth Fallon and they were talking quietly but animatedly. Andy's face still looked worn and sad but from time to time a shy smile flashed across it, as he carried on an earnest conversation with Elizabeth.

Elizabeth's pale face had a smile as well, and as she talked, she would reach down and gently touch Andy's arm from time to time. Her cheeks were flushed, as if she were slightly embarrassed, but happy.

Meg glanced carefully at Andy and Elizabeth. She noticed that their eyes were filled with a closeness, a friendship, a definite caring, and just perhaps, something more.

Then Meg noticed something else. In Andy's right hand there was a little brown bear, just like the one she was holding in her arms. Another little bear from the gift shop, she instantly realized. Andy was gently squeezing the adorable little bear, and from time to time, he would glance down at it and smile. Elizabeth would smile then as well, her cheeks flushing a deeper shade of pink.

Andy and Elizabeth shared a quiet laugh as Andy mouthed the words 'Thank you!' to the young woman sitting close to him on the side of the bed.

Meg stepped slowly back from the door. A wave of emotion swept over her. Her smile vanished as she realized that Andy Morrison had moved on. The young woman sitting next to him on his bed was now the obvious object of his attention and affections.

Human emotions are a funny thing. Even though you don't want someone to be 'that special person' in your life, and are struggling to let them down easy, when they move on from the crush they have on you, it somehow saddens you.

For a few moments, Meg stared down at the darling little bear in her arms and felt both the relief of letting go and the sadness that occurs when someone no longer wants you. Then, she took a deep breath and whispered back toward the doorway, a smile beginning to creep across her face, "Good for you! Both of you!"

Gathering her mixed emotions, Meg walked back up along the corridor, retracing her steps and for once, not really knowing where she was going next. She continued to stare down at the cute little bear still snuggled in her arms.

As Meg stepped out into the waiting room, she saw a young mother with a whiny small child in her arms. Next to the mother was a four or five year old, obviously in distress, crying silently in the chair next to her mother. The mother was trying desperately to quiet the baby in her arms, who was wiggling around and squalling, while the five year old simply sat and cried silently, trying to comfort herself by rocking back and forth in the little chair.

Meg glanced over at Flora Henriksen and realized she was still hugging the little bear tightly. Flora glanced at the stuffed bear and at Meg, again glancing curiously over her half-rim reading glasses.

In Flora's eyes, Meg could see a flicker of compassion and understanding. Flora smiled tenderly and nodded at Meg. The young doctor felt the breath catch in her throat for just a moment. Then, smiling back to her head nurse, Meg turned and walked over to where the mother was preoccupied with her two sick children.

She knelt down and slowly handed the little brown bear to the little girl. The child stopped rocking and her tears stopped as she gazed in astonishment at the cute little bear being held out to her. Her wet, glistening eyes met Meg's. With a glimmer of hope and joy in her shimmering eyes, the little girl put out her small, chubby arms toward the bear.

Meg placed the little bear into the child's embrace and smiled down at her. The child smiled through her tears and hugged the bear tightly, her little eyes now filled with gratitude and delight. Meg touched the child's cheek gently and then stood up, smiling and gesturing for the mother to come with her.

As Meg walked off to the examination room with the mother and her children, she caught Flora Henriksen watching her closely. Meg turned and tilted her head to one side, silently inquiring if Flora needed to tell her something.

Flora compassionately mouthed the words "Happy Valentine's Day!" and then glanced back down at her reports, the moment having come and gone for her.

Meg turned back and nodded to herself as she smiled and followed the mother and her children into the examination room. But in her own heart, she silently declared "Happy Valentine's Day!" to herself as well.

***

All around the town, businesses and community members were getting ready for Valentine's Day. All the shops and stores had beautiful red, pink and white decorations with hearts and cupids while they ran huge sales of up to fifty percent off and gave away delectable chocolates and candies.

The Scoop was giving away small cups of Cupid's Delight ice cream, which was a smoothly whipped combination of cherry, French vanilla and black raspberry, topped off with whipped cream and a real cherry. They also had created a Valentine's Day roll of chocolate where they stacked thin layer after layer of dark, milk, mint and white chocolate, rolling it up and then cutting sections of the roll off for their customers. Norma and Trish were dressed in red and pink aprons and there were dozens of cupids and hearts hanging down from the ceiling.

Burman' Five and Ten Cent Emporium was decorated to the hilt, with red, white and pink streamers, cupids and hearts all around the store. Grandma Burman let every customer choose a scratcher out of a large bowl of scratchers when they entered. Once the top layer was scratched off the small card, it told the customer what percentage off they were entitled to on any one item in the store. Milburn Daily, the first patron to receive a fifty percent off under his lucky scratcher, whooped ecstatically. He promptly bought a new sixty-inch HDTV set, saving himself a bundle, as well as delighting his wife and seven children! Grandma and Grandpa Burman clapped their hands with joy for Milburn and happily helped him pack the new TV in the back of his truck.

Even The Owens Gas Station was having a Valentine's Day sale. Free oil changes went with a fill up, and tires were 'buy one, get one free'. Old Elijah Mendel was the first one in line just past sun up to get four new tires, fill his tank with gas, even though it was almost three-quarters full, and then take advantage of the free oil change. Bill Owens just chuckled to himself as he watched old Elijah, standing by the garage bay, his eyes twinkling, puffing on his pipe and smiling like he had gotten the best deal in the history of the world.

Over at Smith and Peters Super Video Store, the last few contestants entering the archery video game contest were waiting eagerly for their turn to shoot. Jeb and Zeke were content to stand by the counter, letting Geek McCluskey tell the contestants the rules and supervise their turn in the virtual archery contest.

"Well, not a bad turnout," Jeb chuckled, checking the list of contestants smugly. "It looks like we'll have had over four hundred community members, and another fifty or so from Brown Bear Junction and the surrounding farms, involved in our little promotion!" Jeb looked as pleased as punch and his chest swelled with pride.

Zeke nodded, smiling and whistling low, "That's a lot of people! More than I thought we'd have! Just think what it will be like next year if we turn this into an annual event?!"

Jeb stroked his chin, his eyes twinkling and his smile getting bigger all the while, "There's no 'if' about this, my old friend! This has just become one of our most popular yearly events!" Jeb nudged Zeke in the ribs playfully and the two old friends chuckled heartily, watching the last contestant step up to the archery line.

"Okay, as soon as this last contestant finishes, we go to the results and points section of the game and determine who the three winners are, agreed?" Jeb glanced over at Zeke who nodded vigorously and turned back to see who had just come into the shop.

In strode Sean and William Frasier. They walked right up to the two storeowners and glancing at Jeb and Zeke solemnly Sean whispered, "Is there somewhere we can talk for a minute?"

Jeb and Zeke glanced at each other for a moment and then back at Sean, thoughtfully staring at the tall older brother. "Aren't you supposed to be in school, right now, Mr. Principal?" asked Zeke, a little frown on his face, slightly nosy about what was going on.

"I'm playing hooky for a few minutes to come over with William," Sean grinned and glanced at his brother. Turning back to the two old friends, his became face serious and earnest once more. "But really, we need to talk."

Jeb and Zeke glanced at each other, then shrugged and turned back to the two brothers, gesturing politely to the staircase and their office upstairs.

A few minutes later, Jeb, Zeke, Sean and William walked back down the stairs, all of them with large smiles on their faces. After quick handshakes and pats on the back all around, William and Sean took off out the front door and Jeb and Zeke walked over to the game system where Geek McCluskey was getting ready to check the final archery contest scores and see who had won.

Jeb winked at Zeke and patted Geek on the back, and whispered conspiratorially, "We'll take it from here, if you don't mind, young man!"

Zeke winked at Geek who had turned and was staring questioningly at his two bosses, "We want to keep the results a secret from everyone until our grand announcement at seven tonight! You know what they used to say back in the Big War, loose lips sink ships!"

Jeb and Zeke chuckled delightedly at their little joke and Geek McCluskey simply smiled tolerantly and nodded, shaking his head at the shenanigans of his two bosses, which he was more than used to by now. "Sure Mr. Smith, Mr. Peters, whatever you say! I'll get back to work."

As Geek headed back to the repair department and started working on Ellen Burmiester's broken gaming system, Jeb and Zeke glanced at each other and then stared up at the big screen TV. Carefully clicking onto the "Scores and Achievements" section of the archery video game, the two old friends scrolled down through the scores. Immediately, satisfied smiles flashed across their faces and their eyes lit up with delight. Zeke quickly scribbled several names and scores on a small pad of paper as Jeb nodded his head.

After scrolling down through the long list of scores, checking out the relative video gaming skill of the community members who had taken part with a quick grin or a surprised "Not bad!" here and there, they the saved the game's progress and shut down the console. Jeb then made sure that he pulled the game disc out of the disk drive and slipped into his pocket. Walking back over to the front counter, Zeke grinned at his old friend and whispered, "This was awesome! I can't wait to do this again next year!"

Jeb slapped his old friend on the back and nodded emphatically as he turned to carefully adjust the cute cupids and snazzy hearts that were hanging down from long strings attached to the ceiling. The cupids and hearts fluttered gaily over the counter.

With great satisfaction and contentment, Jeb thought to himself, This is going to be a very happy Valentine's Day indeed!

Chapter 30

Mid-morning, Cash disappeared into the back room of the sheriff's office for a few moments. When he walked back out, he had a large cardboard box in his hands. Darlene, Yamato and Horace glanced up curiously from their work to check out what their boss was up to. He placed the box gingerly on his desk and opened it up carefully. Then he glanced up, grinned and pausing for a moment, melodramatically, his eyes twinkling.

The sheriff picked up three packages of slightly varying sizes, each topped with a large red bow, and brought them over to where each of his staff was sitting. Stepping back, he folded his arms across his chest and glanced around the office, with the same lopsided grin on his face.

"Well?" Cash declared, "Aren't you going to open them?"

Yamato, Darlene and Horace smiled, glanced around at each other and shrugged. Glancing back at their waiting boss they each busied themselves with opening the neatly wrapped present that had been set before them.

Horace was the first to open his present, as he eagerly ripped off the wrapping paper and bow. His eyes lit up immediately. Inside his rather large package were several items. There was a large package of Horace's favorite treat, Vermont Beef Jerky. There was also a container of Horace's wife, Millie's, favorite ice cream, Peppermint Candy, straight from The Scoop. The final part of Horace's gift was a big bag of assorted Valentine's Day candies for Hank and Hillary, Horace's two kids.

Horace looked up at Cash, a large smile spreading across his face, his eyes filled with pleasure and gratitude, "Thanks, boss! Millie and the kids will love it! So do I!"

"You're welcome, Horace, Happy Valentine's Day! Hope the kids don't get stomach aches from eating too much candy!" Cash smiled and nodded kindheartedly at his deputy and friend.

Cash had remembered how Hank and Hillary had eaten most of the Valentine's candy their parents had given them last Valentine's Day and then had stomach cramps, preventing Horace from taking Millie out for a special Valentine's Day supper that evening.

Horace immediately responded, getting very serious for a moment, his eyes huge and earnest, "No chance of that this year! Millie's started doling out small amounts of candy to the kids on Christmas, Easter, Halloween and Valentine's Day, just to make sure! She doesn't want to have to clean anymore throw up out of their hair or miss anymore special dinners, no sir!" Horace glanced around at Darlene and Yamato, who both looked up with rather disgusted expressions on their faces for a fleeting moment.

Yamato opened her present next. Her eyes widened as she stared down at her favorite treat of all time. In the top drawer of her desk, she always kept a small box of thin, luscious dark chocolate and mint wavers. They were the one treat she allowed herself whenever she needed a pick-me-up or just to feel a little bit pampered. Yamato glanced back up at Cash with a big smile on her beautiful face and winked her 'thank you' delightedly at her boss.

Cash winked back, and nodded as he smiled broadly, and then turned to the last of his three staff members. Darlene had opened her package and was sitting there staring down at it. Every since she had been a little girl, her favorite treat in the world had been a white chocolate candy log filled with macadamia nuts. They were difficult, if not impossible, to find around that part of the country, and she had always had to send away if she wanted one.

Wide-eyed, Darlene stared at Cash and uttered one astounded word, "How?"

Cash grinned and shrugged, then replied, "I just asked Norma, over at The Scoop, if she could make you one."

Darlene glanced back down at her gift and her eyes lit up as she murmured, "Land sakes! Moses and I will have a really special Valentine's desert tonight! And now Norma and Trish will be getting some special orders from time to time as well!"

Yamato then glanced around at Horace and Darlene, stood up and walked briskly over to the back shelf, retrieving a medium sized box from the top shelf. She quickly walked across the floor and handed Cash the box, her eyes twinkling with anticipation.

"This is to you, from all of us," Yamato took a step back and joined Horace and Darlene as her two colleagues walked up to join her. All three of them glanced around at each other, grinning and anxious to see what their boss thought of their choice.

As Cash pulled a large, oversized coffee mug out of the box, all three of them shouted out a joyful, "Happy Valentine's Day, Boss!" They were obviously thrilled with their gift and hoped he would be as well.

The mug was made of a very handsome and rugged looking stone pottery. On one side of it, the side he would look at every time he drank using his right hand, which he usually did, was a small picture of Cash. Above the picture was the wording in dark forest green, "Cash Green, the best sheriff in all of Vermont!" Down below the picture was the wording, in bright red, "Happy Valentine's day to a real Sweetheart!"

Looking down, Cash admired the mug, which he really liked. He stared at the picture, which he thought was a bit much. He really wasn't into seeing himself on things. Then he stared at the wording both above and below the picture. If the picture made him a tad uncomfortable, the wording definitely was worse. Yet, when he glanced up into the eager, hopeful and delighted eyes of Darlene, Yamato and Horace he realized that he loved it all, no matter what.

With a big grin he reached out and hugged each one in their turn, whispering sincerely, "Thanks! I love it!"

After the hugs, each of his office staff quickly went back to their own desks, eager to sneak a taste of the goodies they had been given. The phone rang, and for once, Cash answered as he watched Darlene sample a smidgeon of her white chocolate macadamia nut roll. Her eyes immediately lit up with pleasure.

"Sheriff's office, how may we help you today?" Cash asked, quietly and professionally.

"Hey! Answering your own phone calls these days, are you?" Doc chuckled.

Cash grinned and glanced over to where his office

THE FALLS: Cupid's Arrow

staff was proudly showing off their treasures to each other. "Yup," Cash responded, "just don't get too used to it, my friend. And Happy Valentine's Day!"

It sounded as though Doc moved a chair, then he declared, "Happy Valentine's Day to you too! From both Meg and me!"

Meg's voice sounded a bit farther away, "Yes! Happy Valentine's Day, Cash! I'm just glad we have no more bodies to deal with now that our Miss Cupid has been caught and is safely locked away in the critical care unit."

Doc broke in, "That's really what we're calling about."

Cash grinned, "It wasn't just to wish me a Happy Valentine's Day, Doc?! I'm crushed!" Cash started chuckling good-naturedly and soon Doc and Meg joined in.

"Well, no, to be honest, Big Guy, it wasn't. It was to fill you in on the status of Wendy Morrison." Doc's voice got back to normal, as he got down to brass tacks.

Cash's chuckle subsided and he began listening carefully, still holding his somewhat outlandish coffee mug fondly in his hand. Even though Wendy Morrison's case was now officially being handled by the Vermont State Police, he had asked Doc to keep him informed of Wendy's condition.

"Well, Dr. Messina was in with her this morning early," Doc began. It sounded like he was stirring his coffee in the background.

"From what Serafina told us, Wendy had no memory of shooting her brother or the state trooper. The last thing Wendy remembers is her brother being upset and driving off after she told him about her awkward meeting with Elizabeth Fallon at the diner in Brown

Bear Junction."

"I guess that's when Adelaide took over, and she remained in control until Wendy lost all that blood and reverted back to herself," Doc was talking quietly, obviously pondering the whole issue of dual personalities as he spoke.

"What's going to happen?" Cash asked curiously.

"Far as I can tell, Wendy has been obsessed over seeing her brother and making sure he's okay. I guess that will happen sometime in the next day or two. I think Serafina has arranged it with the state troopers that they will wheel Wendy's and Andy's beds into the same room for a few minutes," Doc sounded like he wasn't sure that was a good idea.

"Isn't that going to create a problem?" Cash asked quietly, "I mean, Andy is upset that his sister shot him and killed a law officer. How is that going to go over? Won't the shock of knowing what really happened set Adelaide off again and prompt her to take over?"

Doc responded immediately, "From what Dr. Messina said, she's talked to Andy, explained the issue of dual personality to him, and enlisted his aid. He's going to just see his sister, let her make sure he's okay and then, later, when she's stronger, they'll deal with the other issues."

"I'll bet that was a shock for the young lawyer to deal with," Cash remarked thoughtfully. "Don't know how I would react if I suddenly was told that someone I had known and relied on all my life had a nasty, secret personality."

"Apparently," Meg Monroe replied over the speakerphone, "Andy was devastated when he first heard about it. But he has gotten pretty close to Elizabeth Fallon over the last few days. It seems that she has been a really big support and comfort to him." Cash noticed that Meg's voice sounded a bit funny as she talked about Elizabeth Fallon being in Andy's life, but wise man that he was, he didn't mention it.

"So, Wendy stays in your critical care unit until she's recovered enough to be told the truth and moved to a mental institution, where she can get the help she needs, right?" Cash stared at the picture on the mug, shaking his head slightly. He never did like the pictures that were taken of him. He thought that he always looked like his Uncle Ned. No offense to Uncle Ned, who Cash loved dearly, but he was not a handsome man.

"Pretty much, yup," Doc responded. "You heading over to Tina's for the Valentine's Day feast she's cooking up?" Doc sounded much more upbeat talking about food. One thing about doctors and sheriffs, they ate at strange times, and were always a few meals behind. So when a really good opportunity came along to eat well, they were generally more excited and ready than the usual person.

"Are you kidding?!" Cash responded enthusiastically. "Turkey with all the trimmings, two kinds of potatoes, steamed veggies, red colored dressing, homemade gravy, homemade dinner rolls and cranberry sauce shaped in a heart! Wouldn't miss it for the world! We're all going! We'll see you there!"

Cash settled the phone back into its cradle as he glanced over at Darlene, Yamato and Horace. They were all staring at him. Apparently his 'phone voice' had gotten a tad loud and rambunctious!

Cash glanced down at his cup and grinned. "Just time enough to christen my new mug before we head over to Tina's!" he called out cheerfully as he headed for the half full coffee pot.

***

Norma and Trish, dressed up in their red and pink Valentine's Day aprons, had been doing a brisk business all morning. They had sold out of two of their four new chocolate creations and had been creating ice cream cones, sundaes and packing up gallons and quarts of ice cream to go. As Parmenter Jacobsen and his delighted wife, Sheila, left the shop, waving cheerfully and enjoying their Cupid's Delight ice cream cones, the two shopkeepers stepped back from the counter and leaned against the long steel table behind them.

At that very moment, their cheery front door bell jangled and in burst Newt and Remy. The two Brits were each grinning ear to ear and held their hands behind their backs.

"Happy Valentine's Day, Love!" exclaimed Newt as he stood in front of Norma, his eyes sparkling with delight and eager anticipation.

"And a very Happy Valentine's Day to you too, My Darling!" Remy echoed, staring with love and affection at Trish. He and Newt exchanged knowing glances and both of them stood fidgeting around as if they were about to explode with some sort of surprise, while waiting for the loves of their lives to respond to them.

Both Norma and Trish simply couldn't help bursting out with laughter. They loved the two Brits with all their hearts and had come to know their little quirks and eccentricities well. They somehow sensed that their beaus had something to give them and they could hardly wait to do so.

As the two women laughed until tears came to their eyes, Newt and Remy stood in front of them, slightly confused, but filled with eager anticipation. The two balloonists glanced at each other and then back at the girls. Finally, they simply joined in with the laughter.

After all the chuckles and giggles had subsided, Newt winked at Remy and the two balloonists took their hands out from behind their backs. Each of them brought forth a heart shaped red box with a white and pink ribbon tied diagonally across it. They held the boxes out to their respective loves and waited, huge grins spread across their eager faces.

For a moment, Norma and Trish simply stared at the boxes and then they stared at each other. The boxes looked like ordinary candy boxes that you could buy in any pharmacy or convenience store. Could their usually attentive and creative British boyfriends really have decided to give an ordinary box of chocolates to the owners and creators of the best gourmet chocolate and ice cream for miles around? Norma and Trish turned back to their Brits and their eyebrows went up slightly as their arms folded across their chests.

Newt and Remy, winking at each other once again, pushed the boxes out toward the women further and Newt whispered, "Don't judge a gift by its cover, Dearest One!"

Deciding to give Newt the benefit of the doubt, Norma accepted the gift. She placed the box on the counter, and with trepidation, slowly opened it. Inside there were three things. The first was a neatly folded piece of very tough, very lightweight cloth in British racing green. The second was a gift card to an expensive department store made out to her with the sum of five hundred dollars. The third was two tickets. As Norma picked up the tickets, she realized with sudden delight that they were two tickets to The Albuquerque International Balloon Fiesta for the following fall.

Norma glanced up at Newt, her eyes wide with

surprise and delight. Suddenly, she reached across the counter and grabbed the love of her life and kissed him hard, squeezing him tightly.

Trish, having seen what was in her sister's box, eagerly tore open hers to find the identical gift: cloth, gift card and tickets. Without hesitation she screamed out, "You really are going to take us to the balloon festival next fall!" and ran around the counter to leap into her British boyfriend's arms.

At this point, Norma was holding Newt, staring into his eyes and smiling delightedly. Her eyes were filled with love and eager anticipation of the trip to come, "Oh Newt! I've never been farther away than New York and Boston!" she declared, glancing down once more at the tickets to the balloon festival. "How wonderful this will be! I can hardly wait!"

"But see here," interrupted Trish, holding Remy back away from her for a moment, her eyes confused and thoughtful, "what is the cloth for? I mean, I get the tickets. I get the gift card." She kissed Remy on the cheek and grinned, "Five hundred dollars, though? That's an awful lot!"

Remy shrugged and grinned back, "That's so you can get a new Southwestern wardrobe for going to the festival! It's a whole different world out there, my love!"

"And the cloth?" Trish asked once again, a small frown on her beautiful face.

"Ah, the cloth is a piece of leftover material from the new..." Remy started.

"...and improved..." Newt joined in.

"Limey!" all four of them sang out in unison as a flash of understanding crossed Trish and Norma's faces.

"Exactly! We just got back the new envelope and

have outfitted her with a brand new ultra lightweight gondola!" Newt declared delightedly.

"We'll all not only be attending the festival, but we will be in it!" Remy added, his eyes wide with joy.

The laughter and cheers of delight from inside The Scoop could be heard all the way over to the park in the middle of the town square. Eunice McAllister stopped feeding the squirrels for a moment and glanced over at the local chocolate and ice cream shop.

Hearing the cries of delight, she simply smiled and threw a few more peanuts in the shell onto the melting snow, watching the squirrels raced down from their waiting perches in the trees to vie enthusiastically for each peanut shell.

"Now, now," Eunice muttered to the furry creatures, "there's plenty for all of you. Don't be greedy! How many times have I told you that? Harrumph!"

Eunice tried to maintain a straight face, but it was no use. She had always loved feeding the squirrels, as had her late brother, Millard. When they had been children, they had often come to the park to feed the squirrels. It was some of their happiest times together. When they were feeding the furry ruffians as Eunice liked to call them, they had no worldly troubles, and they could simple enjoy the moment.

As the town librarian watched the squirrels, she remembered her brother. She had loved him dearly. He was gone, and she couldn't bring him back, but she could remember him. Every time she came to the park now, she brought enough peanuts for both her and Millard. It was as if they were feeding the furry ruffians together all over again. It made him seem a little closer.

"Hey, Miss Eunice," came an eager young voice from beside her. She turned and saw her honorary assistant librarian, Jeremy Burman, standing next to her, with a cake holder in his hands.

"Jeremy! How wonderful to see you!" Eunice whispered, smiling slightly, her eyes obviously delighted to see him.

"My Grandma B wanted to make sure you got these, Miss Eunice," Jeremy continued on, his voice bright and happy. "When I got back from my early release day at the union high school, I kind of figured where you might be, so Grandma asked me to bring these to you."

Eunice took a long look at Jeremy. He had been a rather short, shy and introverted thirteen-year-old when he had first come to work with her at the town library. Now, he was a rather tall, somewhat gangly, but definitely more self-confident and capable fifteen-year-old. She smiled warmly to herself and then reached out for the cake holder. Peeking inside, she found a half dozen of Lorraine and Grandma B's famous red velvet cupcakes that they made on special occasions. She knew immediately that she was in for a real treat.

Eunice winked at Jeremy and whispered, "Do you think it would be okay if you and I had one right now?" She smiled warmly at her protégé and held out the cake container enticingly.

Jeremy struggled for a moment, but then knowing that it would mean a lot to Miss Eunice if he shared her cupcakes with her, he reached in and eagerly lifted out a red velvet delight. "Happy Valentine's Day, Miss Eunice," he grinned holding up his prize.

"And a very Happy Valentine's Day to you as well, Jeremy!" chuckled Eunice, already savoring the tasty treat.

As Eunice and Jeremy munched their cupcakes contentedly, they each took turns feeding the furry ruffians. The squirrels chittered and chattered joyfully and greedily as they made mad dashes for peanuts and watched the two humans who seemed to find great pleasure in their antics.

***

Jed Farber, Emily Goldstein, Daniel Sturgis and his sister Nancy were in the midst of thoroughly enjoying the turkey dinner special at Tina's. They were seated in the last booth in the back of the diner and every bite of mouth-watering goodness was followed by an enthusiastic comment, a laugh or a contented sigh.

"I'm so glad you suggested an early dinner this evening!" Nancy declared as she buttered a second hot roll from the large basket in the middle of the table and grinned at her younger brother. Her eyes were filled with pleasure and good humor. "To tell you the truth, after supervising and cleaning up after my class's Valentine's Day party, and dealing with all the parents that came in to be a part of the party, I was in no mood to cook dinner!"

Daniel winked at Nancy and grinned back, "I felt it only fair, big sister! You cook and keep me well-fed lots of nights. This time, the treat's on me!" Daniel turned and smiled at Emily.

"Em and I were already thinking of coming here for a Valentine's Day treat after working out in the orchard all day." Daniel nodded toward Jed, raising his eyebrows. "And Jed looked so cold and tired that we compassionately took pity on him as well!"

Daniel chuckled and winked at Jed, who pretended to be offended, a big grin covering a huge forkful of turkey and gravy he had just stuffed in his mouth. As soon as he could politely reply, Jed did so, "Hey! You took pity on me? I'll remember that the next time you get hung up an apple tree after your ladder falls!" Jed chuckled and reached out eagerly to pile more red colored dressing on his plate.

"Still can't quite get used to the sight of red dressing, but it sure tastes good!" Jed exclaimed, glancing over at Nancy and winking at the young schoolteacher.

Nancy nodded, her eyes twinkling gaily, "Yes, I will admit that the color is disconcerting, but the taste is simply heavenly!" Nancy waved to Tina who was going by, grinning and sticking up both thumbs in an approving gesture. Tina smiled back graciously and mouthed the words, "Thank you!"

Emily looked around their happy little group and smiled warmly. In her heart, she was remembering her sweet, younger sister Beth. Beth had been Daniel's girlfriend. Her death had been part of a tragedy that occurred to her family over a year and half ago. Her other cousin, and Jed's half-brother, Amos McElroy, had been involved in an apple stealing, drug smuggling crime ring. Beth was dead, Jed had been seriously injured and Amos was now serving time in a federal prison in New York State.

Since then, Emily and Daniel had grown close, using their friendship and their love for Beth to help each other heal emotionally after her death. Emily allowed herself to gaze thoughtfully at Daniel for a moment. In her heart and soul, she realized that she had come to love him. She felt his love for her, as well. Neither of them had ever spoken the words, but she deeply believed that eventually, they would be together.

"Hey, Cousin!" Jed nudged her teasingly in the ribs, chuckling as he glanced into her eyes, "Penny for your thoughts? You were out of it for a moment there?" Jed smiled warmly and watched his cousin squirm a bit.

Emily shook her head and laughed, "Nope. My thoughts are for another time! Right now, let's just have a wonderful dinner and enjoy Valentine's Day in The Falls!"

Daniel held up his glass of iced tea and winked at Emily, coming to her rescue, once again, declaring loudly, "To a very merry Valentine's day in The Falls! Here! Here!"

At his simple toast, everyone in the diner at that moment turned and raised a glass of whatever they were drinking. From every table in the packed café could be heard robust, enthusiastic shouts of, "To a very merry Valentine's Day in The Falls!"

Emily smiled gratefully as she raised her glass and nodded to Daniel, who winked back as he drank his tea. The two of them exchanged unspoken but understood emotions and thoughts and then turned back to happily clink glasses with their friends.

Nancy Sturgis watched her brother and Emily. She had known for some time now that her little brother was in love with Emily Goldstein, and she with him. She was so happy for them both, but she had the good sense to simply let them be, without voicing her delight.

Watching the two young people laugh and share so much, Nancy couldn't help but hope that somewhere, someday, there would be a valentine with her name on it.

"Yes! A very merry Valentine's Day to everyone!" Nancy declared enthusiastically, her eyes twinkling with happiness, generosity and kindness.

Chapter 31

Jeb and Zeke stood on either side of a six-foot tall cardboard cutout of a grinning cupid with curly golden locks of hair proudly holding a bow and arrow. The caricature was naked except for a large red sash from its left shoulder to right hip and what looked like pink diapers. All around the figure were multitudes of red, white and pink hearts of varying sizes.

Gathered and restlessly milling around in their video store were at least seventy-five people anxiously waiting to see who had won the three prizes from Jeb and Zeke's 'Cupid's Challenge' video game competition.

"Your attention, please, ladies and gentlemen!" declared Jeb loudly, attempting to be heard by everyone in the crowd. "It's just a minute or two past seven o'clock and time for the announcement you've all been waiting patiently..."

"Or impatiently, as the case may be!" yelled out a voice from the back. The crowd chuckled, nodded in agreement and turned to find Leonard Hampton, a clerk at the McDuck's fast food restaurant just a block away, grinning and good naturedly having a little fun with Jeb.

Jeb smiled and winked at Leonard pleasantly, "...or impatiently as the case may be, to hear! Zeke, drum roll please!"

Zeke promptly walked over and sat down at the

drum set used for such video games as Beat to the Music, Dance Rhythm II and Legends of Rock and Roll and proceeded to pound out a snare drum solo ending with an impressive drum roll. As he crashed the cymbals with his sticks, Zeke grinned and gestured dramatically back to Jeb.

"The winners of the first annual Cupid's Challenge video archery contest are as follows..." Jeb turned and glanced across the sea of faces expectantly and eagerly waiting to see if their name might be called.

In the audience, Sean and William stood together, a knowing look flashing across both their faces, as they glanced at each other and winked. Then they turned and glanced a few faces over to where Meg Monroe and Lorraine Burman were standing together, smiling and enjoying the show.

Subtly, William gave Sean a quick 'thumbs up' after glancing back at his brother. Sean smiled and nodded with assurance.

"First of all," Jeb called out to the crowd. "I want everyone to know that there were some excellent scores posted, especially since the game isn't even out yet and no one had a chance to practice beforehand."

The crowd murmured appreciatively, still staring up at Jeb and Zeke, hanging on Jeb and Zeke's every word.

"Second of all," Zeke's voice rang out as he moved back over to center stage with his old friend, a broad smile spreading across his face, "we want you all to know that the scores at the top of the competition were extremely close."

The crowd murmured again and Zeke held up his hand for quiet, continuing, "So, we felt it only fair to make sure that everyone who entered the contest will have a fifty percent discount on their next purchase, whether it be a video game..."

Jeb interjected delightedly, "A video game system..."

Zeke finished his thought, "...or anything else for sale in our magnificent super video store!"

At this, the crowd glanced around at each other, their eyes widening with surprise and excitement as they began to cheer and applaud noisily at the more than generous offer.

After several moments, Jeb raised his hand for quiet once more. "Now, let's get to the winners." He glanced across the sea of faces, and his gaze stopped as he glanced meaningfully at Sean and William. Both Sean and William winked knowingly at the old video storeowner, as he simply smiled back at them

Jeb's voice rose an octave as he called out the first winner, "The first prize, a brand new XBPSIV gaming system with all the bells and whistles, goes to..."

Everyone in the crowd held their breath. The gaming system had only been out on the market for a few weeks and it was by far the best and most expensive gaming console around. Every true gamer in attendance wanted to get their hands on it to truly enhance their gaming pleasure. It was at that moment, in essence, the Holy Grail of the gaming world.

"...Doctor Meg Monroe of the West Sugar Shack Falls Medical Facility! Come on up here, Dr. Monroe!" boomed out Jeb's voice.

The crowd erupted with goodhearted cheers and clapping as Meg Monroe, her face beginning to redden, picked her way through the crowd to come up and stand beside Jeb, Zeke and the outlandish Cupid cutout.

As the crowd continued to clap and cheer, Meg waved, smiled and blushed while Jeb and Zeke each shook her hand. No one's smiles were any larger than those of Sean and William. The two brothers patted each other on the back and nodded in appreciation and satisfaction for Meg's selfless gesture of winning the gaming system for the hospital.

For a moment, as they listened half-heartedly to all the clapping and cheers, their minds raced back to earlier when they had taken the time to sit down in private with Jeb and Zeke. The well-meaning and determined brothers had told the two video storeowners that if either of them won, they wanted to give their prize to Meg. But, Sean and William didn't want to just donate the system, they wanted Meg to think that she had won the system fair and square. That way she would feel that she had done something special herself, not because someone else had given her the system.

William and Sean smiled and nodded their satisfaction over the result of the contest, almost certain that either one or the other of them had won the gaming system and that Jeb and Zeke had done as they had requested.

Meg gratefully accepted the small, but brightly colored, "first prize" trophy from Jeb and Zeke and she laughed joyfully as Zeke gleefully pushed over a handcart with several boxes on it. The boxes held the gaming system, the peripherals and all the cords and power strips needed to get it all ready to go. All that Meg needed to do was add a TV monitor.

"Thank you, Mr. Smith and Mr. Peters," Meg spoke loudly, joyfully, her eyes filled with a few delighted, but unshed tears. "This will mean the world to the kids and the long-term patients at our hospital! I can't even begin to thank you enough for the pleasure and joy that this will bring all of them! This is absolutely wonderful!"

Again, loud cheers and heartfelt clapping filled the room.

"And now," announced Zeke as Jeb and Meg stood slightly off to the side, "for the winner of the sixty-inch HDTV!"

Once again, the assembled crowd murmured in eager anticipation, all eyes craning to see the huge TV box sitting on another handcart just back of the grinning Cupid.

"The winner of the HDTV is..." Zeke hesitated, letting the anticipation build. Then he raised his eyebrows and grinned delightedly.

"...Lorraine Burman, come on up, Lorraine!"

Once again, wild cheering and clapping filled the super video store and Lorraine Burman, her eyes filled with real surprise and astonishment, made her way through the crowd and up to where Zeke was standing.

Zeke hugged Lorraine happily and handed her the second place trophy. Then, as a somewhat embarrassed Lorraine was waving joyfully at the audience who were cheering even louder, Zeke pushed the cart with the huge TV out and proudly handed it to Lorraine.

Sean and William glanced at each other, their faces somewhat surprised. They had naturally assumed that they would take two of the three prizes, given their experience at, fondness for, and expertise in video gaming. But they both shrugged and clapped heartily for Lorraine.

Lorraine waved out at the audience, smiling broadly, then raised her hand for silence, "My brother Jeremy," Lorraine pointed out her brother where he stood with several of his friends near the front of the crowd, "was the one who pushed me to enter!"

Jeremy grinned and blushed as his sister smiled and

stared at him, while his friends poked him in the ribs and teased him good-naturedly.

"He wanted me to enter, because he thought I was a pretty good video game player!" Lorraine grinned and then looked across the crowd once more.

"Well, thank you Jeremy, I appreciate your faith in me. I won because you've done an excellent job at teaching me how to play video games!" Then, Lorraine's smile immediately faded and she turned and glanced solemnly over at Meg Monroe.

"I had thought that if I did happen to win, we could use the TV or the gaming system up at the maple syrup compound. But now, hearing what Dr. Monroe is going to do for the kids and patients that have to stay for an extended time at the hospital, I have a better idea." Lorraine turned and deliberately pushed the large screen HDTV over to where the new gaming system was sitting.

"You need a stunning new TV to use with your new gaming system. Now you have one." Lorraine smiled and reached out to shake Meg's hand. As Lorraine spoke, Meg Monroe's eyes grew huge with surprise and delight.

Instead of taking the offered hand, an overjoyed Meg Monroe reached out emotionally and hugged Lorraine tightly as the crowd cheered even louder.

Several moments later, Jeb was standing back up in front, waving the crowd quiet once again, smiling and nodding, "That was a wonderful gesture Lorraine," he glanced back at a smiling Lorraine who was standing next to an elated Meg.

"I'm sure that somewhere down the road, your good deed will come back to warm your heart, dear," Jeb continued, his eyes twinkling, obviously thrilled with the selfless acts of his two big winners.

"And now, for our final prize, six new games of your choice!" Jeb declared loudly as the crowd once more leaned expectantly forward to see who would win the last prize in the archery contest.

"We have a tie! But it shouldn't be a problem!" shouted out Jeb. "These two gamers play each other almost every day! So, without further ado, Sean and William Frasier, come on up and get your prize!"

The crowd cheered and clapped as Sean and William made their way up to the front. Once they got there, Jeb reached out and handed them the third place trophy, with a big grin and shook both their hands.

Both Sean and William immediately put up their hands to speak. Then William grinned, having realized that his brother was about to say the same thing he was, and gestured graciously for Sean to go ahead.

Sean walked over to Meg Monroe and handed her the trophy. He smiled and spoke quietly, but with clarity so he was heard, "You can't have a gaming system without games. This is from my brother and I. Please allow us to help you choose six games that your kids and patients will love."

Once again, the crowd cheered. This time the clapping and cheering lasted for quite some time as Sean and William hugged Meg and Lorraine, whispering in their ears that they were truly proud of their unselfish and noble actions.

When the crowd had disappeared and Meg and Lorraine had left to take all the prizes over to the hospital, Jeb and Zeke stood in their nearly empty video game store chatting quietly with the two Frasier brothers.

"Okay, I'm dying to know! Which one of us really

won first prize?" William whispered, glancing around to make sure no one heard him. Sean and William stared at Jeb as he got ready to answer.

"There's no doubt that the two of you are the best gamers in town," started Jeb.

"With the exception of us, that is!" interrupted Zeke with a chuckle and a wink.

"But," continued Jeb with a sly smile, "not this time!"

"You mean that..." William blurted out, his eyes stunned.

"I mean that Meg and Lorraine beat you both, fair and square," Jeb declared with a short nod of his head for emphasis.

For a moment, there was silence as the two Frasier brothers processed the astonishing news. Then Sean began to smile. William glanced over at his brother and the twinkle in his older brother's eyes was catching. Soon, the two Frasier boys and Jeb and Zeke as well were laughing and shaking their heads.

As all four of them stood in the nearly deserted video game store, next to the ostentatious Cupid, the sound of satisfied and delighted laughter rang out. Sometimes it isn't who wins or loses. Its how it all turns out that really matters.

***

"Night, Sean! See you tomorrow! Remember, dinner's at six!" Serafina Messina Frasier stood on her tiptoes and kissed her brother-in-law tenderly on his cheek. She gazed into his eyes and hesitated a moment, rather obviously making sure that Sean was doing okay emotionally. It was, after all, Valentine's Day and although his sweet wife Marie had passed on seven years before, Serafina knew only too well how much

Sean still loved and thought of her.

"Thanks, Serafina," Sean smiled with a slight nod of gratitude and affection, "I'll be there tomorrow night with bells on."

William chuckled, "The cat won't like the bells, but she'll just have to learn to deal with it, Big Brother!" He hugged his brother, tightly and lovingly, winking cheerfully at Sean as he let him go and started walking off with Serafina.

As Sean watched the happy couple stroll off through the still melting snow, laughing and holding hands, suddenly oblivious to the world around them, he smiled tenderly. It was the way he had always walked with Marie. They showed the same adoration, intense intimacy and complete togetherness as he and Marie had years before.

Sean turned slowly and started toward home, deciding to take the long way home around the town square. As he walked slowly along in the mild winter temperatures, enjoying the February thaw that the maple syrup companies needed so much, he gazed around at the ending of Valentine's Day in The Falls.

Myron Edelberry and his wife Minnie were walking hand in hand, their three-year-old son perched on Myron's shoulders with a death grip around his daddy's forehead, grinning and hooting with delight.

Old Jonas Ipswich and his wife Ramona were shuffling up the sidewalk each with a cane, animatedly discussing the wonderful turkey dinner they had just enjoyed at Tina's Diner. From time to time, the old couple would stop to look into the shop windows and then look at each other and laugh and hug each other. Jonas and Ramona had been together more than fifty years. They could often be seen bickering and squabbling like hens over feed, but in the end, they were still very much in love.

Penny Okinawa pulled her wailing two-year-old daughter Candice along in a three-sided sled as her husband Icharo walked hand in hand with their scowling five-year-old, who, from the looks of it, definitely was into the 'I do it myself!' stage. From time to time either Penny or Icharo would sigh from the supreme effort it took to raise children, and glance wearily up at their mate. Their glance would be met by a broad, affectionate smile that immediately seemed to boost each other's spirit, and the little parade would once again move happily along.

Everywhere Sean looked in his little town, he saw the real spirit of Valentine's Day come shining through. From the influential selectmen to the poorest farmers and itinerant workers, everyone had found something to be happy about on this special day. Perhaps happiness came in the form of an ice cream treat from The Scoop or a full stomach after a great dinner, or perhaps even a Valentine's card or special little present that made that person's heart feel just a little bit warmer and well loved.

As he passed by The Scoop, he stared in the front window where a thrilled and wide-eyed Trish was enthusiastically hugging her new fiancée, Remy, as she gazed with amazement at the diamond ring he had obviously just placed her finger. Sean grinned to himself, remembering the magical moment he had asked Marie to be his wife.

As Sean walked and glanced around, he began humming to himself. It was a tune that Marie used to hum as she was doing housework, or working with her favorite roses, or just when she was feeling happy and content. As he hummed he glanced into the windows of the businesses and houses that he passed, his heart warm and filled with love. The bright lights, the happy conversations, the Valentine's Day spirit in his small hometown filled him with a deep peace and satisfaction.

"Hey Mr. Frasier!" called out two students from his elementary school as they ran past, giggling and headed for home, their hands clutching red Valentine's Day hearts.

Sean smiled and waved at the kids, then gazed up at the nearly full moon and grinned to himself. There was the North Star, shining brightly in the clear night sky. As he always did, since Marie had gotten him in the habit, he stopped for a moment, closed his eyes and made a wish upon the star.

Then, with a slight mist of tears shining in his eyes, he smiled once more and headed home. As he thought about the word, home, he realized how wonderful the word really sounded to him. It always had and always would. He had been the homebody and Marie had been the traveler. She had teased him about that fact endlessly. She had even given him a children's book that had two cute animated main characters: one a homebody and one a traveler. He remembered how she had laughed delightedly when he had opened it at Christmas time. He smiled warmly at the memory. Then he hastened his gait just a little and strode down the street, more than ready to get home to his own little house. What could be better, he thought? Home.

All around him, the birds and squirrels, who were enjoying the momentary repast from the normally harsh winter weather, chattered, sang and chirped delightedly. Just like him, they were thrilled to be home.

Home in The Falls.

                  The End

GEORGE JACKSON

ABOUT THE AUTHOR

George William Jackson was born November 25, 1947 in the small town of Fair Haven in the Green Mountains of Vermont. He earned a Bachelor's in Education and a Master's in Leadership and Administration from Castleton State College. He spent 40 years in education as a teacher (11 years) and a principal (29 years) in both Vermont and New Mexico. He and his wonderful wife Carolyn, who taught for 30 years, have five children, eight grandchildren and three great grandchildren in their combined family. He is also an artist in oils and loves reading, video games, fishing and the ocean. George and his wife now live in Tradition, Florida. Besides The Falls small town mystery series, he writes The Dragon World Series, Tales from the Principal's Bench, and he has even written a children's book, The Twilight Tea Party, also at the Kindle store. The first seven volumes of The Falls series can be found in paperback at Barnes & Noble and Amazon as well.

CPSIA information can be obtained
at www.ICGtesting.com
Printed in the USA
BVHW031721090622
639374BV00003B/112